I Have No Earthly Idea

S.K. RADHAKRISHNAN

www.skradhakrishnan.com
facebook.com/IHaveNoEarthlyIdea
instagram.com/skrad007
twitter.com/SKRad007

ISBN: 978-1-73365-969-7 (print)
ISBN: 978-1-73365-968-0 (ebook)

Cover art idea and concept by S.K. Radhakrishnan
Editing and cover art designed by PaperTrue Ltd.
Printed in the United States of America

Dedication

To the three wise men in my life.

My grandfather Dr. M. Narayanan, the only primary care physician for 6 villages. The man who taught me the nobility of the medical profession.

My father Dr. N. Radhakrishnan, an ENT surgeon, a tenacious advocate for the wellbeing of his patients, a mentor for his residents and medical students, who was affectionately addressed by his patients, residents, and hospital employees as "Dr. Nice." The man who taught me everything in life—what to do and what not to.

My supervising physician Dr. A. Friedman, the renowned neurosurgeon at Duke University Hospital, who reminds me of my grandfather and father in his work ethic and care for his patients. The man who defined our physician-physician assistant relationship as "residents come and go, but you are family."

Acknowledgment

I am indebted to my mother for her patience and sacrifices, albeit I realized and acknowledged them late in my life. I learned several valuable lessons from her—some of which helped me bring this novel to fruition.

My nephews Ajay, Adithya, and Vaseegaran and nieces Nila and Iniya always keep me on my toes. Their unbridled love, affection, and energy serve a constant source of motivation.

Eric Butler, a fellow neurosurgical PA and Amy Butler have always been there for me unconditionally and were generous with their encouragement and support. Amy's *Butler Law Office* helped me navigate the publishing world.

It is a privilege and an honor to work in the *Department of Neurosurgery at Duke University Hospital*. The neurosurgeons, physician assistants, neurosurgical residents, neurointensivists, nurses, physical, speech, and occupational therapists, nurse practitioners, and the case managers contribute to a great work environment and always go beyond their call of duty to take care of complex neurosurgical patients. Their encouragement in this endeavor is priceless.

Last but by no means the least, my profound thanks to *PaperTrue's* Adrian Slater for being the beacon of light through the publishing journey and Paula Richards and Guy Calvin for their help with editing and feedback. Their professionalism and courtesy could not be overstated. They made my vision for the cover art a reality.

CONTENTS

Chapter 1 — Bon Voyage

December 8, 1993

IT WAS A LONG SHOT. HE HAD NOT EXPECTED HER TO show up.

He would have understood it if she had not. But here she was—as beautiful as ever. With long wavy black hair, a fair complexion, and a willowy frame, she was the envy of Indian women and men alike. Her eyebrows arched perfectly over her soft brown eyes. She was wearing a pink *churidar*[1]—his favorite color on her. A quintessential balance of the traditional and the modern, she was modest yet sexy. To him, she looked like a goddess comparable only to the carvings of Ajanta and Ellora caves and the statues that adorn Indian temples.

She seemed to glide towards him. A breeze trailed her—a much-needed relief in the sultry night at Madras International Airport lit with the neon lights of the city. As she reached closer, her fragrance, like the fresh countryside air, replaced the stench of the people around her. There were all sorts of folks—of different ages, colors, and shapes—waiting to bid farewell to their loved ones. She stood out in the crowd.

1 Traditional Indian outfit

With one look at her, he felt all the weight on his shoulders fall off. He exhaled a huge sigh of relief. His family understood the gravity of the situation. Although it would be a long time before they could see him again—their son, their eldest brother—they took a step back to give him a moment alone with her. After all, they were all too aware of what it must have cost her to be here.

Not knowing what came upon him, he embraced her. For a moment, he forgot the fact that his parents were standing behind him. He did not realize that his brothers and sisters were gawking at him. He held her close, unsure if he was comforting her or seeking solace from her. She did not hold back either and returned his embrace.

To them, it seemed as though they were all alone in the busy airport. Nothing mattered. The fact that they had both grown up in conservative families did not matter. The fact that they had never embraced in their four-year relationship, even in private, did not matter. All that mattered was that they had each other in their arms, even if it was only for a moment.

He tried to be strong, not for himself but for her, but he couldn't. She wiped away the tears that rolled down his cheeks as he dried away hers. His parents adored her; her actions today only made them love her more. They were happy that their son had found someone he called his "soulmate."

He was leaving his life behind, heading to Dallas, Texas, to make a living. They were willing to make this sacrifice at the age when all their friends were getting engaged or married. They were young and madly in love, but both were mature beyond their years. They realized what it meant for them and their families, but this was no rash decision; they had talked about it for a long time and had calculated everything. They had weighed all the paise and rupees and concluded that cents and dollars made more sense. The mighty dollar had the power to make their dream a reality a lot sooner than the rupee could.

The grass was always greener on the other side. Hoping to make a better living, technicians and manual laborers were heading to the Middle East in droves. Professionals, too, were setting up their careers in one or the other affluent Western country. Young students harbored dreams of excelling in the prestigious universities in the land of the free; America gave hope to people's hearts and anticipation to their eyes. He was leaving for America with a similar hope and ambition to make something of himself.

Senthil and Sumathi were a lot alike in certain ways and diametrically opposite in others. Both loved their families but came from very different backgrounds. He was the eldest of five children, and she had two younger siblings. Raised in families that upheld traditional Indian values, both had the sense of responsibility of being the eldest child. They knew they had to be role models for their younger siblings, and when the time came, a crutch for their parents.

Marriage in India wasn't easy. Though the dowry system was declared illegal in India decades ago, it was still very prevalent. The bride was expected to come with a predetermined amount of cash, gold jewelry, kitchenware, and in some cases, a motorbike or even a car for the groom's family. Arranged marriage was still the norm; religion, caste, astrology, and superstitions all played a big role in determining marriages.

In an arranged marriage, the parents of both the boy and the girl sought out compatible horoscopes for prospective matches from families of the same religion, similar caste, and equal economic standard. Then, the prospective groom and his parents would visit the bride's abode for an evening meet and greet. For the occasion, the bride's family would go all out to present to the prospective in-laws a spread of savories and sweets along with piping hot coffee and tea.

The girl would then be brought out—decked in traditional clothes and jewelry. She would pay her respect to the elders and then quietly sit down to be interrogated by the groom's family. The questions asked would range from meaningful to absurd and anything in between. In rare instances, the boy would be allowed to talk to the girl, although never in private. This conversation—if one can call it that—would take place with the elders watching.

The groom's family would then depart, leaving the girl and her family to wonder if he is the one. If the boy approved of the girl or, more importantly, if the boy's family approved, they would get in touch with the girl's family to discuss the dowry. It was customary for the groom's family to express what they expected the girl to bring with her. It had to be enough so she could be welcomed as their daughter-in-law. If the demands were beyond the means of the girl's parents, they could make a counteroffer, and a compromise could be reached. Only then would the wedding arrangements proceed.

It was the norm for the girl's family to foot the entire bill for the wedding ceremony, which could last up to three days. Often, marriages would be forged upon the convenience of the two families even if the groom and the bride did not favor each other. The boy would comply to make his parents happy, and the girl would go along so that she would cease to be a burden to her family. The couple would gradually learn to love each other and move on with their lives. The dowry was the main reason families were less welcoming of a baby girl than a baby boy. Surprisingly, the divorce rate in India back then was negligible in comparison to the Western countries.

Senthilvelan Rajashekaran, twenty-three, was the eldest of five siblings. He was followed by a girl, Eshwari, who was twenty-one. Nandagopal, the next son, was eighteen; Rathi, another daughter, was sixteen; and Balaraman, the youngest son, was fourteen. Whenever his parents spoke about saving money and lectured the kids on why they could not afford to eat out or buy toys or new clothes, Bala always joked, "Why? Is it because you want to save money for Eshwari and Rathi's wedding?"

He followed it up with a solution: "Let's get Senthil *anna*[2] married first. We can use the dowry we get for Eshwari's wedding. Then Nanda *anna* can get married, and we use that dowry to get Rathi married. Finally, I'll get married, and we can keep that entire dowry." This was always met with a smack on the

2 Elder brother

back of Bala's head, usually delivered by Senthil or their *appa*[3]. Both men were strongly against dowries.

Senthil could not think of getting married before helping his *appa* make sure that his siblings' future was secure. It was always all or nothing for him. Once he got married, he wanted to focus entirely on Sumathi and their future. Even though Sumathi was very understanding, he could never ask her to make the same sacrifices his parents had made their entire lives to raise them.

Sumathi had plans of her own as well. Even though girls were not traditionally expected to help their parents financially, Sumathi took on the responsibility as the eldest child. For her, no difference existed between her responsibilities as a daughter and that of Senthil's as a son. She knew that Senthil would definitely help her with her siblings, but she was also aware that he had enough on his plate already.

Sumathi Vaidhyanatha Iyer was twenty-three as well. She had a younger brother and a sister—Subramanian, twenty, and Gauthami, eighteen. Senthil and Sumathi had both earned a Bachelor of Physiotherapy from the Government Institute of Rehabilitation Medicine. Both had given up their desire for a master's degree in Bombay as that meant two years away from their families. The added cost of boarding and tuition was far too high. Neither of them wanted to put their families through that.

They decided to do home visits during the weekends, along with their full-time jobs. Senthil joined the private Apollo Hospital, and Sumathi took a job in the Government Mother and Child Hospital because her parents insisted on stability.

Both lived frugally. Both handed their paychecks over to their families each month and kept for themselves the money they earned from home visits. They barely had any time for each other. At least when they were in college, they could see each other for the most part of the day and spend time at each other's homes studying together on the weekends. Now they only saw each other briefly during the weekends between home visits to patients. Absence

3 Father

only made their hearts grow fonder. Even with working seven days a week for a year, though, they had barely made a dent in the financial goal they had set before they could get married.

Things were going slowly but smoothly—well, until that one fateful Saturday. It was their one-year class reunion in the college where they had met and fallen in love. Even though the school years were stressful, they had enjoyed it; they knew exactly when they would see each other and for how long they could be together each day.

On the day of the reunion, they walked to their classroom, took their assigned seats, and sat looking at each other for a moment. Overwhelmed by nostalgia, they muttered at the same time, "I wish we could go back in time." They chuckled. It was not the first time they had completed each other's sentences. Ever since they had met, they knew exactly what the other thought or felt.

Though they knew the differences between their families, none of their classmates were surprised to see they were still together. Everyone knew they were made for each other. Even the faculty, who frowned upon any kind of hanky-panky between the students, did not mind the fact that Senthil and Sumathi were referred to as "an item." That was how well they had conducted themselves. He was a perfect gentleman and she a proper lady. Both were straight-A students. They were also very respectful.

During their clinical sessions, young and old patients alike would ask for them to be their therapists. Sumathi was particularly good with the infants with Erb's palsy and children with polio; Senthil was good at helping adults with adhesive capsulitis of the shoulder and those with hemiplegia. They had excellent bedside manners and always made their patients feel comfortable. The faculty enjoyed supervising and teaching them as both were fast learners and obedient students.

They walked out of the classroom to join the party and spent the evening catching up with their friends, updating their teachers about their jobs, and sharing stories of interesting patients they had encountered.

One of the teachers asked, "So when are you guys tying the knot?" They replied, "Once we get our siblings and families settled." One of their friends added, "Perhaps you should visit the booth outside and talk to the lady there. She can help you achieve your financial goals faster than you can even dream of."

Curious, they walked over to the booth. There they met Hema, an Indian who was now settled in America. Hema ran a company that recruited physical, occupational, and speech therapists to meet the ever-growing demand in hospitals, nursing homes, and rehab centers across America. Now, Sumathi and Senthil had not even moved to Bombay for their master's degree, and America was not even on the margins of their imagination! They only listened to her spiel to be polite.

"Free ticket to America, a job as a contract therapist with contracts starting from three months and lasting up to a year, free housing, and a salary of $70,000 . . ." They listened to her alright, but none of that information registered in their minds. They accepted the brochure before leaving and thanked her for taking the time to talk to them.

He took her on a ride on his motorbike—his favorite thing to do—and parked it a couple of streets away from her home, walking the remainder of the way with her. This was something they had done for the past four years, from the time that he had inherited the old motorbike from his *appa*. Walking down the street was a good idea since Sumathi's parents were more conservative and wouldn't have liked their daughter to be seen riding pillion. Also, Senthil and Sumathi didn't want to be the subject of her nosy neighbors' gossip.

Two months passed. Both Senthil and Sumathi became busier. Their clientele for home visits continued to increase as their referral base expanded by word of mouth. Senthil was always able to see more patients since he had a motorbike, while Sumathi had to depend on public transportation, the buses or occasionally an auto rickshaw when time was a constraint.

While the added income was welcome, they hardly had any time to see each other. Very soon, they were only restricted to late-night phone calls and occasional visits to each other's homes or dinners during the weekends. In making a future for themselves and their families, they seemed to be losing the most valuable part of their lives: each other.

Chapter 2 — Math Doesn't Add Up

ONE SUNDAY, ONE OF SENTHIL'S PATIENTS DECLINED THERapy, as she had a birthday celebration at home. So, he stayed home and wondered what Sumathi would be doing. Just then, the phone rang. It was her. Sumathi's patient too had canceled the therapy session. She was calling him from a phone booth. He told her, "Stay put; I am coming to pick you up."

He had never driven his motorbike that fast. It had been a long time since they had spent an entire day together. He bobbed and weaved through the traffic. Driving in Madras was not a skill; it was an art. Buses, auto rickshaws, bicycles, motorbikes, lorries, cars, pedestrians, and the occasional cows—none were a match for him.

He saw Sumathi standing at the bus stop. He came to a screeching halt right in front of her. She hopped on the back of his motorbike and held on to him. He knew where she would like to go. Forty-five minutes later, he parked the motorbike at Marina Beach. The weather was perfect. It was the end of July, and the summer was winding down. The sky was clear. The ocean breeze was cool and crisp. Taking his bag off the motorbike, he took her hand. They took a leisurely stroll on the beach until they found a shady spot to sit.

They talked about their work, the interesting patients they had seen, and their families. She was always eager to hear him talk about all the modern electrotherapy equipment he used at Apollo Hospital. He talked about short-wave diathermy, interferential therapy, electronic traction, and combination therapy. Since she worked in a government hospital, Sumathi did not have access to such modern gadgets. In her department, she had an old infrared light, an ultrasound unit, and paraffin wax therapy. She always teased him that while he was busy using machines to treat people, she was healing them with her human touch. He never argued back because he knew she was right.

When Sumathi was least expecting, Senthil pulled out a small box. "Sumi," he said, "I got this for you."

She seemed surprised and asked him, "What is it? The package is so adorable, and I see that you made the wrapping paper yourself."

He had taken a plain white paper, painted it with pink watercolor, and written all over it with a red felt pen. It read "I love you Sumi," with numerous small hearts all over.

"This is so cute!" she exclaimed. "I can't believe you spent so much time making this for me." He was growing impatient. He wanted her to open the packet so that he could see her reaction to what was inside. He did not want to hear her obsessing with the wrapping, though he appreciated it. He had labored over painting the paper and writing and drawing over it. She said, "Thank you, my dear *chella kanna*. It's beautiful, and I love it."

He said, "Thank you? You haven't even opened the box yet!" She was surprised. They had talked about it before they began working: no gifts. They had agreed to be as frugal as possible and save every rupee they earned.

She cried, "What? There is more? I thought the box was the gift! It looks so pretty, and you are so creative."

He stroked her head and said, "Thank you my dear, but enough about the box and the wrapper. Could you please open it? I cannot wait for you to see what's inside."

She opened the box, taking her time with it for she wanted to preserve the wrapper. She folded it and kept it inside her handbag. Finally, she opened the box. There was a smaller box inside. "Senthilvelan Rajashekaran, what are you up to?" she whispered and proceeded to open the smaller box. It was a Titan wristwatch, with tiny black leather straps and a dial with gold trim and a shiny tan and pink metallic sheen. It was by no means an extravagantly expensive watch. It was elegant and beautiful, though. And it was just above their budget.

Her jaw dropped. Her big brown eyes welled with tears that rolled down her rosy cheeks. Sumathi had had the same watch—a hand-me-down from her *amma* who had given it to her when she got into PT school. It was old and tethered, but she had worn it with pride. It had breathed its last about six months ago. Senthil's attempts at resuscitation had been unsuccessful, and the watch repairman had said that it had served its time on Earth and could not be brought back to life.

"Dear, you know I really don't need a watch. I always know what time it is based on the day's schedule. Besides, I was doing a social experiment to see if we really need watches in our lives."

Senthil could sense her disappointment; her clever cover-ups didn't work with him. He knew her all too well—as well as she knew herself. Still crying, she said, "I know you were only trying to make me happy, but you know what, I would have been just as happy with only the wrapper you painted. This will only set us back."

"No, it won't, Sumi," he insisted. "I did not buy this from my paycheck or the money I get from my home visits."

Sumathi tilted her head, confused. "Then?"

"Well," he continued, "I have told you where it didn't come from. So, just enjoy it and think of me whenever you check the time."

A little annoyed, her pretty face now sported a frown. "I don't need materialistic things to remind me of you. You are always on my mind. Now, aren't you going to tell me how you managed to get me this beautiful watch?" she insisted, trying to be stern but she couldn't hide her smile.

"I will tell you, but first, you must promise me that you won't get mad at me."

Sumathi looked at him perplexed. "You didn't steal this, right?"

"Promise me, and I'll tell you."

She placed her hand on his head and vowed, "I promise. Now spill every detail before you get hurt."

"Well, for the last six months," he started, "I did not use my motorbike. I rode my brother's bicycle to work and to see my private patients. I skipped lunch and saved my lunch money. I also gave blood to my hospital's blood bank twice." She was speechless. Her lips started quivering as she gazed at him intensely. Just to make light of the situation, he pointed to his stomach and said, "Look dear, I have a six-pack now and a lot more endurance." He laughed.

Sumathi was not amused. Her first reaction was she wanted to scream at him. *"Are you kidding me? Did I ever complain that I don't have a watch? Why the heck did you put your health and life on the line for a stupid watch?"* was all she wanted to say. However, she quickly realized that doing so would only break the heart of the guy who loved her so much. He had gone to extreme lengths only to see a smile on her face. So, she kissed her fingers and placed them on his lips. Breaking her silence, she said, "My dear, I don't know if I should be elated that I have such a thoughtful sweetheart, who would do so much to make me happy, or be upset that he thinks that I would want material objects over his well-being." She paused for a moment. She did not want to say anything that would hurt his feelings. More than anything, she wanted to make sure he did not put himself in any danger to make her happy. "Senthil, you are the love of my life," she continued. "I love you more than anyone or anything in this entire world. I know that you love me just as much, and there is absolutely no need for you to prove me anything." She looked at him with love and contentment in her eyes and extended her left hand towards him. He took the watch out of the box and wrapped it around her wrist. He rested his head on her knees as she began to stroke his hair gently. She leaned over and softly whispered into his ear, "Thank you. It's beautiful."

They lost all track of time. It was quiet and peaceful, with nothing but the sound of the ocean roaring in front of them and the occasional street vendor hawking their goods for sale. He slowly lifted his head and asked, "You hungry, Sumi?"

She smiled and replied, "Starving."

He pulled out a couple of tiffin boxes and spoons from his bag. "Eshwari made this, and she wanted me to tell you that she misses you and that you should come over sometime."

Sumathi was so excited; she loved chicken biryani. She had been raised in a family of vegans and had chicken for the first time in her life when she had gone over to Senthil's. She had not wanted to appear rude or offend his parents. If she was going to live with them after their marriage, it only made sense that she got used to their customs. It was an acquired taste, but she began to enjoy it.

Once they had finished eating, she asked, "What else do you have?" She reached for the bag, expecting to find Cadbury's milk chocolate bars inside, which she did, and lying inside with the two bars of chocolate was a brochure. She took the chocolates, handed them to him, and proceeded to look at the brochure. "Oh! This is the brochure we got from that lady from America," she said.

Unwrapping the chocolates, he said, "Hope you have your handkerchief. These chocolates have gone a little soft from the heat." Sumathi was busy looking at the brochure. She was more curious about it now than she had been when they had met the lady at the class reunion.

Senthil was busy enjoying his chocolate and licking his fingers. He had a sweet tooth, or as he would say, "sweet teeth." He always lost track of his surroundings when it came to desserts. "You better eat your chocolate before it becomes chocolate syrup," he quipped. He looked up and found her looking intently at the brochure. "What do you have there that is more interesting than chocolate?"

Sumathi looked up and started laughing. "Come here. You are like a little kid." Wiping the chocolate from his nose and cheek, she took the melted bar in one hand and handed him the brochure, proceeding to eat the chocolate.

Senthil looked at the brochure and asked, "What are we looking at this for?"

"Wouldn't it have been nice if physiotherapists here made that kind of money?" she replied. "We could settle down much sooner, and you wouldn't have to literally starve to do something nice for your woman."

Senthil was not amused. "When you factor in the cost of living in America, the pay is probably not that much more from what we make here."

Sumathi was quick to reply, "Unless you make money there and bring it home. With the conversion, one could have five times more." She paused, and then continued, "Maybe we should look into this more—"

"Honey wait a minute," he interjected. "Are you suggesting that we consider taking a job in America and leaving our families behind?"

"No, don't put it that way now," she urged. "We'd be leaving them behind only to make sure that we can take better care of them. Plus, we can also live our lives when we are young and not wait until we are old."

Senthil scratched his head. "What are you talking about, honey?"

Sumathi paused for a moment, stood up, grabbed his hand, and headed towards the ocean.

When they got closer to the water, he rolled his pants as she rolled her *churidar* up to her knees. They picked up their chappals in their hands and walked along the shore, letting the waves caress their feet. They hooked their pinkies and walked for a while. The cool breeze, the sound of the ocean, the wet sand under their feet, and the cool water were all so soothing that they forgot what they had been discussing. They were enchanted by each other's company and their proximity. The breeze blew the transparent *dupatta*[4] over Sumathi's face. They stopped, and Senthil slowly slid the *dupatta* off. Their gazes locked, and they just stood there, lost, with the earnest look of young lovers who longed to embrace and kiss each other. They could see it in each

4 Sheer shawl-like accessory for churidar, worn as symbol of modesty

other's eyes. However, their conservative upbringing, their beliefs, and their culture had made their self-control strong in the most tempting of moments.

Sumathi was unable to look him in the eye any longer. She blushed and became shy, embarrassed that she could not mask her desire. She slowly lowered her gaze and looked at her feet, and she noticed her right big toe unconsciously doodling on the wet sand. Senthil slowly and gently lifted her chin so that he could once again look into her beautiful eyes that were brimming with love for him. Even with the roaring of the ocean and the sound of the breeze, they felt they could hear the other's heart pounding against their chest.

He said, "I wish time would stand still right now. This is the happiest and most content I have been in a long, long time." She opened her eyes that were filled with tears, which he wiped away as he said, "I love you with all my heart."

Wiping the tears rolling down his cheeks, she replied, "I love you more."

With their fingers interlocked, they turned around and headed back to the motorbike. Sumathi asked, "Do you know why this whole day felt special?"

Without any hesitation, Senthil replied, "Because today both of us lived in the present, in the moment, and not in the past or the future."

Sumathi smiled in agreement. "You are right." Then she added, "Ever since we graduated and started working, all we have been thinking about is the future. We think about the past, live in the future, and totally ignore the present."

He knew she was right, but then she always was! They were so attuned to each other that they connected with each other's thoughts, could do anything for each other without being asked, and call when one was thinking of the other.

As they reached closer to the motorbike, Senthil said, "We cannot fast-forward time to start our lives, and I can certainly see that, at the current rate, even while working seven days a week, we will be past our middle age before we can save enough money to get our siblings settled."

Sumathi nodded in agreement. Sadness replaced the joy that was brimming on her beautiful face only moments ago. He noticed it and, squeezing her hand, said, "Let's not think about the future, just for today. Let's just stick to enjoying this day. Everything is going to work out just fine." Even though she knew this was not the end of their discussion, she agreed to his proposal.

They left the beach, Sumathi riding pillion behind Senthil. It was still early in the evening, so they stopped at a temple on the way to Sumathi's house. They prayed and then accepted the *prasadam*[5] that the priest offered. She placed the *vibhuti*[6] on his forehead and saved the rest of it and the *kumkum*[7] in a piece of paper and put it in her handbag. He smiled. She knew very well that he did not believe in the rituals, but she also knew that he was very tolerant and respectful of the culture and beliefs of others.

Senthil had been an atheist until he met Sumathi. He respected the Hindu culture, its teachings, and the morals, but he simply could not wrap his mind around the number of gods. He believed that all religions led to the one Almighty God. His biggest beef with Hinduism was the caste system, as he believed that all human beings were equal in the eyes of God. Sumathi was not so pragmatic; she believed in all the gods but did agree with him about the caste system. They did not let their differences in their religious beliefs stand in the way of their love. They sat quietly, leaning on two pillars on opposite sides of the *mandap*[8] for a few minutes.

When it was time to leave, Sumathi and Senthil got up and walked out of the temple, carefully maintaining a respectable distance between them. They really did not want to give air to the popular notion that young couples come to the temple to hook up. The temple was the house of God and a place for families; they did not wish to tarnish its sanctity. He drove her home, and as usual, they stopped a few streets away and walked to her home as he

5 Sacred food

6 Sacred ash

7 Red dot Hindu women use on their forehead

8 pillared porch-like pavilion leading to the temple

pushed his motorbike along. When they got closer to the house, he parked the motorbike and walked the rest of the way alongside her.

They rang the doorbell, and Gauthami opened the door. Her eyes lit up when she saw him. Exuberantly she said, "Hi *athimber*![9] How are you? It has been a while since we have seen you."

He patted her head and gave her a pen he had got from a drug rep. She was excited and whispered, "Thanks, *athimber*."

Sumathi's parents were sitting on the couch in front of the television. She walked in first and placed the *vibhuti* on her *appa*'s forehead and the *kumkum* on her *amma*'s[10]. Then she went into her room to change. Senthil walked in and greeted them, "*Vanakkam*[11], *appa, vanakkam amma.*" He bent down and touched their feet as a mark of respect.

Sumathi's *appa* blessed him: "Be well." He sat down on the floor next to Gauthami who was doing her homework. Sumathi's *appa* turned off the television and asked, "How is work at that fancy hospital?"

Senthil replied, "Work is going well, *appa*. It's great to work with all the modern equipment."

Sumathi's *amma* interrupted them: "He has come home after a long time. Let me get him something to eat."

Sumathi shouted out from the kitchen, "*Amma*, I am fixing us a plate. You sit down and talk to him." She walked out with three plates of food and sat down with Senthil and Gauthami.

Senthil asked, "Where is Subbu?" Gauthami told him that he was doing some project for school with his friend. They talked as they ate, and her parents enquired about the health of his parents and how his siblings were doing in school. Gauthami showed him her artwork. He was her biggest fan and always encouraged her, and she always liked to have him around, as he made her feel like a princess. He considered her his third sister.

---

9 Elder sister's husband

10 Mother

11 Respectful greeting

Subbu walked in as they finished eating. He greeted, "Hi Senthil, how are you?"

Senthil replied, "Great! Look at you. You are growing taller by the day. Looks like you are taller than me now."

Subbu sat down next to him and whispered, "Every now and then, I eat chicken at my friend's place." Senthil chuckled.

Checking his watch, Senthil told them it was time for him to head home. He thanked them for the lovely dinner, and once again, he bent down to touch Sumathi's parents' feet, who grazed their hands over his head. Sumathi looked at him affectionately. She was extremely proud of him and happy that he treated her parents with such respect and love. Subbu wished him good-night and went in to clean up. Sumathi's *appa* urged him to get back home safely and to convey his regards to his parents.

Gauthami gave him a high-five and said, "Hope it's not months before we see you again." Senthil smiled and proceeded to leave. Sumathi and her *amma* walked down with him.

As they reached the gate, Sumathi's *amma* said, "I am so proud of the gentleman you have grown up to be. You are so responsible and patient with everybody. God bless you."

Senthil replied, "*Amma*, I owe it all to the blessings and well wishes of elders like you."

She smiled and walked back upstairs. Then, she paused, turned to look at Sumathi, and said, "It's misty. Don't keep him standing here for long. I don't want either one of you catching a cold." Sumathi smiled and nodded. He opened the gate, walked out, and turned back to close it. Sumathi turned to make sure her *amma* had gone upstairs, and then caressed his hands that rested on the gate and said, "Be careful on your ride back home. Hope we can do this again soon. Give my respects to your parents, and please thank Eshwari for the chicken biryani."

He nodded, squeezed her hands, winked at her, and said, "Good night, honey."

He walked back to the street where he had parked his motorbike. He drove back home with a big smile on his face. When he pulled into his house, Nanda, Rathi, and Bala scrambled to turn off the television and grab a book. Eshwari was in the kitchen with their *amma*. His *amma* walked out and said, "These kids are more scared of you than they are of their *appa*. Don't let them fool you. They were watching TV until they heard your motorbike."

He turned and looked at them when Rathi spoke out, "But we were done with all our homework, finished our studies, and just wanted to watch a little TV before we went to bed." It was not out of fear; it was out of respect. They felt guilty for watching TV. They all knew that even though he had found the love of his life, even though all his friends were married, their brother had put his life on hold for their sake.

Before going on to take a shower, he reminded them that it was Monday the next day and they would have to get up in the morning to go to school.

Senthil came back in a T-shirt and a *lungi*[12]. Eshwari was setting the table, and he told her that he had had dinner already. She was surprised, being aware of how reluctant he was to spend money eating out. She asked, "Really? Where?"

"At Sumathi's," he answered.

Eshwari was even more surprised by this. She thought he was just meeting her for lunch. But she was happy to know that he had gotten the opportunity to spend the whole day with Sumathi. She asked, "Did *anni*[13] like my chicken biryani? What did she say?"

"She enjoyed it and said that it was the best that you have made so far." This had Eshwari grinning ear to ear.

The other siblings had overheard him say that he had had dinner at Sumathi's. Rathi asked, "So how is *anni* doing? What did you guys do all day? Where did you take her?"

---

12 Sarong wrapped around the waist and extending to the ankles

13 Wife of an elder brother

Senthil always liked the fact that his brothers and sisters addressed Sumathi as *anni.* He replied, "She is doing fine, just busy with work and patients. She asked me to tell you that she misses you all."

Rathi smirked and said, "You didn't tell us where you took her."

Senthil replied, "Okay. We went to Marina Beach."

Bala followed quickly, "Why do boys and girls always go to the beach when they want to be alone?"

Nanda barged in and said, "That's because it is a rich neighborhood. Nobody they know lives there. They can be certain that they are not going to run into somebody they know."

Senthil tapped his head and quipped, "And it is free! Now go brush your teeth and get to bed, you little rascals. You all have school tomorrow." They all scurried away.

Eshwari sat down with a book as Senthil took up the newspaper. *Amma* perched herself in front of the TV with a cup of coffee. Senthil lowered the newspaper and whispered to Eshwari, "Where's *appa*?" She informed him that he was working overtime. Senthil turned to his *amma* and said, "*Amma*, how many times have I told you to ask him to stop working on the weekends? He is not getting any younger."

Amma replied, "I told him what you said, and he answered he has two daughters he would like to see married." She went on to say how happy and proud they are that, as the eldest son, he was so responsible. But he was their son, and they wanted him to settle down in life, too. Knowing it's a no-win situation, Senthil stopped arguing and buried himself in the newspaper.

It was about 10:00 PM when he heard his *appa*'s motorbike. He ran outside to open the gate. *Appa* asked him, "Have you had your dinner?"

He said yes and carried his *appa*'s bag inside. His *appa* came in, washed up, and prayed. Senthil and Eshwari set the table, and his parents sat down to eat. Eshwari joined them. His *appa* asked him, "Where is your plate?"

Senthil replied, "My patient canceled today, and so did Sumathi's. So, we hung out for some time, and I had dinner at her house."

"How is she? It has been a while since we have seen her. Are her folks doing well?"

Senthil smiled, "Yes *appa*, they are all doing well. They asked me to convey their regards."

Chapter 3 — Dollars and Sense

SENTHIL SAT AT THE DINING TABLE, PONDERING. HE could not rid his mind of what Sumathi had said about America. He took the brochure out of his bag and looked at it again, and this time, he read it from front to back. His eyes shone with determination.

As soon as he opened his wallet to copy down some phone numbers, he saw the picture of Sumathi; he had been carrying it for the past four years. It was a simple black-and-white passport-size photo that she had taken for her public transport bus pass. She wore a sari, and her wavy hair was pulled back in a ponytail that cascaded down her right shoulder. There was a hint of a smile on her face. Senthil would always say, "Mona Lisa has nothing on you." He gazed at her photograph, and as he looked back up, he saw the photo mounted on the wall facing him. It was a framed picture of him and his siblings: the two brothers standing on his one side and his two sisters on his other. He shifted his gaze alternatively between the two photos. Finally, he nodded his head as though to acknowledge his thoughts. He wrote down the phone numbers behind a receipt, placed it in his wallet, and kept the wallet and the brochure back in the bag.

He walked into his siblings' room to get his bedding: a few pillows and a sheet. In the faint light, he could see all of them lying on the floor at equal distances from each other. He saw their faces—peaceful and calm. Suddenly, it struck him: the same nightmare that had been plaguing him ever since he was nine years old. Those horrific nights flashed before his eyes. He broke into a cold sweat and began to hyperventilate. He stood staring at his siblings. It was not a matter of one or two nights; the scars had been inflicted over the course of two years that he was hiding from everybody. Nobody knew the pain he harbored. He hastily retreated into the dining room, closing the door softly. He opened the fridge and gulped down cold water.

Regaining his composure, he came back to the living room and lay on the floor with one pillow under his head and another below his knees. He always slept on the cold marble floor; he enjoyed that little chill on summer nights. In the winters, he lay on the sheet. He turned on the cassette player next to him to the lowest volume setting and played a favorite tape as he gradually drifted off to sleep, unmindful of the tears that rolled down his cheeks. This had been a routine for him for many years now.

He woke up early the next morning. He wanted to meet his friend Shiva before leaving for work. Shiva was a senior who he had heard was going to America in a month as a contract physical therapist. He found Eshwari in the kitchen, making coffee for *amma* and *appa* and preparing breakfast for others before she headed out for college. Carrying the pillows and the sheets, he tiptoed into his siblings' rooms. It was a Monday, and they could not sleep in. He always wondered how his siblings rose early on Sundays or holidays, never needing a wake-up call, and yet, come a school day, they needed to be pushed into waking up on time. After placing the pillows and the bed sheet in a corner, he turned the ceiling fan off. Then, he fetched some water from the bathroom and sprinkled it on his siblings. Startled, they sat up one by one. They fixed him with a cold stare, which soon turned into a fit of giggles.

"It's time to get ready for school," he told them and walked out.

Eshwari had already made a batch of *idlis*[14] with coconut and green chili chutney. Senthil gobbled up three *idlis* with the chutney and said, "Eshwari,

14 Savory rice cakes, a popular breakfast in southern India

the chutney is out of this world. You do so much work around the house, and you are such a great help to *amma*."

She smiled and said, "Just like you are for *appa*. Thank you *anna*."

She had always been a girl of few words. Always soft-spoken, Eshwari gladly took the backseat when it came to her siblings.

"Some guy out there will be lucky to have you as his wife," he added.

Mid-way through washing the dishes, Eshwari turned around, sprayed some water on him, and smiled. "When I am married and gone, who is going to make you *idlis* and chutney? Anyway, aren't you leaving a little early today?"

"Yes, I am going to stop by Shiva's place before heading to work. I have a few things to discuss with him."

Rushing out, he yelled, "Have a nice day Eshwari." He hopped on his motorbike and rode away. Shiva was two years senior to Senthil and Sumathi in college. He had come to Madras to study physiotherapy from a village close to the village of Senthil's grandparents. That was one of the reasons they became fast friends. Shiva lived in a small one-room apartment in Mylapore. To reach there, Senthil had to ride his motorbike through a few narrow streets and navigate his way through the hustle and bustle of pedestrians, street vendors selling tea, coffee, *idli*, and *vada*[15], parked auto-rickshaws, and the cows that had free reign over the streets. When he reached Shiva's complex, he parked his motorbike and ran upstairs.

Shiva was getting ready to go to work. He was standing in his room in his pants and a *baniyan*, combing his hair, when Senthil knocked on the half-open front door. Shiva opened the door and was delighted to see Senthil. "Hey *kulla*[16]," he greeted. "C'mon in! How are you?"

Senthil walked in. Though the papers said it was an apartment, it was, in reality, just a single room. In one corner, there was neatly rolled up bedding. A built-in bookshelf had a bunch of physiotherapy books and some Tamil magazines. There was a small stool on which sat a small statue of Lord Ganesh, with

15 Savory fried snack

16 Shorty in Tamil

a few incense sticks smoldering away. Interestingly, a photo of Jesus Christ sat on top of a small shelf that housed a Bible and a candle. Shiva was in love with a Christian girl, Maria, who was a nurse in the hospital where he worked.

Senthil sat down on the bedding. Shiva said, "I was going to come to your house to personally convey the good news to your parents and get their blessing."

Senthil asked, "So, when are you leaving?"

"In three months. I just have to return to the village and resolve some family property before I leave."

"So, what is the pay? What are the benefits? Where are you going to be working? How long is the contract—"

"Calm down *kulla*!" Shiva interrupted. "What's up with all these questions?"

"You may be a giant, but I am not short," Senthil snapped back. "Anyway, Sumathi and I are thinking about America."

Shiva jumped up in joy. "What? I can't believe this! Are you serious, or are you just pulling my leg?" Senthil went on to narrate the *beach incident.* When he was done, Shiva tapped him on his head and said, "I can understand you doing crazy things for Sumathi. I have done my fair share for Maria, but why in God's name would you *tell* her about giving blood?"

"I just cannot lie, let alone to her," Senthil replied.

Shiva looked at his watch. "Hey, it's getting late. I have to catch the bus for work. I'll come home after work, and we'll continue."

"I'll drop you. Don't worry about catching the bus," Senthil said.

Shiva locked his room, and both hurried down the stairs. "If you guys are serious about this," Shiva continued, "I'll postpone my flight, and we can all fly out together maybe. That would be so much fun, and if Maria knows that you are coming with me, she would be so relieved. She worries that I will get lost or something." Senthil nodded and said that he was going to discuss the idea with Sumathi.

That night, Shiva came over. Over dinner, he told Senthil's parents that he was leaving for America on September 15. They wished him the best and asked him if Maria was accompanying him. He informed that he was going first and that his company had promised him to help find a nursing job for her. After dessert, Senthil walked Shiva out. They stood outside and talked for a while as Senthil scribbled down everything Shiva told him on a notepad. He did not want to miss any detail for when he would tell Sumathi. Once Shiva had shared everything, he prepared to depart, but Senthil offered to drop him off on his motorbike. Shiva said, "Hey, you don't have to drive me all the way to Mylapore. Just drop me off at the bus stand."

"Okay, as you wish," Senthil said.

Senthil could not sleep that night. He tossed and turned and dreamed of nothing but numbers. He could see dollars and rupees raining around them as Sumathi and he ran together in slow motion, holding hands like they did in Indian movies. He could see their sisters getting married and their brothers going off to colleges. He could see himself marrying Sumathi while they were still young. He could not wait any longer. It was still 3:00 AM in the morning, but that didn't stop him. He got up, washed his face in the kitchen sink, and made sure the doors to both his parents and siblings' rooms were closed. He then turned on the light and sat at the dining table with the notepad to make a budget. The more he wrote, the bigger his smile grew.

Once satisfied, he sprang up, took a quick shower, got dressed, and headed out. He hesitated for a moment on his way and quietly peered into his siblings' room. It was 5:15 AM, and he did not want to wake them up this early. But he knew that Eshwari would be up soon; she was usually the first one to wake up and start the kitchen work before she went off to college. He tapped her shoulder. She turned, and Senthil immediately put a finger to his lip, signaling her to be quiet.

She gestured: "What?"

Senthil whispered, "I just wanted to let you know that I'm leaving early. Tell Rathi and Bala to get a ride to school. I'll explain later." She gestured to ask if he wanted to eat anything. He shook his head and whispered, "Thank you." He hurried out and almost reached the gate before realizing that he had forgotten something. He ran back inside and grabbed the notepad. Opening the gate, he pushed the motorbike out; he started it only as he reached the corner of the street.

He rode his bike to the bus stand in Mogappair from where Sumathi took the bus to go to work every day. He knew that he was way too early, but he could hardly wait to sec her and did not want to risk missing her. He parked his motorbike by the sidewalk and waited, staring at the notepad, still making corrections. He checked the time intermittently. He knew she would be there at only around 6:45 AM; he also knew that staring at his watch would not make time move any faster. But he could not help it.

He had been waiting there for almost an hour when he saw Sumathi walking through the early morning fog towards the bus stand. It was only 6:20 AM; she was early, as though she had known he was waiting. When she looked up and noticed him, her face lit up like a 1000-watt bulb, and she ran towards him. Even her run looked elegant to Senthil.

She came to a halt by his motorbike. Catching her breath, she exclaimed, "What a surprise! I was wondering why I was so restless this morning. I got up earlier than usual and just couldn't stay home any longer."

"I am glad you are here early. I just wanted to talk to you," Senthil replied.

"How are Rathi and Bala getting to school today?"

"Oh, they can manage one day. I have something important to share with you. I spoke to Shiva last night."

"How is he doing? How is Maria?"

"They are doing fine," Senthil said impatiently. He knew they could not discuss something of this magnitude in a hurry, so he said, "I'll drop you off to work. Do you have a case this evening?"

"Not today, but tomorrow and every day for the rest of the week."

She hopped on behind him. It was still early for the morning traffic, and roads were quiet. Street vendors were setting up their stands. Coffee and tea stalls were preparing for morning customers, and the crowd at the bus stand was gradually swelling. Senthil said, "My case for this evening is coming to the hospital for a follow-up. I'll tell him I won't be coming today when I see him. I'll come and pick you up at work this evening."

"Sounds good." Sumathi smiled.

He drove to her hospital. The place was always crowded, but he found a corner to stop his motorbike. Sumathi got off the vehicle. Both checked their watches and smiled as they had some time on their hands. He parked his motorbike.

"I miss being in college," she started.

Senthil nodded in agreement. "Me too."

"What time do you get off work this evening?"

"I can manage to get out at around 5:00."

"Perfect. I'll try and get out a little earlier than that and just meet you at your hospital, and then we can go to Alsa Mall."

Senthil agreed. They wished each other a good day, and Senthil drove off.

In the evening, Sumathi came to Senthil's physiotherapy clinic at Apollo Hospital as he was treating his last patient—a young woman with childhood polio resulting in deformities of the leg. She had undergone correctional surgery. An open-reduction and external fixation fitted to her leg would straighten her limb. Senthil was stretching the weak muscles to prevent contracture of soft tissues as the bones grew in length.

Sumathi walked into the reception and told the receptionist that she was there to see Senthil. She also told the receptionist not to disturb him if he was with a patient. The receptionist said, "You can go inside, madam. Sir is with his last patient and asked me to send you in when you come." Sumathi smiled and walked in to see Senthil standing next to a table upholstered with dark brown leather. The floors had dark brown and orange tiles—so clean and shiny that one could see their reflection in them. Compared to her clinic in the government hospital, this was light years ahead. Senthil saw her coming and signaled her to enter.

Senthil smiled. "Sumi, this is Florence. She is from Kerala." He then turned to Florence and said, "This is Sumathi. I told you about her?"

"Hi, I have heard a lot about you," Florence smiled.

"Oh, oh!" she hesitated.

Florence replied, "Don't worry; it's all good. The only thing that is wrong is that you are way prettier than he described."

Sumathi blushed and said, "Well, I don't want to disturb your session. I'll wait in the staff room while he finishes your treatment."

"Don't be silly," Senthil objected. "Pull up that chair and sit down. You can distract Florence while I finish stretching her gastrocs. She hates this part."

Florence replied, "Sumathi, please stay. He is brutal and has no mercy."

Sumathi pulled up a chair and sat facing Florence. She kept Florence distracted while Senthil completed the stretching. He instructed Florence to slide to the edge of the bed, let her leg hang by the side, and lift her leg on to the bed, repeating the action fifteen times.

In the meanwhile, Senthil took Sumathi around the integrated ultrasound and interferential therapy unit and then showed her the short-wave diathermy machine and the electronic traction units. "This is nice," she nodded. "Wonder how many years it would take for all this to be available in every hospital." They walked back to Florence. Senthil helped her off the exercise table and told her he would see her tomorrow. Florence told Sumathi it was nice to meet her, and Sumathi replied, "Likewise. All the best with your therapy and recovery."

They then headed out to Alsa Mall, an upbeat West-style shopping complex. The mall housed boutiques catering to upscale clients, supplying clothes, leather bags, imported toys, and gourmet snacks and ice cream. The floors were of marble, and the best feature of the mall was that it was completely air-conditioned. It had a big courtyard in the middle, with a raised platform where people could sit. Stores surrounded this center. Sumathi and

Senthil went there for two reasons: to seek a respite from the heat and to window-shop. She sat down at one corner of the platform, right across from the popular snack shop "Hot Breads." Senthil went into the store and came out with a slice of black-forest chocolate cake and two spoons.

As they shared a slice of cake, Senthil pulled out the little notepad he had been obsessing over since last night. He said, "Honey, after talking with Shiva and getting all the information about the job as a contract physical therapist, this is what I have come up with." He showed her the notepad.

Sumathi, licking her spoon, reached for the notepad and asked, "Physical therapist?"

Senthil told her that physiotherapists were apparently referred to as physical therapists in America. Sumathi was amazed at the detail of the plan in the notepad. She could clearly see the time, effort, and thought he had invested in his deliberations. She felt grateful that Senthil was not a typical Indian guy who expected her to just listen to him after he had made all the decisions. When it came to their present or their future, Senthil always came to her for discussions and never with a decision. He valued her opinion and trusted her instincts. Senthil's notepad had this written down:

America:

Contract physical therapist monthly salary ($62,000 ÷ 12)	$5,166.67
After tax and deductions of approximately 40%	$3,100.00
Monthly allowance for living expenses – tax-free	$1,000.00
Total monthly income	$4,100.00
Health insurance, licensing exam, and PT license paid by the company	
Flight ticket Rs. 55,000 ÷ $43.45 = $1,265.82 (initially paid by the company and then deducted from monthly paycheck until paid in full)	–$105.49

Expenses: apartment rent, food, electricity, water bill, phone bill, transportation, miscellaneous, and unexpected Goal to keep within the monthly allowance	-$1,000.00
Net possible savings each month after expenses	$2,994.51
Monthly savings in rupees: $1.00 = Rs.43.45; $2,994.51 × 43.45	Rs. 1,30,111.46

India:

Monthly salary in India	Rs. 1,750.00
Private practice/Home visits averaging 2 patients a day at an average Rs. 50/visit × 30 days	Rs. 3,000.00
Average monthly expense in transportation and miscellaneous	Rs. 150.00
Net possible savings each month after expenses	Rs. 4,600.00
The time it would take in India to save the same amount saved in America: Rs, 1,30,111.46 ÷ Rs. 4600 = 28.29 months	2.36 years
Multiplying everything by 2, the time it would take us to make what we can make in 1 year in America	4.72 years

Senthil was anxious. The whole time she was reviewing the notepad, he studied her face cautiously. He did not want to disrupt her thought process, but he could hardly help feeling like a kindergartner who had submitted his homework to his favorite teacher and was impatient to hear the four magic words: “You got an A.” He could see her pupils dilate, and he was happy to see a smile that touched the corner of her beautiful lips and gradually spread across her face.

As much as it was about money, it was not about the money. That was merely a means to an end. To Senthil and Sumathi, it wasn’t about how much they could earn or save for themselves. It was about how much and how fast they could give to their families to ensure their bright future and finally start a family of their own. They were perfectly happy with starting together from scratch, without having to worry about the future of their siblings or the welfare of their parents.

Halfway through his notepad Sumathi looked up at Senthil, her eyes filled with tears. She exclaimed, "I cannot believe this! This is amazing. According to this calculation, we could get married before we turn thirty. We can actually have kids of our own, and they'll call us *appa* and *amma* rather than *thatha*[17] and *patti*[18]." Senthil was glad and relieved to hear her approval. He laughed as she echoed his sentiments. As she continued reading, her smile receded. She paused and sighed. What she said next with a sympathetic smile put an abrupt end to his laughter. "Honey, what do you mean by multiplying everything by two?"

He was surprised that she had not got it. "I did the calculation based on the numbers I got from Shiva, but that was only for one person. I multiplied it by two for the both of us," he said.

Sumathi said, "Honey, I am sorry to put a damper on this, but do you think my parents would be okay with us taking off together halfway across the globe before we are married?"

Senthil had to sit down. He felt weak. He felt that the mat underneath his feet had been pulled out. In a quivering voice, he asked, "What do you mean, Sumi? We are so close to making all our dreams come true—the ones we have for our families and the ones we have for ourselves. That too in half the time we thought it would be possible! Well then, if it is like how you say it, we'll get married first and then go to America."

She could sense the disappointment and the desperation in his voice. She could also see that he had forgotten they were in a public place.

She tugged at his hands, urging him to sit. She looked at him intently as he sat next to her, his head bent. He was ashamed of losing his cool as much as he was disappointed. She gently placed her hand over his and said, "Look at me, Senthil." When he looked up, his eyes met hers. She continued, "I want this as much as you do. But this is something we have to think about. We must think about the ramifications of our actions, and about what would happen

17 Grandfather

18 Grandmother

to our sisters. We have been patient for so many years. Now is not the time to become selfish in the name of making a sacrifice."

He understood exactly what she meant. She always knew what to say, when to say it, and how to say it. If they got married first, it would be extremely difficult, if not practically impossible, to find good suitors from respectable families for their sisters. Nobody would want to accept a girl whose elder sibling had an inter-caste marriage. That was one of the main reasons Senthil and Sumathi had decided to wait at least until Eshwari and Gauthami were married. Also, when there was a younger sister who had come of age, it was a common tradition in South India for the brother to wait to get married until the sister's marriage. What she said about being selfish in the name of making a sacrifice resonated with him.

Senthil came to terms with the situation. This was a nice dream, and that was all it was—a dream. It was time to wake up. That was when she said something he had never even thought of. "Honey, it is a wonderful opportunity, and times one is definitely better than times zero. Why don't you go to America? I can stay back and take care of our families here. It'll be only for a few years and—"

He interrupted her, "I don't think so, honey. I don't think I can be so far away from you for that long. I'll go insane." Sumathi was glad to hear that; it brought a smile to her face. She also knew that this was an emotional decision and not a rational one.

They just sat there silently, watching the people walking by.

The ride back home was quiet. Neither of them said a word. It was not awkward, though. Silence is never awkward when two hearts beat in harmony. They just enjoyed each other's proximity, the quiet road, and the gentle monsoon breeze. The roads were also quiet. Senthil adjusted the side mirror of his motorcycle to get a better view of her face. She had her eyes closed as the breeze tussled her hair and her pink-and-purple dupatta placed securely across her chest; it did not put up a fight and swayed with the breeze. A small smile lit her face, reflecting her contentment.

As usual, he stopped a few streets ahead of her house. As they strolled homewards, she broke the silence. "Senthil, I love you a lot, and I cannot picture my future with anyone apart from you. I know you love me, too. Our love for our families and our commitment to them is nothing less than our love for each other. And we have decided to unite only after ensuring their welfare. Distance, even if it is as great as the Atlantic Ocean, is no match for the love we have for each other. If staying away from each other for a few years means that we can achieve our goals and make our dreams a reality a lot sooner, then it is worth a try."

Senthil just nodded in response.

Sumathi did not expect him to say anything. She knew he always became quiet when he was in deep thought. She was glad that he was not angry with what she said. After all, she was suggesting that he make the sacrifice of leaving his family and her behind while she stayed home. But Senthil shared the same sentiment. He was sure that their love was much stronger than the strains of separation. He had a decision to make, but he also had the assurance that he did not have to make it alone. As they reached her house, he stopped. Sumathi said, "Aren't you coming up?"

Senthil said, "I need to go home. I promised Rathi to help her with a school project." Sumathi nodded her head and smiled, trying to hide her disappointment. He squeezed her hand and said, "I love you."

"I love you too," she replied.

Senthil turned around and walked away. After crossing a few yards, he slowed and turned back to see her still standing by the gate, looking at him. They waved at each other. She opened the gate and walked up the stairs. When she entered the house, she saw her *amma* sitting and reading a magazine. Gauthami was sitting at the dining table and writing something. Sumathi did not say anything to them. She just went to freshen up and did not come out.

She had her bed, and just as she was about to lie down, Gauthami peeked into her room. She was surprised to see her sister go to bed already and asked, "Are you okay?"

"Yes, I just have a lot on my mind," Sumathi replied.

Gauthami tiptoed into the room, kneeled beside Sumathi as she lay on her side, and whispered, "Did you see *athimber* tonight?"

Sumathi turned her head, smiled, and said, "Yes."

Gauthami was not going to accept a one-word answer. Giggling, she sat on the floor and said, "Tell me more. What did you talk about? Where did you go? What did you do?"

Sumathi was in no mood to entertain her. She just replied, "We talked about the future and what we are going to do with you."

Gauthami pouted her lips and said, "You are no fun." She got up to walk out.

Just then, Sumathi turned around and said, "You are beautiful." Gauthami blew her a kiss. Sumathi added, "I see you are wearing my *churidar*." Gauthami laughed out loud and ran out of the room.

After returning home, Senthil washed up and sat down to help Rathi with her science project. He had always considered his parents to be a little more liberal than Sumathi's parents. As his *amma* walked by, he asked her if she and *appa* would be okay with Eshwari going abroad for a job if it were safe. She replied that they were comfortable with that idea. He nodded and asked her how they would respond if she were to go with a good guy whom she intended to marry in a few years. She said, "Why do I get a feeling that we are not talking about Eshwari?" Senthil asked her to just humor him. She answered, "Well, it would be better if they got married and then went together. I don't think we would be comfortable with them leaving together no matter how good the guy was." She knew that was not the answer he wanted, but she did not want to lie to him.

Senthil was surprised at the answer, and not pleasantly. He knew it had to do a lot with the society they lived in. Western civilization had made an impact and was continuing to do so in the traditional Hindu culture. Some people had embraced them, but many of them were concerned by the pace of the changes. The major metropolitan cities of India, namely Delhi, Bombay,

Calcutta, Ahmedabad, Bangalore, Hyderabad, and Madras—all northern cities—were changing more readily than their southern counterparts.

Arranged marriages were still the norm in India, but society had begun accepting love marriages if they met the criteria of similar caste and family backgrounds. Inter-caste marriages were still frowned upon. Women had achieved great strides regarding rights to education and employment; boys and girls alike traveled overseas for both, and America was the prime destination for these trailblazers. However, while bachelors were bid farewell readily, some families still considered it too modern or liberal to send a bachelorette away.

The next day, Senthil called Sumathi at her workplace during his lunch break. "I am sorry I could not stay last night."

"Don't be silly. I understand. Was Rathi happy with her project?"

Senthil laughed and said, "She was, but we were up until midnight." She was glad he called, and he was happy to hear her voice. They talked about taking Shiva out for a meal before he left for America. Sumathi said that she would talk to Maria and check with her if she had any plans and would call him back tomorrow.

Sumathi called the next day and asked Senthil to keep the 22 of August free. She told him that Maria had arranged all the details for the day. Both scheduled their private patients for 7:00 AM that Sunday morning. Sumathi had a patient in Kilpauk. It was an eight-year-old girl with polio who had undergone surgery to release a flexion contracture of the Achilles and hamstring tendons. After the treatment session, she went to the Kilpauk bus stand from where Senthil had promised to pick her up at around 7:30 AM after finishing his session with his patient.

Senthil reached the bus stand on time. He picked her up and drove to Mylapore terminus bus stand where Shiva and Maria were waiting for them. The plan was to go to Besant Nagar—a place with rich history and famous landmarks in Madras.

Besant Nagar set along the shores of Bay of Bengal, the home of Elliot's Beach, was named after Annie Besant, the prominent British socialist, women's rights activist, and a big advocate for India's liberation from the British Empire.

Besant Nagar also housed the world famous Kalakshetra Academy: a dance school that was established in 1936 to preserve, teach, and promote Indian classical dance and music. It was an affluent neighborhood, and the tranquil area with the large banyan trees was home to many leading movie stars. In contrast to Marina Beach, Elliot's Beach was quieter and cleaner. There were several restaurants, but Maria, Shiva, Sumathi, and Senthil came to Besant Nagar for two other reasons: the Annai Velankanni Church and the Ashtalakshmi Temple.

The plan was to attend the Sunday morning Mass at the Annai Velankanni Church, say a prayer for Shiva's safe trip, have brunch, offer a prayer at the Ashtalakshmi Temple, followed by a stroll at Elliot's Beach before heading back home. The Annai Velankanni Church, with its magnificent 97-foot belfry, opened in 1972. The church was built in honor of the Virgin Mother Mary, who is portrayed with Her infant son Jesus, and people worship her and seek her blessings regardless of caste or creed.

The Ashtalakshmi Temple was built in 1976 to worship Goddess Lakshmi and was the only one of its kind on the East Coast. Ashtalakshmi literally translated to "eight Lakshmis," and the temple held all the eight forms of this Hindu goddess in her glory. People sought the blessings of Ashtalaksmi to secure all eight forms of wealth: health, wealth, knowledge, happiness, parenthood, courage, power, and long life.

Senthil had grown up with Anglo-Indians as neighbors. Celebrating Christmas or going to the church was nothing new for him. He constantly struggled with his beliefs. After an intense internal struggle, he embraced atheism until he met Sumathi. Even though he was raised a Hindu, he believed in one God and also that Jesus Christ was born to save humanity. He had two theories for the number of Hindu gods: either it was the people who had created the different versions to understand God better, or it was God who had sent these different versions to India, just like how He had sent Jesus to Jerusalem. Regardless, Senthil did not care much for organized religion. He did not think he needed a middleman in the name of a religion to mediate between him and God.

His parents did not oppose his beliefs. They were glad that he was no longer an atheist, and they believed that Jesus was also an incarnation of God. For Sumathi, on the other hand, this was the first time she was in a church. She was raised in a very religious Hindu Brahmin family and preferred to pray to her Hindu gods. But like many Hindus, she believed that the church is a holy place and Jesus is another version of God. Shiva had been to church many times with Maria and embraced Christianity as much as Hinduism. He was even ready to convert to please her family.

They all prayed for Shiva's safe trip and their future. Following this, they walked to Elliot's Beach. They were hungry and decided on a non-vegetarian restaurant. Sumathi had gotten accustomed to eating chicken. Lamb was too strong for her, and she had not been able to get past the smell of fish. They ordered some tandoori chicken, chicken tikka masala, chicken vindaloo, and chicken biryani. When the bill came, Senthil and Sumathi grabbed it, refusing to accept Shiva and Maria's offer to split it. It was their treat. When they came out of the restaurant, they got some ice cream and walked towards the beach.

They found a shaded spot and sat down. Shiva explained his itinerary. He was flying out of Madras, to Bombay, on an Indian Airlines flight. From there, he was to take the Lufthansa Airlines to Amsterdam, Netherlands, and then a connecting flight to Dallas, Texas. He told them that Hema, the lady with the recruiting company, was going to pick him up and take him to the company's apartment in Lewisville, Texas. He had to be there for a few weeks for his orientation, setting up a bank account, and getting his driver's license, and then go to Jefferson City, Missouri, as a contract physical therapist in a rehabilitation facility.

The whole thing sounded like a fairy tale. Sumathi changed the focus to Maria, saying, "So Maria, what are your plans? How are you going to handle the separation? Please feel free to call us anytime if you need anything."

Maria replied, "Thank you so much. I am counting on your moral support when Shiva leaves."

Shiva chimed in, "I hope it's not for too long. Hema is looking for a nursing job for Maria as well. With America's critical shortage of nurses, I am hoping she'll come to America soon."

Maria said, "I am studying for my *CGFNS*[19] exam, and once Hema finds a job for me, I can prepare for the *NCLEX-RN*[20]."

"Wow!" Sumathi exclaimed. "That's wonderful! If you don't mind me asking, are your parents okay with you going to America before you get married?"

Maria laughed and said, "I don't know. I have a cousin in Missouri. I am hoping my parents wouldn't mind if I get a job in Missouri."

If Sumathi and Senthil's was an uphill battle for an inter-caste marriage, Shiva and Maria had an epic battle ahead of them with inter-religion marriage. But they were in love with each other. Maria and Shiva were determined to elope if their parents did not approve of the match. Shiva was hopeful that going to America, gaining financial independence, and converting to Christianity would be enough to convince Maria's family to accept him as a son-in-law. Maria also knew that a man could do only so much for love. She respected his commitment to her and was willing to break ties with her family if needed.

Maria was the youngest of three children. She had two married elder brothers. Shiva had an elder brother and a younger brother, and he had no sisters that were yet to be married. So, they had the choice of eloping if it was absolutely essential. Senthil and Sumathi did not have that luxury to fall back on. They had younger sisters. Sure, they could always hope to win back their

---

19 Commission on Graduates of Foreign Nursing Schools

20 National Council Licensure Examination for Registered Nurses

parents' acceptance if they eloped. Historically, Indian parents remained estranged only until the time they became grandparents. Once a grandchild was born, they tended to melt, forgive, and accept their defiant children back into their families. However, Sumathi and Senthil could not expect the same acceptance from the potential suitors for their sisters.

At about 4:00 PM, they walked to the Ashtalakshmi Temple. Shiva and Sumathi wanted to walk up all the four levels, to all the eight shrines, to worship the eight forms of Goddess Lakshmi. Senthil and Maria followed.

It was getting late. They walked back to the Besant Nagar bus stand. They were happy that they had a good day, and no one said much on the way back home. The bus was not crowded. The men's seats in the bus were empty. Shiva and Maria sat in the front, and Senthil and Sumathi sat behind them. The bus reached the Mylapore terminus. Shiva was going to take Maria home and then head back to his place. Senthil shook his hand and wished him luck. He told him that he would go to the airport to see him off. Sumathi wished him the best as well. They both turned to Maria and asked her to call them if she needed anything.

Senthil got his motorbike, and Sumathi hopped on. They bid farewell to their friends. As Senthil started his bike, Sumathi whispered, "It's only 5:00 PM. I told my parents I'd be back between 7:00 and 8:00 PM. We can go to your house and then you could take me home if you don't mind."

Senthil said, "Are you kidding? That would be wonderful." He kick-started his bike, threw it into gear, and took off. He parked his motorbike at the bus stand close to his house, and they walked the remaining way.

When he opened the gate, he saw his family was watching the Sunday night movie on TV. Rathi spotted them first. She came out running and yelled, "Sumathi *anni* is here." Sumathi touched Senthil's parents' feet to pay her respects. "Long live my child and may God bless you," they blessed her. She exchanged pleasantries with his siblings. The movie was about to start. Senthil kneeled beside his parents and asked them if it would be okay for him and Sumathi to go up to the terrace to talk.

His parents nodded, and he signaled Sumathi to follow him as he climbed the stairs.

On reaching the terrace, Sumathi saw some bricks arranged in a long triangle. She looked puzzled and asked, "What are those bricks for?"

"That's where I do my pushups, and the bricks add some depth and range of motion, Sumi," he replied. Sumathi laughed and reached out to feel his biceps. He obviously had to tense his arm, and that made her laugh even more. The weather was just perfect; the sun had set, and stars were beginning to appear in the clear night sky. A gentle breeze turned the air around them chilly. Senthil grabbed one of the saris hanging on the clothesline and wrapped it around her.

She smiled, and said, "Only you can do something like this for me without me even asking for it. Only you can answer the question I am mulling over, and only you know what I need or want."

Senthil smiled and whispered, "My sentiments exactly. You just took the words right out of my mouth."

As they were talking, Bala, standing at the top of the stairs, cleared his throat and called out, "*Anna*, can I come up for a second?"

Senthil rolled his eyes, but Sumathi said, "Come up, Bala." Bala came up with a platter bearing two cups—one filled with water and the other with tea— and some onion *pakoras*[21] and *kesari*[22]. Sumathi asked, "Bala, is there enough for everybody?"

Bala replied, "Don't worry about it, *anni*. We all had our share." He then turned around and told them that he was going down before the commercials ended.

Sumathi reached for the cup of tea. Senthil grabbed her hand and asked, "How do you know that the tea is not for me?"

---

21 Fritters

22 South Indian dessert

Sumathi replied, "Everybody knows you don't drink tea or coffee. I don't know how you do it." Senthil smiled and said, "I like the smell of tea and coffee but just can't drink them."

Sumathi took a sip of the tea, cleared her throat, and softly asked, "So, did you give it any more thought?"

Senthil knew what she was talking about. He replied, "Yes, I am trying not to think about it."

"I feel guilty and sad that I am holding you back, that I am holding us back," Sumathi said.

Senthil replied, "Please don't say that or feel that way, Sumi. We are in this together."

Sumathi knew he was trying to make her feel better. She looked at him and said, "I think you should go—for our sake, our families' sake. I'll miss you terribly, but we will get through this. I am not sure how absence can make my heart grow fonder of you than it is now, but I believe in our love, and I believe we can survive this temporary separation." Senthil remained quiet. He did not know what to say. One part of him knew she was right, but another part could not bear to imagine being so far away from her.

Sumathi said, "Honey, please say something."

Senthil lowered his head and mumbled, "I am scared."

Sumathi put her hand over his and asked with genuine concern, "About what, honey?"

His voice cracked as he said, "I don't know . . ." She could not bear to see him breaking down like that. She knew that he was emotional and was not afraid to show it. That was one of the things she liked about him. She kissed her fingers and planted them on his cheek and ruffled his hair.

Senthil said in a somber voice, "The thought of us being together forever, the thought that we don't have to worry about our siblings and can focus on our lives is probably enough to carry me through our temporary separation for a few years."

Sumathi echoed his sentiments, saying, "I can't agree more."

They sat there, lost in thought, basking in their togetherness. Senthil broke the silence. "It's getting late. I better take you home." Sumathi let out a long sigh and stood up.

They both walked downstairs. Senthil's family was still watching the movie. He gestured to Eshwari that he would be back in ten minutes. She nodded to say that she would let *amma* and *appa* know. They opened the gate quietly and walked towards the bus stand where he had parked the motorbike.

As they parked the motorbike again and walked towards her house, Senthil told Sumathi that he would look into the application process and talk to Shiva before he left. Sumathi nodded. They realized that they were doing the right thing. Finally, they were on the same page, or as Senthil usually said, "on the same sentence." They felt at ease as they reached her house. He opened the gate for her, and she asked him if he was coming up. He was sure that her family too was watching the Sunday night movie, and he did not want to disrupt that.

That night, after the lights were all turned off, Senthil found it hard to fall asleep. After making several attempts to fall asleep, he gave up. He knew what he wanted to do, and it made sense. He jumped off the floor. It was just past midnight. He tiptoed out of the house and opened the gate as quietly as he could, hoping it would not squeak and wake everybody up. He took his bike out, pushed it fast as he ran beside it, and just like a western cowboy, he jumped on it, threw it into gear, and took off.

Before he knew it, he was in Mylapore, parking his bike in front of Shiva's place. He ran up the stairs and repeatedly knocked on Shiva's door. He did not care if the neighbors woke up. The complex housed a bunch of bachelor pads, and they were used to midnight ruckus. A half-asleep Shiva answered the door. He'd expected it to be one of his neighbors who was half drunk and wanted to borrow money to get something from the street food vendors. He opened the door partly and was surprised to see Senthil standing in his *baniyan*[23] and a pair of shorts.

---

23 Sleeveless undershirt

Shiva's first thought was that something was wrong. He asked, "Shorty, what are you doing here at this time of the night? Is everything okay?"

Senthil pushed him aside, walked into the room, turned the lights on, and sat down. Shiva had to squint to adjust his eyes to the bright lights. He looked at Senthil, puzzled. Senthil said, "Nothing is wrong. I want to come to America."

"What? Now? Are you crazy?"

Instead of answering his questions, Senthil asked if Shiva had an application packet. Shiva looked through his suitcase and found one. He told him that the packet contained a complete application form. All he had to do was to fill out the form, get two original transcripts from the college, four passport size photos, and a copy of the passport, and then wait a couple of months.

Senthil grabbed the packet. He wanted to get started on it right away. His goal was to complete everything so that instead of mailing everything to Hema in America, he could get it hand-delivered by Shiva. That was exactly what he did.

On September 15, Shiva was to fly out of Madras International Airport at 1:45 AM. This was the first time he was boarding a flight. His parents and his two brothers had come from his village to see him off. Senthil came to the airport with the application packet. Shiva promised that he would personally deliver it to her and request her to expedite the process. Shiva's parents told Senthil that they wished he were accompanying their son so that they could take care of each other in a foreign country.

Shiva was glad that Senthil came. He asked him to look after Maria. Senthil promised that Sumathi and he would check on Maria often. Although Shiva's parents were brimming with pride since he was the first in their family to board a plane or go overseas, they could not hide their anxiety. But it was a great opportunity, and they wanted the best for their son.

The next day, Senthil went to back to work knowing he had a busy day ahead of him. He had promised Shiva to take over two of his private practice patients. He was trying to make and save as much as possible so that he would not have to impose on his *appa* for the air ticket fare.

The following Sunday, he returned home from seeing a patient and noticed that everybody was at home. He had not told anybody that he had sent an application with Shiva and thought this would be a perfect time to break the news to his family. But he did not know how to begin. He had no idea how his parents or siblings would react.

He wanted to tell his parents before telling his siblings. His *appa* was reading the newspaper on the front porch, and his *amma* was in the kitchen with Eshwari. Sunday lunch was usually a big event since that was the only time everybody sat down to eat together. They always had something non-vegetarian. Chicken, lamb, fish, shrimp were all expensive, and middle-class families could not afford them daily. This luxury was reserved for Sundays in Senthil's house.

Senthil freshened up and went into the kitchen. He told his *amma* that he had something important to say to her. She gave him a puzzled look, washed her hands, and drying her hands on the *pallu*[24] of her sari, walked out behind him.

On reaching the porch, Senthil stopped and stood behind his *appa*. His *amma* went and sat next to his *appa* and said, "Senthil wants to say something."

His *appa* looked up and said, "What is it? Where is he?" He turned around and said, "Hey, what are you doing back there when you want to talk? Come up to the front."

Senthil's head was lowered. He walked to the front and found a corner. With his head still lowered, he said, "I am thinking about going to America to work as a physiotherapist. It pays well, and it's a great opportunity. I have sent an application with Shiva and hope to hear from them soon."

There was a pause. All Senthil heard from his *appa* was an elongated "hmmm."

---

24 Part of the sari draping the shoulder

His *amma* looked stunned. She said, "Are you telling us that you are going to America or asking us if you can go?" There was no anger in her voice—just concern.

His *appa* said, "Shh. Let him speak. What is this suddenly?" Senthil explained to them what he had learned from Shiva about the job opportunities, pay, and how much he could save in a year. The financial aspect made sense to his *appa*. After all, he was a working man. Senthil's *amma* was completely emotional and was only thinking with her heart. She could not bear the thought of him going so far away.

With tears in her eyes, she said, "I can't believe you are ready to leave us all behind."

His *appa* interrupted her, "Does Sumathi know about this?"

Senthil nodded, "Yes."

Eshwari yelled out from the kitchen, "*Amma*, the masala is ready, and I have ground the garlic and ginger." His *amma* got up, but his *appa* motioned her to sit down. He told her not to get emotional or question Senthil's motives. He explained to her that Senthil was sacrificing a lot by going to America and that he was doing this more for them than himself. He asked her to think that even if she believed he could happily leave them behind would she believe that he would also happily leave Sumathi behind?

She got up, rubbed her hands on Senthil's face, and then cracked her knuckles on her head. This was a gesture performed in India to ward off evil spirits. She asked him to come and have breakfast. Senthil replied that he did not want to ruin his appetite by eating a late breakfast, as he was looking forward to the chicken biryani and chicken korma.

Senthil's *appa* gestured him to sit down to talk about it in greater detail, while his *amma* walked into the kitchen. Eshwari saw her tearful expressions and knew something was wrong. She had always been perceptive and a stabilizing force—be it listening and counseling her *amma* or taking care of the conflicts between her siblings. His *amma* told her that Senthil was thinking about going to America.

Just then, Bala walked into the kitchen to get a snack, and he could not believe what he heard. He ran out yelling, "*Anna* is going to America!" That was all it took to send Rathi and Nanda in a frenzy. In a second, a pandemonium broke. They were all screaming, "What?", "Really?", "When?", 'Who is going with him?", "Why?" "He is going to see snow."

Senthil's *appa* told him, "You better go inside and take care of it before they run around and break something." Senthil nodded and walked inside the house. His siblings were all over him like little paperclips attracted towards a magnet. He placed his index finger over his lips, asking them to be quiet, and then said, "I have sent an application packet with Shiva. Let's see what happens."

Eshwari asked, "If everything goes well, when do you think you will leave?"

"Hopefully in December. So, in two and a half to three months."

A collective "Wow, that soon!" resounded across the room. He asked them to run along and finish the homework and get things done for school the next day so they could all sit and eat lunch together, play *carrom board*[25] afterward, and then watch the Sunday night movie on TV together.

He then changed his clothes, grabbed his motorbike keys, and headed out. His *amma* stopped to inform him that lunch would be ready in an hour. Senthil promised that he would be back before that. Eshwari knew exactly where he was going and told him that if he went after lunch, he could perhaps take Sumathi some chicken biryani, korma, and raita. He shook his head and said, "No, that's okay. I don't have time."

He hopped on his motorbike and drove to Sumathi's house. He drove past her house and honked his horn twice. Sumathi was inside the house, helping her *amma* in the kitchen. She recognized that sound; it had been their signal to meet for quite some time. The honks brought a smile to her face. She washed her hands and told her *amma* that she suddenly remembered a phone call she had to make to one of her patients. Her *amma* said, "Can't you do it

---

25 Cue sport-based tabletop game

later when the sun sets?" Sumathi replied that she had promised to call them at the earliest hour possible and assured her that she would be back shortly. Her *amma* said, "Don't forget the umbrella."

It was not raining, but Indian girls were more afraid of the sun than they feared the rain. They would rather get drenched in the rain than turn a shade darker under the sun. Fair complexion was desired by all, especially girls of marriageable age; it was a big advantage in arranged marriage matches. Brides' parents tended to get a better deal in dowry if the girl had a fair complexion.

Sumathi grabbed the umbrella, and then ran down the stairs and hurried to the local telephone booth where Senthil was waiting for her. He jumped off his parked motorbike the moment he saw her and said, "I filled out the application and was able to get all the supporting documents including the transcripts from our college in time to send the entire packet with Shiva. He is going to deliver it to Hema."

Sumathi replied, "That's great. That'll save us time, and we don't have to worry about whether something happened to the mail." She told him that she could not stay longer. Senthil nodded and told her that he had just wanted to see her and tell her about the application. He made his way back home, counting the number of possible days it would take to hear something back from America.

Chapter 4 — Waiting for the Visa

IN THE NEXT THREE WEEKS, NOT A SINGLE DAY WENT BY without Senthil checking the mail. The night of Saturday, October 9, Senthil came home late after treating three private patients. He entered the house, tired, and found all his siblings sitting at the dining table. They were unusually quiet for a Saturday night; even the TV was off. As he walked inside to freshen up, he asked, "Where's *amma* and *appa*?" Eshwari said that they had gone shopping for Diwali. Diwali is the festival of lights that celebrates the triumph of good over evil. This year, it was on November 3. It is one of the elaborate festivals of Hindus that is comparable to Christmas. People wear new clothes, make a lot of sweets and food, and light fireworks.

After a shower, Senthil came out and was perplexed to see everybody still so quiet. Parents' absence, combined with no school the next day, was usually a recipe for disaster—not today, though. He asked, "What are you all up to?"

They could not hold it in any longer and screamed in unison, "You got a letter from America!" His eyes widened. "Where is it?"

Bala took out the letter from inside his book, and holding it up in the air, said, "What are you going to give me in return?" Senthil lunged to grab the letter from Bala who ran around the house. The other kids thought it was funny and cheered Bala on. As Senthil caught up with him, Bala threw the letter to Nanda, who passed it on to Eshwari, who then tossed it to Rathi, and eventually, it came back to Bala.

Senthil stopped chasing and warned, "I am going to count to three, and by then, if the letter comes to my hand, I'll spare you all. If not, no one's going to watch any TV for a week." Before the sentence was finished, Bala surrendered and handed the letter to him. Senthil was visibly nervous as he opened the letter. His hands trembled. He sat down to read it, and his siblings stared at him. They were patiently waiting for him to say something. After he finished reading, he put back the notes in the envelope and silently walked into his bedroom.

They looked at each other and mumbled. They hadn't expected this somber reaction from Senthil. They stood in the doorway of the room, worried. Eshwari was brave enough to ask, "Is everything okay?"

Senthil was grinning from ear to ear and screamed, "Gotcha! Yeah, everything is fine. That was a note from Shiva and Hema. Shiva said that he reached safely and is over the jet lag and is on orientation. Hema said that my application packet was complete and that she has filed for my visa and the temporary license."

They all screamed and began to jump up and down in joy. In the noise, they did not hear their parents open the gate and come in. They were surprised to see Eshwari, who was usually a little more reserved, taking part in the shenanigans. Their *appa* shook his head, while their *amma* exclaimed, "What is going on?" Everybody stopped suddenly.

After a moment of silence, Rathi ran up to their parents and announced, "They have accepted Senthil *anna's* application for America."

His *amma* did not want to hear any more. She walked into the room with the bags. His *appa* sat down in the middle of the hall, and asked, "So, when do you have to leave?"

"I don't know. Hema has filed for my visa and temporary physiotherapist license. Based on the time it took Shiva, I am guessing early December," Senthil replied.

Senthil woke up early in the morning. Everybody was still asleep. He got ready and drove to Sumathi's bus stand first to catch her before she went off to see her patients. He waited for no longer than ten minutes when he saw Sumathi walking towards him in a hurry. She told that her first patient was in Aminjakarai. His first patient was in Kilpauk, and since her place was on his way, he said he would drop her off. She was excited and hopped onto the motorbike behind him.

The roads were quiet, as it was a Sunday morning. He asked her where her last patient was, and she said it was in Arumbakkam and that she should be done at around 2:00 PM. He asked her if she would be interested in going to his place with him. She said yes, but she had to be back home by 7:00 PM since her relatives were coming to visit. She said, "My *periyamma*[26] and *periyappa*[27] are very conservative. My parents told me to come home before they arrive." Senthil asked her not to worry about it and promised to drop her back in time.

He dropped her off in front of her patient's house and left to go see his patients. Even though they both had three patients to see, Senthil had a motorbike and was able to be back at the Arumbakkam bus stand by 1:30 PM. He was surprised to see Sumathi standing at the bus stand already. He pulled up close to her and asked, "How did you beat me here?"

Sumathi laughed and said, "Well, you may have a motorbike, but I have a helicopter."

He laughed, "Very funny."

She said, "Two of my patients were on neighboring streets, and I just had to walk for ten minutes instead of waiting for the bus."

As they drove towards his house, Sumathi saw a street vendor sitting on the platform selling flowers. She tapped Senthil's shoulder and asked him to stop. The woman had a big basket with *Malligai*[28], *Kanakambaram*[29], and

26 Mother's elder sister

27 Mother's elder sister's husband

28 Jasmine

29 Firecracker flower

Samanthi[30]. They were tied into strings and sold by length. Women adorned their hair with these flowers. In Hindu culture, widows were prohibited from wearing flowers on their heads and from wearing a *bindi* on their forehead. It is customary to bring these garlands of flowers while visiting a family with wives and girls of age.

She got down from the motorbike, and after a little haggling with the woman, she bought some *Malligai* and some *Kanakambaram*. The flowers were wrapped in a moist banana leaf so they would stay fresh longer. When Sumathi returned, he said, "You sure did give her a hard time." She replied, "I can't believe she was going to charge me an arm and a leg for these. I talked her down." She sounded proud of securing a good deal. Senthil stopped a street before his house. Sumathi got down so she could walk the rest of the way home. Just before he took off, she asked, "Is your *amma* making chicken?"

Senthil replied, "Of course; it's Sunday." He went into the house and washed up in haste, and before he went to change his clothes, he rushed into the kitchen and whispered in Eshwari's ear that Sumathi was coming.

She looked at him excitedly and said, "Oh no! You should have told me earlier. We made chicken korma, chicken masala, and coconut rice. If I knew Sumathi was coming, I would have made her favorite chicken biryani." Senthil said that it was okay and that it had been decided at the last minute.

She winked and said, "I think I can still whip up something really fast."

He said, "You are a Godsend. Thank you!"

Eshwari told her *amma* that everything was almost done and asked if *appa* was ready to eat and whether she could set the table. *Amma* was reading the newspaper. She looked up and said, "You have done enough. Call your brothers and sisters to set the table so you can go freshen up." Eshwari went back to the kitchen to check on the cooker. Senthil came into the kitchen and told her, "You go. I'll take care of the rest."

She said, "Okay, just make sure you turn the stove off after the pressure cooker whistles thrice. If you leave it any longer, the rice will become mushy."

---

30 chrysanthemum

He nodded and then called out for Nanda, Rathi, and Bala to set the table. Just then, Sumathi reached the house. Bala saw her first and was about to run to open the gate. Senthil stopped him and said, "Go help set the table like you were asked to. I'll take care of the gate." He opened the gate. Sumathi took off her sandals at the porch and walked in. Hearing the gate open, his parents came out to see who it was. Sumathi bent down to touch their feet to pay her respects and gave *amma* the flowers.

Everybody sat around the table. Sumathi headed into the kitchen to help. Eshwari warned her that they had been cooking chicken all day and the smell could be too strong for her. Sumathi told her it smelled very good and that she had gotten used to chicken. It was the smell of fish that churned her stomach.

Their *appa* said the lunch was totally worth all the wait. They all thanked their *amma* and Eshwari for the delicious lunch. Sumathi thanked them for their hospitality and gave Eshwari a special thanks for making her favorite chicken Biryani. Eshwari looked at Senthil and winked. Bala said, "There was Biryani? I thought we had coconut rice." Eshwari said she had made only a small amount for Sumathi, and there was a collective "Oh!"

Sumathi felt shy and got up to help clean up, but Eshwari told her that she and Rathi would take care of tidying up the kitchen. Their parents and Bala sat in the living room to watch TV. It was too hot to go up to the terrace, so, Senthil and Sumathi walked out to the porch. His *appa* asked Senthil to close the door since there was too much glare on the TV. He smiled and mouthed the words "Thank you," as he knew that his *appa* had said that to give some privacy to them. He closed the door behind him and handed her the letter. Sumathi looked at him in puzzlement. "What's this?"

He only gestured her to open the letter. She read the letter and said, "This is great! It's good to know everything is going well. But when will you . . ."? Her voice cracked, and she could not finish the sentence.

Senthil said, "Probably December." They sat quietly for a few minutes, which felt like an eternity to both.

Sumathi said, “I understand that it’s hard to be excited and sad at the same time. We have talked about it. We think it is the most rational thing to do. We love each other and know that the distance is not going to change anything. We could be gloomy until the day you leave, or we could just look at it positively, as a sacrifice for our bright future, approach it happily, and enjoy the time leading up to it.”

Senthil reached for her hand, and her first response was to gasp and turn around to make sure the door was still closed. She clasped his hand briefly, smiled coyly, and winked at him. He said, “Your face . . .” and paused.

Sumathi tilted her head and asked, “What’s wrong with my face?”

“Nothing. It’s just perfect. It’s the most beautiful thing I have ever seen. It’s also what I am going to miss the most.”

“Well, we’ll have to make an album with pictures of my face before you go to America, so you can look at it whenever you think of me.”

“Sweetie, if I want to see your face, all I have to do is close my eyes.”

She smiled and said, “That’s smooth; you are a real charmer.”

He grinned and said, “I can’t argue with that.”

Senthil showed his watch to Sumathi: it was 6:30 PM. She walked into the house to take leave of his parents. She touched their feet, and they asked her to convey their best to her parents. Then she said goodbye to Senthil’s siblings.

Senthil pushed his motorbike along, walking on Sumathi’s side, until they reached the corner of the street. Then she got onto his motorbike, and he dropped her off at the usual spot near her house.

Senthil kept up his feverish pace of working with his private patients to earn as much as he could. He had four patients now, and even saw one early in the morning before going to work. Weeks went by. He managed to see Sumathi at least once a week. He kept everybody updated regarding the correspondence from Hema and Shiva—from getting approved for the temporary license, receipt of the application by the United States INS[31], to the approval of the labor certification.

On Thursday, November 18, he came home at around 10:00 PM. Everybody was already in bed as it was a school night. He tried to be very delicate with opening the gate and parking his motorbike. He reached the front door, and as he was fumbling with his keys, the door opened. It was Eshwari. She had the habit of staying up for him or their *appa*. She told him to go wash up as she set up his plate for dinner. He said, "Thank you Eshwari. You shouldn't have stayed up, but I appreciate it. I'll clean up after myself."

She just smiled. As he was walking to the bathroom, she said, "Oh, I have left something for you on the shelf above the TV."

After his shower, he came straight to the dining table. He was famished. He had skipped lunch at work so that he could leave an hour early to see his private patients. He gorged on the rice and the potatoes and peas curry and finished his meal with rice, yogurt, and mango pickle.

He walked towards the TV. His heart skipped a beat when he saw the Express Mail envelope with a large eagle on it. He realized why Eshwari had said "something above the TV" rather than a packet or letter from America. She wanted to make sure he ate his dinner after the long day he had. He picked up the packet and came back to the dining table. He paused for a second before opening the envelope. There it was: approval of his H1-B visa by the INS and instructions to go to the American Consulate in Madras.

Eshwari peeked out of her room. She wanted to make sure she that did not disturb their siblings' sleep. Senthil saw her and waved her to come out. He said, "My visa has been approved. I have to go to the American Consulate on the 26 with my passport to get the visa stamped."

She replied, "Wow! That was fast. So, when will you leave for America?"

"As early as the first or second week of December if I have enough for the flight ticket," he replied.

"Aren't they paying for it?" she asked.

---

31 Immigration and Naturalization Service

"Yes. Hema will reimburse the airfare after I get there, but I have to buy the ticket first."

He told her to go to bed and that he would talk to *amma* and *appa* in the morning. Eshwari said, "I am happy for you; I am happy for all of us. I know you are doing this to take care of us, but all of it is just happening too soon." He assured her that it was all going to be okay and that he was going to be gone only for a few years. He sat down to read the letter all over again, to make sure that he had not misunderstood anything.

When he was satisfied, he walked into his siblings' bedroom to fetch his bedding. He closed the door partially so that the light did not wake them up and moved to the corner to pick up his bedding. In the faint light, he was able to see all of his siblings lying on the floor. Suddenly, it hit him—the nightmare that had been plaguing him ever since he was nine flashed before his eyes. He broke in a cold sweat. He knew he could not stand there all night. He dropped his bedding in the middle of the room and headed to the sink in the dining room.

He splashed some cold water on his face and gulped down a glass of cold water. Then, he lay down on the floor, blankly staring at the ceiling. He must have eventually fallen asleep because he woke up to rattling noises from the kitchen. It was Eshwari getting an early start. He got up and headed to the shower. He was hoping his *appa* would wake up before he left, as he wanted to share the news about his visa.

It was 6:10 AM when he was ready to leave. He found his *appa* reading the newspaper on the front porch. Eshwari knew he would not have the time to eat breakfast, so she had packed some *idlis* and chutney for breakfast and some rice and leftover vegetable curry for lunch. He grabbed the boxes and said, "Eshwari, you are the best. Ask *amma* to come to the porch." He then walked out with his bag and stood in the corner of the porch.

His *appa* lowered the newspaper, and peering above his eyeglasses, he said, "Looks like you are heading to work. Did you have breakfast?"

Senthil replied that he had not but that he was taking along the breakfast Eshwari had packed for him. Just then, his *amma* walked out to the porch with two cups of coffee. She handed one to his *appa* and sat down with the other. Senthil said, "My H1-B visa has been approved. I must go to the consulate next Friday with my passport to get it stamped."

His *appa* looked surprised and said, "That was fast. Congratulations! You are a hard worker, and you will do well, no matter where."

Senthil replied, "Well, I learned from the best."

His *amma* did not seem too thrilled about it. She said, "But what does this mean that you are getting something stamped on your passport?" Senthil replied that he would be leaving to America soon, perhaps as early as December. His *amma* said, "That early? You wouldn't even give us enough time to get used to the thought that you are going away?"

His *appa* interrupted her, "Okay, you don't start now. Don't make him late to work. We'll talk about it tonight." He then gestured Senthil to go on.

His *amma* drank her coffee in silence, while his *appa* read the rest of the newspaper. Knowing that she was not going to get anything from her husband, she got up and went to the kitchen. The moment she saw Eshwari, she said, "I cannot believe he is so anxious to leave us all behind to go and enjoy in America! I didn't know he could be so selfish."

This angered Eshwari, and she lashed out. "Selfish? *Amma*! Do you really think he wants to go to America to get away from us and have fun? He is doing this for us. He is putting his life on hold for us. I am actually happy that he is going so he can achieve his goals sooner and can move on to live his life."

Her *amma* was speechless. She had not expected that from her mild-mannered daughter. She knew Eshwari was right. Eshwari saw her *amma* tear up, and this calmed her down. She put her hand on her *amma*'s shoulder and said, "I know you are sad to see your eldest son go so far away, but you are going about it the wrong way." She gave her *amma* a much-needed hug.

During his lunch break, Senthil called Sumathi's hospital and asked to be connected to the Physiotherapy Department. He wanted to tell her about the approval of his H1-B work visa. She could not come to the phone as she was with the mother of an infant with Erb's palsy due to a breech delivery. She was teaching her some exercises and proper positioning to help the weak muscles of the shoulder, elbow, and wrist. So Senthil left a message that he had called. He was a little disappointed that he could not share the news with her, but he understood that she was busy.

His afternoon turned out to be quite hectic, and he did not get any time to think. He had a couple of stroke patients. He then had to juggle between a patient with back pain who required intermittent traction, interferential therapy, and back exercises and a patient with plantar fasciitis who needed phonophoresis with ultrasound and dexamethasone gel and stretching exercises. Just when he was going for a break, he had a patient with an ACL repair who required pain management, mobilizing, and strengthening exercises. By the time he had to run up to see a couple of patients in the ICU for chest physiotherapy and cardiac rehab after open heart surgery, he was beaten. Before he knew it, it was 6:00 PM, and it was time to leave.

He bid his colleagues goodbye and walked up to the front desk to hand over his patient notes to the secretary. As he came to the front, Sumathi, who was reading a magazine in the corner, got up and said, "Hi."

His face lit up like Diwali firecrackers. He dropped his notes on the table, and said, "Hi. When did you get here?"

She smiled and said, "About twenty minutes ago."

He turned to look at the secretary who said, "I got your notes. Don't keep that pretty girl waiting."

He said a big thank you and turned around to walk out with Sumathi. As they exited the hospital and hurried to the parking lot, Senthil said, "I am so happy to see you."

Sumathi replied, "I am sorry I couldn't come to the phone. When they said I got a call from you, I managed to work through lunch and get out early so I could catch you before you left." He asked her if she had any patients to see. She said she had one to see that evening. Senthil had two. He said that he would drop her at her patient's house and then go to see his. She said, "That would be great. So, are you going to tell me why you called? Or do you want me to guess?"

"Hmm . . . take a guess," he said.

"Well, you seldom call me at work. So, it must be something important. I am going to guess that you heard from either Hema or Shiva." Senthil was not surprised that she got it right away. He told her his visa had been approved and he had to go to the American Consulate to get his passport stamped. Sumathi was relieved to have crossed the first hurdle and to see they were one step closer to their goals. He asked her if she could take the upcoming Friday off and go to the American Consulate with him, and she agreed.

Chapter 5 — The American Consulate

ON FRIDAY, NOVEMBER 26, EVERYBODY GOT UP EARLY IN Senthil's house. His *amma* had arranged a pooja for the gods. She made offerings to all her favorite gods and goddesses: Lord Shiva, Ganesh, Krishna, Lakshmi, and Sarasvati. Senthil did not want to hurt his *amma*'s feelings, so he joined them.

Sumathi joined in on time to take part in the pooja. She helped with making the flower garlands while Eshwari and her *amma* made the food for the pooja. After the pooja, the food would become the divinely blessed *prasadam* that would be eaten to invoke the blessings of the gods. After attending the pooja and having the prasadam as breakfast, Senthil's siblings went off to school, Eshwari to college, and his *appa* to work. They all wished him the best before they left. Sumathi helped his *amma* clean up while he was at the dining table, checking his file to make sure he had everything in place. He wanted to make sure he had his passport, his bachelor's degree certificate, college transcripts, the approval of the I-129 petition for the non-immigrant worker that Hema sent, his proof of residence, and his birth certificate.

He was a little anxious. He dressed in a light blue shirt, black pants, and his *appa*'s red, white, and blue checkered tie. He had polished his shoes last night. He called out to Sumathi from the porch and told her it was time to go.

Sumathi came running out, and with one look at him, she gasped. She had never seen him in a tie. "You look very handsome!" she said.

He blushed and said, "Thanks, honey. I am a little nervous." She assured him that he was going to do great in the interview. Sumathi was holding on to his folder as they headed to Mount Road where the Madras American Consulate was located. There was no parking near the consulate, so they parked in the Parson Shopping Complex on Nungambakkam High Road and walked to the consulate.

The consulate sat inside a 12-foot-high compound wall. When they reached, Senthil knocked on the small glass window and handed the I-129 petition for non-immigrant worker approval and his passport to the guard. Once that was checked out, he was asked to enter through the small narrow gate. He and Sumathi tried to enter, but the guard stopped them and said, "Only the applicant. Your wife should wait outside." They both smiled at each other. He took the folder from her and asked the guard how long it would take to get his visa stamped in his passport. The guard told him that it could be anywhere between four to six hours. He asked Sumathi what she was going to do for the next few hours. He apologized to her and said he would never have asked her to come if he had known that she would have to wait outside.

"Don't be silly," Sumathi replied. "I would have come with you even if you hadn't asked me to. I can go see two of my patients and be back by the time you are done."

The guard was getting impatient, so Senthil said, "Okay. I'll see you soon. Thanks again, honey." He walked in, and the guard closed the gate. Sumathi walked to the bus stand.

Inside the compound wall, a courtyard led to the consulate. When Senthil entered the room, he saw almost a hundred people there, each anxiously waiting with a ticket in their hands. Senthil noticed a little machine under the sign that read "Take a ticket and wait to be called." He pulled out a ticket: number 76. He sat down in an empty seat, not knowing what to expect. He kept to himself and continued to quietly look at his folder. Students were waiting for their student visas. Some people were waiting for a visitor's visa. Some men and women were anxious to get their dependent visa or fiancé visa so that they could join their better halves. There were even older parents looking forward to visiting their children who had settled in America.

From their faces, their body language, and the tone of their voices, it was easy to distinguish between people who were there for the first time and those for whom it was not their first rodeo. Senthil had repeatedly heard that if he came across as a potential immigrant to the consular, he could kiss his visa goodbye. It was the burden of any applicant under the non-immigrant visa to convince the consular that they indeed intended to return to India at the end of the visa term. This could be done by showing documentation of property ownership in India, a potential employment offer on return, and other strong family ties. Senthil had a copy of the "ration card."

Even though this was called card, it was a booklet issued by the state government. It had the householder's name and age, the spouse's name and age, and the children's names and ages. This would be issued when officials went door to door to assess census and were used as a proof of residence, to get rice, wheat sugar, and oil at subsidized rates.

While the others tried to talk to each other and find out the kind of visa that they were there for, the way to get a good deal on the airfare to America, and the best airlines to fly, Senthil remained quiet. For the next four hours, he anxiously waited for his number to be called. Every time the monitor went "ding, dong" he straightened himself up in the chair and looked up. The next few hours felt like a few years for him. It was about 2:30 PM when the monitor chimed "76." It took him a couple of seconds to figure out that he had been summoned.

Senthil got up hurriedly. A shiver took over him, and his hands trembled. He paused, took a deep breath, walked to the glass window, and sat on the stool across from the consular. The consular was a female in her twenties. She had wavy blonde hair and was wearing a white shirt with a dark blue blazer. On her left lapel was an American flag pin.

"Good afternoon," Senthil said.

"Good afternoon to you too," she replied. She asked him for proof of residency other than his passport. He slid the ration card under the slot in the glass window. As she was looking through, she asked him why he wanted to go to America. Senthil replied that he was going to gain some experience working with the latest technology and earn some money. She asked him how long he planned to live in America, and he quickly replied that it would be two to three years. She asked him if he would change his mind after living in America for a few years and want to settle down there.

Senthil replied, "No way. My family is here. My parents and my brothers and sisters are here, and I am leaving the love of my life behind only so that I can earn enough money and come back to settle down with her." His voice cracked as he got emotional when he said that.

The consular said, "Lucky girl. What is her name?"

Senthil replied, "Sumathi, and I am the lucky one."

She smiled and slid the passport and the ration card back to him. He fixed his gaze on her, anxiously waiting to hear what she was going to say. She gestured for him to look down, so he slowly picked up his passport and nervously opened it. She congratulated him as he saw the H1-B Temporary Work Visa stamp on it. His face lit up, and he had a grin from ear to ear. She said, "You are all done here. Have a safe trip and good luck."

He thanked her profusely and rushed out of the building. He stopped at the gate at the edge of the compound. As soon as he exited the gate, he loosened his tie and began to gasp for air. He was elated that the wait was over, but at the same time he was also apprehensive of what the future held for him. That was when he heard an all-too-familiar voice call out, "Hope your interview went well." He turned to the left, and there was Sumathi, standing on the sidewalk with an umbrella in her hand to block the sun's rays from her fair complexion.

He was extremely glad to see her, but he remained quiet. He was still catching his breath. As she came closer to him, he further loosened his tie and hunched forward. He then handed her his passport. She looked at him with concern and slowly reached for it, hesitant to open it. She slowly opened it, and as soon as she saw the H1-B Temporary Work Visa stamped on his passport, tears rolled down her eyes. Senthil lifted his head to look at her and smiled.

He then stood up straight and arched his back to stretch himself. Sumathi said, "Honey, this calls for a celebration."

"Of course! What do you have in mind?" he smiled.

She said, "I know just the right place." They began to cross the road. Senthil reached for her hand. Sumathi smiled and clasped her hand around his. They walked hand in hand, with Sumathi leading the way. She stopped at *Archana Sweets and Chaat Palace*. It was a place where all dessert lovers' dreams come true. The store offered a wide range of both North Indian and South Indian sweets and savory snacks.

She asked him to sit and walked up to the counter. She spoke to the guy at the counter and came back and sat across him. The aroma of all the spices and desserts was mouthwatering. The myriad of colorful desserts of all shapes and sizes inside the glass cases looked like beautiful paintings. Senthil was salivating. Just the thought of desserts could make his mouth water. A few minutes later, a server brought out a tray with an array of desserts and set it in front of him.

In front of Senthil were a *jilebi,* a kesar pistha roll, a Mysore *pak*, a *kaju katli*, a *rasamalai*, a *kala jamun*, *besan burfi, motichur ladoo, kesar chum, and badam halwa.* His eyes widened as wide as the *jilebi* in front of him. Sumathi smiled and said, "It's all for you, honey. So, eat to your heart's content."

Senthil joked, "What? You think I can't put this away?"

"No honey, I want you to."

Senthil offered to share it with her, but she insisted that he should eat as much as he could, and she would help him finish it if necessary. She got a cup of hot masala chai for herself. She patiently drank it sip by sip as she enjoyed watching him indulge his sweet tooth.

Senthil had no trouble finishing the desserts. Sumathi had never doubted that he could. She told him, "I am so happy to see that smile and look of contentment on your face."

He was quick to reply, "It is all because of you."

She called the server and ordered two of their two-kilogram boxes of assorted desserts. As Senthil reached for his wallet, Sumathi tapped his hand and said, "Put your wallet away. This is my treat."

He replied, "Well, thank you, my dear. Are those boxes for us to eat on our way home?"

Sumathi said, "No little piggy, those are for our families. We cannot share this great news empty-handed."

Senthil replied, "You are always so thoughtful. Thank you."

First, they went to Senthil's house. As usual, she got off two streets ahead of his house, and instead of driving home, he parked his motorbike on the side of the road. She looked at him in confusion. He said, "I am not going there and telling them I got the visa without you by my side."

She smiled, "That's so sweet!"

He chuckled and added, "Besides, you have the boxes of sweets, and I can't trust you alone with them." He winked. She wanted to pinch him but restrained herself.

Nanda, Rathi, and Bala were all on the terrace of the house, eagerly anticipating his return. As soon as they saw him around the corner, they ran down to tell their parents and Eshwari. By the time they reached the gate, his family had already gathered at the door. They waited with bated breath. Senthil was enjoying this suspense his family was going through. He kept quiet and hung his head low. There was a small smirk on his face, but they could not see it. Sumathi tried to stay out of it, but she could not bear their plight any longer. She slapped him on the shoulder and said, "It's not fair that you are putting your family through this. Tell them already."

He looked up with a big smile and announced, "I got the visa."

His siblings surrounded him, congratulating him and bombarding him with questions. Questions flew from all directions, and he did not even know who was asking what. He did not even have the time to respond. All he heard was this: "Are you going to get a window seat on the airplane?", "What is the first thing you are going to do when you land in America?", "Will you play in the snow?" "Can you take a photo with KITT, the car from Knight Rider?"

Sumathi moved to one corner of the room. She wanted to make sure he got all the attention and adoration from his family that he deserved. She watched him with pride and joy. Suddenly, it dawned on her: she wanted to capture these moments so that they would last forever.

She pulled out her little point-and-shoot camera and walked around them, taking pictures. She wanted to capture the moment from all angles. Senthil freed himself from his siblings; he walked towards his parents and touched their feet. His *appa* lifted him by grabbing his shoulders and said, "I am proud of you my son."

Senthil replied, "I am in this position today because of you, and all the credit goes to you."

His *appa* replied, "It's all your hard work and God's blessings." There was not a single pair of dry eyes in the room.

Sumathi wiped her tears and walked into the kitchen. She took a few small plates and placed on them the desserts she had bought. She placed the plates on a serving tray and walked out. "*Laddu* and *jilebi* anyone?"

All his siblings turned around and yelled, "Me!" They all sat down to eat.

Sumathi gave a plate each to his parents, but they said, "Just give us one plate, and we'll share it."

"It's not every day that you get news like this, and there is enough for all of us. So please enjoy it," Sumathi insisted.

She fixed a plate for herself and turned around to Senthil and asked, "Do you want more or are you sick from the sweets you ate earlier?"

Senthil laughed and quipped, "Does the fish get tired of the water or does the bird get tired of the sky? I'll have some if there are any left."

They all sat down and enjoyed the desserts. Eshwari came to Sumathi and said, "*Anni*, thank you for the sweets and for being so thoughtful."

Sumathi smiled, "It's my pleasure. It's nothing compared to your delicious cooking. I am glad we were all able to share this moment, and I hope I can draw strength from all of you while we all wait for him to come back."

Eshwari gave her a hug and said, "We are lucky that you are here for us."

Sumathi was busy socializing, when Senthil saw the time. It was 7:00 PM. As much as he enjoyed having her over, he wanted to make sure that he took her home on time. He just wanted to make sure that he did not offend her conservative parents by keeping their daughter out too late. He was so proud that she was the center of attention and that his siblings and parents adored her. He did not want to rain on her parade, but he had to make her aware of the time. He cleared his throat somewhat loudly. She got the cue and looked at her watch, only to jump up in shock.

His siblings thanked her again for coming and for the desserts. Sumathi sought his parents' blessing before she took their leave. She grabbed her bag and bid farewell to everyone. On the way, Senthil asked her if there was any dessert left for her family. Sumathi reminded him that she had bought two boxes—one for his family and one for hers.

He parked the motorbike away from her house as usual, and they walked to her house. They walked in, and to their surprise, they saw that her family was entertaining. But it was not a pleasant surprise—Sumathi's *periyamma* and *periyappa* were visiting. They had been very vocal in their criticism against Sumathi being involved with Senthil, as he belonged to a lower caste and was a non-vegetarian. They did not seem too thrilled to see Sumathi walk in with him. However, Gauthami and her *appa* made up for their lack of enthusiasm. Since *periyamma* was the matriarch of the family, Sumathi's *amma* showed some restraint in her enthusiasm. Senthil whispered to Sumathi to ask her if he should just leave and come back another day. Sumathi said that it would not be necessary and insisted that he stayed.

Sumathi told everybody that Senthil had got his visa and he would be going to America very soon. Gauthami was excited, and she jumped up and down shouting, "Congratulations *athimber*!" Senthil stepped forward and touched Sumathi's parents' feet to seek their blessings. They both congratulated him and said that they were very happy for him.

The visiting *periyappa* warned him: "Be careful. America is full of alcohol, drugs, and loose women, and you may come back with a white woman." That put a damper on the spirits. Gauthami retaliated saying, "How do you know *periyappa*? You have never been there. In fact, you have never been outside Madras." She was aware of their dislike for Senthil and thought she had to take a stand for him.

Senthil did not think it would be wise to respond by taking offense, so he only smiled. He paid his respects to Sumathi's parents and took leave. Sumathi and Gauthami walked him down the stairs. As they were walking out, he could hear *periyamma* say, "I cannot believe you let Sumathi be friends with that boy and Gauthami call him *athimber* even for fun. If this progresses to more than friendship, it will not sit well with our family or relatives."

Sumathi and Gauthami apologized for their *periyappa* and *periyamma*'s ignorance. He just shrugged and said, "I care about only what your parents think. I am not worried about your extended family."

Meanwhile, upstairs, Sumathi's *amma* tried to explain to *periyappa* and *periyamma* that Senthil came from a respectable family and that he was a gentleman. They paid no heed to her and only focused on the fact that he was born in a lower-caste family. It was a futile exercise, like playing the flute for a deaf person.

Gauthami asked Senthil to promise her that he would return again soon so that they could do justice to the good news and celebrate the proper way. He agreed and took leave. When he got home, his parents asked him what Sumathi's parents had to say. He said that they were happy for him and that they wished for his parents to be proud of him too. He left out the details about the encounter with Sumathi's *periyamma* and *periyappa*. He did not see any good that would come off it.

The next day, Senthil went to work as usual. When he came back late at night after seeing his private patients, everybody in his family had gone to bed. He had instructed Eshwari not to wait up before leaving in the morning. Senthil quietly entered and went straight to the dining table.

He spent the next few hours writing out a list of things he would need for his big trip and a budget for them.

Flight ticket	Rs. 55,000.00
New clothes	Rs. 3000.00
New suit	Rs. 2000.00
Dress shoes	Rs. 250.00
Sneakers	Rs. 200.00
Two suitcases	Rs. 1000.00
Pressure cooker	Rs. 170.00
Rice: 5 kg	Rs. 50.00
Dhal (Lentils): 2 kg	Rs. 75
Spices: 500 g	Rs.200
Chilli powder: 500 g	Rs. 20
Cumin seed powder: 500 g	Rs. 20
Garam masala: 500 g	Rs. 30
Turmeric powder: 250 g	Rs. 30
Roundtrip taxi to the airport	Rs. 100

That budget totaled to ₹62,145. He included spices, rice, and lentils in the list since he was not only going to the land of the free but also, for him, the land of the unknown. He wanted to make sure he had something to survive on until he grew accustomed to the food in the new country. He pulled out his bank passbook and saw that his net savings totaled at ₹27,700.00. This meant that he had to ask his *appa* for ₹34,445.00. Just the thought of it made him sick to his stomach. He racked his brain, but finally realized the harsh reality that he had no other choice. He went to bed thinking about how to pluck up the courage to broach the subject with his *appa*.

Chapter 6 — Siblings' Surprise

SENTHIL WOKE UP EARLY THE NEXT MORNING. AS USUAL, he rode his motorbike to Sumathi's bus stand. She beat him in the task that morning and was already waiting for him there when he reached. She again apologized for her *periyappa* and *periyamma*'s comments, and for the fact that her parents did not speak up against them. He reassured her, telling her that he understood her parents' predicament and was just thankful that they did not share her *periyamma* and *periyappa*'s sentiment. Relieved, she said, "You are so understanding and have such a big heart. I love you."

"I love you more," he replied. They compared their patients' locations and appointments, following which he took her to her first patient and then went off to see his own.

He picked her back up at 2:30 PM. He asked her if she wanted to go somewhere to eat. "And ruin Gauthami's plans?" she rejoined. "That'll break her heart, and besides, she'll never forgive you, and I'll never hear the end of it for being selfish." Senthil looked perplexed. "Remember you promised her to come back to celebrate the visa approval?" she added.

He nodded. She continued, "Well, she planned something and asked me to bring you home when we were done."

Senthil asked nervously, "What is she up to? Is she going to embarrass me?"

Sumathi tapped his shoulder and said, "Give her a break. She is looking forward to this. She even went to the library to look up—" She broke off. She put her hands on her mouth and said, "Oh my goodness! I almost gave it away. She would have killed me."

"What's going on?" Senthil asked. "And why did she go to the library?"

Sumathi looked mortified and said, "I have already said too much. I promised her that we'd be back as soon as possible. So, mister, hop on your chariot and whisk me away to my house."

As they headed home, Sumathi said, "I've never said this before, and this is going to be the first and the last time I ever say this—"

Senthil interrupted her and asked curiously, "What's it dear?"

Sumathi said, "Could you go faster?"

He was surprised and exclaimed, "Come again! Did I hear you correctly?"

Sumathi chimed in, "This is only a one-time pass, dear. So, enjoy it."

Senthil said, "Don't you worry. I am carrying precious cargo. I'll be extra careful."

He then increased the throttle with a big smile on his face. The vehicles on the road were so full that some of the men were hanging out of the auto rickshaws, bicycles, tempos, and lorries. She was giggling the entire time, perched nervously behind him. Her left hand had a death grip on the handle behind the seat, and her right hand dug into his right shoulder.

He slowed down as they came close to her house, and he parked his motorbike two streets ahead as usual. They walked to her house. As they got closer, Sumathi said, "Remember, I didn't tell you anything, and you don't know anything."

"But you really didn't tell me anything, and I really don't know what I am walking into. I'm actually nervous."

Sumathi laughed out loud and said, "Oh dear! Don't be nervous. It's all good."

Upon reaching the house, they found it empty. The house was quiet and spotlessly clean. It was also unbelievably fragrant, as though somebody had been cooking all day. He inhaled deeply and said, "Wow! It smells delicious. I am hungry already!"

Sumathi smiled and said, "Take a seat, and I'll be right back." Sumathi motioned for him to sit down and walked into her room.

As he took a seat, he noticed something peculiar. The living room was decorated with colored papers of red, white, and blue. Before Senthil could realize that the colors were those of the American flag, he was startled by a loud noise. It was the cassette player blaring Michael Jackson's song "I just can't stop loving you" in full volume. He was a huge Michael Jackson fan. With a big smile on his face, he kept looking inside the house to figure out where everybody was.

Just at the moment the chorus started, Gauthami, Subbu, Eshwari, Nanda, Rathi, and Bala rushed into the living room and screamed: "I just can't stop loving you and if I stop then tell me just what I will do." Shocked, surprised, and amazed, Senthil started in his chair. Sumathi captured all of it with her camera. When they finished singing the chorus, she turned the volume down.

Senthil was grinning from ear to ear, and at the same time, he was crying. Wiping away his tears, he said, "Will somebody tell me what's going on?" Looking at his siblings, he added, "When and how did you all get here?"

Eshwari was the one to speak first. "This was all Gauthami's idea. She wanted to celebrate your visa approval and throw you a surprise party."

Senthil looked at Sumathi and asked, "You knew about this?"

Sumathi was quick to reply, "Oh no! All I knew was I had to make sure to bring you back here today for a surprise, but I did not know any of the details."

He turned around, looked at Gauthami, and stretched out his arms. She ran to him for a hug. He said, "Thank you very much." Then, with her on one side, he motioned to his siblings to come to him for a group hug. Sumathi had her camera ready to capture the moment.

"Who's hungry?" Gauthami asked. Everybody raised their hands.

Senthil said, "I am starving, and the aroma is only making it worse. What's on the menu?"

"Since you are going to America, Eshwari and I made you food that you'll eat there, just to get you prepared."

"Really? How do you know what Americans eat?"

As she walked to the kitchen, Gauthami replied, "I did my research. I went to the British Council Library on Mount Road and read some books."

"I am impressed."

"You know what's impressive? An Indian going to the British Council Library to read about American food and cooking a meal for another Indian. And they say World Peace is difficult!" Gauthami quipped.

He knew she was too wise for her age, but he had to agree with what she said. He too believed that complicated problems sometimes had very simple solutions.

"Wait a minute! Where are your parents?" Senthil asked, noticing that Sumathi's home was being run by the exuberant siblings.

Gauthami replied, "We gave them a day off, and they are out to watch a matinee movie so that we can celebrate in our own way." Senthil thought that it was very magnanimous of them. Sumathi told him that she was not sure what her sister had told her parents for them to entrust the entire house to a bunch of teenagers, but she was glad that all the siblings had been able to come together for the afternoon. She was happy that they all got along so beautifully. After all, this was her future family, and she was very happy with the prospect.

Once they all gathered around the table to eat, Gauthami and Eshwari revealed their spread, introducing to him things he had never seen before. Gauthami announced, "These are French fries, these are chicken nuggets, and these are veggie burgers. For dessert, we cheated and got a store-bought cake and ice cream." Senthil just stared at the spread of food, completely speechless. He did not have the words to describe his feelings.

Gauthami told him that she had picked out what seemed like the popular foods that were easier to make. She exclaimed, "Americans eat a lot of meat, especially cows and pigs. Are you going to eat cows when you go to America?" Her voice cracked at the end as she sounded very serious and genuinely concerned. Cows are considered sacred in Hinduism, and she knew that Senthil was not as religious as her family.

Understanding the gravity of her question, Senthil hesitated to answer. He did not want a serious conversation, neither did he want to ignore her question. He always believed that a good sense of humor could diffuse the stickiest of situations, and so he patted Gauthami on her head and said, "I'll make sure I do not eat any meat from Indian cows, but American cows are going to be free game," and winked at her. To his relief, Gauthami laughed, as did the others.

Senthil then asked Gauthami if her parents knew that chicken was sitting at the top of their dining table. She said that she had checked with them before they left, and they had told her it was okay if they did not cook it inside the house and if they did not use their dishes. Eshwari jumped in and told him that she had made them at their house and brought some banana leaves to serve them on.

Senthil said, "I am impressed. I can't thank Gauthami and Eshwari enough for the trouble they went through in making this beautiful spread of food and for bringing all the siblings together." Eshwari said, "Most of the thanks should go to Subbu as he was our errand boy, taking us to the library, running back and forth to the store for all the ingredients, and cleaning the house after we were done with the kitchen."

Senthil looked at Subbu, smiled, and saluted him. Subbu, who was usually quite reserved and did not talk much, said, "It's the least I could do for a dear brother who cares so much for us, and besides, I got plenty of help from Nanda and Bala."

Sumathi and Senthil had a smile on their faces. They knew exactly how the other felt. They were happy that their siblings had worked as a team. Eshwari summoned them all to sit on the ground as there was not enough room at the dining table: "This may be an American style spread of food, but you are all going to eat it the Indian way." They all laughed and scurried to sit on the floor.

Gauthami then said, "For the final touch, everybody closes their eyes."

They all looked at each other, and Eshwari repeated, "C'mon now. Close your eyes!"

They all shrugged and obliged her. The two girls tiptoed to the kitchen refrigerator and returned with glass bottles of *Thums Up*[32]. They placed one bottle next to each one and said in unison, "Okay, you can all open your eyes."

When they opened their eyes and saw Thums Up instead of the usual tumbler of water, their jaws dropped. They all yelled out, "Yay! Now, that's American style!"

They all thanked Gauthami and Eshwari for the delicious and thoughtful meal and most of all for bringing everyone together. Senthil stood up and asked them all to gather around. He then said, "I am so proud of each one of you. Leaving you all behind is going to be the hardest thing I'll ever do in my life. I hope you all know that I am doing this to make sure we all have a bright and prosperous future. I am going to America not just for Sumathi and myself but for every one of you. In return, I just ask that you all study hard, do well in school, stay out of trouble, and help our parents." They all promised that they would do just that.

"How about dessert? Gauthami asked. Senthil asked if she had bought eggless cakes and she replied in the affirmative. He suggested that they should have dessert once her parents returned, and everyone agreed. They spent the next couple of hours playing cards, goofing around, and just enjoying each other's company. It was about 6:15 PM when they heard the gate open. Gauthami said, 'They are back. I am going to set the plates for dessert."

---

32 Indian version of Coca-Cola

Eshwari got up and said, "I'll help. I'll make some tea for *appa* and *amma*."

Sumathi's parents came up the stairs and walked in. They were pleasantly surprised to see that the kids had managed to not bring the roof down. The house was spotlessly clean, and everyone was sitting down and playing cards like one big family. Senthil bent down and touched their feet to show his respect. As they raised him up, Senthil said, "Thank you so much for opening your home to us. We had such a great time." They replied that they were happy to see all the siblings under one roof and it was a pleasure to have them over.

Gauthami walked in from the kitchen with a tray that had small plates with a slice of a cake and a scoop of ice cream. She offered it to her parents, who said, "Kids first." As she was busy passing the dessert plates, Eshwari came out with cups of tea for the adults.

Sumathi reached for a cup before her parents could and asked, "Is this your masala tea?"

Eshwari smiled and nodded, "Yes."

Sumathi then turned to her parents and said, "Eshwari makes the best tea in the world, and you are in for a treat."

Sumathi's parents took a sip of the tea, and her *appa* was the first one to comment: "Did you make this tea with the ingredients in our kitchen or did you bring something from home?"

"Everything in that tea came from your kitchen," Eshwari replied, sounding nervous.

He laughed, "I didn't know tea could taste so good and just wanted to make sure you didn't bring any exotic ingredient with you."

Eshwari exhaled a sigh of relief and said, "It just has tea leaves, some cardamom, coriander, ginger, milk, and sugar."

"And Eshwari's magical touch," Sumathi's *amma* added.

Eshwari blushed and said, "You all are too kind."

Senthil and the rest of the gang were busy enjoying the vanilla cake and *kesar pista* ice cream. Sumathi asked her *amma* if it would be okay for her and Senthil to go up to the terrace to talk. After her *amma* gave permission, Sumathi motioned to Senthil that she was going up to the terrace. Senthil acknowledged the gesture and followed her.

The sun was setting in the horizon, and the sky had turned yellow and reddish-orange close to the setting sun. The sky was getting darker. Dusk was falling upon them. There was a cool breeze in the air. There was the familiar smell—a cocktail that included the fragrance from the neem tree, hibiscus flowers planted in little pots on the surrounding terraces, petrol fumes being spewed by cars, buses, lorries, and auto rickshaws stalling in the traffic, and aromatic foods sold by street vendors. Somehow all these unrelated smells came together to create a sweet fragrance.

Sumathi and Senthil stood next to each other on the terrace, looking out at the main road. Sumathi studied his face as he stared into the distance. She could see that even though his lips remained unmoving, his eyes and the silence were speaking volumes. She slowly asked, "Are you worried about the expenses and the cost of the airline ticket?"

Senthil was never surprised by her ability to exactly know what he was thinking, but this time, he was taken aback. He turned to her and said, "You are amazing!"

She just smiled and looked at him endearingly. He explained to her the expenses, including the price of the ticket. Even though the fare for the ticket was going to be reimbursed by Hema when he reached America, he still had to pay it up front. He told her that the mere thought of asking his *appa* for money made him sick in his stomach.

She told him, "I know how you feel. I have ₹22,000 in my account, which I can withdraw tomorrow and give it to you. And if we skimp on the shoes and clothes, it should be just enough to get us through and get you to America."

He looked at her, and shaking his head in disbelief, he said, "No, that would make me feel worse than asking my *appa* for money."

Sumathi was disappointed. "You may be the one going to America, but we are in this together. Please don't count me out or think that this is not my problem too." He could sense the pain in her voice, and when he saw tears well up in her eyes, he could not hold back his tears either. He told her that he was not trying to exclude her, but he did not want to touch the *nest egg*, in case there was an emergency. He did not want her to be without any reserve or any back up to fall back on when he was on a different continent.

She tried to explain to him that he would be the first person she would turn to if she needed something. Senthil immediately replied that even if she did, it was going to take him some time to send her money from America.

They talked about it, discussing all the possibilities including a bank loan or borrowing from friends, and Sumathi eventually said, "As much as you hate asking money from your *appa*, did you ever think how he'll feel when he learns that you looked everywhere but to him in your time of need?"

"But I am just trying to spare him—"

Sumathi interrupted Senthil and said, "I understand that dear. But you need to look at it from his point of view. You may be the eldest son who is trying to assume all the responsibilities, but he is still the man of the house."

Just like lightning, it hit him. He realized that his attempt to spare his *appa* from a financial burden would only hurt him or bruise his ego in the very least. He promised to discuss the expenses with his *appa*. He thanked Sumathi for helping him see the whole picture. She assured him that she had faith in God and in him.

It was getting dark, so they went downstairs. Everybody was watching the Sunday night movie. They quietly joined the others, and when the movie ended, Senthil and his siblings thanked them for a wonderful evening and took leave. Sumathi walked down the stairs to the gate to send them off. His siblings bid Sumathi goodbye and walked towards the bus stand.

Senthil stood outside the gate while Sumathi stood inside. He told her how lucky he was to have her in his life and how she always helped him look at things with clarity. He thanked her for being so understanding and loving.

Smiling, Sumathi said, “I am just a mirror, dear,” and followed it with a wink.

He got on his bike and caught up with his siblings at the bus stand. He summoned his sisters to hop behind him on the bike and asked his brothers to catch the bus.

Chapter 7 — Thoughtful Parents

BY THE TIME THEY GOT HOME, SENTHIL'S PARENTS HAD finished dinner and were waiting for them to return. Hearing the motorbike, their *amma* opened the gate. "Where are the boys?" she asked.

Senthil replied, "They took the bus and should be here shortly."

Their *appa* asked if they had a good time. Rathi sat down by his feet to recount the day, while Eshwari followed her *amma* into the kitchen to finish cleaning up. Senthil parked his motorbike and walked in. His *appa* said, "I want to talk to you."

Senthil answered that he would be right back after he washed up. By the time he came out, Nanda and Bala had returned. *Amma* was telling them to clean up and go to bed as they had school the next day.

Appa was sitting on the porch. Senthil sat down on the stairs. His *appa* said, "I was asking around about the airline ticket, and one of my friend's brother has a travel agency. He has promised to give us a good deal. Other than the airline ticket fare, how much do you need?"

Senthil was speechless. Here he was thinking of how to broach the subject, while his *appa* was one step ahead of him!

Realizing his *appa* did not have his reading glasses on, Senthil ran into the house to get them and his budget and handed them to his *appa*. He sat down on the steps beside him. His *appa* looked through the list, and Senthil said, "I have saved ₹27,000 from treating private patients after work."

His *appa* took off his glasses and holding them in one hand and the paper in the other, he chuckled. Senthil was not amused. He was not expecting such a reaction. He leaned forward to peek at the piece of paper to ensure it was his budget his *appa* was looking at and not one of his love notes to Sumathi.

He did not think his *appa* would stop laughing anytime soon. So, he interrupted, "Why are you laughing? What's so funny? Did I write something wrong?"

Amidst a fit of laughter, his *appa* said, "Go get your *amma*." Senthil had no idea what was going on, but he obliged. His *amma* followed him to the porch, drying her hands on her sari. His *appa* was still chuckling away. She looked at him, and Senthil just shrugged. His *appa* motioned them to sit down and handed the piece of paper to her. As soon as she glanced at it, she started giggling as well. His parents were entertained by his well-thought-out budget, amused at his expense, and Senthil was annoyed.

When he had had enough of the ridiculousness, he demanded, "What's so funny?"

His *appa* turned to his *amma* and said, "Tell your son what you have done to prepare for his trip to America."

She said, "Well, I bought a pressure cooker and sealed little packets of all kinds of spices, pickles, and curry powders. I also got an accessory for the pressure cooker for making idlis."

Senthil looked at her gratefully and said, "I don't know what to say."

His *amma* replied, "You children think we parents are clueless and that you all know more than us. Parents know what their children want and need even before the child does."

And that was the truth. He turned to his *amma* and said, "Thank you."

She smiled and said, "As much as I hate to see you go, I want to make sure that you have some basic things that will get you started in that new world." Senthil's eyes filled with tears. He leaned over and hugged her and kissed her head. She wiped his tears with the *pallu* of her sari.

Senthil's *appa* said, "Stop by the travel agent's office next week to confirm the date and to pick up the ticket." Senthil, still emotional and overwhelmed, nodded in reply. His *appa* added, "Looks like everything other than your clothes and shoes is taken care of, and you certainly do not want me or your *amma* to pick them out for you."

His *amma* fired back, "Speak for yourself. I know what looks good on my son." Finally, Senthil laughed, and then he said to his *appa*, "I can withdraw all the money from my savings account and take it to him as cash or as a cashier's check."

His *appa* said, "I have already paid for the ticket. You are not the only one who knows how to save around here. You keep that money and use it to buy some new clothes and any last-minute expense that might pop up."

Senthil told his *appa* that he would send him a check as soon as Hema reimbursed him for the ticket. His *appa* replied that he could worry about it later.

Senthil stopped accepting new clients, as he thought it would be unfair to leave them in the middle. He was hoping that his three current clients would no longer need physical therapy by the time he had to leave. Senthil and Sumathi spent the next few weekends shopping for clothes.

They went to Purasaiwalkam, where two big retail clothing stores were known for their discount prices and wide selection: Madhar Sha and Sree Krishna Cut Piece Junction. Their first stop was Madhar Sha. Sumathi helped him pick out some clothes. Choosing the material for pants was a no-brainer. They covered all the basic dark colors: black, brown, navy blue, olive green, grey, and khaki. They got 1.2 meters in each color so that they could take it to a tailor for a custom fit. Unlike in Western countries, getting clothes made for one's measurements was cheaper than buying readymade clothes in India. Their next stop was for materials for shirts at Sree Krishna Cut Piece Junction, which was a gallery of shirting material precut; it was 1.5 meters for half-sleeved shirts and 2 meters for full-sleeved ones.

Senthil tried to stick to conservative pastel shades and pinstriped shirts, but Sumathi protested, "Are you going to dress like an old man in a new country? You are young and handsome, and you need something that reflects your personality." She then asked the salesman to give her a piece of shirting that had a light blue background and streaks of black specks. She spread the piece out, laid it across Senthil's chest, and said, "Now that's you."

Senthil slid the material off his shoulder and smiled. "Don't you think it's too flashy?"

Sumathi and Senthil settled. For every pant they bought, he would get two shirts: one for business and one for parties. He picked out the more traditional shirt with either plain pastel shades or stripes, while she picked out materials with a little more flamboyant pattern, intended for a more casual occasion. In all, they got materials for six pants and twelve shirts. He then bought two leather belts—one in black and the other in brown. Then they headed to Bata from where he got a pair each of black and brown shoes.

The shoes fit in the side box of the motorbike, and Sumathi hugged all the other bags close to her as she sat behind him on the motorbike. He went to his usual tailor whom he had befriended over the years. Venkat was an honest and hardworking man in his early thirties, who always kept his promise on the delivery date. He was also an expert in his craft and kept himself updated with the trends in Bollywood. Senthil always admired his hard work and honesty and was an unpaid ambassador who always directed his friends and patients to this store called Masculine Tailors.

Venkat came from humble beginnings. He had to quit his education after high school to put food on the table for his *amma* and two sisters after his *appa*'s death. He began working at a local tailor's shop, initially as a helper—sweeping, cleaning, and running errands. He slowly worked his way up by learning to hem, attaching buttons, sewing shirts, and pants, and eventually learning the whole trade—from taking measurements to cutting patterns and using the sewing machine. In time, he was able to successfully establish his own store and secure a loyal customer base.

Their friendship blossomed when Senthil came to him to have a white coat made. Venkat asked him if he was a doctor, and Senthil replied that he was a physiotherapist. Venkat mentioned that his *amma* was recovering from a stroke. Senthil asked who her physiotherapist was, and Venkat replied that they took her to the Government Institute of Rehabilitation Medicine once a week and then, at home, his sisters helped her with the exercises and movements they had learned. He told Senthil that taking an auto or taxi to the institute was expensive, and with him having to manage the store—their only source of earning a living—and the sisters going to school, they could not take their *amma* to therapy sessions every day.

Senthil told him that he had recently graduated from that institute and offered to evaluate his *amma* at home and treat her if they were willing to be flexible with the time. So Senthil visited her late in the night, after finishing with all his private patients and before heading home. By the end of three weeks, he had her walking, with functional use of her left hand. Venkat and his family were extremely appreciative of his efforts, and when Senthil declined to accept any fee at the end of the month, they were speechless. He said that he was glad to be of help.

Ever since then, Venkat and Senthil had become friends. When Venkat offered to tailor his clothes for free, Senthil declined the offer politely, but when Venkat insisted, they agreed on a 25 percent discount.

As soon as Venkat saw Senthil walking towards his store, he ran up to the counter to greet him. Senthil introduced Sumathi to him, and Venkat said, "You are a lucky girl."

Venkat was surprised when they emptied the bags on the counter. "Who is getting married?" he asked.

"This is not for a wedding," Senthil replied. "I am going to America to work."

Venkat's jaw dropped. "Did you say America? That's great! When are you leaving?"

"December 8. I hope you can have this ready by then."

"That soon? Do not worry about this. I'll have all of it ready for you in four days."

He asked Senthil to step into the store for measurements and asked Sumathi if she would like some tea or coffee. Sumathi politely declined, thanking him for his hospitality. Venkat was excited that his friend was going to America, and Senthil joked that he was going to recommend his tailoring services to the people there.

Venkat said, "Well, if they pay in dollars, then I can maybe get my sisters married." As he noted down the measurements, he said, "I am going to stitch each pant slightly differently. One with two pleats, another with three pleats, another with box pleats, and so on." He then clipped the corner of each piece of clothing and stapled them to a card with the order number.

On a Sunday morning, two weeks before he was to take his flight, Senthil was surprised to see his *appa* up early in the morning.

"Are you free this morning for a few hours?" his *appa* asked. Senthil confirmed that he was and that he had finished with all his private patients. His *appa* took him to Raymond Suiting, an upscale clothing store on Mount Road. As Senthil wondered why they had entered this store, his *appa* confirmed his suspicion: they were going to get a suit made.

They walked through the large glass doors and stepped onto the black marble floors with golden flecks. The floor was shiny, and even with his shoes on, Senthil could sense it was cool to touch. The store was air-conditioned, and a pleasant smell lingered in the air. The store had two levels and a high roof. From the second level, one could look down to the atrium. There were two staircases on either side of the store with gold-tone rails. The salesmen were all dressed in shirts and ties.

Senthil felt a little intimidated. He had never been inside an upscale store such as this one. He had no idea what to do. He stayed one step behind his *appa* as he walked up to a salesman and asked for the tailor.

The salesman escorted them up the stairs. While the lower level showcased clothing materials for shirts and pants and accessories, mannequins dressed in suits stood in the upper level. The place looked sterile with glass showcases. Senthil was afraid to touch anything; he did not want to smudge the spotless glass countertops.

The salesman introduced them to a bespectacled older man with silver hair. Senthil's *appa* said, "We would like to get a suit made. Could you deliver it in ten days?"

The tailor raised his glasses, looked at him with pouted lips, and nodded. He took his measuring tape off his neck and asked, "Who is the suit for?"

Senthil's *appa* turned around, grabbed Senthil by his shoulders, and dragged him forward. Senthil hesitated, and then digging his heels into the ground, he protested, "But I had decided against a suit to save some money."

His *appa* replied, "Well, you are going to America, and you should have a basic suit for any special occasion, interview, or any meeting with your superiors if one should come up." He nudged Senthil towards the tailor, who took Senthil's measurements and noted them down in his little pocket notebook.

The tailor then looked up and said, "Now let's select the material for the suit." He walked behind the glass counter and asked them to sit on the high padded stools by the counter. He proceeded to remove the bales of clothes stacked up in shelves and place them on the counter. He then unfurled a few of the bales and began to inspect the material proudly.

Senthil's *appa* felt the material between his fingers, looked up, and said, "These are blue and black shades. Please show us grey." He turned to his son and said, "Grey will suit any occasion."

They perused a few grey colored fabrics. Senthil checked the price tag each time his *appa* asked him whether he liked a particular material. He settled on the one that had the lowest price. He still could not believe how good the material felt.

He looked at his *appa* and asked, "Do I have to get a suit? Can we afford this?"

His *appa* said, "Yes and yes. It's not every day that my son goes to America. Besides, you are going to be working in the health-care field, and a suit will come in handy. Don't worry about the added expense. Some expenses are worth it."

There was a dark red tie that caught his *appa*'s attention, and he asked the tailor to add that to the order.

Senthil quietly listened to his *appa*. He did not know what to say. His *appa* paid the deposit, and the tailor asked him to come in a week for a fitting before the suit was finally stitched. They walked out of the grand store, and Senthil immediately covered his face with his hands as he felt the scorching heat. Laughing, he turned to his *appa* and said, "A few hours in the air-conditioned store makes the heat more intense than it is."

Senthil's *appa* laughed and replied, "I wonder what you will say when you come back after a year in America where even the bathrooms are air-conditioned."

He patted Senthil on his shoulder as they walked to the nearby bus stand.

The next stop was Burma Bazaar in Parry's Corner. A strip of makeshift stores lined either side of the road in front of the Beach Railway Station. These stores had been in operation since the 1960s, having been set up for the Tamil refugees from Burma by the State Government of Tamil Nadu. These street vendors traditionally specialized in cheap foreign goods that included audio cassettes of movie songs, perfumes, watches, tape records, transistor radios, shoes, sunglasses, hats, toys, luggage, VCRs, color TVs, pirated VHS tapes, and anything in between. Many of the goods were smuggled out of countries such as Malaysia, Singapore, Dubai, and the Gulf countries. If one was not careful, one could easily be stiffed with a duplicate or a defective product. The vendors employed pressure tactics and pushed their products aggressively.

Haggling was the norm, and shoppers always had to remain vigilant. The stores lining the roads always bustled with people, courtesy of the proximity to the railway station. The place especially attracted youngsters, especially college kids looking for a cheap bargain. All the goods were sold as is, and there were no guarantees or returns. Shoppers bought the goods at their own peril. There were two extremes: either one would be lucky and got an extremely good deal, or one got stiffed. This was a lucrative business and had flourished for years.

Senthil's *appa* had brought him here to get a pair of suitcases. He wanted to get his son sturdy suitcases that would withstand the inter-continental flight. As they waded past stores that had invaded the broad sidewalks by encroachment and reduced it to a narrow two-way path, they were thronged by vendors calling out for their attention. Luckily, Senthil's *appa* knew exactly where he was going. One of his friends had told him about his cousin who ran a shop that sold goods imported from Singapore.

Senthil was still puzzled. He had never been to Burma Bazaar before and felt like a tourist. He asked his *appa*, "What are we doing here?"

His *appa* smiled and said, "Just follow me."

They walked down a narrow strip for the next fifteen minutes, dodging aggressive salesmen trying to persuade them to stop and take a look at the merchandise such as new movies in VHS tapes, perfumes, and watches. Senthil did not stop, although he was tempted to take a look at the movie *Devar Magan*, which starred his idol Kamal Hassan, the versatile Tamil actor. He did not want to lose sight of his *appa*.

His *appa* finally stopped in front of a vendor. Saleem greeted them and said, "*As-salāmu 'alaykum*![33] Imran *bhai*[34] said you would be coming. What can I get you?"

---

33 Greeting in Arabic meaning "peace be upon you"

34 Brother

Senthil's *appa* replied, "*Wa Alaykum as-salam*![35] We are looking for some good suitcases. My son here is going to America."

Saleem's eyes grew wide. He looked very excited, and reaching out to shake Senthil's hand, he said, "America! That's great news. I am going to find you the best suitcases." He then added, "Let's see. You are going to need two big suitcases to check in and one small carry-on."

Senthil and his *appa* knew they had come to the right person.

Asking them to wait, Saleem took off in a hurry. He came back in twenty minutes with a young man, and between the two of them, they had four big suitcases. Saleem carefully laid them down. He opened two of the suitcases and pulled out a smaller carry-on from each. Looking at Senthil, he said, "Senthil *bhai*, these are the best suitcases. You pick the ones you like."

Senthil took a step forward. He looked at the suitcases in front of him and liked a pair of brown ones. He lifted the handle to check the number lock and noticed the label SAMSONITE below it.

Saleem said, "Senthil *bhai*, that's the name of the company. It's made in America. Very good strong suitcase. Look, it has wheels and a handle that can be pulled out, so you can just drag or push it around and never have to carry it."

Senthil looked at his *appa* who nodded in approval. Saleem put the carry-on inside the smaller suitcase and the smaller one into the larger suitcase. He then wrapped that suitcase with old newspapers and tied it up with a thick jute string. Senthil's *appa* asked Saleem how much they owed him. Saleem replied, "Whatever Imran *bhai* said, sir."

Senthil's *appa* hesitated and said, "But these suitcases look expensive."

Saleem replied, "Oh, you don't worry about it, sir. Imran *bhai* had instructed me to find whatever you want and give you the best deal."

Senthil interrupted, "It just wouldn't be fair if you took a loss on our account."

35 "And peace be upon you"

Saleem laughed and said, "Senthil *bhai*, this is Burma Bazaar. Even with that price, I am still making a profit. I'll double my profit with the next customer. Please don't worry. Good luck in America."

Senthil carried the suitcase and walked behind his *appa*. His *appa* thought it would probably be better to take an auto rickshaw back home, but Senthil insisted on taking the bus. He could carry the suitcase. Auto-rickshaw rides were expensive. They walked to the bus stand and caught a bus that was not crowded; they got home in time for dinner.

Tuesday, November 30, was the last working day at the hospital for Senthil. He bid farewell to the patients he saw regularly. Florence, while upset that he would no longer be treating her, wished him the best. She gave him a card that wished him bon voyage, and also a pen. His fellow physical therapists threw him a farewell party. Sheela, Indira, Uma, Varalakshmi, Xavier, Ramesh, Vidhya, and Vasudevan took him to Connemara—a legendary upscale restaurant that dated back to 1854 and was a prominent landmark of Madras.

Senthil hesitated when they mentioned that they had made reservations at the Connemara. It was a five-star restaurant and was extremely expensive.

"Come on," Indira urged him. "We know you are frugal, but this is our treat. You don't have to worry about it."

They all left work on time and went straight to the Connemara. Uma led them in. She had a flair for things like this, and she was the one who had made the reservation. As they walked in, Senthil was astonished to see Sumathi waiting inside. She was nervous and was relieved to see him.

Sheela, Indira, Uma, Vidhya, and Varalakshmi turned around and yelled, "Surprise!"

Indira turned to Senthil, and said, "We figured we should invite her too. I hope you don't mind," and winked.

Senthil walked towards Sumathi and said, "This is a pleasant surprise, and I am so happy to see you."

Sumathi replied, "Thanks to your colleagues. I am so glad to spend the evening with you." They sat down at their table. Indira took a picture of Sumathi and Senthil sitting next to each other. She then asked one of the waiters to take a group picture and motioned all the others to huddle behind Senthil and Sumathi.

As they were eating, Sumathi leaned in and whispered to Senthil, "This was unexpected, and I couldn't say no when Indira called. My parents don't know I am out. They are probably worried, and it would be nice if I could make it home by 9:00 PM."

Senthil replied, "I understand; I am in the same situation. I'll drop you home right after dinner."

The food was delectable. At the end of dinner, when the bill arrived, Senthil reached for his wallet. But Indira looked at him, cleared her throat, and said, "Put that away. I told you this is our treat."

"Well, for Sumathi—"

Indira interrupted him, "She is part of the treat, and everything is taken care of."

Uma echoed, "Yeah, don't worry. We all chipped in."

Sumathi and Senthil thanked them profusely and took their leave, when Xavier called out, "Hey, why the hurry? Let's go get some ice cream."

Senthil said it was a great idea, but he had to go pick up his *appa* from work. He turned to Sumathi and said that he could drop her halfway home. They both thanked everybody again for the wonderful treat and walked to the parking lot.

As they were walking towards his motorbike, Sumathi asked, "You have to pick up *appa*?"

Senthil replied, "No, but it was the best way to shake off Xavier. Can you imagine how much grief he would have given us if we had just said that we had to be home in time?"

Sumathi chuckled. "You are right. Thank God for your presence of mind."

On the ride home, Senthil said, "One more week, dear. Next Wednesday, I'll be on my way to the airport."

There was silence. Sumathi grasped his shoulder and leaned in on him. He did not mind the silence with her proximity.

As they got closer, he broke the silence and said, "My flight from Madras Airport is at 11:30 PM. I'll have to be at the airport by 9:00. Will you be able to come to the airport?"

"Yes, with Gauthami and my *appa*," she replied.

Senthil said that it would be wonderful to see her before he took off. She also said that she was not seeing any patients the upcoming weekend and could come over to help him pack. He was glad to hear that and thanked her for her thoughtfulness.

It was 8:25 PM when he dropped her two streets away from her house. She told him that she was looking forward to spending the weekend with him. "Ditto," he smiled and watched her walk away.

Tears trickled down his cheeks with the thought that he would be thousands of miles away from the love of his life the next weekend.

As she was about to turn into the next street, she turned around to wave at him. Senthil wiped away his tears, waved back, and started his motorbike.

Saturday, December 4, was the last weekend before Senthil left for America. So, his brothers and sisters took the day off from school. They figured that since it was only half a day worth of classes, they could catch up with the stuff they would miss from their friends. They planned to make breakfast for their brother and go shopping when Sumathi came. They wanted to buy little things such as handkerchiefs, socks, pen, and so on for their brother with whatever little they had managed to scrounge. These were monies they had got for their birthdays or had been given to them by their grandparents.

Senthil was sleeping in the living room as usual. Since nobody was going to school or work that day, his parents and his siblings were all sleeping in. Senthil woke up at 4:30 AM and just lay there staring at the ceiling fan. He got up, unplugged the tape recorder lying by his pillow, and put it on the shelf. He stacked his pillows, folded his cover, gently nudged the door open, and walked into the room where his siblings were asleep. He placed the pillows in the corner, and as he was tiptoeing back out, the light through the open door gently lit up the room, and he saw his siblings all lying down in a row.

As he looked at their peaceful sleeping faces, he assured himself he was doing the right thing by leaving. It was for their welfare. He worried about their future, thanks to the Indian culture that put all the responsibilities on the eldest male child of the family. As he watched their peaceful faces, his heart grew heavy. The same nightmare that had been plaguing him ever since he was nine flashed before his eyes.

He prayed that they would never recall or realize what had happened. There was a peculiar constriction in his chest. Clutching at his chest, he left the room. He walked to the sink in the dining room and splashed some cold water on his face. Staring at his reflection in the mirror, he hoped that this was the last time he would have this nightmare and that the new country would give him some inner peace.

Suddenly, he heard the gate open. For a second, his heart skipped a beat, thinking that Sumathi had arrived early. He ran to open the front door. It was Subbu, Sumathi's brother. He halted at the gate when he saw Senthil at the door. Senthil waved at him to come in.

They sat down on the porch. Senthil was worried. He asked, "Is Sumathi okay? Is everything all right?"

Subbu assured him: "She is fine. Everything is fine." Senthil let out a sigh of relief, but his solace was very short-lived.

"Our *periyamma* and *periyappa* from hell are visiting," Subbu continued. "They are here with their son and daughter to check out a few alliances for their son."

This meant only one thing, and Senthil immediately realized what it was: Sumathi was not coming to see him this weekend.

He asked, "When are they leaving, Subbu?"

Subbu said that they had mentioned something like a week, but he knew that they had an alliance to meet the next Friday. Senthil felt sick. He was flying out on Wednesday, and he would probably not be able to see Sumathi before he left India. Subbu profusely apologized for being the bearer of bad news. Although he was devastated, he patted Subbu's shoulder and said, "It's okay. It's not your fault. Thank you for coming to let me know."

He asked Subbu to step in so that he could fix him a cup of coffee or tea. Subbu declined the offer saying that he came under the pretense of going to the milk booth and must return home with milk to make morning coffee for the guests. Senthil asked him if he could drop him on his motorbike, but Subbu again declined, saying that he had come on his bicycle. As he headed to the gate, Senthil said, "Hey Subbu, tell Sumathi I understand, and everything is going to be all right." Subbu nodded and left.

Senthil returned to the porch and plopped down on the chair. He shut his eyes and sat there motionless. He could not imagine how he was going to leave the country without seeing Sumathi once more. He also knew that her *periyamma* and *periyappa* were very conservative when it came to caste. There was no way her parents were going to do anything that would cause drama or let the relatives chastise Sumathi for leaving home late at night to see Senthil.

Chapter 8 — Maiden Flight

AND YET, AGAINST ALL THE ODDS, HERE SHE WAS ON 8 December 1993. Senthil did not think of how she got there, what she had risked in coming to the airport at this hour, or what excuses she must have made. He was just overjoyed to see her. But his joy quickly gave way to concern for Sumathi. He turned to his parents and asked if they could drop her home.

His *appa* said, "Of course. You don't worry about it. We'll take her in our taxi and stop a street before. We'll have Nanda and Bala walk her home."

Sumathi reassured Senthil that Gauthami had it all covered at home. She said, "Gauthami and I volunteered our room to our relatives, and they are sound asleep. We are sleeping in the living room. She'll quietly let me in. Please don't worry about me."

Senthil's *amma*, who was holding back her tears, added, "At least we all are here together and have each other. My son is going to be all alone in a strange place."

Sumathi turned, and wiping her tears, said, "Please don't worry about Senthil. He knows what he is doing. He is very smart. He's going to be back in no time."

Senthil was proud to see Sumathi's resilience as she comforted his *amma* though she was vulnerable herself.

As they sat there, talking about how much they were going to miss each other, the overhead speakers came on: "Attention passengers. Indian Airlines Flight 6766 bound for Bombay will be ready to board in fifteen minutes. Passengers are requested to proceed to the gate."

The family looked at each other. There was not a single pair of dry eyes.

Senthil's *appa* finally announced, "This is it. It is time."

Since Senthil had checked in his two big suitcases when they had first arrived, he now had only his carry-on. He leaned forward and touched his parents' feet for their blessings. His *appa* held his shoulders and pulled him up. His *amma* cried as he hugged her. His siblings tried to smile but failed in holding back their tears. They all took turns to hug him. It was finally Sumathi's turn. As he stood in front of her, tears ran down his cheeks. She reached for them with her handkerchief as he wiped her tears with the back of his fingers.

As the other passengers headed to the gate, his *appa* gestured to him that it was time for him to leave. Senthil reached for his pocket while Sumathi reached for her purse. They both pulled out a letter, surprised to see the other holding a similar envelope. After exchanging the envelopes, he held her hand and walked with her by his side until a guard stopped her.

"I love you so much, Sumathi," he said as he reluctantly let go of her hand.

"I love you too, dear," she replied. "Have a safe flight and please take care of yourself."

He kept walking forward with his head turned in her direction. His family had walked up behind her, and he was reassured to see Eshwari's arms around Sumathi and Rathi holding her hand. He waved one last time before he turned the corner and disappeared from their line of vision.

Senthil and the other passengers walked up the runway towards the Indian Airlines aircraft. The thrill of boarding his first flight was overshadowed by his distraught thoughts about Sumathi and the anxiety of what awaited him. His heart felt heavier than his carry-on.

As his thoughts swirled around Sumathi, he remembered her words. "I'll be traveling vicariously through you and imagine being with you everywhere. I want you to be brave and friendly. Don't be shy."

Even in her imagination, he didn't want to disappoint her. He wanted to make sure he remembered as much as he could of his first flight, so he could later share this experience with her.

Fluorescent lights illuminated the clear night. He had never seen an airplane from this close. He didn't know it was this big! He climbed the stairs, and just before he stepped into the cabin, he turned around to take one more look at his beloved Madras. He found 16A, his seat. He was happy it was a window seat. He remembered his childhood trips to his grandparents' house in the village and how all the siblings would fight for the window seat on the train. The overhead bin was open. He looked to his side, and the air hostess, sensing what he wanted to ask, nodded her head. He placed his carry-on in the bin and sat down.

Within fifteen minutes, all the seats were filled. It was a two-hour-and-five-minute flight to Bombay. Two middle-aged men were sitting next to him. From their body language, Senthil guessed that this was not the first time they were flying. He was too nervous to make small talk or be friendly. Three air hostesses, dressed in red saris and beige long-sleeved blouses and their hair pulled up in a bun, moved quickly across the aisle, checking the overhead bins and reminding passengers to buckle their seat belts.

A few moments later, it was time for take-off. Senthil didn't realize he was clutching the armrests until his hands cramped up. He had no idea what to expect. He could not move. From looking out the window, he could see the plane gaining speed. He slowly glanced at the man sitting next to him, to get some idea of what he should do. The man asked, "First time?"

Senthil's mouth was so dry that he couldn't speak; he nodded in response. The man reached into his shirt pocket and pulled out a piece of gum and asked him to chew on it to prevent his ears from stuffing up. Senthil gratefully accepted it. He looked at the flat yellow strip with the words "Juicy

Fruit" on it. Senthil subtly glanced at his neighbor to see if he was looking in his direction and smelled the piece of gum. It did smell fruity. He unwrapped it and popped the gum into his mouth. The burst of flavor in his mouth made him smile.

The plane reached take-off speed and left the tarmac below, gradually climbing up. Senthil felt queasy. He was glad to have the gum. He felt his stuffy ears getting better each time he swallowed. He gratefully looked at his neighbor and did the classic Indian nod. His neighbor acknowledged his gratitude and smiled.

As the plane reached cruising altitude, the captain turned off the seat-belt sign. Senthil was beginning to get comfortable. The queasiness in his stomach eased. He looked out the window and could see thousands of tiny lights. It looked like a Diwali—the festival of lights—of the grandest scale. As he continued to look out the window, he heard "Chicken or vegetable?" He turned around, confused.

His neighbor said, "They are serving food, and the air hostess is asking if you want chicken biryani or vegetable biryani."

Senthil was not expecting food. With all the anxiety of leaving behind his loved ones, he had hardly eaten anything. As the air hostess came closer with the cart, the aroma rekindled his hunger. Even before she could finish repeating the question, he blurted out, "Chicken." He thanked the air hostess as he received his tray and laid it on his lap. His neighbor pointed to the seat-back tray. Senthil followed the cue and opened the tray to place his food on it.

He was surprised to see an entire meal arranged so compactly in such as a small container. The chicken biryani was hot, but the *raita*[36] was cold. And there was a *laddu* for dessert, along with a cup of water. The plastic cutlery was wrapped in a paper napkin, and salt and pepper packets were tucked into the container.

Senthil peeled open the aluminum foil covering the chicken biryani over the small tray and was pleasantly surprised again. Half the tray contained

---

36 a yogurt side dish with onions, tomatoes, and cucumber

chicken biryani, and the other half had chicken korma. Senthil ate every morsel, and then, he savored the dessert. After he was finished, he did not know what to do with his food tray. As he was checking the size of the seat pocket to see if his food tray and the little containers would fit in there, the air hostess returned to collect the trays.

The timing was just perfect. As soon as all the trays had been collected, the seat-belt sign came back on. The air hostess on the overhead speaker instructed the passengers to secure their trays, bring their seats to an upright position, and fasten their seat belts. Until then, Senthil had not known that his seat could recline.

The plane began to descend. The lights below began growing bigger and bigger. Senthil's neighbor asked, "Where are you going? Dubai or Saudi Arabia?"

With a hint of pride, Senthil replied, "America." He explained that he was taking the Lufthansa Airlines flight from Bombay to Frankfurt, Germany, and from there to Dallas, Texas, in America. From the look on his neighbor's face, Senthil could tell that he was impressed.

Eventually, the plane touched down. Senthil thanked his neighbor for the gum as he exited the plane. His neighbor smiled and handed him a new pack of juicy fruit gum and wished him good luck. Senthil thanked him profusely. He carried his suitcase and followed the signs to Baggage Claim. As he waited to pick up the two large suitcases he had checked in, he remembered the instructions the travel agent had given him. He placed his suitcases on a cart and proceeded to the shuttle headed to the international terminal.

He had only heard about the glamor and glitz of Bombay—the home of Bollywood—but now he was riding a shuttle through the streets of the city. Even in the wee hours of the morning, Bombay was lit up like the scenes in the cinemas. There was only one tall building in Madras—the fourteen-floor Life Insurance Corporation building. It was a skyscraper in its own right in Madras. Bombay had many buildings that dwarfed the Madras LIC building. Senthil peered out through the large glass windows of the shuttle. He looked in awe as the bus glided through roads and approached the international terminal.

He waited for his turn and took the heavy suitcases out of the shuttle bus to place them on the pavement. He walked around looking for a luggage cart and kept turning to keep an eye on his suitcases. Even though the suitcases were heavy and there was no way anyone could just pick them up and run off, he did not want to take any chances. He found a cart, piled on his two check-in suitcases and the carry-on, and followed the signs leading to the Lufthansa terminal.

On reaching the Lufthansa section, he saw several kiosks and joined the hundreds of other passengers in a queue. His suitcases were placed on a conveyer belt that went through an X-ray machine. He walked past the metal detectors, joined his suitcases, and then proceeded to the counter. Once it was his turn, he handed his passport and the ticket to the lady at the counter. She asked him to place his suitcases on the scale one at a time. One weighed 69.93 kg and the other 69.98 kg. The maximum weight allowance was 70 kg per piece.

She smiled and commented, "Nice packing."

She handed him his boarding passes along with his passport and Senthil smiled. "Thank you. Do I pick up the suitcases in Frankfurt?"

She replied, "No, sir. They are checked in for Dallas, Texas." He was relieved.

Senthil joined the line, got past the security, and walked towards the gate. His jaw dropped when he saw the 747 Jumbo Jet. He had never seen anything this big! He wondered how such a massive thing could soar in the sky like a feather. After what seemed like a long wait, he boarded the flight past midnight. The interior of the 747 was even more impressive. It was like entering a huge house.

As he came to his row, he opened his carry-on, removed a small bag from it, and put it in the overhead bin. As he sat in his window seat, he thought about Sumathi and his family. He placed the small bag in the seat pocket in front of him and closed his eyes. He was more exhausted emotionally than physically and dozed off. He woke up to some shuffling next to his seat and an announcement that declared, "Ladies and gentlemen! Welcome aboard flight 757 bound to Frankfurt with a flight time of ten hours and forty minutes." She continued to go over the instructions and made sure everyone had their seat belts on.

An elderly woman was sitting next to Senthil. She had salt-and-pepper hair and wore glasses. A big red *bindi*[37] adorned her forehead. She was dressed in a sari in the North-Indian style and seemed a little nervous, fidgeting with her delicate hands. She had on a cardigan. Next to her sat a middle-aged European male, probably a German returning home. He had either partied too much or worked too hard. Maybe he was recovering from the *Delhi belly*. With his head tilted back, he put a small hand towel over his face, looking ready for a nap.

It was cold inside the plane. The crew must have cranked up the air-conditioner. Senthil noticed a blue blanket with the Lufthansa logo wrapped in a plastic bag tucked in front of each seat pocket. He was not that cold. It was refreshing to be in this atmosphere compared to the sultry air outside. The lady next to him would probably disagree. She went from fidgeting with her hands to crossing her arms and rubbing her shoulders. Senthil asked in his rusty Hindi, "*Aap thande rahe hai*?"[38] Her face lit up like a 1000-watt bulb. She heaved a sigh of relief and nodded.

Senthil reached for the seat pocket in front of her, pulled the blanket out, and wrapped it around her. She looked at him gratefully and said, "*Dhanyavad*."[39] She proceeded to talk in Hindi, but Senthil interrupted her and said, "I only know a little Hindi. Do you speak English?"

She smiled and answered, "A little."

---

37 Red dot

38 Are you cold?

39 Thank you

Senthil said, "That's good. It's probably good for you to speak a little English than for me to speak a little Hindi." They both laughed.

Not realizing it was his first time too and that a short flight from Madras did not make him a seasoned traveler, he asked, "First time flying?"

She replied, "Yes. Going to be with daughter for delivery."

"That's wonderful! Congratulations!" he smiled.

The lights dimmed, and they could feel the huge plane gently roll down the runway. Senthil reached into his pocket and pulled out the juicy fruit gum. He gave her a piece, and she looked at him, puzzled. He popped a piece into his mouth and said, "It'll prevent your ears from getting blocked."

He felt good sharing his newfound wisdom. It was his way of solidifying anything he learned. If he learned a new word, he would immediately start using it in conversations. He used to drive Sumathi nuts with this habit, but she still found this idiosyncrasy of his cute.

The huge beast gained speed and pushed off the ground. Senthil looked out the window, and as the plane rose higher and felt lighter, his heart sank lower and became heavier. Except for a gentle hum, it was eerily quiet around him. Senthil was surprised. This was in stark contrast with the flight from Madras to Bombay. The smaller plane had been much louder. He turned to the side to see the lady drifting off to sleep. A nap sounded good to his weary heart, so he leaned back and closed his eyes.

A couple of hours went by, and Senthil woke up. The window that was dark when he had closed his eyes was intensely bright now. He looked out the window to see the plane flying above the clouds. It looked like a fluffy white carpet beneath them. He stared in awe. He reached for the seat pocket, grabbed his bag, and pulled out a small photo album. He flipped through the pictures of his loved ones.

Staring at Sumathi's photo, he was lost in thoughts until a gentle voice brought him back to reality: "Vegetarian or non-vegetarian?" He turned to see the air hostess standing there with the food cart. She was talking to the European on the aisle. Senthil woke up the lady next to him. He brought down the small table for her and himself. The air hostess handed her a tray saying, "This is a special Indian food that was ordered with your ticket." The lady acknowledged with a nod and accepted the food tray.

It was Senthil's turn. He stated, "Non-vegetarian."

Senthil looked at his tray: strawberry yogurt, cream cheese, orange juice, thick round bread with a hole in the middle, a thin pink soft piece of something and a white color soft piece of something, a bowl of fruit, and a cup of water—all of which was arranged neatly in a small rectangular tray. He did not know where to begin. He knew orange juice, and he had read about strawberries and had seen them in movies but had never eaten them. He knew yogurt was like curd, but he had no clue what the rest of them were. He leaned forward and peered at how his European neighbor was faring with his tray.

The gentleman on the aisle seat must have felt Senthil staring at him. He leaned forward and said, "You need some help with your breakfast?"

Senthil smiled and replied, "They look pretty, but I don't know what some of the things are."

"I get it. It's the same for me with Indian food. Let's see. This is a bagel. It's like bread; you split it and smear it with the cream cheese. The pink stuff is ham, and the white thing is cheese. Make yourself a bagel sandwich and enjoy."

Senthil pointed to the fruit cup, and the gentleman told him that it had honeydew melon, cantaloupe, pineapple, and grapes. Senthil thanked him and proceeded to eat.

He played it safe by trying the strawberry yogurt. It was sweet like a dessert. He was accustomed to eating plain yogurt. He had no idea what ham was. He made the bagel sandwich and took a bite. It was nothing like what he had anticipated. He thought the bagel was a stale imitation of bread, as it was dense and a little hard. The ham had a weird taste, and he had to spit it out. The pretty pink slice was deceptive. He then tried the orange juice and found it to be sour—nothing like the hand-squeezed orange juice he usually drank. He then tried the fruit cup and finally smiled. He knew pineapple and grapes, but he was impressed with the melons. Finally, he gulped down some water and called it quits.

The lady next to him said, "My daughter ordered special Indian food while booking the tickets."

Senthil smiled and said, "Good idea. I like to try new things. Hope I get used to American food."

He leaned forward and asked the European, "Sir, what is ham?"

The man laughed and said, "It's the meat of a pig and—"

Senthil interrupted, "I thought pig's meat was called pork."

The man laughed again and said, "Well, ham is pig too. It's a certain part of the pig and processed in a certain way. Did you like it?" Senthil said that he didn't.

The air hostess came around and collected the food trays. Senthil again immersed himself in the photo album, while the lady next to him buried herself in a Hindi novel. The European went back to sleep. Senthil gently stroked Sumathi's cheek in the photo. He must have stared at it for an hour when he suddenly mumbled, "The letter!"

He quickly put the photo album back. Reaching into his bag, he pulled out a diary and flipped through the pages until he saw that envelope Sumathi had given him.

He was not in a hurry anymore since he had the letter in his hand. He looked at the envelope, caressed it, and looked at the back of it. He wanted to open it, but on second thought, he figured that once he opened and read it, there would be nothing to look forward to. The idea sounded silly even to him, but it was a long flight, and the idea of anticipation was more appealing than instant gratification. However, he caved and opened the envelope.

The letter was written on a piece of pink paper, Senthil's favorite color. He teared up as he read the letter.

My dearest Senthil,

Whoever said that absence makes the heart grow fonder must never have experienced true love. I don't know how my heart can grow any fonder of you than it already is. Just the thought of not being able to see you breaks my heart. At the same time, I take solace in the strength of our love and know deep down in my heart that we can endure this temporary separation.

I am so proud of you and admire your courage and sacrifice. Please don't worry about our families or me. I'll take care of them. I am aware you are going on a mission and know how focused you can be. Living in America is an opportunity of a lifetime. I have a request: please don't bury yourself in work and try to enjoy your stay there. Let me live vicariously through you.

I look forward to hearing about your adventures. Take a lot of pictures. I am sorry that I was not able to go to America with you. I hope you understand.

I love you with all my heart and look forward to the day you come back. Until then, please know that though miles and continents apart, when others have my company, it's you who has my heart.

Yours ever loving,
Sumathi.

His tears fell on the letter. It was sealed with Sumathi's kiss. He wiped his tears away, folded the letter, and placed it back in the diary. He glanced to his side to make sure his neighbors had not seen him crying and was relieved to see both asleep.

Another meal was served. Senthil was losing track of time. This meal was not bad. He had some bland potatoes and meat, but he liked the cake that was for dessert. Another couple of hours passed with him drifting in and out of sleep. He woke up to the overhead message for fastening the seat belts and sitting upright. The plane was on its descent to Frankfurt.

He remembered the touchdown in Bombay. It was a small plane, and he had felt the impact of the landing. He braced himself for this beast to hit the tarmac. As the plane got closer to the ground, he clenched the armrests, anticipating a big thud. To his surprise, he did not even realize they had landed until all the passengers clapped, applauding the pilot on a safe landing. The plane taxied the runway and eventually came to a standstill.

He helped the elderly lady with her carry-on and escorted her out of the plane. As they came out of the gate, he wanted to check the gate for his connecting flight to Dallas, Texas. But first, he wanted to make sure that Mrs. Agarwal, his fellow passenger, was okay.

He asked, "Where are you going from here?"

"My daughter lives in New York," she replied.

Senthil took her boarding pass and walked her to the series of computer screens displaying the departures. He looked for her flight bound for New York. They were at B8. The flight to New York was departing from gate B46, and his flight to Dallas was leaving from E9. Her flight was departing a little earlier than his. He carried her luggage and boarded the skyline—the shuttle train—with her. She was nervous, and since she could not read the signs, she appreciated his help.

Frankfurt airport was huge. It seemed at least fifty times bigger than the Madras Airport. They got off the shuttle, and Senthil helped her find a seat right next to the check-in counter at her gate. He talked to the lady at the counter to make sure they were in the right place. He then wished her good luck and said goodbye.

She thanked him for being so kind to her, and he replied, "You are just like my grandmother. I am glad to help."

He hurried back to the skyline and boarded the one headed to E9. He realized that he had a long way to walk after he got off the shuttle train. He picked up his pace as he was a little nervous about getting lost in the massive airport. He finally reached his gate and exhaled a sigh of relief when he realized that he had four hours to spare before his flight's departure. He double-checked to confirm he was at the right place and plopped into a chair by the huge glass walls so he could see all the flights gliding down the runways, landing and taking off.

After a while, he decided to walk around the airport to see what Frankfurt had to offer. Since he knew where he had to be and had enough time on his hands, he walked around with his carry-on. His was amazed at the wide array of eateries in the airport, the electronic stores, clothing stores, and the toy stores. He finally walked to a store that made his jaw drop and his mouth water. It was a huge store with nothing but chocolates of a hundred different kinds.

He had read about strawberries as the fruit of passion and had only seen them in Hollywood movies. Here, he saw chocolate-dipped strawberries—luscious, fresh, and bright red juicy strawberries half dipped in milk chocolate, dark chocolate, white chocolate, and half-dark chocolate and half-white chocolate. Some were decorated to look like they were wearing a suit. He was tempted to get some. He pulled out his wallet and moved closer to look at the price. There were small boxes of six strawberries, with the boxes marked with "8.00 DM / $6.00." He had exchanged some ₹2,000 to get $50 just in case he urgently needed something when he landed in Dallas. Those six strawberries would roughly cost him ₹270. His wallet sheepishly found its way back into his pocket.

He found himself taking a deep breath as though he was trying to inhale as much of the flavor in the air possible as he walked out of the store. He had had enough of window-shopping and hurried back to his gate. He took out the photo album to look at Sumathi. The time change was getting to him. He fell asleep as soon as he boarded the plane.

He woke up to a tap on his shoulder. It was a fellow passenger. He was sitting by the window, the middle seat was empty, and she was sitting on the aisle seat. Senthil could not believe his eyes. With her big wavy auburn hair, she looked like April Curtis, from the American TV show *Knight Rider*.

She said, "Sorry to wake you up, but you missed breakfast, and I didn't want you to miss lunch either. Not sure if you are hungry."

Senthil sat up and wiping off the drool from the side of his mouth, smiled and said, "That's okay. Thank you for waking me up." Then he added, "Excuse me. I need to freshen up." She smiled and leaned back so he could pass by. When he returned, she was in his seat.

As soon as she saw him, she said, "Oh, I am sorry. I just wanted a peek at the sea of white clouds below."

She hurried to move back into her seat, but Senthil motioned her to stop. "It's okay. You can sit there as long as you want. I'll take your seat."

She replied, "That is very nice of you. Thank you."

She looked out the window for a moment and then turned to him, saying, "Hi, I am Amy." She extended her hand towards him.

Senthil shook it, and said, "Hi, I am Senthil."

Amy asked him where he was coming from, where he was going, and what he was planning to do. She told him she was from Dallas and was visiting her sister who was married and settled in Germany. She talked non-stop—telling him about her Indian friend Vanaja with whom she had been friends since they were little girls. She talked about her favorite Indian foods and how much she admired Indian culture. Finally, she stopped talking and asked, "Why are you looking at me like that?'

Senthil said, "Forgive me for staring, but you look so much like April Curtis from the TV show *Knight Rider*."

She burst out laughing. She tried to control her laughter but could not. She finally managed to say, "Me? I'll take that as a compliment I guess."

Senthil said, "If I don't count the lady at the American Consulate in Madras, you are the first American I have had a conversation with."

"Oh! Really? So, what do you think of Americans?"

He smiled and replied, "Friendly."

As they were talking, the food carts arrived. She explained to him what his tray contained. Beef stew, mashed potatoes, salad with lettuce, tomatoes, and cucumber, and a piece of chocolate cake. As the air hostess walked by, Amy asked for a beer and turned to Senthil, who shook his head and asked for a Coca-Cola.

As they began eating, she suddenly squealed, "Hey Senthil, you know beef is meat from a cow, right?"

Senthil smiled and said, "Yes, of course." She said that she was surprised he was eating beef, as cows are considered sacred in India. Senthil teased, "I don't think this is an Indian cow."

She laughed and exclaimed, "You are so funny!"

The team of air hostesses came by to collect the trash. Amy asked Senthil if he would like to play cards. He nodded yes. She pulled out a pack of cards from her handbag, moved to the middle seat, and flipped down the food tray. "What game shall we play? Do you know rummy or poker?" Senthil replied that he was familiar with rummy, and so they started playing. He won three games in a row.

Amy started to complain, "This is not fair. That's the third game in a row that you have won."

Senthil replied, "I think I just got lucky. Besides, I never win. Sumathi always won when we played."

"Who's Sumathi?" she asked.

Senthil's face brightened. For the next few hours, he told her everything about Sumathi.

Eventually, she interrupted him and said, "Your face lit up the moment you mentioned her name, and the way you talk about her can make any girl jealous. I hope my boyfriend James feels the same way about me. She is very lucky!"

He replied, "No Amy, I am the lucky one."

She asked, "Do you have a picture of her?"

Senthil grinned and nodded. He showed her the photo album of Sumathi's pictures. "Wow! She is beautiful!" Amy exclaimed.

Senthil said, "She is also the kindest and smartest person you will ever meet. Now you know why I am the lucky one."

A few more hours passed, and the plane was on its descent to Dallas. Amy asked, "Do you have a ride from the airport?" Senthil said that Hema or someone from the rehab company would be there to pick him up from the airport. She told him it was great he did not have to take a cab. She mentioned James would come to pick her up and she was excited to see him after two weeks.

As the flight descended, Senthil gave her a piece of the Juicy Fruit gum and said, "It's good for your ears and prevents them from getting blocked." He popped one into his mouth.

The plane taxied to the gate, and Senthil and Amy walked out towards Baggage Claim. They waited near the carousel, looking for their luggage. Senthil spotted one of his suitcases coming towards him on the carousel. He reached for it, and with a little difficulty, lifted it off. Amy was busy putting on lipstick and fixing her makeup, and when she looked up, she noticed that she had let her duffel bag go past her. She exclaimed, "Oh my goodness, I missed my bag."

Senthil asked her which one it was, and she pointed to a black-and-yellow duffel bag. "Please watch my suitcases," Senthil told her and ran past the other passengers. He was able to catch up with the bag before it reached the end of the carousel. She smiled and clapped in joy. Finally, Senthil saw his second suitcase coming down the carousel. As he reached down to pick it off the carousel, Amy went to get him a cart.

As they approached the gate, they saw three lines: one for American citizens, one for green-card holders, and one for visa holders. Amy wished him the best of luck and a successful career. Senthil said, 'Thank you, Amy. Good luck to you too. I hope James knows how lucky he is."

Amy laughed, and Senthil reached out to shake her hand. Amy gave him a big hug saying, "You are in America now, and you better get used to this greeting."

Senthil blushed and patted her shoulders. He wasn't awkward, but he had no idea how to reciprocate properly. She bid adieu as she walked towards the counter, and Senthil joined the others in the immigration clearance line.

When his turn came, Senthil handed his passport to the immigration officer who opened his passport, looked him up and down, and flipped to the page where the H1-B visa was stamped. Once that was verified, the officer asked, "Do you have any fresh fruits or vegetables?"

Senthil replied, "No sir, but I do have some dried spices, some pickles, and some raw rice."

The officer asked him to step aside and follow him.

Senthil obliged, and as he began walking, the officer turned around and said, "Bring your suitcases with you." Senthil apologized, turned around, grabbed his cart, and followed him.

The officer gestured him to enter the room and walked back to his counter. Senthil entered the room. There was a female officer with blue latex gloves on her hands, standing behind a table. She pointed to his big suitcases and patted on the table. Senthil picked up one of the suitcases and placed it on the table. She said, "Open it."

Senthil placed his carry-on suitcase on the floor, bent down, opened it, and took out a small keychain. He stood up, fumbled with the keys, and finally managed to open the suitcase on the table. Although he was not afraid, he was a little anxious about the procedure, monotone instructions, and expressionless faces.

Once he opened the suitcase, the officer asked him to step back and began to go through its contents. She rummaged through his clothes and the sealed bags of spices and rice. She picked up the pickle bottle, sniffed it, and looked at him as though to ask him what it was.

Senthil said, "It's mango pickle."

She asked, "Spicy?"

He nodded yes.

She lifted a small sealed plastic bag and Senthil said, "Cumin seeds." For the other one, he said, "Star anise and fennel seeds."

She asked him to move this suitcase to the side and place the other suitcase on top of the table. This suitcase just contained clothes and his books, his pressure cooker, and an extra pair of shoes—nothing edible. She asked him to close the suitcase and head out towards the right. She walked towards the sliding door. He had to rearrange some things so he could close the suitcases again. He then slid them back on to the cart, placed his small carry-on on top, and proceeded to the sliding door.

As the door opened, the female officer smiled and said, "Welcome to the United States of America. Enjoy your stay."

He felt relieved. With a big smile, he said, "Thank you very much, ma'am."

The door opened, and he squinted from the bright sunlight filtering through the big glass windows. He did not know where to go. He looked left and right. Christmas trees and decorations adorned the airport. People were dressed up. The scene reminded him of the movie *Home Alone*, which he had seen with Sumathi and his siblings. The air smelled like cake, vanilla, apples, and cinnamon.

He followed the signs for "Ground Transportation" and followed the people exiting the airport. Families and friends were waiting to greet their loved ones; a lot of hugs and laughter followed the greetings. As he looked around for Hema, a sign caught his eye: "Senthil, Therapy Solutions."

He walked towards the gentleman holding the sign and said, "I am Senthil."

The gentleman said, "I am Walter. I am one of the recruiters working for Hema."

Chapter 9 — The Land of the Free

SENTHIL EXITED THE AIRPORT, AND THE CHILL IN THE AIR made him shiver. He was surprised at how deceptive the bright sun was. As he followed Walter to the car, he was amazed to see the different makes and models of the cars, the cleanliness around him, and the organized traffic. Everything seemed to be in its proper place—a sharp contrast to how things were back home.

Walter walked ahead as Senthil followed him with his cart. Walter stopped near a large black sedan. He opened the trunk and helped Senthil with the suitcases. Senthil pushed the cart back to the designated area and got into the front seat. Walter asked him if he had a good flight, and if everything was okay. Senthil replied that everything had gone well. He asked about Shiva, and Walter told him that Shiva was working at a rehabilitation facility in Jefferson City, Missouri.

They left Dallas Airport and headed to Lewisville, Texas, where the company had two three-bedroom apartments. The one on the first floor was for boys, and the one above it was for the girls. It served as the home for the contract therapists. They could stay there between their assignments and have that as their permanent mailing address for their paychecks and tax purposes. All utilities were paid for. The apartment had all the basic amenities, and Hema always kept the fridge stocked with necessities. There was a cordless phone, a fax machine, a computer, a printer, and a VCR, and a big TV in the living room. There were two full-size beds and a safe in each bedroom.

The therapists who arrived from India stayed there before embarking on their first assignment. Hema helped them get a driver's license, a social security card, and a checking account. She also provided them with a basic orientation to the American health-care system, including Medicare, Medicaid, and insurance. She took them to grocery stores and department stores to familiarize them with shopping in America. Sometimes, these were done by therapists who were already here and were between their assignments.

In the car, Senthil was fascinated by everything: the wide spacious roads, the speed at which they were going, the buildings, and the different types of vehicles. He turned to Walter and asked, "Excuse me, Walter, what kind of a car is this?"

Walter smiled and replied, "Oh, this is a 1994 Eagle. I just got it brand new last month. What's your favorite car?"

Senthil exclaimed, "KITT from *Knight Rider*!"

"You should get a Pontiac Trans Am. And a 1982 model, if I might add," replied Walter.

Senthil saw the exit sign for TX -121 BUS N to Lewisville. He remembered Hema mentioning that the apartment was in Lewisville.

Walter told him they were almost there as he turned into the apartment complex. It was a gated community that was beautifully landscaped with manicured lawns and a large swimming pool. As Walter approached the gates and slowed down, Senthil said, "Walter, I'll get the gates."

He tried to open the car door, but Walter laughed and said, "That won't be necessary Senthil, but thank you for the offer."

He pulled closer to the security gate. "You press 9357 and hit "Enter" to get in." Senthil was struck dumb when the gate opened automatically.

Parking the car, Walter helped Senthil get out his suitcases from the trunk and said, "I guess one can't pack light when going from a continent to another." They rolled the suitcases to the apartment door, and Walter pressed the doorbell. Hema opened the door.

Senthil was very happy to see her. He removed his shoes and walked in with his socks on. She asked him about the journey and if everything had gone well with customs and immigration. Senthil said he had a smooth journey without any problems. Hema gave him a tour of the apartment. She showed him the TV and the VCR and also how to operate the remote controller. In the kitchen, she pointed to the containers on the counter and asked him to help himself to the Indian food she had cooked for his dinner. She showed him the fridge, the toaster, the dishwasher, and the microwave. She emphasized that he should not put any metal in the microwave.

Senthil had to interrupt, "You have a machine that washes your dishes, and you can cook and eat your food in minutes and can even do it on paper or plastic?" Hema laughed and nodded.

She showed him the bedrooms and the bathroom and taught him how to operate the shower. She showed him the safe and gave him the combination to open it, advising that he lock his passport and valuables in the safe. She told him that since no one was there now, he could pick his bedroom. She told him to relax and rest for the day and that she would come by the next day, Friday, at 9:00 AM to take him to get an ID card and his social security card and visit the bank to open a checking account.

Senthil asked Hema about Shiva and how he was doing. Hema replied that he was doing well and was currently on a six-month contract with a rehabilitation facility in Missouri.

She showed him the phone and the computer and told him the password for the computer and the long-distance code for the phone. She then gave him a piece of paper with the phone numbers for the apartment office, her home, and her office. She laughed and acknowledged that she had given him an overwhelming amount of information in a short period but reassured him by asking him to eat something and get some rest to overcome the jet lag.

Senthil asked Hema if he could call his home and tell his parents that he had arrived safely. She said, "Of course, and your first call is on me. Just call after 9:00 PM, as the AT&T world savings plan is effective from 8:00 PM to 8:00 AM."

Senthil thanked her, and she showed him how to operate the cordless phone and the base.

When Hema and Walter left, Senthil locked the door behind them. He removed his socks and walked on the plush soft carpet. He had never walked on a carpet before! It was incredibly relaxing to curl his toes into it. He brushed his teeth and took a long hot shower. It was much more rejuvenating than the shower he was used to—with freshly pumped water out of a bucket.

He changed into his pajamas and walked out to the kitchen. He was famished. He looked at the containers on the kitchen counter and found to his happy surprise that Hema had made him chicken tikka masala, mutton curry, basmati rice, green beans stir fry, and mixed vegetable curry. There was enough food for four people. He fixed a plate with a little of everything and popped it into the microwave. He opened the fridge to get some water and was surprised to find the fridge completely stocked with all the staples. He poured himself a tall glass of orange juice. His food was ready—nice and hot—in two minutes.

Smiling, he walked with his plate and the orange juice to the dining table. He felt like royalty. His taste buds relished the spices they had missed the past few meals. He savored every bite of it. He finished his dinner, washed his plate, and set it up to dry on the kitchen counter. He opened the fridge to snoop around and found something that caught his eye right away: a sampler cheesecake. He picked up the box and carried it to the dining table. The box had pictures of twelve wedges. There were four varieties with three slices each. They were plain, turtle, chocolate, and raspberry. He took a slice of the raspberry, not because he knew what raspberry tasted like, but because the cheesecake was pink—his favorite color.

He took a slice of the raspberry and a slice of turtle cheesecake in a plate, walked to the living room, and plopped into the recliner. The lever on the side caught his eye. He pulled on it, and the chair reclined, elevating his legs. He was startled and thought he was going to fall, but he was surprised at the position he ended up in. It was very comfortable. He cut into the raspberry cheesecake. Interesting texture, he thought. With the first bite, he thought he had died and gone to heaven. It was delicious and reminded him of the North Indian desserts made of *khoya*. The sweet, tangy nature of the cheesecake and the layer of sweet raspberry topping complemented each other.

The last bite of the heavenly cheesecake brought him back to reality. He looked at the time. He had another hour before he could call home, so he turned on the TV. He was amused by the commercials that were so different from the ones he was used to. A song with a fast beat and catchy tune came up, and all he could make out was the line that repeatedly came up: *"It's alright, 'cause I'm saved by the bell."* The song piqued his interest, and so he decided to watch it.

It was about a school and seemed to revolve around a few kids. He was surprised to see the clothes the kids wore to school. Even more surprising was how the lead character Zach Morris interacted with the school principal and how the kids behaved in the classroom. Screech made him laugh, and he was surprised to see a cafeteria in the school. This show was the first culture shock for Senthil. It was fun, nevertheless. There were two shows back to back, and he watched them both. He looked up to see the clock on the wall, and it was 9:01. He ran to the phone. It was 7:30 AM the next day in India.

He dialed the international code, the Indian code, then the code to Madras, and finally the phone number. His heart was racing. There was a pause, and after a few seconds, the phone rang. It hardly rang twice, before his *appa* answered. He must have been sitting right by the phone.

"Hello, Senthil! Did you reach safely?"

Senthil replied, "Yes. It's 9:00 PM here, and I am in the apartment. Hema came to the airport and picked me up. Where is everybody?"

His *appa* said that they were all standing around him and pointed the phone receiver towards the awaiting ensemble. He heard all his siblings screaming, "Hello! How are you? How is America? How was the plane ride? Is there snow?" He had to speak loudly so they could all hear him through the phone receiver.

Finally, his *amma* grabbed the phone to talk to him. "Did you have dinner? What did you eat? Are you getting used to the weather?" He tried to answer all her questions but could sense some anxiety in her voice. He sensed relief when he told her that he had rice, chicken, and mutton curry.

She said, "This is an international call, and we have been talking to you for an hour but hang on for a second."

There was a brief pause, and then he heard his parents say, "Take care of yourself, eat on time, take time to enjoy your stay, and don't just work."

All his siblings screamed, "Bye, take care! Eat a lot of chocolates, go see the Disneyland, we miss you."

He screamed back: "I miss you all too. Take care, be good, and do well in school and . . ."

As he was talking, there was a gentle "Hi!" on the other end. This whole time he had been pacing the living room while talking on the cordless phone, but that simple hi made him go weak and he had to sit down. He sat down and said, "Hi! How and when did you get there?"

Sumathi replied, "I told my parents that I had to be at work early and came to your house at 7:00 AM. How are you?"

Senthil said, "I am doing fine. The flights were on time, and everything went well. How are you doing?"

She replied, "I am fine too. Thank you for the lovely letter. I thought I was reading mine."

Senthil said, "Same here. We pretty much wrote the same thing. I don't think it's a coincidence. I miss you, dear. I wish you were here with me."

Sumathi replied, "I know. I miss you too."

They talked for another five minutes, and Sumathi said, "I know you don't want to hang up, but I should let you go. Take care. I can't wait to talk to you or read your letter again. I love you, Senthil."

He replied, "I love you too, Sumathi. I'll talk to you soon. Take care."

He stayed slumped in the recliner for a few minutes. He was beginning to drift off and decided to go to bed. He checked the door to make sure it was locked and walked to the bedroom. He locked the safe and got into bed. He was so exhausted that he fell asleep almost as soon as his body hit the bed.

Chapter 10 — Adventures: Embarrassing and Interesting

SENTHIL WOKE UP TO THE TELEPHONE RINGING. HE found himself lying on the carpet near the bed, with a pillow under his head and one under his knee—just like in India. The only difference was that he used to lie on the cool marble floor in India, and here he was lying on a carpet and was cold enough to cover himself with a comforter.

He felt disoriented. To his left, there was the bed, and to his right was the wall. He felt as though he was sleeping in an alley, and he panicked and sat upright. He got his bearings once he sat up and could see the whole bedroom over the bed. He had no idea about when or how he got to the floor. Just then he remembered: "The phone!"

He ran to the living room, and answered the phone in a groggy voice: "Hello?"

It was Hema. He heard could hear the enthusiasm in her voice as she said, "Hello Senthil, good morning. Hope you got some rest and are getting over your jet lag. I told you I'd be there at 9:00 AM, but it'll be around 10:30 before I reach. I have a conference call with a client in Missouri; it's about a potential assignment for you. It's only three hours away from Shiva and—"

"What day is it?" Senthil had to interrupt her as she was talking a mile a minute.

Hema laughed and said, "I am so sorry. It's 7:30 AM on Friday here. Wow, I am so jealous if you slept through Thursday."

Senthil could not believe it and told her that he must have gotten up at least once. She laughed and said, "Hope you feel rested. I'll see you around 10:30."

Senthil walked back to the bedroom, picked up the pillows and the comforter, and made the bed. He sat on the edge of the bed and tried to recollect the events of the past twenty-four hours. He had only a vague memory of getting some water to drink and going to the bathroom.

Senthil was famished. He decided to get ready, eat some breakfast, and then fill out the form Hema had asked him to complete before she arrived. After a hot shower, he walked into the kitchen. He took out the bread, the strawberry jam, and the orange juice out of the fridge. He looked for butter but could not find any; just as he was about to give up, he noticed a glass bottle and read the label out loud: "Mayonnaise." He had no idea what it meant. He opened the bottle and saw something creamy yellow that resembled soft butter.

He made two sandwiches with a lot of strawberry jam on one slice and an equal amount of mayonnaise on the other. He was surprised by the consistency of mayonnaise and wondered if it was some really good butter that was so smooth and silky. He poured himself a tall glass of orange juice and sat at the dining table. Bread and butter sandwich was a special treat growing up as it was different from the routine savory *idli*, *dosa*, *uppuma*, or *pongal* they had for breakfast. His siblings Nanda and Rathi liked butter and jam sandwich a lot.

He took a big bite, and a small frown spread across his face. Instead of the big burst of sweetness exploding in his mouth, he was surprised to find a little sourness along with the sweetness of the strawberry jam. He stared at the sandwich. His first idea was that the butter was spoiled, but he dismissed the thought as he had opened a brand-new bottle. He took another bite, and by the third bite, he got used to this *American* butter.

Once he was finished, he washed the plate and the glass and put them in the dishwasher to dry. The clock read 8:45 AM. He had time to fill the form. He walked to the safe in the bedroom and tried to open it. He got a sick feeling in his stomach when he realized that he had forgotten the code. The forms were inside. He racked his brains and tried entering the numbers that popped into his head but to no avail.

He walked to the living room and searched the coffee table, the side tables, and the other bedrooms to see if any code had been written down. No luck! There was a notepad on the table that had the phone on it, but there was only the office phone number and the apartment office number there. He thought of calling the office and asking Hema, but he was afraid that she would think he was stupid for not remembering three simple numbers. Finally, he decided that he would rather look stupid than unreliable by not being ready when Hema arrived. So, he called the office to talk to Hema but got an engaged tone.

He checked the kitchen drawers and the cabinets. On the fridge was a magnetic whiteboard with some numbers on it. This gave him a glimmer of hope. There was the office phone number, Hema's home phone number, apartment office number, and below that was written "Emergency 911."

He knew about the area codes in America and that all phone numbers were ten-digit numbers. He, however, did not recognize the phone number that stood at only three digits.

He was in a state of emergency all right. The safe had to be opened, the forms had to be filled, and the passport taken for identification purposes. After all, the number was meant for emergencies. So, he got the phone and sat down at the dining table with a piece of paper and a pen and dialed 911. The phone rang, and a female voice answered.

911 Dispatcher: "Denton County 911. Where is the emergency?"

Senthil: "In my apartment."

911: "What is your emergency, sir? And please talk slowly."

Senthil: "Yes ma'am. I need the code for my safe."

911: "What?"

Senthil: "My passport and some forms are in the safe."

911: "Are you alone in the apartment? Is somebody holding your passport against your will?"

Senthil: "Yes, I am alone. I put the passport in the safe and locked it last night. And I forgot the code to open the safe. Could you please help me?"

911: "What else is there in the safe?"

Senthil: "My passport, some forms for a bank account, my degree certificates, and $50."

911: "What is your name, sir?"

Senthil: "Senthil."

911: "Is that your first name or your last name?"

Senthil: "It's my first name. My full name is Senthilvelan Rajashekaran."

911: "Can you spell it?"

Senthil: "S as in summer, E as in elephant, N as in necklace, T as in tiger, H as in horse, I as in ice cream, L as in London, V as in violin, L as in London, A as in apple—"

911: "It's okay. That's enough. Wherc are you from?"

Senthil: "India. I came here on Wednesday evening. Oh, somebody is knocking at my door."

911: "Is your phone cordless?"

Senthil: "Yes, it is."

911: "Okay. Don't hang up. Walk with your phone, unlock the door, and step back."

Senthil walked to the door and opened it and stepped back as instructed. Two police officers were standing at the door.

"May we come in?" asked one of the officers.

"Yes, please come in. Can I get you something to drink? Water? Orange juice?" Senthil asked.

His hospitable nature remained unaltered even in this moment of crisis—a reflection of his Indian sensibilities. The officers entered the apartment and said, "No, thank you. That won't be necessary."

One of the officers walked into a bedroom, but Senthil redirected him, saying, "No sir, it's not that room." He pointed to his bedroom, and the officer turned, stared him down, and walked inside.

The other officer signaled for the phone and spoke into it: "Officer Cooper here. Everything is fine. Thank you." He hung up the phone while the other officer walked back to the living room after checking all the rooms.

Everything was not fine; the safe was still locked. While Senthil stood there puzzled, Officer Cooper approached him and asked why he had called 911. Senthil tried to explain, telling them that he had just arrived from India and that he was just trying to get his passport and the forms to fill and be ready when Hema arrived. Officer Cooper asked him if he had forgotten the numbers, to which Senthil replied, "I thought I remembered the numbers 25, 27, 33."

Officer Cooper said, "Try it again." Senthil walked to the safe, bent down to look at the knob, and turned it clockwise to 25, then to 27, and finally to 33.

Officer Cooper was looking over his shoulder the whole time. He said, "Looks like you turned it clockwise for all three numbers."

Senthil looked at him puzzled, and Officer Cooper added, "In these number combination locks, the second number is usually turned counterclockwise."

Senthil looked up at him in surprise. Officer Cooper said, "Go on, try it."

Senthil turned the knob again. Only this time, he turned 27 counterclockwise, and to his relief, the safe opened. He turned to the officer with a stupid grin on his face.

"Could you get your passport out?" Officer Cooper asked. Senthil handed his passport to Officer Cooper who flipped through it to the page with the picture and looked at Senthil.

Satisfied with the comparison, he asked, "What's your date of birth?"

Senthil replied "April 14, 1969, sir." Officer Cooper verified the date on the passport and handed it back to Senthil.

Officer Cooper continued, "Sir, 911 is for life-threatening emergencies only." He then walked towards the door where the other officer was standing. Senthil apologized for his ignorance.

Officer Cooper turned and said, "Have a nice day." He looked at the other officer and remarked, "Fresh off the boat." Senthil followed him to the door. But he had not come by boat; he came in a Jumbo Jet.

He thought he'd clear the air, just in case. "Thank you. But officer, I came by Lufthansa Airlines."

Senthil quickly shut the door and hurried to the safe. He collected his passport and the forms and promptly filled them in. He was all set for Hema's arrival when there was a knock on the door. Hema entered in a hurry with a concerned look on her face. As soon as she stepped in, she closed the door behind her and asked, "Arc you okay? Is everything all right?"

Senthil replied, "Yes Hema, but—"

"I got a call from the cops that they were here," Hema interrupted. "I am sorry. It's my fault for not telling you about all the important phone numbers."

"Don't worry about it, Hema. I am fine. I feel a little stupid, but I am fine."

"That's good. Okay then, maybe I can take you out for breakfast to shake this off?"

"I ate breakfast already, Hema, but thank you," Senthil replied.

"What did you have?"

Senthil told her that he had made himself a bread, butter, and jam sandwich and washed it down with some orange juice. He had liked the strawberry jam, but the butter needed some getting used to. Hema asked him what he meant by that, and Senthil explained that while he had liked the consistency of the butter and the fact that it spread easily, the American butter, unlike its

Indian counterpart, was a little sour, and despite having been stored in the refrigerator, the consistency remained creamy.

Hema told him it was not butter but Country Crock Spread. Senthil protested, "But the bottle read—"

"Bottle? You mean a brown plastic tub?"

Senthil insisted that it was a bottle. Grabbing the bottle of mayonnaise from the refrigerator, he said, "This is the one I used in my sandwich."

Hema grabbed the bottle and started laughing. Senthil was not amused. Finally controlling her laughter, Hema said, "That's mayonnaise." She explained what it was and what it was used for.

Senthil shrugged and said, "Oh well, I am still alive."

Laughing, they both walked out of the house. Their first stop was Bank One. Hema helped Senthil set up a checking account, get a box of starter checks and a Bank One ATM card. The next stop was the social security office to get Senthil a social security card. From there, they went to the DPS. On the way to the DPS, Hema asked him if he knew how to drive a car. Apart from the motorbike, Senthil had learned to drive a car by taking driving lessons. He procured a car driver's license after his move to America was finalized, but he had never regularly driven a car. Hema picked up a book to help Senthil with the driver's license test.

After they were done, Hema asked Senthil, "So, what cuisines have you had other than Indian?" Senthil told her that a lot of fusion restaurants and street vendors in India served Indo-Chinese food. She suggested they get something to eat before she dropped him back. She asked him what he would like to try, and he asked what the choices were.

"Well," Hema started, "there is Mexican, Italian, Japanese, Chinese, Greek, and—"

Senthil interrupted her: "Hema, what are some classic American dishes?"

"Well, there's fried chicken, apple pie, macaroni and cheese, hot dogs, burgers, potato salad . . ." Senthil asked, "Can we get some fried chicken?"

Hema drove to the Kentucky Fried Chicken on Main Street. Hema explained to Senthil how the fast food joint worked. She paid for two KFC buffets, and each of them got a food tray and a glass. They found a place to sit by the large windows. Senthil was surprised to know that they could help themselves to their food, pay $6.95, and eat and drink as much as they wanted to. He could not comprehend how this could be a profitable business idea. He had never heard of this concept in India.

Hema grabbed a plate to fix herself lunch, but Senthil decided to walk around the food stations in the middle to look at all the items that were on offer. Hema followed close behind, telling him about the types of fried chicken: original, crispy, extra crispy; the sides: mashed potatoes, corn, biscuits, green beans, stewed tomatoes, baked beans, collard greens, pickles and carrots, coleslaw; and desserts: apple pie, cherry pie, Jell-O, chocolate, vanilla, and butterscotch puddings. The list refused to end.

Senthil again asked, "I can eat however much of anything I want?" Hema smiled and nodded.

Senthil had grown up eating spicy food. He filled his plate with a couple of pieces of chicken thighs and a bit of each vegetable. He was surprised to find that the chicken was not spicy—flavorful, yet not spicy. Hema told him about the hot sauce and ketchup. After he had finished eating, he took his plate to get seconds. Hema stopped him and pointed him to a sign that read, "Please use a new plate each time."

He was surprised to learn that the plates were disposable and that wasting them was encouraged. He wanted to make sure he got Hema her money's worth, so he grabbed a new plate and loaded it with more fried chicken. The coleslaw was interesting, as he had never had raw cabbage. Other than cucumber, coconut, onion, and an occasional carrot and tomato, he had never had anything raw. The steamed green beans and carrots tasted better the second time around.

Hema looked on amazed at the amount of food Senthil was able to put away. She just watched him finish his second helping. Just when she thought he was done, he announced, "Time for dessert!" Senthil got himself some apple pie and some vanilla, chocolate, and butterscotch pudding. He told Hema he had never had a cooked apple before. He tried the apple pie first: after a bite, he was convinced that it was the best thing he had ever had. It was even better than the cheesecake!

Hema interrupted him: "If you like this so much, we have to get you some real warm apple pie with ice cream."

Senthil found it hard to believe that it could get better than this, but he was very open to the suggestion.

Hema brought him back to the apartment. Before she left, she said, "I almost forgot to tell you that Brent and Peter are stopping by tonight."

Hema explained that Brent and Peter were contract physical therapists who worked for her and were stopping there on their way to the next assignment. She told him, "They are finishing their six-month-long assignment in Wichita, Kansas, and are driving through Dallas to their next assignment in Houston, Texas."

Senthil was excited about meeting American physical therapists. He bid farewell to Hema and sat down at the dining table. He was curious to see what was included in the knowledge test for the driver's license. He perused the guide and tried to memorize the signs and the questions and answers.

About 7:15 PM, when Senthil was engrossed in yet another episode of *Saved by the Bell*, the doorbell rang. He opened the door to find Brent and Peter, standing with a shoulder bag and a six-pack in their hands.

"Come in, come in. You must be Brent and Peter. Hema said you'd be coming."

Brent reached out and shook Senthil's hand and said, "I am Brent Miller. You must be the new PT from India."

Senthil grinned and nodded.

Peter introduced himself. "I am Peter Robinson. Welcome to America."

Peter grabbed the six-pack from Brent's hand and walked to the refrigerator. Senthil asked, "Can I get you anything to drink? Water, orange juice, or coke?"

They said no, thanked him, and settled down in front of the TV.

Brent asked, "What's your name again?"

"Senthil Rajashekaran."

Noticing the puzzled look on their faces, Senthil added, "*Senthil*. It rhymes with lentil."

Brent said, "That works, Senthil. Do you mind if we change the channel to watch some football?"

Senthil handed him the remote and said, "Sure! Go ahead." Brent said that the game would start at 8:00 PM and that they could watch it then. Senthil asked them about their work and the type of patients they treat. Brent worked as a PT in an acute rehab facility, and Peter was a PT in a skilled nursing facility.

Peter wanted to order pizza for dinner and asked Senthil if he would like some. Senthil told him he had never had pizza before but would be happy to try some. Peter looked at Brent, who said, "I am down for the usual. Make it two large ones."

Peter grabbed the cordless phone to call Pizza Hut and stepped out.

Brent changed the channel to watch the football game. The game was about to start, and the players started running down the field. Senthil was puzzled; he had not expected to see players running down the field with pads and helmets looking more like gladiators than athletes. It looked as though they were preparing for war and not a game.

Senthil asked, "Brent, what's the ball made of?"

"Pig's skin. Why do you ask?" Brent said.

Senthil told him he did not understand the pads and helmets. Now it was Brent's turn to look puzzled.

Dallas Cowboys won the toss and elected to receive. Buffalo Bills started the game with the kickoff. As soon as the receiver caught the ball, Senthil yelled, "Foul! He touched the ball."

When he saw the receiver run with the ball, he turned to Brent and said, "What is he doing? This isn't football."

Very soon, they figured out that Senthil was talking about soccer and that he had no clue what American football was. Both started laughing as Peter walked back in.

"What's so funny?" Peter asked.

Brent said, "Our Indian friend here has never watched a football game before and thought we were settling down to watch soccer. You should have seen the look on his face when he saw the players with pads and helmets and when Dallas received the kickoff."

Peter joined in the laughter and asked Senthil if he wanted a beer. Senthil declined politely, saying he did not drink. Peter grabbed two cold ones and joined them in front of the TV, when a knock sounded on the door. "That must be the pizza guy," said Peter.

He brought in two large pepperoni pizzas with extra cheese, and Senthil offered to get some plates, but they asked him to grab some paper towels and a couple of beers. Senthil brought those and a glass of orange juice for himself.

When Brent opened the box, Senthil exclaimed, "Oh my goodness! It smells great and looks like a big beautiful cake!"

He took a slice of the pepperoni pizza and relished it. They asked him if he liked it, and he only nodded in reply, as he had stuffed his mouth. For the rest of the game, Peter and Brent took turns explaining to him how football was played. By the end of the game, Dallas Cowboys and Pizza Hut had both gained a new fan.

The next day, Brent and Peter drove off towards their next assignment. Hema called Senthil to let him know that he would not be starting his first assignment until January 3 the next year as all existing contracts were set to last until the end of the year. Also, he would be going to Detroit, Michigan, and not to Missouri as planned earlier. Hema had been unable to secure that contract.

Senthil spent his time studying for his national licensure exam for physical therapy, watching TV, and walking around the apartment complex. Hema brought him groceries on her way back home so he could cook. A week went by. Hema visited the following Friday and took him to the DPS. He passed his knowledge test on the computer and the eye test and made an appointment for the driving test for Monday. She asked him if he needed a driving lesson. Being frugal, Senthil told her he had learned to drive a car in India and that if he could drive a stick shift on the congested roads back home, he would have no trouble driving an automatic in the organized roads with lanes and proper traffic. He just had to remember to drive on the right side of the road instead of the left.

Since it was the weekend, Hema came over the next day. She let Senthil drive her car inside the apartment complex. He had pretty good control over the car and a good sense of the road. Hema said she was relieved and felt confident that he would do well in the road test on Monday.

As he parked the car, Hema asked him what his plans were for the rest of the day and the weekend. He told her he was going to study for the PT exam, write letters home, and watch some football. Hema looked surprised when she heard him say football. Senthil told her how Brent and Peter had educated him about the game and introduced him to pizza. Senthil told her he was going to order pizza for dinner.

"Wow," Hema smiled. "You are getting Americanized pretty quickly. Be careful when you order pizza though. They may try to talk you into ordering more than what you want."

Senthil assured her that he would be careful. Hema gave him some money and told him that she would be there on Monday morning to accompany him to the road test. He would need to bring his international driver's license for the test.

Senthil was reviewing some anatomy in neurology when the phone rang. It was Shiva. They talked for more than an hour—about home, Sumathi, Mary, and Shiva's job. Senthil was very happy that Shiva had called. He shared the bad news of his assignment being in Detroit, Michigan. Shiva told him he was hopeful that his next assignment would be in Michigan and that they would be able to get together soon. He gave Senthil his phone number and told him to call after nine in the evening or at any time during the weekends.

Senthil sat down to finish his reviewing. Reading it reminded him of the times he spent studying with Sumathi. They used to learn by teaching each other. Eventually, he realized that he had fallen into a reverie of his time with Sumathi; he had not read anything. He decided to catch up with his studying later. It was time for some football.

He dialed the Pizza Hut phone number. "Hello!" a female voice came on. "Thank you for calling Pizza Hut. Our special today is two medium specialty pizzas, an order of breadsticks, an order of cinnamon sticks, and a two-liter coke for $15.99. May I take your order?"

Hema was right. He replied, "I just need one large pizza and nothing else."

"Okay. One large pizza it is. What toppings do you want?"

"No toppings. I just need a large pizza."

"Excuse me, no toppings?"

"That's right, ma'am. I just need one large pizza."

"Okay, let's try this again. What crust can I get you?"

"I don't know what you mean by that."

"I mean, pan, hand-tossed, or thin crust. Sir, this is a busy night. Can I get your order, please?"

"I don't want any crust; I don't want any toppings. I just need one large pizza. Could you please take my order?"

"Sir, is this a joke? You picked the wrong night for that. We are very busy." The connection went dead.

Senthil looked at the phone in confusion. "She didn't take my order!" he exclaimed.

He was disappointed. He fixed himself a plate with leftovers, poured himself a glass of water, and sat down to watch the football game. To his surprise, he was able to follow the game. Although he did not know the intricacies and all the nuances of the game and the fouls and penalties, he nevertheless enjoyed watching it.

He woke up early Sunday morning to pick up his studies from where he had left it off the previous night. He finished reading about neurological conditions and the exercise principles and decided to tackle the topic of electrotherapy next. He took a break to have breakfast before starting on the new topic. He went to the kitchen and began looking through the cabinets. A big plastic jar labeled "Peanut Butter" caught his attention.

He opened the lid and the seal and was surprised to find a smooth, creamy paste that smelled like peanuts. It reminded him of the day Sumathi had made him a dessert made of peanuts. He had been studying at her place for an exam. After lunch, Sumathi realized there was no dessert at home to serve him. She knew of his sweet tooth, and even though he insisted that it was okay, she was insistent. He asked her for a glass of water, which she fetched him. Then he asked her to stir the water with her fingers. He then took a sip of the water and said that it was as sweet as *payasam*[40], and his sweet tooth was immensely satisfied.

She smiled and said, "You are such a romantic. But I love it. Why don't you take notes for the next chapter while I whip up something sweet for you in ten minutes?"

Senthil asked her not to worry about it. Besides, making a dessert in such a short time was impossible.

Sumathi felt challenged. She winked at him and said, "Let's see about that."

---

40 Rice and milk pudding

She ran to the kitchen and looked through the cabinets in a hurry. As she was about to close the last cabinet, a jar of roasted peanuts caught her eye. She stared at it for a second and grabbed the jar. She put two handfuls of peanuts into the blender and ground it. Senthil, curious to see what she was up to, walked to the kitchen, but Sumathi motioned him to go back to the study table. He reluctantly obliged. Sumathi emptied the blender into a bowl. She then added a couple of spoons of ghee and sugar and mixed it with the powdered peanuts until it had a dough-like consistency. She took a small plate and patted the peanut mixture into a nice big circle. Just before she could take it to him, she had another idea. She took a knife and carved a heart from the center of the circle. She tasted the piece of the mixture that she had carved out, and it brought a big smile to her face.

Senthil had been impressed. He could see the pride in her face as he asked her what it was. She said, "It's my invention. Try it."

He took the spoon from her hand and cut a piece of the heart and tasted it. She was looking at him in anticipation, awaiting his reaction.

"Wow! This is amazing," he exclaimed.

"And it only took me seven minutes," she winked.

He thought to himself that the ingenious Americans had stolen Sumathi's invention and figured a way to produce her idea by the jars. He could not wait to tell her about this peanut butter he had just discovered.

Senthil made himself a sandwich. He smothered a lot of peanut butter on two slices of bread, found some sugar and sprinkled it generously on each slice, and then slapped the slices together. He grabbed a glass of orange juice and sat down in front of the TV.

Senthil was neck-deep in nostalgia and eagerly took a big bite of the sandwich. He nearly choked on the bite. He did not realize that peanut butter would be so difficult to swallow! Also, it was not as sweet as he had expected it to be. Then again, coming from India, he did not believe in wasting food. He gulped down some orange juice, only to realize that it clashed with the taste of peanut butter. So, he covered the glass of orange juice and placed it back in the refrigerator. He came back with a glass of water and more sugar.

He sprinkled more sugar on the slices of the sticky sandwich and tried taking a much smaller bite. This time, he enjoyed it. While it did not exactly taste like Sumathi's ground peanut sweet with ghee and sugar, he liked the convenience of readymade peanut butter and the fact that something so American reminded him of her. He resumed studying. At one point, he started feeling stiff and decided to take a walk to get some fresh air. It was about three in the afternoon, and the sun was shining brightly.

He locked the apartment, put the keys in his pocket, and started walking around the complex. Only a minute into the walk he realized that the sunlight was deceptive. It was rather cold. He was wearing a T-shirt, a pair of shorts, and *chappals*. He began to walk faster. He was determined to finish the walk around the apartment complex. He noticed it was colder in the shade. By the time he came back to the apartment, his nose, ears, fingers, and toes were as cold as ice. It was a relief just to step back into the apartment. He thought a hot shower would help, and it did.

On Monday morning, Hema came to pick Senthil up, and together they headed to the Department of Public Safety. On the way, she asked him about his weekend. He told her about his experience ordering pizza and with peanut butter. Hema started to laugh so hard that she had to pull over. Senthil tried to ask her why she was laughing, and Hema tried to answer, but the more he asked, the more she laughed. She asked him what the pizza he had had with Brent and Peter looked like. He said that the pizza was round and had lots of red circles on top. She informed him that those were pepperoni and explained to him the different types of crusts, cheeses, and toppings. She then asked him to try the peanut butter sandwich with the strawberry jam and a glass of cold milk.

They reached the DPS. Senthil told Hema that he had always experienced test anxiety and was feeling nervous. She encouraged him, telling him he would do just fine. She was right. He passed his knowledge test and eye exam without any trouble.

As he waited his turn for the road test, Hema took a small envelope, put his passport and a copy of the insurance for her car in it, and told him that he must show them to the trooper overseeing his driving test. She reminded him that he was supposed to drive on the right side of the road, unlike in India.

When his turn came, he led the trooper to Hema's car. The trooper inspected his passport and the insurance for the car and sat in the passenger seat as Senthil started the car. The trooper gave him directions as Senthil drove the car out of the DPS. He stationed his hands at the 10 o'clock and 2 o'clock position on the wheel. He used the indicator and signals correctly. He kept his eyes on the road, checked the blind spot, and then changed lanes. Everything was going according to the textbook.

On the way back to the DPS, the trooper instructed, "Please parallel park by that yellow car," pointing to a car that stood about a hundred feet away on the right.

Without taking his eyes off the road, Senthil asked, "Parallel park? Next to the yellow car?"

The trooper confirmed, "Yes."

Senthil slowed down and checked the rear-view mirror to make sure there were no cars behind him. He pulled up next to the yellow Mustang.

He asked once again, "Parallel park?"

The trooper was now getting annoyed, and in a stern voice, he replied, "That's right."

Senthil pulled the car up next to the yellow Mustang, perfectly parallel, and checking the rear-view mirror once again to make sure there was no car behind; he shifted the car to park and killed the engine.

The trooper looked at him and said, "Are you kidding? What are you doing?"

Senthil leaned over the trooper to make sure his car was parallel to the Mustang. He was happy with his parking and said, "You asked me to park parallel to the yellow car, and I did, sir."

The trooper shook his head and asked him to pull into the DPS. Once there, the trooper walked out, with Senthil following close behind. He walked to the counter and was shocked to hear that he had failed the road test. He turned towards Hema, and she was alarmed to see tears streaming down his face. He told her he had failed the road test. Hema asked him to sit down and went to talk to the trooper.

She came back smiling and said, "It's my fault. I should have encouraged you to take at least one driving lesson. The good thing is that your driving skills are just fine. It's just a misunderstanding." She explained to him what the trooper had meant when he had asked him to parallel park his car.

Still upset, Senthil said, "But Hema, isn't that serial parking?"

"Oh Senthil, you are parking parallel to the curb," she replied. She said that the trooper had asked him to come next Monday to retake the road test.

Hema wanted to take him to the grocery store to cheer him up, but Senthil was in no mood for that. He had never failed in anything before this and did not quite know how to take it. He felt bad that Hema had to pay for the driving test again. She told him it was not his fault and talked him into going to the grocery store.

Senthil was awestruck when he walked into Kroger. To begin with, this was the biggest store he had ever seen. He was surprised to see everything under one roof. He was used to separately going to the vegetable market, the meat market, and then a grocery store for rice, grains, and spices, and a department store for all the other essentials. This was a one-stop shop. He was amazed to see the size of the vegetables. The tomatoes, onions, potatoes looked huge in comparison with the ones in India. He found the chicken and the eggs to be bigger too, and he had never bought eggs by the dozen before. Hema got him some vegetables and some chicken and took him to the frozen-food section. He could not believe his eyes when he saw the variety of ice creams available. He did not know which one to try, and Hema told him he could pick whichever he wanted.

He walked along the aisle, amazed by the different names until he saw a sign that read, "Breyer's ice cream: Buy one, get one free." Never had he heard of a sales pitch like this in India. He decided to go with it, as he did not want to pass up on this extraordinary deal. He would get to have two while saving money for Hema. It was a win-win situation. He picked butter pecan and chocolate chip cookie dough. Hema told him she had a surprise for him and took him to the bakery section. She picked up a freshly baked apple pie and placed it in the cart.

Senthil came home happy as a clam. He was excited with the prospect of eating warm apple pie with butter pecan ice cream. Hema told him that she would be busy for the rest of the week and would see him again the next Monday to accompany him to his test. She asked him to call the office in case he needed anything. Senthil spent the rest of the week studying, watching TV, and cooking. Other than trips to the apartment office for borrowing free videocassettes of movies, he did not venture out much. The cold weather kept him inside. It was nothing out of the ordinary for Dallas and ranged in low 60s. However, as he was from India, it felt quite cold to him.

Every time he ate something he enjoyed, whether it was apple pie and ice cream or peanut butter and jelly sandwiches, he thought of Sumathi and his family. He wished they were with him to share his new experiences.

Hema called on Friday afternoon and told him she was coming over to pick him up so they could practice parallel parking. She took him to her office building. Walter and Margie came out of the office to greet them. Hema introduced Margie to Senthil and told him that she helped her run the office and kept track of all the paperwork.

Margie and Walter wished him good luck, and as they went back into the office, they yelled, "Senthil, please don't hit our cars! Just kidding."

Senthil laughed and said, "Thank you, I won't."

Hema showed him how to parallel park, explaining all the nuances. After a few demonstrations, she asked him to get behind the wheel.

Senthil parked the car exactly how he had observed Hema doing it. The very first time was a success. He practiced a few more times. Hema told him that he could drive the car back to the apartment and stayed seated in the passenger seat. When he got out of the car, she said, "You got this. Enjoy your weekend. I'll pick you up bright and early Monday morning at 7:00 AM."

It was the same trooper administrating the test. Instead of asking him to get out on the road, the trooper asked him to drive to the back of the DPS. Senthil obliged. The back of the DPS had the appearance of a small race track. There was a special place to test parallel parking.

The trooper smiled and said, "That was smooth."

"Thank you, sir," Senthil replied. The trooper asked him to the exit the car, and they walked into the DPS.

Hema was worried to see them back so soon. Senthil walked towards Hema as the trooper walked to the counter with his clipboard. Senthil told a worried Hema, "It went fine. I passed."

Hema exhaled a sigh of relief. He got his picture taken and was handed a temporary driver's license. The original driver's license would be mailed to him in a week.

When she dropped him back to the apartment, Hema said, "We are having a Christmas party this Friday, then going to the Christmas Eve mass at the church. You are invited."

Senthil excitedly replied, "Oh great. That sounds amazing."

Hema was glad to hear his enthusiasm and said, "Walter will come to pick you up at four."

His first party in America! Senthil did not know what to do. He decided to cook some Indian food and take it with him. He checked the refrigerator, the kitchen cabinets, and the spices in his suitcase and decided to make chicken biryani. It was 3:00 PM by the time he was done with a nice big pot of chicken biryani. Once he was satisfied with the dish, he began to get ready.

He took a shower, shaved, and wore a blue shirt, his red tie, and the grey suit his *appa* had got him.

Walter was on time. Senthil opened the door on hearing the doorbell, and Walter said, "Merry Christmas, Senthil," and then exclaimed, "You look dapper!"

Senthil looked at him in confusion and said, "Happy Christmas."

Walter added, "Oh my goodness! You must have been cooking. It smells wonderful."

Senthil replied, "Yes Walter, I made chicken biryani for the Christmas party. By the way, what did you mean by dapper?"

Walter laughed and said, "You look sharp."

Seeing the puzzled look Senthil still had, he said, "Dapper, sharp all mean that you look great in your suit."

Senthil smiled, "Thank you, Walter. You look great as well."

Walter drove to Argyle, where Hema lived. It was a nice big house, away from the hustle and bustle of the big city, and her house was in the middle of a big property with trees surrounding it. The driveway leading up to the house was quite long.

Walter parked the car and said, "Looks like we're the first ones."

Senthil walked to the door with the pot in his hand. Walter rang the doorbell, and Hema greeted them at the door with a "Merry Christmas" and welcomed them in. "What's this, Senthil?" she asked.

"Oh, nothing much, Hema. I just made some chicken biryani for the party."

Senthil attempted to remove his shoes, but Hema said, "Don't worry about it. You can leave your shoes on." And then she exclaimed, "Oh my goodness! It smells delicious and looks so good. I better keep this in the oven, so it stays warm. You know you didn't have to bring anything, right?"

Senthil said, "Yes Hema, I know I didn't have to, but I just wanted to bring something to the party. Hope that's okay."

"That's perfectly fine, Senthil. Thank you for being so thoughtful."

He followed her into the kitchen as Walter walked into the living room.

The house was vast and spacious with an open floor plan and high ceilings. There was also a fireplace in the family room. A large Christmas tree with presents all around it was placed next to it. The kitchen was huge with a built-in refrigerator, oven, and a large island in the middle. The countertops were made of granite. Senthil said, "Hema, you have a gorgeous home. It looks like it's right out of *Home Alone*."

"Thank you, Senthil," Hema smiled, and called out to her husband: "Sampath! Honey, this is Senthil. Senthil, this is my husband, Sampath."

They shook hands, and Sampath wished him a Merry Christmas, and Senthil returned the greeting.

"Honey, could you entertain Senthil and Walter while I go get dressed?" Hema asked.

"Of course, dear," he answered.

Hema ran upstairs, and Sampath escorted Senthil to the family room. "What would you guys like to drink? We have red and white wines, beers, eggnog, and sodas."

Walter said, "I'll take a glass of red wine please."

Sampath replied, "Sure, Walter. What about you, Senthil?"

"I'll take anything without alcohol in it," he replied. Sampath went to the kitchen and came back with two glasses of red wine and a glass of sparkling apple cider.

Senthil took a sip of the cider and asked, "Wow! What is this?" It was sweet, bubbly, and tangy. Sampath explained that it was made from apple juice and had no alcohol in it.

Senthil asked Sampath about his work, life in America, and what it meant to be a first-generation American of Indian descent. Sampath told him he was an electronics engineer working for Texas Instruments. His parents had come to Dallas in the 1950s. His dad had come as a physician after graduating from Madras Medical College to pursue a residency in nephrology.

His mother was a homemaker, and he was the only son. He had been brought up with the best of eastern and western cultures.

Sampath added, "Hema told me about your 911, pizza, and the road test. Not to be mean, but it's funny. I can only imagine what my parents went through when they first came here. My dad used to tell me he failed his road test because he drove on the left side of the road."

Sampath took their glasses and went to the kitchen to get a refill. Hema walked down the stairs in a black dress; a red and green scarf adorned her neck, and she had her hair up in a bun.

As she walked into the family room, Senthil said, "Hema, you look dapper."

Hema laughed and said, "Thank you, I guess."

Walter interjected and said, "It's my fault. I told him that he looked dapper when I picked him up."

As Hema explained to Senthil that dapper was reserved to describe a male, Sampath walked in with three wine glasses, a bottle of red wine, and a glass of sparkling apple cider. He looked at Hema and said, "You look lovely, dear."

Hema hugged him and said, "Thanks, honey."

She then looked at Senthil and said, "That's how you compliment a lady."

Senthil replied, "I learned a new word and had to use it in a sentence so that I would remember."

She and Walter laughed, and Sampath asked, "Did I miss something?"

Hema explained to him what had just happened. Sampath said, "Leave Senthil alone. His English is very good. He must get used to the phrases and slangs that we take for granted." He asked Senthil how they complimented people in India.

Senthil said, "For a man, we say you look smart or handsome, and for a woman, you look beautiful or gorgeous."

"Smart for good looking? Interesting. What else is different?"

Senthil said, "Well, you wouldn't wear black on festivals or happy occasions. Black is for mourning."

"I am glad I am not in India. I would be offending the Christmas spirit," jested Hema.

The doorbell rang. It was Margie and a few of the neighbors. They were all dressed in red and green and looked merry and festive. They all carried wrapped gifts in their hands. "Merry Christmas everybody," they said, and as the first order of business, they walked to the family room to place the gifts under the tree.

They talked, laughed, and sang Christmas carols. Hema had made a roast leg of lamb with lots of sides. They all held hands and stood in a circle while Hema said a prayer. After grace, they filled up their plates and settled down to eat. Everybody complimented the leg of lamb and the chicken biryani. Senthil was more interested in the sweet potato casserole, ambrosia salad, macaroni and cheese, and the variety of Christmas cookies.

Hema's guests were interested in the Christmas traditions in India. Senthil talked to them about growing up with an Anglo-Indian family in his neighborhood. His childhood friends were Mohan, Shankar, Madhu, and Rochelle.

Senthil and his siblings celebrated Christmas with Rochelle and her family, just like she and her siblings celebrated Diwali with them. There was no concept of Christmas tree or Santa Claus, but a star made up of colorful construction paper with a bulb that lit it from the inside adorned the entry door. It symbolized the Star of Bethlehem. Senthil went to the midnight mass at their local church on Christmas Eve. Every Christmas, Rochelle delivered a plate of cakes and biscuits each to her friends' house.

Similarly, for all the Hindu festivals, she received a plate of food from Senthil, Mohan, Shankar, and Madhu's house. So, growing up, religious festivals had involved new clothes, family, friends, good food, fellowship, and well wishes. They focused on God and people rather than on gifts or presents.

Hema's friends said that they liked the tradition of family, friends, and fellowship and the lack of commercialism associated with Christmas. Senthil went with them to attend the midnight mass at Saint Mark Catholic Church in Denton, Texas, which was a short drive from Hema's house. Having seen churches in Madras, Senthil was expecting a huge church with a bellowing cathedral. To his disappointment, the exterior of the church was more like a big house. However, the interior, the festive mood, and people inside made up for the lack of edifice. After listening to an inspirational sermon and bearing witness to God's word, Walter and Senthil went back to Hema's house while the others returned to their homes.

Senthil and Walter spent the night at Hema's. When they woke up early the next morning, Sampath was in the kitchen making coffee and eggs for breakfast. They added the leftovers from the previous night's dinner to the breakfast spread. After breakfast, Walter dropped Senthil at the apartment on his way home.

Senthil spent the next week studying for his tests and writing letters to his family and Sumathi about the Christmas party, the new foods he had tasted, and life in America in general. Hema and Sampath left to spend the rest of the holiday season in Hawaii and had plans of ringing in the New Year there. The office was closed, as Walter and Margie were out of town, too. They made sure that Senthil had enough groceries and that the refrigerator was stalked before they all left town.

On New Year's Eve, as usual, Senthil walked to the apartment complex office to check his mailbox in the evening. He was elated to find a card with Sumathi's handwriting on the envelope. He hurried back to the apartment, and as he eagerly turned the envelope to open it, he noticed a note on the flap of the envelope: "Please do not open until midnight." He could not be mad because he had sent her a letter with a similar note on the envelope.

Shiva called late in the evening. He shared his experience of working in a skilled nursing facility and asked Senthil about his preparation for the board exam. "Did you get the study guide from Hema?"

Senthil replied that he had not, and he was studying from the books he had gotten from India.

"You are in for a surprise when you get it."

"Really? What is it?" asked Senthil.

"Oh, you'll find out soon," Shiva replied.

After Shiva hung up, Senthil had dinner and sat down in front of the TV with Sumathi's card in his hand. He spent more time looking at the clock than the TV. Even though continents separated them, she wanted to be the first one to wish him a happy new year, as did he.

Dick Clark was counting down the crystal ball drop in New York Times Square amidst an avalanche of confetti. Just as he counted down "5, 4, 3, 2, 1 and Happy New Year!" Senthil opened the envelope to read Sumathi's card.

Chapter 11 — Dire in Detroit

ON RETURNING FROM VACATION, THE FIRST ORDER OF business for Hema was to secure a contract for Senthil. On Thursday, January 6, Senthil heard a knock on the door. It was Hema.

She walked in and said, "Well Senthil, I have some good news and some bad news."

"Let's hear the good news first," he said.

"The good news is I have a contract for you at a major hospital, and you start Monday, January 10."

"Really? That's awesome. Thank you so much. This is great. I was beginning to get bored in the apartment." Senthil kept talking and forgot all about the bad news.

Hema had to interrupt: "I am glad you are excited, but here is the bad news. The assignment is at Detroit Receiving Hospital in Michigan, not Missouri."

"How far is it from Shiva?" asked Senthil.

"Six hundred fifty miles away, I am afraid," she said. Senthil looked at her confused. She said, "That's around 1000 km or about a ten-hour drive."

"Oh," Senthil said. It was, indeed, bad news.

Hema reassured him that she would work hard to get them closer for the next assignment. Senthil had the next two days to get ready. He was set to leave on Sunday. Hema booked him a flight to Detroit, arranged a rental car from the airport, booked him a hotel for Sunday night, and got him TripTiks for directions from Detroit airport to a hotel in Dearborn and the hospital from there. She had arranged an apartment for him, but the apartment office would not be open until Monday and so he would have to spend the Sunday night at a hotel.

She dropped by the apartment on Saturday to give him the flight ticket, the TripTiks, and the contract papers. She also handed him a packet with a study guide to help him prepare for the national board exam for the permanent physical therapy license and study material for the Michigan jurisprudence exam. The temporary physical therapy license for Michigan and Missouri would be valid for one year. The goal was to work for at least six months and get to know the Medicare and Medicaid and insurance rules and regulations and patient population, which would help with both the physical therapy licensure exam and the jurisprudence exam.

He was excited, anxious, and nervous all at the same time. Shiva had been working there for the past four months, but it was a skilled nursing home in a small city. Everything was of a much smaller scale and ran at a slower pace. He talked to Shiva on Saturday, and his friend reassured him that the experience in Apollo Hospital with the state-of-the-art equipment would come handy while working in an American hospital.

Sunday came, and Walter took Senthil to the airport. He told him that he was in for a big shock with the change in weather—it was snowing in Michigan. He told him that the secret to driving in snow was to drive slowly, pump the brakes, and watch out for the crazy drivers. He showed him how to read and navigate with AAA's TripTiks.

It was 5:28 PM on Sunday when Senthil landed in Detroit. He picked up his suitcases at Baggage Claim and checked in at the rental car counter. He was given the rental agreement and pointed to the way to the shuttle.

He was surprised at the stark difference in weather that morning in Texas and Michigan the evening of the same day. He was thankful that Walter had given him a heads-up, and he had dressed in layers accordingly. The sides of the roads and parked cars bore marks of recent snowfall. It was only 6:15 PM, and he was surprised that it was already dark. Michigan air smelled different too. People talked differently and dressed differently. As the shuttle bus carried him away, the only thing he noticed that was common was the chain of fast food centers that it passed by.

Senthil, though a novice, felt like a seasoned traveler. He was amazed by the organization and intuitiveness involved from the time he got out of the plane to the time he got into the white Toyota Camry. He put one of the big suitcases in the trunk, the other on the back seat, and the carry-on suitcase on the passenger seat. He picked out the AAA TripTiks marked "To the hotel"; he was to take I-94 East.

As he exited the parking lot, he asked the attendant at the gate how to get to I-94 East. With the instructions, he pulled out of the parking lot. His heart was racing, and his palms were sweaty. He wished the seats were a little higher so he could see past the hood. He saw the exit for I-94 East, took the ramp, and joined the traffic. This was his first time driving on the interstate highway, and he felt intimidated by the speed of the cars and the trucks that zipped by.

As he entered the highway, it started to snow. Senthil turned on the windshield wipers. Visibility dropped, and he slowed down, only to be honked at by a truck behind, which startled him. He turned on his blinkers to move to the rightmost lane. He flipped the TripTik booklet and was looking for the exit for John C. Lodge Freeway going north.

As he stayed on the right lane, he noticed the sign above the right lane read, "South, Exit only." He needed to take the one going north. He turned on his left blinker to move over one lane but did not think he had enough room to move over, as the vehicles on the left lane kept coming. He was getting nervous as the right lane was coming to an end at the exit. He was eager to move over to the left lane. He had only a few yards left, and there was a semi-truck on the left. He slowed down significantly to let the truck pass so he could move over before he had to take the wrong exit. But the car behind him almost rear-ended him and honked.

He had no choice but to take the wrong exit. Intuitively, he thought that all he would need to do once he was on the M-10 road heading south was to turn around and go the other way. M-10 road had a median in the middle. He had to make a U-turn or turn left on to one of the streets, and then turn around and turn right on M-10. Unfortunately, each time the median ended, there was a sign that read "No U-turn" or "No left turn." He had to drive further until a point the median gave room for a left turn. As he drove further, he saw a sign that read "Detour." The road ahead was closed, and he had to turn right.

He told himself that he just needed to follow the signs to get back on the M-10 road, head north, and go past the I-94 exit, and the TripTik would take it from there. The snow was coming down harder and harder. There was no place to stop to ask for directions. Turn after another, due to the snow and low visibility, he could not even make out the names of the streets. He was lost. He made another turn and ended up on a small street. There were cars parked on both sides of the street, making the street narrower than it already was. The houses seemed run-down. He was astonished that a neighborhood like this existed in America.

On the right side of the road, he saw a car with the hood popped open. As he reached closer, he saw a pregnant woman standing in the snow. He stopped the car, ran out to her, and asked,

"Ma'am, are you okay?"

"Thank you for stopping. My stupid car died on me, and I need to get to the hospital."

"I am new to the country ma'am and I don't know where the hospital is, and I am lost."

"Where do you have to go?"

"To a hotel on M-10 road tonight and Detroit Receiving Hospital tomorrow. I am going to work as a physical therapist."

"I need to go to the hospital now. I think my water broke."

"Ma'am, if you can tell me how to get to the hospital, I'll drive you there."

He threw his carry-on suitcase on the back seat and helped her get into the car. He shut the hood of her car and hurriedly got into his car.

"What's going to happen to your car?" he asked.

"My husband will get it towed to the mechanic."

Taking the wheel, he looked at her. "Go straight and take the first left," she said.

He drove, and as he took the first left, he saw a sign that read, "Dead end, No outlet."

He turned to her and asked, "Are you sure about this turn ma'am?"

At that instant, she pulled out a pillow from underneath her shirt and said, "Stop the car. Give me all the money you got, or else I am going to scream that you are going to rape me."

He could not believe his ears. His voice trembled as he spoke. "Wait! What?"

"You heard me. Get your wallet out," she screamed.

"Please ma'am. I come from a respectable family. I will get deported; my family will die . . ."

She cut him off saying, "Stop blabbering and get your wallet out."

Senthil took his wallet out of his back pocket. She grabbed it from his hand, as he said, "Ma'am please, I have my driver's license and social security card in there." He started crying. She asked him to shut up and looked in the wallet. There was $250 in the wallet, which she shoved inside her bra and threw the wallet in the back seat. "Is this your car?" she asked as she opened the glove compartment. "No ma'am, it's a rental car," he said, sobbing.

She got out of the car and warned him to stay quiet and drive away quietly, or she would scream that he was going to rape her. Senthil just nodded and sat there shivering while she got out of the car, slammed the door, and walked back to her car and drove away.

Senthil sat there in shock. A few minutes later, he gathered himself and reversed his car out of that street. He just started driving and eventually came across a gas station. There was a pay phone outside. He grabbed his wallet from the back seat and ran to the phone. He looked in the wallet, but there was no money. Luckily, he remembered the 1-800 number for the company. He prayed that someone was still there and dialed the number.

As soon as he heard "Hello" from the other end, he started sobbing. All he managed to say was, "I just want to go home." He kept repeating it over and over again. It was Hema on the other end.

Luckily for him, Texas was an hour behind, and Hema was staying late to catch up with some work after her vacation. She could not understand anything he was saying.

"Senthil, is that you? Are you okay? Take a deep breath, calm down, and tell me what's going on."

He finally calmed down, and with his voice trembling, he said, "Hema, I just want to go home."

"Home? What do you mean? What happened?"

"I don't want to work here. I just want to go home."

"Home? You mean come back to Texas?"

"No, home to India. I can't work here."

Hema eventually calmed him down enough to make him tell her what happened. She said that she was sorry and asked him to go into the gas station and ask for directions to get to the hotel. She asked him not to make any rash decisions, and they could talk about it. She promised to call him at the hotel.

Senthil agreed. He walked into the gas station and got the directions to get to M-10 and the hotel. He managed to find his way to the hotel and checked in. He felt emotionally drained. He was hungry but in no mood to eat. Besides, he did not have any money. He just lay on the bed, staring at the ceiling.

A loud knock on the door startled him. He jumped out of bed but did not know what to do. He stood against the wall, not taking his eyes off the door. First, he thought he had imagined the knock and no one was at the door, but just as he was convinced of that, there was another series of knocks.

"Who's there?"

"It's the pizza guy. I have your delivery" came the response.

Senthil was puzzled, almost to the point of being scared. "It must be a mistake. I didn't order any," he said, standing by the door.

"It was ordered to this room by someone by the name Hema," the voice responded.

Senthil was reassured by that name, even though the pizza guy pronounced the name wrong: "he-ma" instead of "hey-ma." He opened the door and received the box of pizza. He said, "I am sorry I don't have any change." The guy said that everything including his tip had already been taken care of and left.

Senthil locked the door behind him and sat at the table by the bed. He turned on the TV, and the local news came on. It talked about drive-by shootings, gang-related violence, and the weather. He heard nothing that could change his mind about Detroit. When the phone rang, he was not startled; he knew it was Hema. He thanked her for the pizza and gave her a detailed account of what had happened. This time, he did not cry but told her the events matter-of-factly. She listened patiently and told him she would book him a ticket to fly him back to Texas. But he also had the option to work at Detroit Receiving Hospital as scheduled if he chose to. She asked him to sleep on it and reassured him that his experience was very rare and not the norm.

He went to bed but could not sleep. He tossed and turned, thinking of Sumathi. He thought about his family and his siblings. He thought about his reason for coming to America. He knew what he had to do, and a sense of calm took over him.

He woke up early in the morning with the alarm he had set for 5:30 AM. It was 6:30 AM when Hema called. She must have woken up early too, as she was an hour behind.

She asked him what he had decided. Senthil said that he wanted to stay in America and work but not in Detroit. He asked Hema if it would be possible for her to get him a contract in a smaller city. Albeit disappointed that she had lost the contract with Detroit Receiving Hospital, Hema was glad to hear that he had decided to stay in America and not leave the country. She asked him if he would consider working in Detroit Receiving Hospital and live in one of the suburbs of Detroit instead of living in Detroit and commute about thirty to forty-five minutes to work every day. Senthil said that he would get an ulcer just driving back and forth to work.

Hema agreed. He was sorry that Hema was losing a contract, but she asked him not to worry and told him that she could explain it to the hospital and send a replacement in a couple of days.

Margie was waiting for him at Dallas airport. As soon as she saw him, she threw her arms around him and said, "I am glad you are okay."

"Me too. It was a nightmare, but I am glad it's over."

"I can't even imagine what must have been going through your head at that time."

"Mostly, me getting deported and unable to face my family or Sumathi."

"Oh, you poor thing. Well, let's go to the office first before I drop you off to the apartment."

Hema and Walter were on the phone when Senthil and Margie walked in. Hema motioned for them to take it to the adjacent room. She hung up the phone as soon as she could and hurried towards Senthil.

"Are you okay?" she asked as she hugged him.

"I am fine now, Hema."

Walter came in and joined in the conversation. Senthil explained his experience to them. He realized that the more he relived the moments, the less traumatic it became. In fact, by the time he finished, he was laughing out loud. Hema, Walter, and Margie were relieved that Senthil was feeling better. He stayed in the office and helped around while he waited for a ride to the apartment.

They took him out to eat, and then Hema dropped him back to the apartment on her way home.

"I am sorry you lost a contract, Hema."

"Don't be silly. It's not your fault. I am just glad you are okay."

"When do you think I'll be able to get another assignment?"

"Don't worry. By next Monday, you'll be in your new job." Her confidence reassured Senthil. "Just make sure you don't pick up a pregnant woman on your way," Hema joked.

On Wednesday evening, Hema came to the apartment. As she entered, she said, "I have some good news for you."

"Really? That's great. Let me hear it please."

"I have two job offers for you to choose from. One is in an acute rehab facility in Indianapolis, Indiana, and the other is in a skilled nursing facility in Glasgow, Missouri."

"That's great, but I'll go wherever you recommend, Hema. I don't know any difference."

Hema told him that an acute rehab facility was a place where patients, both young and old, usually came from a hospital with good rehab potential for a few weeks before they went home. A skilled nursing facility, also known as a nursing home, was a place for elderly patients who were ready to be discharged from the hospital setting but unable to care for themselves or lack the social support to return home with assistance. They would either be unable to participate in intense therapy provided in acute rehab or lack the rehab potential. She said that acute rehab was fast paced and had a more diverse patient population.

Senthil said, "Looks like they are completely different from each other. Before I go back to India, I would like to gain experiences in all therapy settings. It doesn't matter in which order. So, please Hema, you choose for me."

"Well Senthil, you are eventually going to be working in all different therapy settings. So, for now, you can decide based on the location."

"Hema, I am not good with American geography. I have no idea where these places are. So, you choose whichever option you think is the best for me."

"Okay Senthil, I'll tell you about these places, but you have to decide."

She told him Indianapolis was a big city with a lot of activities for young people. It was a diverse place, with a sizable Indian population. Glasgow, on the other hand, was a much smaller town with a population of only about 1100. It had nothing much to offer in terms of social life. She told him Glasgow was such a small place that no contract therapist wanted to go there, and many contract companies found it difficult to staff the nursing home.

"I'll go to Glasgow. I want to make sure you secure a new contract," said Senthil.

"C'mon now, Senthil. What happened in Detroit is not your fault. You don't have to do this."

"No Hema, it's not just for that. I don't think I feel safe in a big city. I prefer a smaller place. Besides, my social life is in India. I should be studying for my board exam and don't want any distraction. Also, I'll be in the same state Shiva is in. It's a win-win choice, Hema. Please send me to Glasgow."

Chapter 12 — Merry in Missouri

THERE WAS NO DIRECT FLIGHT TO GLASGOW. THE CLOSEST airport was fifty-six miles away in Columbia, Missouri. As the owner of a contract company, Hema had two options for her contract therapists. One, she would find them a furnished one-bedroom apartment, pay for it for the entire duration of the assignment, and provide them with $360 as food allowance. Otherwise, she would give them a $1,000 tax-free allowance each month. Senthil opted for the $1,000 tax-free allowance, thinking he could save money by being frugal and living in a non-furnished apartment.

The itinerary was all laid out. Senthil would fly out to Columbia on Sunday, January 16. He would pick up the rental car from the airport, stay in a motel, and drive down to Glasgow Monday morning to report to work. Hema would pay for the two nights in the motel and the two days of rental car service. After that, Senthil would be on his own.

Columbia Regional Airport was much smaller than the airports in Dallas or Detroit. The TripTik with directions to the motel was only three pages long. By evening, Senthil was on his bed in the motel room, too anxious to eat or sleep. He just wanted to get to work. He hoped his luck from Detroit had not followed him. The night seemed to last forever.

Hema had given him an MCI calling card. The moment the clock struck nine, he called Hema to let her know he was fine. He then called Shiva and told him that he had taken the $1000 allowance option. Shiva told him he had done that after the first month when he got to know the place better. He told him about free apartment guides that were available in front of grocery stores and gas stations and the listings in the yellow pages in the telephone directory.

After he hung up, Senthil recalled he had passed a gas station at the corner of the street where his motel was. He drove to the gas station and got the free apartment guide. Lying on the bed, he browsed through the guide. He had no idea what he was doing, but the amenities provided by some of the apartment complexes amazed him. From the address, he could not tell how far these apartments were from the nursing home. He did not see any listing for Glasgow.

He checked the TripTik Hema had given him for directions from the motel to the nursing home. It was forty-four miles, and it would take him fifty-three minutes to get there. He was to report to the administrator of the Haven on the Hill Nursing Home at 8:00 AM. He set the alarm for 5:00 AM. He also called the motel's front desk and requested a wake-up call for 5:00 AM. He did not want to take any chances.

Sumathi had recommended that he wear the black pants, the light blue shirt, and the red and blue tie she had picked. He took them out of the suitcase. Even though the clothes had been pressed before he had packed in India, being in the suitcase the entire time meant they needed ironing again. The motel had the facility, and Senthil pressed his clothes and his white lab coat again and hung them on the hotel hangers.

He planned to leave the motel at 6:15 AM and hoped to reach the nursing home well in time. He did not want to risk being late. He was an exception to the *Indian Standard Time*, the stereotype that Indians were never punctual.

The motel had a free breakfast bar, but it would only open at 6:00AM. He woke up at 5:00 AM, showered, and got dressed. He walked down to the lobby at 6:00 and headed to the breakfast bar. Grabbing a couple of donuts, a banana and an apple, and a small orange juice bottle, he headed back to his room.

He packed the donuts in one plastic bag and the apple, banana, and the orange juice in another. Then, he grabbed his folder with his certificates and his passport and walked out. He did not want to leave them in the motel. He flipped through the TripTik booklet. He was to take the Providence Road to I-70W/US-40W and then to MO-240W into Glasgow. He placed the TripTik on his lap, fastened his seat belt, and with butterflies in his stomach, pulled out of the motel's parking lot.

Unlike Dallas and Detroit, there were no huge buildings here. Columbia was a university town. It looked simple and unpretentious. Unremarkable buildings lined the street he was driving through. MO-240W reminded him of his grandparents' village. It had farmlands with large bales of hay scattered across the land. It must have been a hilly terrain because the road went up and down. He felt nauseated as if he were riding on waves.

He was relieved to see the sign on the road: "Welcome to the Historic City of Glasgow, MO." He picked up the TripTik for further instructions. The nursing home, aptly named Haven on the Hill, was on a hilltop. It was a curvy uphill road, but not too steep. He thought this place would literally be a haven on the hill in spring, summer, and fall. Winters did not do justice to the place. Abundant trees and shrubbery lined the road, but they were all barren. He pulled into the quiet parking lot at 7:20 AM.

The nursing home was sprawled out on a single floor. He walked to the entrance and pulled open the large glass door. Another set of glass door to the foyer greeted him. The foyer was full of life. It smelled pleasant with potpourri and big vases filled with large arrangements of freshly cut flowers. A big aquarium with exotic fish decorated the place. In one corner, there was a large bird cage with colorful little birds perched on little swings and branches. Four elaborate antique chairs faced the aquarium and the birdcage.

As soon as he opened the door, the birds came alive. They flew around the cage, startling Senthil who paused for a minute and stood there until they calmed down. He walked past the foyer that led to a hallway with large paintings on the walls. The hallway opened to a nurses' station. Three hallways were leading up to the nursing station—from the left, the right, and the front. From the middle of the nurses' station, one could see down all three hallways.

Penny spotted him first. "Hello there. Can I help you?" she smiled. Penny was dressed in a white shirt and white pants, with a cloth belt around her waist. She had a nurse's cap over her thick, wavy blonde hair. Short bangs fell across her forehead to meet the rim of her large tortoiseshell glasses. Tiny freckles spread on her nose and across her cheeks, giving them the appearance of a butterfly. A big smile lit up her face, and her green eyes shone mischievously.

"My name is Senthil," he replied. I am the new physical therapist assigned to this facility. I am supposed to meet Ms. Kathleen Richardson, the administrator."

"Really? Are you our new physical therapist? So glad to meet you. Our residents have not had physical therapy for the last two weeks." She shook his hand.

"Kathy should be here any minute. I am Penny, the charge nurse here. I must relieve the night crew, but I'll take you to her office, where you can wait. Could I get you some coffee?"

"No, but thank you. It's nice to meet you. I am looking forward to working with you."

"What's your name again?"

"Senthil. It rhymes with lentil."

She laughed. "Senthil like lentil. This is going to be fun," she said walking down the hall. Senthil followed her. He had a gut feeling that Penny would be a troublemaker but in a good way. She opened a door and said, "You can wait here for Kathy."

"Thank you," he replied.

A few minutes later, Kathy walked in. She was slender, tall, and elegantly dressed, with shoulder-length curly blonde hair. She had her hands full with her handbag, folders, two bags, and her coffee mug. Senthil got up to greet her. She dumped the stuff she was carrying on her table and turned to give Senthil a handshake. "It's a pleasure to meet you, Mr. Bean."

He shook her hand and said, "Nice to meet you too, Ms. Richardson."

"Please call me Kathy. So, you'd like to be called Mr. Bean?"

"Excuse me? My name is Senthil Rajashekaran. People call me Senthil. I am not sure who Mr. Bean is."

Kathy shook her head and said, "I am so sorry." She muttered, "Damn you, Penny."

They both heard Penny laugh. She was standing by the door. Kathy rolled her eyes and said, "Get in here now."

"I am sorry; I couldn't help it. He said his name is Senthil, like lentil, and I thought Mr. Bean would be funny as a name."

"Oh, I get it. That is funny," Senthil smiled.

"See, Kathy, he thinks it's funny too. No harm done." Penny grinned.

"Shame on you Penny for teasing the physical therapist who has come to help us."

"Please don't worry about it, Ms. Richardson. It's just a practical joke. One of these days, I'll get back at her with a practical joke of my own," Senthil said.

"I am glad you have a good sense of humor. Please call me Kathy," she said.

"I am scared now," said Penny.

Kathy escorted Senthil and gave him a tour of "The Haven," showing him the common areas such as the Therapy Department, the activity room, the dining hall, and the courtyard. She introduced him to Linda Campbell, the social worker; Patricia Turner, the activities director; Darlene Gibson, the secretary; Larry Smith, the maintenance supervisor; Phyllis Anderson, the dietician; and Loretta Clark, the head cook. Everyone was very cordial.

They came back to the Therapy Department which, he learned, was shared by the physical therapist (PT), the occupational therapist (OT), and the speech-language pathologist (SLP). Since they did not have a full-time

PT, the OT and the SLP visited only three days a week. Now that Senthil was starting full-time, the OT and the SLP would also be there five days a week. She told him to look at the patient folders on the table that were marked "PT Eval pending" and "Pending PT screening." She also assured him that when the OT and the SLP came in, they would help him with seeing the patients.

"Before I leave you here with the folders, do you have any questions?" asked Kathy.

"No, ma'am. Thank you for the tour. Well, actually, I do have a question if you don't mind me asking."

"Sure Senthil, and please call me Kathy. I am not old enough for you to address me as ma'am."

He felt strange calling his boss, the administrator, by her first name. He came from a culture where elders and people in authority, even if they were younger, would be addressed as sir or madam. Even in a social setting, children addressed perfect strangers as *athai*[41] *and mama.*[42]

"Oh, I am sorry Kathy. Why is it hard for a beautiful place like this with all these wonderful people to find and keep a physical therapist?"

"Well Senthil, we are in the middle of nowhere. Glasgow has nothing to offer in the form of social life. Almost all the contract therapists are young, like you, and do not find Glasgow appealing. We don't have any schools for married folks with young children to settle down. All of us working here in Haven commute at least an hour from the places we live. We solely depend on contract companies who provide us with a therapist on a three-month contract basis. A therapist wants their contract extended here very rarely."

"I see. I hope I can find an apartment here in Glasgow. I don't need a big social life. The days off work, I study for my board exam so I can get my permanent license."

"I am afraid Glasgow does not have any apartments. This is a farm town, you see. But I know a friend who wants to rent the upstairs of his house. It

41 Aunty

42 Uncle

is vacant since his son and daughter-in-law moved to Springfield. It's on 1st Street, and it's only a mile and a half from Haven."

"That sounds great," he said.

She left, and Senthil stood in the middle of the room, looking around. The room looked like it had not been used in a while. He took a towel and dusted the therapy bed, the sandbags, the ankle weights, the walkers, and the canes. He turned on the wax therapy unit, put on new pillowcases, and as he was fluffing up the pillows to lay them on the therapy bed, he heard a knock on the door.

"Hi, I am Amanda, the OT. You must be the new PT."

Senthil put the pillow down and reached out to shake her hand. "Yes, I am Senthil, the new PT. Nice to meet you. I look forward to working with you."

"Likewise. I am sorry, your name again?"

"Senthil, rhymes with lentil."

"Senthil! Got it," she nodded.

Amanda made Senthil's brown complexion look fairer. Her pearly whites were a stark contrast to the complexion of her beautiful face. Her natural soft tiny curls looked like a hat made of black cotton candy. She was very energetic and could never sit still.

Amanda showed him the list of patients who needed a PT evaluation and treatment. As they perused the folders, prioritizing them in order, Rachel, the SLP walked in. Amanda did the introductions. The difference between Amanda and Rachel was like night and day. Rachel was petite with light brown hair and hazel eyes and was very soft-spoken. Both then introduced him to the paperwork, including evaluation and progress notes.

Rachel went to the dining room to work on her patients who were on a modified diet. Her goal was to upgrade their diet gradually from pureed through different textures to a regular diet. When she worked with them to improve their cognition, memory, or language function, she sometimes worked with Patricia in the activity room while they had Bingo or other games. Occasionally, they brought the patients to the therapy room to work one on one with them, without any distractions.

Since it was breakfast time, most of the nursing home residents were in the dining hall. Amanda decided to go see her patients there and help them with breakfast. She worked on activities of daily living and taught the patients to use adaptive equipment to feed themselves. Senthil thought that it would be wise to start with patients who had a peg tube and were on tube feeds and hence did not join the others in the dining room. He put on his white coat and walked out to find Ms. Marjorie Jones in Room 48. He followed the signs in the hallways and walked past the nurses' station.

"Who are you looking for, Mr. Bean?" Penny asked, walking out of the med room with the med cart.

"I am going to get Ms. Jones from Room 48 for her therapy, Ms. Moneypenny," replied Senthil.

"My, oh my! Somebody didn't waste any time coming up with a nickname for me!" she laughed. "Follow me, Mr. Bean, or should I say, Mr. Bond?"

He followed her as she walked down the hall with the med cart. She introduced him to Ms. Jones, a sixty-six-year-old lady who had suffered a hemorrhagic stroke that left the left side of her body paralyzed. She needed a PEG tube in her stomach for nutrition. Once stable, she had been transferred to the Haven a week ago. The nurses performed passive range-of-motion exercises and got her up in a chair twice a day. That was the most they could do. Penny was glad that Ms. Jones was finally getting the therapy she needed.

You could tell by looking at Ms. Jones that she was a special and well-cared-for lady. Even now, her hair was colored blonde and done in perms. Her fingernails were painted. Her room was decorated with pictures of her children and grandchildren. There were fresh flowers and hand-made get-well-soon cards. Senthil helped her shift from the bed to the wheelchair.

"Are you ready for a workout, Ms. Jones?" Senthil asked.

"Where are you taking me, young man?" she said in a perplexed, feeble voice.

"To the therapy room, Ms. Jones."

"I can't go out like this. I have no makeup on." She might have been weak, but she was stern.

"Really, Ms. Jones? You look so beautiful, I thought you had skipped breakfast to get ready for your therapy. We need to get you stronger and walk these halls again."

She blushed, impressed by his optimism. Giving up the attempt to hide her smile, she pointed to the table by her bed and said, "Get me my bag." Senthil brought her the bag, which she put on her lap, and took out a small mirror and her lipstick. She gave the mirror to him and gestured him to open it. He waved his hand in dismissal, and to her astonishment, he picked up the large mirror off the wall and held it in front of her.

This time she could not control herself from laughing. She could not see Senthil's face as it was hidden behind the large mirror. She applied her lipstick, paused, and then leaned to the side to ascertain if he was looking. Once she was satisfied that he was not, she hurriedly powdered her face, applied some mascara, shoved everything in her bag, and closed it shut.

"Are you just going to stand there?" she asked, feigning anger.

"Oh, I didn't realize you were done." He turned around and hung the mirror back on the wall.

"Marilyn Monroe! Where is Ms. Jones? She was here just a few minutes ago!"

"I am Ms. Jones!" She tried to look mad but could not keep a straight face.

"Ms. Jones, you look amazing!"

He got behind her wheelchair and pushed it into the hallway and towards the therapy room.

Penny was impressed to see him bring Ms. Jones out of her room. She winked and flashed him a thumbs-up. Penny followed them to the therapy room and pushed Ms. Dorothy Hillman's wheelchair to the dining room.

Ms. Hillman was seventy-four years old and had come to the Haven nine years ago. She was the first resident who came to live in Haven after her husband passed away. Ms. Hillman had sustained a fall, and her osteoporotic right hip snapped at the neck of the femur, requiring a total hip arthroplasty. She too needed physical therapy. As they passed him, Ms. Hillman touched his arm and said, "Hi, young man! You must be new here!"

"Keep your hands to yourself, Dora; he's mine," snapped Ms. Jones.

"C'mon now, Ms. Jones, play nice," Penny interrupted. Penny introduced Ms. Hillman to him and said, "Senthil is our new physical therapist. He'll be working with you too."

"Nice to meet you, Ms. Hillman," he smiled. "Enjoy your breakfast. I'll see you later."

As they entered the therapy room, Ms. Jones mumbled, "Be careful with Dora. Don't be fooled. Just because she has lived here the longest, she thinks she is entitled to everything."

Senthil replied, "Ms. Jones, I must take care of all the patients in Haven who need me, but I'll make a deal with you. I'll take care of you first every day." Ms. Jones smiled.

He helped her shift from the wheelchair to the exercise mat. The left side of her body was significantly weak. It was a little rough, as the exercise mat was lower than the beds in the room. Ms. Jones sighed heavily and looked disheartened.

"C'mon now, Ms. Jones. You just try hard and work with me, and I'll get you walking again." His optimism was refreshing.

He started treating her with motor relearning program (MRP), an Australian technique used to treat stroke. He and Sumathi learned this technique from a book he had borrowed from the British Council library. They were impressed by the principles of MRP as it emphasized active movements rather than passive range-of-motion exercises. Even with flaccid paralysis, the goal was to focus on recruiting as many muscle fibers as possible during the eccentric phase or lengthening of the muscle. He explained to her that unlike the range-of-motion exercises that the nurses did for her, with him, she needed to focus, and participate.

He narrowed in on her shoulder and worked on trying to establish proximal control by focusing on shoulder protraction and flexion. Then, he worked on her triceps to help her gain some elbow control. He encouraged her loudly as she tried to control her nearly flaccid arm.

He could see her getting discouraged, and he did not want to push her too much on the first day. He helped her sit up by the edge of the exercise mat with her feet on the ground. He stretched her left arm and placed it on the exercise mat. He then asked her to lean on it and bear weight.

"You are doing very well, Ms. Jones. Let's work those legs now. Time to stand!"

He transferred her to the wheelchair and took her to the parallel bars. He unveiled the large postural mirror at the other end of the bars. He then wheeled Ms. Jones into the parallel bars from the other end. He asked her to push on the armrest of the wheelchair with her right hand and helped her to stand up with a gait belt around her waist. She was not able to bear any weight with her left leg. He stabilized her knee from the front with his knee and asked her to lean slightly and shift her weight on her left leg. Once she had mastered that, he moved on to the outside of the parallel bar so that she could see herself in the mirror for visual feedback.

He asked her to focus on symmetry and posture and asked her to adjust while he supported her knee. Again, he stopped before she got frustrated. He lowered her to the wheelchair, asking her to reach for the armrest and control herself from plopping down.

"You did great, Ms. Jones. You are going to be my model patient. I can tell."

She shook her head and asked, "Is this going to be a waste of time? Am I going to be like this for the rest of my life?" She did not intend to appear vulnerable to him, but her voice trembled, and tears welled up in her eyes.

Putting his hands on the armrests of her wheelchair, Senthil bent forward, looked straight into her eyes, and said, "Ms. Jones, this is not going to be easy, and you may not become normal, but I am confident that I can get you functional, independent, and walking again. We are partners in this. I am going to give you all I have, and you do the same, and we'll have fun doing it. Deal?" He reached out his hand.

Shaking his hand, she said, "Deal."

He wiped her tears and said, "Now, if you mess up that makeup, you are on your own. I have no idea what to do."

She smiled as he wheeled her back to her room. "Have a nice day Ms. Jones. I'll see you bright and early tomorrow."

As he turned to walk away, she grabbed his hand and, in a voice trembling with sincerity, said, "Thank you!"

"You are most welcome, Ms. Jones," he replied with equal sincerity.

Senthil walked back to the therapy room, and as he was cleaning the exercise mat and changing the pillowcase, Amanda came in wheeling Ms. Hillman.

"Look who I have for you."

"Hi there again Ms. Hillman! Hope you had a good breakfast," said Senthil.

"Yes, I did, young man."

"Where's Ms. Jones?" asked Amanda.

"She is back in her room. I can go get her for you," Senthil said.

"No thank you. I am going to work on dressing and grooming, and Ms. Jones would rather do it in her room anyway," Amanda said and left the therapy room.

"Ms. Hillman are you ready to get working?" he asked.

"You betcha! I can't wait to walk again. I have to go to my granddaughter's high school graduation this summer and don't want to go in this damn wheelchair."

"That's a great attitude. You are not only going to walk to your granddaughter's graduation but also dance at her wedding whenever she gets married," Senthil replied encouragingly.

"You think so? If I live long enough, you can escort me to the wedding."

"You got yourself a date, Ms. Hillman. Now, let's get to work."

Senthil assisted her transfer to the exercise mat. He taught her hip precautions and worked on a range of motion and strengthening exercises. Ms. Hillman had some weakness in her right leg, and weight-bearing caused her some pain. Senthil picked up a walker for Ms. Hillman and adjusted it for her height. He secured a gait belt around her waist and instructed her to place her body weight on to the walker during the stance phase of the right leg while she swung her left leg forward.

They came to the door, and he asked her if she wanted to turn around. Ms. Hillman said, "I am not tired. Are you?"

"No, ma'am."

"Let's keep moving. I want to go show off to Margie."

"Now, Ms. Hillman, I don't think that would be very nice."

"I am only trying to motivate that old woman. She's only going to get more determined when she sees me sashay down the hallways."

She had a point, Senthil thought. This could be a healthy rivalry that could serve as motivation. There was more to Ms. Jones and Ms. Hillman than what met the eye. Even though they bickered a lot, both cared about the other's well-being. As they crossed Ms. Jones' room, Ms. Hillman stopped to peer inside and yelled, "Hey grandma! I am taking a stroll with your man."

Ms. Jones was working with Amanda and yelled back, "I had him first. You always go for sloppy seconds."

Senthil kept quiet; he wanted to stay out of this feud.

When he returned to the therapy room, Amanda was sitting in front of a few charts. She told him she could spare a few minutes to show him the documentation and how to write a progress note. Senthil appreciated the gesture and sat down. As per her instructions, he documented the therapy session on Ms. Jones and Ms. Hillman's charts. As he was finishing up, Kathleen walked in.

"It's music and activity time with Darlene, and we encourage all our residents to attend. This would be a good time to take a drive down to have a look at that house if you are interested. I am going to the post office down the street from the house. You can ride with me."

"Thank you so much. That sounds splendid."

Kathy had called the homeowner and talked to him about Senthil. When they arrived at the house on 1st Street, they found Mr. Spencer waiting for them outside. They got out of the car, and Kathy introduced Senthil to him. She told them she had to go to the post office and would pick him up on her way back. Mr. Spencer took Senthil upstairs to show him the place.

The door opened to a small walkway. To the right was a large kitchen. The kitchen had a door on the far side that opened into a deck with wooden stairs going down to the backyard. One could get into the house from the back. The left of the hallway led to a large living room. The entire length of the wall on the street side consisted of glass windows that opened up to a river. "That's the Missouri River. My son used to sit by the window all the time. It's usually just gentle waves on the water, but every now and then, one can see a tugboat or a barge on the river," said Mr. Spencer.

"It's a beautiful view," Senthil replied.

The place was huge. But other than the kitchen appliances and light fixtures, the house was unfurnished. This did not bother him. He was used to sleeping on the hard floor, and the carpet was actually an upgrade.

When Mr. Spencer told him that the rent was $200, Senthil was convinced. He could save $800 from the tax-free allowance Hema was giving him. He asked about the utilities, and Mr. Spencer told him that water and trash were included in the rent, but the tenant was responsible for the electricity and the phone bill. He wanted to keep the electricity bill in his name and asked Senthil to pay the amount along with his rent. "I'll take it, Mr. Spencer," said Senthil.

They came down the stairs just as Kathy rolled to a stop. Senthil asked Mr. Spencer if there was a lease or a contract he needed to sign. Mr. Spencer gave him the keys and said that he did not need to sign anything. He just needed a month's rent as a refundable deposit and the first month's rent. Senthil told him his checkbook was at the Haven. Mr. Spencer said that he could move in anytime and just leave the check in the mailbox. Senthil thanked him and got back to the Haven with Kathy. He thanked her again and went back to the therapy room.

Amanda and Rachel were in the therapy room, finishing up their documentation over a cup of coffee. They were surprised to hear that he was going to live in this little town rather than in Columbia. They warned him about the lack of social life in Glasgow, telling him he would get bored easily. Senthil told them that his visa would be canceled if he did not pass his board exam, and he would thus be better off without any distraction while he prepared for the exam. Rachel offered to give him a ride the next day, as he had to return to Columbia to drop off the rental car.

The employees of Haven could opt to get a lunch tray from the kitchen for $2.00. It was the same lunch tray served to the residents on a regular diet. Senthil decided to forego lunch. In his mind, $2:00 a lunch translated to ₹86.90, and he could not fathom spending that much on a single meal. He decided to review some more patient charts. Amanda and Rachel went to work with the patients in the dining hall. As an OT and an SLP, they had more opportunities to provide therapy during meal times, and at times the nurses got the residents up and ready for them in the morning.

As he was reading the charts, he heard a voice at the door, "Are you, my papa?"

Senthil looked up and saw an old man in his late 70s sitting in a wheelchair. He had his arms crossed over his pot belly. He wore a round pair of glasses. His face was smooth and round and had no teeth but refused to wear dentures. He must have served in the army; he was wearing a blue and white hat with a spread-eagle, underneath which "USA Army" was embroidered. He was dressed in a checkered blue full-sleeved flannel shirt, a pair of dark blue jeans, and a pair of white and blue sneakers. His voice was peculiar: croaky, brittle, and adenoidal—all in one. The seat was set low so that he could propel his sports wheelchair with his feet.

Senthil said, "Hello sir! How are you?"

William Rutherford, affectionately referred to as "Billy" by all, inched closer. He just swung his legs twice, and he was there by Senthil's table. His wheelchair was like a little sports car.

"Are you my papa?" he asked again.

"I am afraid not, sir. My name is Senthil. I am the new physical therapist. It's lunchtime. You should be in the dining hall. Let me take you there."

He turned the wheelchair and pushed Billy towards the dining hall as he lifted his legs off the floor. Billy had a big grin on his edentulous mouth.

Rachel pointed to Billy's table. Senthil parked the wheelchair and said, "Enjoy your lunch, sir." He turned around to walk back to the therapy room.

"He is Billy," Penny said. She told him it upset him to be addressed by anything else. Billy had dementia and was only oriented to himself. He thought of every man as his father and every woman as his mother. He was confused but perfectly content in his wheelchair, even though nothing was wrong with his legs and he did walk around in his room. He loved sitting in the foyer and talking to the birds. He would talk to anyone who came and went, even if they did not notice him. His laugh was infectious.

Senthil sat at his table, and as he reviewed the charts of patients to be evaluated and those that were to be screened, he noted a priority list according to the patients' needs, based on the nursing documentation.

It was around 2:00 PM when he heard Penny's voice at the door. "Wanna give us a hand in bringing back our residents from the dining room?"

"Well yes, of course," he said as he got up and walked towards her.

As they walked to the dining hall, Penny squeezed his arm, shrugged her shoulders, and said, "I am so glad you are here at the Haven!"

Senthil smiled and replied, "Me too!"

Lunch was over. The residents were sitting quietly at their table. Most of them were peaceful and appeared to reminisce about their glory days. Some had fallen asleep with their heads hung over their half-eaten lunch trays. Some of them were already back in their rooms for a quick nap. Penny made a note of the residents who had not finished their meals so she could offer them a snack during the afternoon activity hour.

After all the residents were accounted for, Senthil returned to the therapy room. Rachel told him she was going to the grocery store and Walmart in Columbia before heading home and that she would be happy to help with dropping off the rental car. She invited him to join her for shopping.

Later that afternoon, at around 4:00 PM, Amanda, Rachel, and Senthil said their goodbyes to Penny and Kathy and left the Haven. Senthil followed Rachel in his car. Rachel had quite the lead foot. She was zipping through the curves and flying through the ups and downs of the road. Senthil would not have dared to drive this fast, but since he was following someone, he was able to shake off his fear somewhat. He was still cautious and kept a safe distance behind her. He couldn't deny the exhilaration of speed. Rachel kept an eye on him via the rear-view mirror and slowed down each time he fell back.

He dropped the car off at the Columbia Regional Airport. He checked the car twice to make sure he had not left anything behind. Rachel was patient. He hopped insider her car and went shopping. He bought some vegetables, onions, tomatoes, green chilies, some chicken, yogurt, and buttermilk. Rachel picked up some salsa, avocado, and chips. Senthil was intrigued by salsa, especially because of the "buy one get one free" label. After she explained to him what it was, he decided to get a couple of them, too. He was getting two for the price of one!

As they walked down the aisle, he was ecstatic to see the sign "Ramen noodles 10 for $1.00." "Wow! This is incredible. These are like Maggi noodles in India!" he exclaimed and proceeded to pile on ten packets of Ramen noodles. Maggi noodles were a luxury in India, and they had it only as a special treat since it was expensive.

He was thrilled that he could get ten meals out of $1.00. Rachel looked at his cart and said, "I have no idea what you are going to do with these and how all these are going to become part of a meal."

Senthil laughed and replied, "I'll cook some Indian food for you and Amanda one day."

Excited at the prospect, she replied, "That would be great. We could have a potluck. Amanda and I could cook some American food. I've never had Indian food before, but you have to promise me to tone down the spices."

The next stop was Walmart. Rachel had to pick up some film rolls for her camera. She was going to a baby shower. Senthil bought himself some soap, shampoo, laundry detergent, toothpaste, and cologne. He also got a pillow and a comforter. He told Rachel he was frugal, so she helped him stay with the store brand whenever possible, but she told him that he was on his own for the cologne. He restricted himself to the body spray aisle, as the products there were cheaper than cologne. He finally decided to settle with Brut, which seemed to be the best bargain.

Walking out of Walmart, Senthil noticed the Dollar Store on the other side of the street. Curious, he asked Rachel, and she explained that everything in the store cost no more than a dollar. Senthil's eyes widened.

"Would you like to take a peek inside?"

"Only if you don't mind, Rachel. I don't want to hold you up."

"I don't mind. Besides, it's so much fun seeing your reactions. You are like a kid in a candy store."

He dumped the bags from Walmart in the car and crossed the road enthusiastically. Rachel tried to keep up with him. He walked around the store and was impressed to see everything that cost just one dollar. He picked up a knife and a cutlery set, a ladle, a spatula, and a plate. A plastic box caught his eye, and he thought it would make the perfect lunch box to take to work.

It was time to go home.

Rachel said, "Since you are staying in a motel, I'll keep your groceries in my refrigerator."

"That sounds like a great idea. You are so kind, Rachel. I don't know what I would have done without you," he replied.

"It's no big deal. Besides, you are going to cook some Indian food for us. So, I need to make sure the groceries stay fresh," Rachel laughed.

Chapter 13 — Gleeful in Glasgow

THE NEXT MORNING, SENTHIL GOT READY BY 6:00 AM. HE checked out of the hotel and waited in the lobby with his suitcases. He ate a couple of the donuts that were being served in the lobby, wrapped two more in paper towels, and put them in his bag. When he saw Rachel pull up in front of the hotel, he walked out with one of his suitcases.

"Good morning, Rachel. Thanks again for picking me up."

"You are welcome, and good morning to you too!"

She popped the trunk open, and Senthil placed his suitcase inside. He went back into the hotel and came out with his carry-on and the other suitcase, which he put on the backseat.

"Be careful not to squish your groceries. I don't want anything to happen to my first Indian meal," Rachel laughed.

Rachel drove off, and Senthil felt like he was in a race car. There was hardly anybody on the road to Glasgow.

"You are a good driver," he said.

She laughed and thanked him. They were talking about work and the staff at Haven when Rachel suddenly exclaimed, "Well, wait a minute! How are you going to cook an Indian meal? You didn't buy any Indian spices."

Senthil smiled and said, "Don't you worry. I brought all the basic spices from India."

"Is that what's in the suitcases?"

"Well, in one of them. The other one has my clothes and some books."

"Are these the only things you brought over from India? I am afraid I pack more for my weekend visit to grandma's, and she lives in Branson, Missouri."

"That's funny. I wish I could have gotten more, but airlines have strict restrictions when it comes to the number of suitcases and the weight you are allowed to carry."

"That's so sad. Hey, we are almost here. You need to tell me how to get to your place."

Senthil told her that his place was the third house on the left on 1st Street. A few minutes later, Rachel parked in front of his house and popped the trunk. Senthil hurried up the stairs with one suitcase at a time. Rachel carried his groceries upstairs. He took off his shoes and walked in, carrying the suitcases to the bedroom. When he came back for the carry-on, he saw Rachel removing her shoes to get in.

"Thank you for taking off your shoes," Senthil said. "You didn't have to, but I appreciate it."

"Of course, I am aware of that Asian tradition. I think it's neat."

They walked into the kitchen, and Rachel placed the kitchen bags on the counter. Senthil put the chicken, the yogurt, and the vegetables in the refrigerator and left the rest of the things on the counter.

"I'll see you downstairs, Senthil. Take your time," Rachel said and walked down to her car. Senthil took out the checkbook and wrote out the check for his landlord. He locked the house and ran down the stairs. He placed the check in the mailbox and got into the car.

During lunchtime, Senthil called the telephone company to establish service. Hema had told him to choose MCI as his long-distance company as they had the best plan to call India. He called Hema and gave her his house address and his home phone number.

That evening, he walked back home after work. He took out his pressure cooker and the stir-fry pan he had got from India, along with the bag of rice and all the spices. He carried everything to the kitchen. He made some chicken biryani with vegetables. It was a one-pot dish. He made enough to last him for a week.

The rest of the week kept Senthil busy with treating his patients. Penny continued to tease him, but he did not mind it. She helped him by introducing him to his new patients. Of course, he did not need any help with Ms. Jones or Ms. Hillman, as they both fought over who he would see first. Senthil managed to keep both the ladies happy by giving equal attention to both.

He usually left after Amanda and Rachel as they were able to treat their patients during breakfast and lunch. He walked back and forth to work. It was a good hike, and the uphill climb was a bit challenging, but he was fine with it.

Friday came around, and Amanda and Rachel were getting ready to leave a little earlier than usual. They had plans to go out on the town to eat and then to a sports bar to watch a football game. They invited Senthil to join them. Rachel said that he could crash at her place and she would bring him back on Saturday. Senthil politely declined; he had a lot of catching up to do with studying for the board exam, writing letters, and calling home. Penny had plans for the weekend too. She was going to Moberly to visit her friend and go watch *Mrs. Doubtfire.*

It appeared that everybody had something planned for the weekend and it was sacrilege to not do anything fun and just stay home.

He was not used to two-day weekends. In India, the workweek was six days, and Sunday was the day off. This was his first weekend off work. Before he left, he stopped by Ms. Jones and Ms. Hillman's rooms and taught them a few exercises that he wanted them to practice over the weekend. He did not want them to lose the gains they had made with the therapy sessions. As he was walking out, Penny stopped him. "I've got to say you have made an impression on all of us."

"Really? I hope it is a good one."

"Of course, it's good, Senthil. You may not know this, but all the residents have told Kathy how good you are and what a great therapist you are."

"It's a privilege to work here at the Haven. Everybody is so kind."

"You know, Senthil, we have never had a therapist come to work in a shirt and a tie and a white coat. They usually come in khakis, a polo shirt, and sneakers. It is refreshing to see someone take their role seriously."

"I don't dress up for vanity. I think it's a way of showing respect to my patients, and being a foreigner, I have to try harder to earn their trust."

"You are no foreigner, Senthil. You have become one of us. I am so happy to work with you."

"Thank you, Penny. The feeling is mutual."

It was getting dark quicker with each passing day. When Senthil walked out of the Haven, it looked like it was already night although it was only 5:00 PM. As he walked down the hill, he felt a shiver. It was finally time to take out the leather jacket.

That night, he called Shiva. They talked about work first. Senthil told him how happy he was in Glasgow and how well-received. He went on and on about how friendly people were, and he did not feel like he was in a foreign country. Shiva agreed. He, too, had noticed that people were warmer and friendlier in smaller cities. They talked about their families, about Maria and Sumathi. Shiva told him that he had received a letter from Maria. It was comforting to him to hear that Maria and Sumathi met regularly. They talked about meeting up. Shiva told him that one of the therapists he worked with had some family in Moberly and had offered to give him a ride sometime in February when he would come down to visit them. Both were excited about that prospect.

They talked about the preparation for the board exams. Senthil told Shiva that he was going to start studying tomorrow. Shiva told him he was in for a surprise when he took a look at the study material Hema had given him. Senthil again asked him what the surprise was, but Shiva refused to give him any clue.

"You'll find out tomorrow," he said.

"Is it a good or a bad surprise?"

"It depends. Call me tomorrow after your study session," replied Shiva.

Since it was a weekend, he did not have to wait until 9:00 PM to call him.

Senthil had brought some old newspapers from the Haven. He spread those out when he sat on the floor to eat so that he did not accidentally spill anything on the carpet. He usually preferred being in the kitchen as it was warmer than the rest of the house. He did not want to turn the heater on and get a higher electricity bill. Cooking and heating leftovers on the stove did a good enough job of warming up the kitchen.

He slept in the kitchen too. He had brought two sheets over from India. He spread one on the floor and covered himself with the other. He used his books as a pillow and slept close to the baseboard heating unit to keep himself warm. Since he did not have to wake up early the next day, he decided to stay up and write letters to Sumathi and his family. He would mail them the next morning as the post office stayed open until noon on Saturdays.

It was way past midnight when he finished the letters. He told them his address and phone number and wrote about his new job, his colleagues—Penny, Amanda, Rachel, Kathy—and his patients, especially Ms. Jones and Ms. Hillman. Both the letters essentially contained the same content, but he enjoyed writing them.

In the letter to his family, he wrote a separate paragraph for his parents and a different one for his siblings. He let his parents know that he was doing fine with the grace of their blessings. He asked his siblings about school and advised them to make poor Eshwari's life easier by helping with the chores. In the letter to Sumathi, he added how much he missed her and how he wished she had been there by his side on this journey. He told her how much the Haven would have loved her. It was a fine line he was treading. He wanted to tell her how much he missed her, but at the same time, he wanted to make sure that he did not make her feel bad or sorry.

He wanted to sleep in, so he turned off the alarm clock when he went to bed. Yet, he woke up at 6:00 AM. He tried but could not fall back asleep. He finally got up, folded the sheets, and put them away. After completing his morning rituals, he sat down to study. He realized that he had not bought any breakfast food. On weekdays, he hardly missed breakfast as he was so busy with work. Today, however, he felt hungry. He wanted to go to the grocery store to get some cereal or bread, but he knew the post office would not be open and he did not want to go out twice.

He ate some chicken and rice and sat down to study with his back against the wall. He opened the study material packet Hema had given him. He remembered what Shiva had told him. The packet had a study guide inside. It was divided into sections according to systems: orthopedics, neurology, rheumatology, cardiology, pulmonary, and so on, and therapeutic interventions: electrophysiology, exercise physiology, heat and ice therapy, and the like.

He wondered what Shiva had been talking about until he saw something below the study guide. It was a booklet titled "Sample test questions and Sample test." He was happy to see it, as he had no idea what type of questions he would encounter in the board exam.

But his happiness was short-lived. His smile dropped into a frown as soon as he read the instructions on the first page of the booklet. "Multiple Choice Questions: Read the questions and the answer choices correctly and choose the most correct response by filling the bubble sheet. Fill the appropriate bubble completely with a #2 pencil. If you need to change your response, erase your choice completely and fill the appropriate bubble." Confused, he flipped the pages of the booklet to get a look at the actual question. The instructions made sense. There was a question, and following the question were four choices marked "a," "b," "c," and "d." He had to pick the correct answer.

This perplexed him. He had never taken an exam where he had been given the answers. All through his school, he had been required to write the answers. His tests until middle school had included questions related to choosing true or false, filling in the blanks, matching correct options, and short answers. After middle school, depending on the section, he had to write a short paragraph, a couple of paragraphs, or an essay.

For some reason, this multiple-choice-question format seemed much harder. The choices looked very similar. One could argue for two answers for the same question. There was no room for providing any justification for your choice. Also, "the most correct response" indicated that there could be more than one choice but only one correct answer. Senthil was tempted to call Shiva immediately, but thought maybe he was still sleeping.

He continued to read the questions and the choices provided. He was beginning to get a grasp of the nature of the test, but he still was not convinced that this method was the most appropriate tool to test his knowledge. What if he misunderstood or misread the question? His wrong answer would suggest that he possessed no knowledge of the subject.

On the contrary, if he could write a paragraph or two, or an essay, it would reveal his command of the topic in question. This format only made him nervous. Now he understood what Shiva had been trying to tell him.

He looked at his watch. It was 9:30 AM. He could finally mail the letters and stop by the local grocery store. He got dressed, grabbed the letters, and walked down the stairs. He opened the glass doors and realized it was freezing. He knew that he would not be able to keep himself warm even if he ran. The temperature had plummeted overnight.

He ran upstairs, went through his suitcase, and took out a pair of long johns. He put on his leather jacket and exchanged his chappals for sneakers. He then stepped out feeling better. He walked to the end of the street—past the laundromat, the barber shop, the crafts store, the gas station, and the local diner. Across the street, there was a mechanic shop, a bookstore, and a tavern.

He stopped by the post office first and mailed the letters. The clerk asked if he was new in town, and Senthil replied that he was the new physical therapist at the Haven. He then walked to the IGA grocery store. Unlike the ones in Dallas and Columbia, this was a small grocery store. It had all the basic groceries, but not the range of options. He found bread, eggs, peanut butter, and strawberry jam. He made sure they were all from the store brand. He got some chicken to make another batch of chicken biryani for Rachel and Amanda. The cashier, too, asked him if he was new in town. Everybody knew everybody in this small town.

He walked out with plastic bags; lucky for him, the cashier had double bagged everything. The sun was out from behind the clouds. Senthil hurried back. He realized as the winter progressed, his two sheets are not going to keep him warm. He would need to take out the comforter he bought and also raise the temperature setting of the thermostat.

Putting the groceries away, he turned on the stove for some heat. He stood with his hands over the stove for a few minutes, and then turned it off. His phone rang as he sat down to study. Since he spent all his time in the kitchen and slept there as well, he had plugged his phone into the socket in the kitchen. It was Shiva.

He said, "Did you just wake up? I called you a few times, and you didn't answer."

"I went to the post office and the grocery store."

"You should get a phone with an answering machine."

"This is the phone the landlord left in the house, but next time I go to Walmart, I'll get one."

They talked about the study material, the exam format, and the questions. Both agreed that they had a steep learning curve ahead. After chatting for an hour, Senthil studied for the rest of the day. The only breaks he took were when he went to the bathroom or got up to drink water. He planned to study the familiar books he had brought from India and tackle the study guide later. He would practice the test questions a month before taking the actual exam.

Chapter 14 — Studying in the Snow

SENTHIL'S SCHEDULE, PREDOMINATED BY WORK AND studying for the board exam, remained unchanged for the rest of January. February arrived, and winter took a bitter turn. He continued to walk up the hill to the Haven every morning. On Friday, February 11, Senthil went to bed as usual in the kitchen. He planned on starting the study guide. Even with two layers of clothing and a comforter, it was cold, and he had to turn on the electric baseboard heating. The warmth, the softness of the comforter, and the carpet made him drift off to sleep—it was as though he was sleeping on a cloud.

It was the weekend, and he had turned off the alarm. Being a creature of habit, though, he still woke up at 6:00 AM. He could not believe his eyes when he looked outside the big window in the kitchen. The brown tree branches had turned white. He rushed to open the back door of the kitchen. Everything was plain white—there was not a drop of color. It looked like someone had taken a giant fluffy white blanket and covered the deck, the rails, the stairs, the ground, and the trees overnight.

He was mesmerized. He has seen this only in the movies. He shut the door and hurried to the living room to get a look at the front of the house. The road and the cars parked on the streets were blanketed with snow. Running down the stairs, he pushed opened the door and stepped outside. For a minute, he forgot he was in his pajamas and wearing only a pair of socks. As he stepped on to the snow-covered sidewalk, his feet sunk up to his ankles. He pranced a few steps down the sidewalk, scooped up the snow, and threw it up in the air.

Grinning ear to ear, he was about to grab another handful of snow when he realized how cold it was and how soggy and cold his socks had gotten. His hands were freezing. He scurried back indoors. Indian movies would sometimes depict the hero and the heroine frolicking in the snow in fancy dresses, without any jackets or gloves. *How misleading.* While the scene was picturesque, the cold was unbearable. He went upstairs, removed the wet socks, and ran warm water over his hands. He brushed his teeth and changed his clothes. He wore his leather jacket and his sneakers and went to the backyard.

"I am going to build a snowman, just like the one in *Home Alone*," he said out loud. He did not have a pair of gloves, but he had come down prepared. He wrapped his hands with a couple of T-shirts and also a couple of plastic bags he got from the grocery store.

As he was piling the snow in the middle of the backyard, he heard a voice: "What are you doing?"

It was Mr. Spencer, the landlord, who had come to check on the house and plow the sidewalks.

"I am trying to build a snowman like the one you see in the movies."

Mr. Spencer saw his excitement. "How old are you? I have never seen an adult this excited about snow."

"Not if one is seeing snow for the very first time!"

"Really? You have never seen snow before?"

Senthil shook his head no.

"What's that on your hands?"

"Oh, these! They are my makeshift gloves. The snow is pretty, but it sure is cold."

Mr. Spencer turned around and started walking towards his truck, smiling.

"Are you leaving, Mr. Spencer?"

"Yes. Why don't you go upstairs and get warmed up? I'll be back in half an hour. I have something important to talk to you about."

"Sure, Mr. Spencer, but I am building a snow—"

Mr. Spencer interrupted him, "Don't worry, the snow is here to stay. It's not going to melt anytime soon. I'll see you upstairs soon."

Senthil glanced at his alien-like hands and ran upstairs. He walked into the living room and stood by the windows, looking at the street. Soon, he heard a knock on the back door. He hurried back to the kitchen and opened the door to find Mr. Spencer walking down the stairs.

"Mr. Spencer? I thought you wanted to talk to me."

"C'mon down, big fella."

Senthil followed him down the steps. As they reached downstairs, two kids jumped out from the side of the house.

"This is Brittany and Johnny, my grandchildren. They are here to help you build a snowman."

"Wow! That's amazing! Thank you!"

"Kids, this is Mr. Senthil. He has never seen snow before."

Brittany was an eight-year-old little girl with freckles, wavy blonde hair under a pink beret, and pretty, big blue eyes. She was all bundled up in a pink and purple jacket, pink ear muffs, purple knit gloves, and purple and pink boots. Johnny, a ten-year-old who also had freckles, was dressed in black and blue.

"You have never seen snow before? How old are you?" asked Brittany.

"I am twenty-five, but I just arrived from India where it's hot or warm all the time. So, we don't get snow."

Brittany's jaw dropped, and her eyes grew big. Johnny did not say much.

"Okay, grab the little shovel and let's roll," said Mr. Spencer.

Mr. Spencer had brought little snow spades and let Senthil borrow his spare gloves. Together, they built a snowman—five feet tall and three feet wide. It was impressive! Brittany whispered something into her grandpa's ears. He nodded and walked towards his truck as Brittany and Johnny stood there, watching Senthil and giggling. Mr. Spencer returned with a bag. He handed a packet of Oreo cookies to Brittany, who in turn handed it over to Senthil. Senthil thanked her and opened the bag of Oreos. Brittany grabbed a couple of them and motioned for Senthil to pick her up.

Senthil, puzzled, picked her up, and she lunged forward with her outstretched hands to give the snowman cookie eyes.

"That's a great idea," Senthil said as he lowered her. Johnny picked up some Oreo cookies to make buttons on the snowman's belly. Brittany grabbed the bag from her grandpa and pulled out a carrot. She gave it to Senthil and pointed at her nose. Senthil placed the carrot on the snowman's head to form a nose. She then handed him a red scarf and a black hat. They used a pack of Mini Oreo cookies to form a big smile on the snowman's face. Johnny scoured the backyard while Senthil and Brittany decorated the snowman. He came back with two skinny tree branches and stuck it on either side of the snowman to form its arms.

It was a masterpiece. Senthil stepped back to look at it and exclaimed, "This looks better than the ones I have seen in the movies!"

Brittany and Johnny clapped their hands. Mr. Spencer said, "Okay kids, it's time to go. Oh, I forgot. Let's take some pictures."

He took a camera out of his coat. Senthil and the kids posed with Frosty, as Brittany called the snowman. Mr. Spencer then took a picture of Senthil alone with the snowman. "I'll get these pictures to you once the weather gets better and I can go to Walmart."

"Thanks again, everyone. This is awesome." The children waved him goodbye and hurried back to the truck.

Senthil stood in the backyard and waved until the truck disappeared around the corner. He took a long look at Frosty and hurried back up the stairs. He could barely contain his excitement. He wished Sumathi was here to share this experience with him. They had watched many movies together in which the hero and heroine played in the snow.

He was too excited to study. He sat down and wrote a letter to Sumathi and then one to his family, describing his day. He studied for the rest of the weekend.

On Monday, he got ready for work. He peeked at the backyard, and to his joy, Frosty was still there. As he walked up the hill, he realized his ears and nose were beginning to hurt, and even though he was wearing a leather jacket, he was shivering. His regular dress shoes could hardly protect him from the cold snow. His pinky toe started aching. He tried to walk faster, but the pain only worsened. By the time he reached the parking lot, he was hobbling.

Pat, the activities director, was at the bottom of the path that curved up the hill, leading to the Haven, and saw Senthil hurriedly limping ahead. Senthil walked into the Haven and waved at Penny as she tried to talk to him. Once she learned what had happened, she took him to the bathroom and asked him to take off his shoes and socks.

His feet looked pale; he could not feel them. His little toes on both feet were paler than the rest. She turned on the warm water in the tub and asked him to immerse his feet in it. He sat at the edge of the tub, rolled up his pants, and put his feet into the water. The pain worsened at first, but, in a few minutes, he could wiggle his toes and the intense pain he had suffered just a few minutes ago dissipated.

Penny left to check on her patients. He heard Pat's voice, "Where is he? Has he gotten frostbite? Is he okay?"

Senthil was putting on his socks when Pat entered. "What are you doing walking in this weather, young man?" She had a big frown on her face, and her hands were perched on her waists. However, there was only concern in her voice. Senthil told her that he could not afford a car right now, and since he lived so close by, he had decided to walk.

"But it's freezing out there. Can't you get a used car? My husband Donald knows a used-car dealer. He can get you a good used car for a good price."

"Oh, thank you, Pat. That is very kind of you. I just have to be very careful until I take my board exam and get my permanent physical therapist license."

"What's that got to do with your car?"

"Well, you see, I am working with my temporary physical therapy license. If I fail my board exam, I cannot work until I retake my board exam three months later."

"I don't see you fail, but I see your point. Well, this is what we are going to do then. I drive past 1st Street to come to work every day. Be ready by 7:45 AM, and I'll pick you up."

Pat was not asking him but telling him. Senthil was touched. His eyes welled up with tears, and he told her he did not know how to thank her. She replied, "Well, you can thank me by passing your board exam."

Amanda and Rachel had called in to inform that they would not be able to make it due to the bad weather and unplowed roads. From that day on, Pat picked up Senthil and dropped him back at the end of the day. He got ready in the morning and waited by the window in the living room. The moment he saw Pat's blue Chevy Lumina come down the street, he ran down the stairs. He did not want her to wait or get out the warm car. Amanda and Rachel came to work on Tuesday. They planned to work the next Saturday to make up for their absence on Monday so that the Medicare patients could get their five days of therapy.

That Friday, Amanda and Rachel asked Senthil to accompany them to Columbia for a night on the town. Since they were coming to work on Saturday, they could drop him back. They insisted that he could take a break from studying. Since it was only one night, Senthil agreed.

First stop was dinner at Chi-Chi's, a Mexican restaurant in Columbia. This was not a fast food restaurant but a sit-down one. Senthil looked at the menu and was taken aback by the prices. Amanda and Rachel ordered cocktails, while Senthil settled for water.

The waiter asked, "Do you want lemon with it?"

"Is there an extra charge for the lemon?" asked Senthil.

"No, sir."

"Sure then, I'll have lemon with my water."

The waiter came back with chips and salsa, and Amanda and Rachel dove right in. Senthil did not know who had ordered it and kept staring at the menu. He did not understand many of the entrées. This was not the same menu he had seen in Taco Bell, and the price of a burrito was five times more than that at Taco Bell. The waiter brought them the cocktails and asked if they were ready to order. Amanda and Rachel were busy talking and asked the waiter to give them a minute.

The waiter brought a new bowl of chips and salsa, and Senthil, curious, asked him who had ordered it. To his pleasant surprise, the waiter said, "It's on the house."

Senthil had not touched the previous bowl since he thought either Amanda or Rachel had ordered the chips. Now he got his fill of chips and salsa. It was delicious, and he could not believe that the restaurant was giving it away for free. It was time to order, and Amanda ordered a chicken quesadilla while Rachel ordered a beef fajita. Senthil decided on the southwestern egg roll from the appetizer section because it was the least expensive item on the menu. He was hungry, but he could not justify spending $13 for a meal, which translated to ₹564.85 to him.

The waiter said, "If you place your entrée order too now, it will be ready by the time you finish your appetizer."

Senthil replied, "I am just going to have that as my entrée." Amanda and Rachel looked at him in confusion, and he said, "I am too full from eating the chips and salsa." He did not want them to think he was stingy or have them assume that he thought they were spendthrifts.

After dinner, they went to a bar. "What would you like to drink? It's on me," said Amanda.

"I don't drink."

"Is it against your religion?" asked Rachel.

"No. I have had a sip of beer and whiskey once. I just didn't like the taste."

"Well, that was Indian beer. Here, try this American beer," said Amanda. Senthil hesitated, but then he took a small sip, and from his facial expression and body cringe, Amanda knew he was not a fan. She laughed and said, "It's like giving a baby some new food and watching their reaction."

Rachel said, "Here, try my Long Island Iced Tea."

"I don't drink coffee or tea but thank you."

"What? You are from India, and you don't drink coffee or tea? Strange! Anyway, this is a cocktail drink."

Senthil took a sip of that too and hated the taste of it as well. He had to drink a glass of water to get the taste off his mouth.

"You don't drink coffee or tea or alcohol. So, what is your vice?" asked Amanda.

"I like sweets—a lot of it."

Amanda and Rachel laughed.

He sipped his ice water as they finished their drinks. They had to work the next day and had to call it a night early; otherwise, they would have stayed out a lot longer and hit the dance floors. Senthil was glad. He felt out of place in the bar, and he certainly did not know how to dance. They spent the night at Amanda's place. Senthil slept in a sleeping bag on the floor, and Rachel took the couch.

The next day, they dropped him off at his place on their way to work. On his way up, Senthil checked his mailbox. It had an envelope with the pictures Mr. Spencer had taken of him with Frosty, Brittany, and Johnny. Mr. Spencer was kind and generous enough to include two copies of each photo. He placed a copy of each photo in the envelopes with the letters for his family and Sumathi. He went to the post office in the afternoon to mail them. Even though there was snow and it was cold, the sun was up, and it made the weather bearable. He stopped at the IGA grocery store and bought some groceries.

Apart from work, he spent the rest of the winter studying for the board exam. Nothing distracted him other than the regular letters from Sumathi and the letters he wrote back every two weeks. He had reviewed the books he had brought from India and the study guide provided by Hema. He was ready to take the board exam in June. Working at the Haven helped him learn about Medicare and Medicaid and some other health-care laws. Senthil called Hema to tell her that he would be ready to take the board exam in June. He only needed two months to practice the multiple-choice questions.

Shiva too had called her to say the same thing. She sent them another study guide with more questions and bubble sheets to keep them busy until June. Snow led to rain as spring came and March ended. Pat continued to pick up and drop Senthil off from work. In return, Senthil frequently packed Indian food for her. She and Donald became a big fan of his chicken biryani.

Senthil started practicing the multiple-choice questions with the bubble sheets. As June 3 approached, he got more comfortable with the format. He learned to look for buzzwords and twisters like "all," "except," "but," "none," which could completely change the answer. He resisted the temptation to look at the answer choices until he had carefully read the question and come up with an answer in his head. He timed himself taking the mock exams to improve his time management skill.

Chapter 15 — Linguistics: Fallacies and Foils

THREE WEEKS REMAINED UNTIL THE BOARD EXAM. THE exam would be held in Jefferson City, so Senthil planned to go to Shiva's place on Thursday night before the exam and share a cab ride with him to the exam center. He had to figure out a way to reach Shiva's place. He received a packet from Hema with the examination entrance ticket and the instructions. He had to carry two forms of photo-bearing government-issued identification, report forty-five minutes early for registration, and only use #2 pencil on the bubble answer sheet.

Senthil called Hema to ask about #2 pencils. He did not know what that meant or where he could find them.

"It's the darkness of the graphite in pencil. #2 pencils are used to fill out answer sheets, as the computers used to score the bubble sheets read the #2 pencil's shade correctly."

"What if I make a mistake and need to change my answer?"

"Don't worry. You'll do well. In case you make a mistake, just make sure you erase your first choice thoroughly. You don't want the computer to read two answers for the same question and earn zero points. Anyway, go with your gut instinct and the first impression. Don't read too much into the question and second-guess yourself."

"Where can I get this #2 pencil, Hema?"

"Walmart or any store would have it, I am sure."

Kathy was getting the Haven ready for summer. Some landscaping work was underway. The patio and the courtyard were getting a facelift. Kathy got a vending machine installed in the activities room so that the visitors could get a cold drink on hot summer days.

Work at the Haven was getting busier. Since they had a full rehab team available five days a week, a lot of Medicare patients were being admitted for subacute rehab from the hospital. Penny told him that her sister had recently got herself an intermediate driver's license and had a friend in Moberly. If he paid her gas money, she would drive him anywhere in their grandma's car. With gas at $0.99, it would be a lot cheaper than getting a cab or renting a car. Penny's sister would get to drive a car, and Senthil would save some money.

That Saturday, Senthil was studying in the morning when the phone rang. It was Melissa, Penny's sister.

"Hi, Penny said you would like a ride to Walmart. Would you like to go there today?"

"Oh hi, Melissa. That is very kind of you. Yes, it would be great. What time did you have in mind?"

"How about I come to pick you up at noon? And please call me Mel."

"Sure. By noon. Thanks, Mel, I appreciate it."

"You are welcome. See you then."

Mel was on time, and Senthil was ready. He gave her $10, but Mel told him that Moberly was only thirty-five miles away and accepted $5. Mel was meeting her friend for lunch in Moberly and asked if he wanted to join them for lunch or just get off at Walmart. Senthil did not wish to impose and asked to be dropped off at Walmart. He told her he had eaten just before they left Glasgow.

Walmart was on US-24. There was a Dollar General nearby, and across the street, there was Lowes. Mel said that once he was done with his work at Walmart, he could walk around these stores to avoid boredom. It was 12:40 PM when they reached Walmart. Mel told Senthil that she would be back to pick him up at 3:00 PM. He stepped out of the car in front of a plain, unassuming brown building, but when he walked into the store, he was amazed by the aisles after aisles stacked with products.

He decided to explore since he had over two hours before Mel picked him up. He grabbed a cart and started on the left side of the store with the produce section. This store offered more choices than his local IGA and was cheaper too. He got some vegetables, plain yogurt, milk, and eggs. He then headed towards the office supplies section.

Senthil picked up a pack of # 2 pencils. He remembered what Hema said about erasing the bubble thoroughly if he had to change his answer. He wasn't too confident about the little pink eraser at the tip of the pencil, so he took out his wallet and took out his company's business card to test the eraser. He wrote "Sumathi" on the back of the card and tried to erase it with the eraser attached at the tip. The result was a light smudge and streaks. This eraser would not do on the bubble sheet that was going to determine his fate.

He set out to find a better eraser. He looked at his watch, and it read 2:15 PM. He did not want to keep Mel waiting when she got back. He rushed to buy a good eraser but could not find any that was not attached to a pencil. He saw a young girl in a Walmart smock; leaving his cart on the side, he ran towards her. "Excuse me," he said.

"Hi, my name is Becky. How can I help you?" This was Becky's first job, and her enthusiasm showed.

"Yes, please. I am looking for a good rubber. Could you help me find one?"

"Excuse me?" Becky turned red and tried to control her laughter.

Senthil thought his accent was the cause of her confusion or amusement. So, he repeated himself slowly and loudly, making sure he enunciated every syllable. "Could you help me find a good rubber?"

Turning redder by the minute, Becky replied, "Walk down that way and turn right. I am not sure which is a good one, but there is quite a selection for you to pick from."

Senthil walked down the path Becky pointed to and turned right. He was surprised to find himself in the middle of the pharmacy. He did not think he would find his rubber in the pharmacy. Puzzled, he looked at his watch. It was 2:30 PM. He turned around and hurriedly walked back towards Becky. She covered her mouth with her hand, not wanting him to see her laughing.

"Excuse me. I couldn't find it, and I am in a hurry. Could you help me find a good rubber?" Senthil pleaded.

Becky could no longer contain herself. She started laughing and called over her colleague. "Hey Samantha, this guy wants me to find him a good rubber."

Samantha hurried over asking, "Are you serious?" She joined in Becky's laughter.

Senthil thought they were making fun of his accent and felt a little hurt. He slowly said, "Yes ma'am. I have a big exam next week, and I need a good rubber."

Becky and Samantha laughed and exclaimed, "What kind of exam do you have that you need a good rubber?"

Senthil still thought they were mocking him. He felt humiliated, and with his voice cracking and tears welling up in his eyes, he said, "If you do not want to help me, it's all right. I'll ask someone else."

"Oh no, we are sorry. I'll walk you to the rubbers, but you pick which one you want," said Becky, walking in front of him.

Senthil grabbed his cart and followed her. She walked to the end of the hallway and turned right. And they were back at the pharmacy. Becky pointed to a shelf with rows of condoms and said, "There, you can pick what you like. I don't know which one is good. My boyfriend buys them."

Senthil looked at the shelf she pointed and alarmingly exclaimed, "These are condoms. I am looking for a good rubber."

"*These are rubbers*, and yeah, they are called condoms too."

"Oh no!" Senthil exclaimed. Grabbing the pack of pencils, he pulled one out; pointing to the pink eraser, he said, "I am looking for a rubber that is not attached to a pencil. This pink rubber is not good."

"Oh, I am so embarrassed. I am so sorry we were talking about two different things. In America, we refer to condoms as rubbers," Becky explained.

Senthil told her that in India, erasers were referred to as rubbers. Both had a good laugh, and Becky walked him to the office supplies section to show him the "erasers." They were on the aisle opposite the pencils; Senthil had somehow overlooked that section.

Becky pointed to a white eraser labeled "Hi-Polymer" and said, "I used that in high school, and it's pretty good."

They came in packs of three. Senthil grabbed one, thanked her, and walked towards the check-out counter.

"I am sorry again for the misunderstanding. It was the funniest thing ever. Good luck with your exam," Becky yelled after him.

Senthil laughed and replied, "It's funny now. Thank you for your help."

It was 2:55 PM when Senthil stepped out of the Walmart with his cart. He picked up the bags and sat on the bench outside the store. Mel stopped in front of him. Senthil put all the grocery bags in the trunk, except the one with the pencils and the erasers, wanting to keep them in sight.

When he got home, he called Shiva to let him know that he had enough #2 pencils and erasers for the both of them and he should not worry. He told Shiva that Mel and her boyfriend were going to drive him to his place the Thursday night before the exam and pick him back up on Sunday evening. They had a couple of friends in Saint Martin, Missouri, which was only ten miles west of Jefferson City. Senthil did not share his embarrassing experience in Walmart with Mel or Shiva. In fact, he was not going to reveal his ignorance of American lingo to anyone. Little did he know how fast news traveled in little towns where everyone knew everyone.

The following Monday, when Penny saw him, she could not contain her laughter.

"Good morning, Penny," Senthil said.

All Penny did was cover her mouth to control her laughter. Finally, she managed to ask, "So, you asked Becky to find you a good rubber?"

Senthil was shocked, but to his own surprise, not offended or embarrassed. He started laughing too. "You should have seen the look on her face," he shot back.

He told her what happened, and Penny said, "That's the funniest thing I have heard in my entire life. You are too precious!"

That day at the Haven, Becky and the rubber formed the topic of conversation all day. Senthil learned to laugh at himself and with them.

Senthil left the Haven a little early on June 2. He was excited to spend the weekend in Jefferson City with Shiva, but he was also nervous about the board exam the following day. Mel and her boyfriend Ryan came to pick him up. Senthil was all ready and packed. It took Mel about an hour and a half to get to Jefferson City.

It was around 6:30 PM when they reached Shiva's apartment to find him anxiously waiting downstairs. As soon as he saw Senthil get out of the car, he ran towards him to give him a hug. Senthil introduced him to Mel and Ryan.

Shiva asked them to stay for dinner, saying that he had made some Indian food. Mel and Ryan told him they had another twenty-minute drive to Saint Martin and had promised to meet their friend for dinner. They said they would be happy to have the Indian dinner on the way back to Glasgow on Sunday evening.

Unlike Senthil, Shiva had gotten a furnished apartment with a TV and a VCR. Senthil and Shiva talked about Maria and Sumathi and their families, and then they talked about strategies for the test. Both decided to get a good night's rest instead of cramming at the last minute.

They woke up early in the morning. Shiva had some leftover sambar, and he made some *dosa* from an instant mix for breakfast. The last time Senthil had *dosa* was at Hema's place. Shiva told him there was a local Indian grocery store and there he was able to get Indian spices and groceries that were not available in IGA. Since Shiva knew about Senthil's sweet tooth, he had also gotten some assorted donuts. Senthil grabbed a sour cream donut on the way out.

Shiva had taken a few walks to the exam site and timed himself. It took him thirty-two minutes—a brisk walk just enough to wake them up and get the juices flowing to have them stimulated enough to tolerate sitting down for four hours during the test. They had three #2 pencils and two erasers each. About thirty therapists were waiting to take their exam. They decided to meet outside after the exam.

The next four hours were a blur. Senthil was the last one to finish. When he walked out, he saw Shiva sitting down by the stairs. They both exhaled a sigh of relief. They had no idea how they had fared and decided nothing good was going to come from discussing the exam or their answers. They walked to the Indian grocery store, and along with some grocery and frozen mackerel, they got a couple of movies: *Devar Magan* with Senthil's favorite actor Kamal Hassan and *Thalapathi* with Shiva's favorite actor Rajinikanth. On their way home, they stopped at IGA and got some chicken as well.

When they got home, both of them felt exhausted—more mentally than physically. Shiva plopped on to the recliner, and Senthil settled on the sofa. Within a few minutes, Shiva was snoring. Senthil was exhausted but couldn't fall asleep. His thoughts were on Sumathi.

Shiva woke up and made some coffee while Senthil had another donut.

"Why the long face, Senthil? Aren't you relieved the exam is over?"

"Oh yes, I am. I was just thinking about Sumathi."

"I know how you feel. I wish I could talk to Maria and tell her about the exam. Anyway, why don't we get cooking and then we can watch the movies during dinner?"

Shiva made fish curry, while Senthil made chicken korma. They got carried away sharing stories of patients and ended up cooking all the vegetables in the refrigerator. They made tomato *rasam*, green beans *varuval*, carrot *porriyal*, and chayote *kootu*. Finally, they made some rice. This was the most elaborate cooking they had done since they had arrived from India. They managed to set off the smoke alarm twice during their cooking and could not stop laughing. Shiva had to fan the air under the smoke alarm with one of his books, and he eventually ended up taking out the battery to shut the smoke alarm down.

They had enough food for the next three days. They arranged all the food on the table, fixed their plates, and sat down in front of the TV. They watched *Devar Magan* first, as it was Senthil's favorite movie. Later, they cleaned up the kitchen, kept the leftovers in the refrigerator, and got ready to watch *Thalapathi*.

Senthil was very excited to see Shiva come out of the kitchen with a cake with pink icing and a tub of butter pecan ice cream. It was about 10:30 PM when the movie ended.

"I saved the best surprise for the last," said Shiva.

"What surprise?"

Shiva picked up the phone and dialed. When the phone rang, he passed it on to Senthil. Recognizing the voice on the other end, Senthil felt his knees go weak and eased himself to the floor. Shiva had talked to Maria the week before and told her about the board exam they would be taking that day. He had asked Maria to bring Sumathi to Senthil's parents' house. Senthil was speechless. It was an emotional conversation. Even though Senthil was not sure about the results, Sumathi told him she was confident he would pass the boards and encouraged him to be positive. He asked Sumathi about her family.

Senthil then talked to his parents and siblings about the exam, the snowman, his work at the Haven, and his new friends.

He briefly talked to Maria, who was very excited that her two favorite people were spending time together and relieved that the dreaded board exam was over. Eventually, Shiva got his turn. He said quick hellos to Sumathi, Senthil's parents, and his siblings, and talked to Maria for a while. By the time they were done, they had been on the phone for two hours. As soon as Shiva hung up the phone, Senthil gave him a bear hug and thanked him for the phone call.

Mel and Ryan joined them for dinner on Sunday evening. Shiva and Senthil had enough leftovers to host them with a nice spread. Both Mel and Ryan were sweating and sniffling the entire time they ate. This was the first time they had tried Indian food. It was extremely spicy but way too good to stop eating. They downed a bottle of Coke with the chicken korma and fish curry with rice. It was around 9:30 PM when they dropped Senthil back to his place.

The next day, Pat came to pick him up as usual. "I was praying for you all day Friday. Hope your board exam went well."

"Oh, thank you, Pat. I think I did okay. It's a waiting game now."

"When do you get your results?"

"In four weeks. I am just not going to think about it anymore. I did the best I could."

"You don't have anything to worry about, Senthil. I am sure you'll pass with flying colors."

He went straight to Penny as soon as he entered the Haven. They talked about the exam, his time with Shiva, and the phone call to India. She told him that Ms. Hillman slipped and fell over the weekend and was unable to walk. She was pretty upset that she might not be able to walk to her granddaughter's graduation. Senthil went to visit her in her room.

He did an orthopedic assessment of her leg. She was sore in her hip and had pain with weight-bearing.

"I am so depressed," she said.

"Don't worry, Ms. Hillman. As long as you have not broken anything, we can get you walking again. We have three weeks until graduation."

"Bless your heart. My family is coming to pick me up today to go see a doctor and get an X-ray done."

"Great. I'll come and see you as soon as you get back."

The weather was warming up, and Amanda and Rachel were treating patients out in the courtyard at lunchtime. Senthil conducted gait training for his patients out there too. Penny came out to let him know that Ms. Hillman was back and did not have a fracture. She also told him that she had been given an order for physical therapy and occupational therapy.

Senthil brought Ms. Hillman to the therapy room.

"My doctor said the X-ray of my hip did not show any fracture. He prescribed some Ibuprofen for me."

"That's great. We'll start with some hot packs and TENS therapy for pain and some gradual mobilization exercises. You can bear as much weight as your right leg can tolerate." He reassured her that he would see her in therapy every day.

On the way back home that evening, Pat drove him as usual.

"Since my exams are over, I don't know what I am going to do when I get home, Pat," he said.

"That's right, Senthil. You were studying all this while. What are you going to do?"

"The weather is so nice. Maybe I'll jog down to the river and explore a little bit of Glasgow. I feel so sluggish. I haven't exercised for the past five months."

"That sounds like a good idea, Senthil."

"Besides, the sun sets late, and there is light outside until 9:00, which is unbelievable. In India, even in the summers, the sun sets by 6:00 or 7:00 PM the latest."

"Really? I thought it would be the opposite. I wish Donald and I could go visit India someday. Speaking of Donald, would you mind if I use your phone to call him? I forgot to tell him that I have to stop by my hairdresser. He was planning to fire up the grill tonight for supper."

"Not at all, Pat. You are welcome to use the phone."

He also asked Pat if she would be offended if he walked to the Haven and back since the weather was nice and he was in no hurry to get back home to study. He told her he could use the exercise, and Pat agreed with one condition. If it rained or the weather worsened, he had to call her for a ride before he decided to walk to the Haven in bad weather.

Senthil removed his shoes as soon as he entered the house. Pat was fumbling with her heels, and Senthil said, "Oh Pat, you can leave your shoes on."

"No Senthil, this is your home, and I want to respect your customs. Oh my, this is a big house for one person. Where is the furniture?"

"Yes Pat, it is huge for me. This is an unfurnished place, and if I was afraid to buy a car, you could understand why I didn't want to buy any furniture."

"That I do. How about renting some? There is a Rent-A-Center in Moberly that'll deliver."

"Being the eldest son, I just want to save as much as I can so that I can help my family."

"Your parents and siblings should be proud of you, Senthil. I have never met anyone quite like you."

She called Donald and took Senthil's leave. Senthil changed and put on his sneakers. He jogged down to the river and sat by the bank, watching a few old men fish. They were sitting on folding chairs, with beers in one hand and fishing poles in the other. They seemed to be enjoying the company and the beer more than focusing on catching a fish. He was not the only one out jogging. He saw quite a few people jogging about, taking advantage of the wonderful weather.

Jogging back home, he saw a guy coming from the opposite direction. As they got closer and were about to cross each other, Senthil smiled and greeted him with a "Hi." At the same time, the other guy said, "What's up?" Senthil stopped to ask what he meant, but the guy ran on. Senthil was confused why someone would ask a question like that and not wait for a response.

It happened again as he crossed the road and set his foot on the curb in front of his house. As a guy passed him on the sidewalk, he said, "Hey what's up?" Senthil answered with more of a question, "Hi, my house?" He meant that he lived upstairs, but he wondered why the other guy wanted to know or why he did not even bother to stop to hear the answer.

The next day, as soon as he entered the Haven, he went straight to Penny and asked her why those guys had asked him "What's up?" when they did not wait for a response.

Penny doubled over in laughter. "If I laugh any harder, I am going to pee my pants," she said. Senthil looked at her puzzled. "I am not laughing at you, Senthil. It's just that we take so many things for granted and forget how hard it can be for someone from another country, even if they speak good English, but it is so funny—the way you say it and your honest reaction." She wiped her tears and said, "Those guys were just saying hello. They were not asking you what is up as in "what is above?" It is not a literal question, and what they actually meant was what is new or what's happening in your life now."

"Really? That doesn't make any sense at all, Penny. Isn't hi or hello a lot simpler, especially when they don't wait for an answer to such a loaded question? Anyway, what do you say in return?"

Penny laughed and said, "Well, you can say not much or nothing, and ask back what's up with you."

Senthil still did not understand and went back to the therapy room to get the hot pack ready for Ms. Hillman's therapy session. As he waited for the hot pack to be ready, he sat down to write some progress notes and review the orders for new evaluations.

Amanda walked in, and out of curiosity, Senthil said, "Hey Amanda, what's up?"

"Nothing much" was her initial instant reply. She did not pause; she did not think—it was like a reflex. He did the same thing with Rachel when he saw her, and she replied, "The usual. What's up with you?"

Senthil was fascinated. He had attended an English medium school in India, had Anglo-Indians for neighbors, and spoke English growing up. Coming to America with a good command of English, the last thing on his mind was that he would have trouble conversing with people. Little did he know that this was only the beginning.

When he returned home from the Haven, he was surprised to see Larry from the Haven climbing down the stairs with Mr. Spencer close behind.

"What are you doing here, Larry?" asked Senthil.

"You'll see when you go upstairs. I got to get something from the truck. I'll be up in a second."

He looked at Mr. Spencer who just shrugged and asked Senthil to go into the house. As he entered the house and went to the living room, he saw a futon against one wall and a table and a chair by the window. He turned to Mr. Spencer, who pointed to the bedroom. There was a mattress on a box spring in his bedroom. He stood speechless, only to have his jaw drop when Larry walked up with a small 13-inch TV.

"What's going on, Larry?"

"Well, they asked me to drop all this off here, and I am just doing what I was told."

Larry explained that since he was living without any furniture, Pat had talked to Kathy and Penny and all of them got together and asked Larry to pick up some of their spare furniture and drop it off here. The table and chair were from Kathy, the futon was from Penny, the mattress and TV were from Pat.

After Larry left, Senthil immediately called Pat. He thanked her profusely. He couldn't find appropriate words to appreciate her kindness and generosity. The more he talked, the more overwhelmed he got. Pat told him they all were glad to help, and it was just a way to say thank you for all that he was doing. He gave Penny, Kathy, and Pat all a big hug when he saw them the next day.

The TV came with a rabbit antenna, and he was able to get some local channels. He got hooked on three TV shows: *Seinfeld*, *Home Improvement*, and *Saved by the Bell*. These became his guide to American pop culture. He did not miss out on a single episode that aired and watched them all religiously. He became a big fan of Kramer and Wilson. Elaine's hair reminded him of Sumathi's hair. He was not sure if it was because they looked similar or because he thought about Sumathi all the time and tried to see her in everything that even had some remote likeness to her.

As the weather grew warmer, the Haven had more and more visitors. Amanda and Rachel invited Senthil to Columbia for the weekend. He appreciated their offer, but he was focused on getting Ms. Hillman back on her feet. He visited the Haven on the weekend on his own time to work on Ms. Hillman's mobilization, strength, and gait training. She was very thankful for his commitment to getting her ready for her granddaughter's graduation at the end of the month.

One weekend, after working with Ms. Hillman, Senthil went jogging down the 1st Street, all the way under the historic Glasgow Bridge over the Missouri River and ended at the Stump Island Recreation Park. He did not know about the park and ventured in. It was lush and green with trails, a shelter house with park benches and grills, and public fishing access spots. As he was running along one of the trails, he saw two girls moving towards him on bicycles. As soon as they spotted him, they split to either side of the trail to let him run through the space between them.

Senthil stayed in the middle of the trail. As the girls rode past him, he waved hi. One of them said, "How's it hanging?" They rode off before he could think of a suitable reply.

When he got back to work the following Monday, he went straight to Penny and asked her how to respond when someone asked, "How's it hanging?" He also wanted to know what it meant. Penny asked him where he had heard that, and he told her about his run-in with the girls on the bikes. She laughed and told him that it was just like "What's up."

He said, "That doesn't make any sense. How is how's it hanging the same as saying hello?"

"I don't know, Senthil. It's just something people say. It's slang and popular culture. I am sure you have something unique like this in India which I wouldn't understand."

"I guess that's true, but please tell me how I should respond in case someone else says how's it hanging."

Penny laughed and said, "Well, the next time someone asks you how's it hanging, just respond by saying low and a little to the left." She could not stop laughing as she said it.

"Why are you laughing?"

"It'll just be funny to see a foreigner speak American slang, that's all."

It was the end of June, and graduation weekend was here. Ms. Hillman was able to walk to the graduation and back. She proudly attended her granddaughter's graduation and thanked Senthil for his dedication. Senthil told her that his work had been easy because he had a highly motivated and hard-working patient.

It was the week before the Fourth of July. The Haven was preparing for the annual Fourth of July barbeque. Senthil was excited. This was his very first American holiday and barbeque. Fourth of July fell on a Tuesday, and Amanda and Rachel planned on taking Monday and Tuesday off and make it a long weekend to celebrate with their respective families. Penny and Kathy were the organizers of the celebration at the Haven. The Haven was going to buy all the meat, and all the staff working that day were supposed to bring the sides, desserts, soda, and beer. The families of the Haven residents were welcome to join their loved ones, and Kathy had arranged for fireworks in the evening.

Senthil offered to make some *tandoori chicken* and *potato masala*, an Indian style mashed potato. The weekend preceding Fourth of July, he walked to the IGA grocery to get 10 lbs of chicken drumsticks, lemon, onions, potatoes, and plain yogurt. On Monday night, he marinated the chicken drumsticks in the yogurt mixed with Indian spices. He went easy on the chili powder for his American friends.

On Fourth of July, Senthil finished treating his patients early so he could get back home to make the mashed potatoes and bring it along with the marinated chicken drumsticks to be grilled at the Haven. Penny gave him a ride to his house and told him to call her as soon as he was ready to leave so that he did not have to carry all the food uphill.

He boiled the potatoes with a teaspoon of turmeric powder and salt and then peeled and mashed them, leaving behind some lumps. He sautéed some onions and jalapeno peppers with mustard seeds and added the mashed potatoes. The end result was nice mild yellow-colored lumpy mashed potato with translucent sweet onions. He removed and discarded the jalapeno peppers. Once he was done, he called Penny, who picked him up.

He was gone for only a couple of hours, but when he arrived at the Haven, the driveway up the hill was lined with cars, minivans, and trucks. The front of the Haven itself looked like a carnival. Half of the parking lot had been cleared, and there were a lot of people in front of the Haven and tables decorated in red, white and blue. At the far end, he saw Larry standing by two big grills. Penny took the potatoes inside and asked Senthil to take the chicken drumsticks to Larry, who placed them in a cooler.

Senthil went inside to help the staff transfer the residents who could not ambulate to wheelchairs and assist people who needed help walking out to join the party. He helped carry the food out to the tables. Larry asked Senthil if he had any special instructions for cooking the chicken drumsticks. Senthil said that they were grilled like any other chicken. He had cut up lemon wedges to be squeezed over them if people preferred a little tang.

There was a lot of food: assorted veggies with dips, salads, pasta, mac and cheese, and along with Senthil's Indian style lumpy mashed potato, there were German potato salad, American potato salad, watermelon, and other fruits, and lots of cookies, pies, and cakes.

The staff had set up music to be played by loudspeakers. The mood was festive. After making sure all the residents and their families had food to eat and had settled down, the staff formed a line towards the grill. Senthil got a couple of hamburgers with cheese. He politely declined when Larry offered him hot dogs. As he sat down with Penny, she pointed to his hamburgers and asked, "You are eating that? I thought people from India considered cow as sacred and didn't eat beef."

"Yes, Penny, cows are considered sacred in India because they provide us with milk. But I had many Anglo-Indian and Christian friends growing up and got used to it. My family is okay with it as long as I don't bring it to our house. But why you do you ask? I am only eating a hamburger."

"What do you think is in a hamburger, Senthil?"

"Ham, which is pork, right?"

Penny laughed and said, "No! It's beef, not pork."

Senthil thought she was teasing him. Why would it be called hamburger if it had no ham in it? He tried to argue with her but learned that he was wrong and that the hamburger indeed had beef. When he told them why he had declined hot dogs, Penny and everybody at the table lost it. They could not stop laughing over the fact that he thought hot dogs were made of dog meat. He took a bite of Penny's hot dog and found it delicious.

Senthil helped clean up and get the residents ready to watch the fireworks. Larry was the master of ceremonies, and he was directing where the residents were to be seated. They were all moved to one side. Kathy turned off the floodlights when Larry gave her the signal. The place became dark.

Larry put on quite a show. The fireworks looked brilliant. Coming from India, Senthil was used to fireworks on the Hindu religious festival of Diwali—the festival of lights, but most of the fireworks were lit on the ground and made loud noises. Only a few simple fireworks lit up the sky.

In contrast, Larry created a dazzling display of fireworks in the sky. There were shimmering swirls, cascading waterfalls, sparkling showers, and mesmerizing explosions of colors. It was amazing, and everybody enjoyed it immensely. Senthil stayed back to help take the Haven residents back to their rooms and tuck them in.

Senthil was not merely a physical therapist at the Haven; he had become an integral part of it. He voluntarily participated in all the activities and helped everyone as much as possible. It was his way of repaying for their kindness and generosity.

Senthil was walking down the hall when he heard his name. He turned around, and it was Ms. Hillman. She was walking down the hall holding a young girl's hand. "Senthil! Come here. Meet my granddaughter. She is visiting from Chicago. Janna, this is Senthil, my physical therapist. He is from India."

"Hey, how's it hanging?" said Janna.

"Low and a bit to the left," replied Senthil.

Ms. Hillman was furious. She could not believe her ears. "How dare you talk to my granddaughter like that?"

"But Ms. Hillman—"

"Don't you ever talk to me again. I thought you were a gentleman. Janna, take me back to my room."

Senthil was confused. He tried to talk to her and followed them as Ms. Hillman hobbled back to her room and shut the door in his face. Senthil tried to talk to them but to no avail. Ms. Hillman asked him to leave.

He walked straight to Penny and told her Ms. Hillman was mad at him, and he did not understand why. He was in tears as he talked to her. Penny tried to calm him down, but Senthil just kept on rambling.

Finally, she said, "Stop it, Senthil. You are not making any sense. Please tell me what happened."

Senthil told her what had happened. Penny's jaw dropped. She said that it was her fault and ran to Ms. Hillman's room. She explained to Ms. Hillman and Janna that she had put him up to it and that it was her fault. Like a bag of marbles on the loose, they came out laughing. Senthil was not amused when he learned about Penny's prank, but he could not stay mad at her.

With the board exam under his belt, the rest of the summer looked as bright and warm as the long sunny days. Since he no longer had to study for the boards, he asked Hema if there were any opportunities for overtime or some other part-time job. Every dollar he earned or saved had the potential to cut short the time he had to spend away from Sumathi and his family.

The Haven was a small nursing home and had just enough patients to keep him busy. There was no room for overtime. However, Hema said she could find him a PRN assignment on the weekend in a facility either in Moberly or Columbia. He would need a car, as Glasgow did not have any opportunity for home health-care services.

Senthil was apprehensive about buying a car before securing his permanent license. So, he spent the weekends exploring Glasgow on foot, watching TV, and writing long letters to Sumathi and his family. He wrote a letter each weekend, as did Sumathi. His was more of prose, and hers more poetry. The long distance did not dampen their romance.

His siblings also wrote to him. He was very fond of Rathi for her innocence and free spirit and always read her letters first. He was especially proud of Eshwari, who at that young age when all her friends had a carefree life, shared all the household chores with her *amma*. She shepherded all the younger siblings and took care of them—beginning with helping them with their homework to getting ready for school.

It was already August of 1994. One day, Senthil was finishing up his progress notes on a Friday evening, when Hema called the Rehab Department of the Haven. Amanda answered the phone. "Senthil, it's your boss lady for you," she yelled.

"Hello Hema, how are you?"

"I am doing well. Hope you are too. I called to tell you something very important. Hope you are sitting down for this."

Her tone made him uneasy. She sounded very serious. "What is it, Hema?" he asked.

"Well, I am not quite sure where to start or how to tell you."

"Hema, just say it. Is it family? Is it Sumathi? What's wrong?" His voice trembled.

"Oh, I am so sorry I scared you. You passed your boards. Your letter just arrived. You have your permanent PT license."

"Oh, my goodness Hema! This is wonderful! Thank you very much. I was so scared something bad had happened."

Hema apologized for the stunt she had pulled. "What about Shiva?" he asked. Hema told him he had passed too, and she was going to call and let him know as soon as she hung up the phone.

Like a little kid who just had his cake slip and fall into a bowl of ice cream, Senthil leaped in joy.

"What was all that about?" asked Amanda.

"I passed my boards! I got my permanent license!"

Amanda and Rachel ran over to give him a hug. "We had no doubts," they said.

The news spread like a summer brushfire in California. Penny and Kathy were the first to congratulate him. Pat announced the news on the overhead speaker for all of the Haven to hear. Senthil looked at his watch: it was midnight in India. Even though it was happy news, he did not want to wake up his family in the middle of the night. He wanted to share the news with Sumathi, but he knew it had to wait.

Like an army of ants marching towards a pot of honey, the residents of the Haven came to congratulate him on passing his boards.

Senthil called Shiva that night to congratulate him. He told him he was going to wait until tomorrow night to call home, as it would be Sunday morning in India. Shiva did not have his patience. He had already called Maria. Senthil had the most relaxing Saturday morning ever. He wrote a letter to Sumathi, explaining the emotional roller coaster he had felt when he heard

Hema tell him about the results and the reaction of his colleagues and the patients at the Haven.

Senthil could not wait for night to set in. He called home at 9:00 PM. His heart revved like his motorbike as the phone rang. It was 6:30 AM on a Sunday morning in India. Eshwari would be up early to get a head start with breakfast, and Senthil was expecting to hear her voice.

"Hello!"

It was not Eshwari. Senthil felt his knees go weak at the voice. He lowered himself to the carpet.

"Hi, Sumathi. I was not expecting you. How are you?"

"Hi, dear! I am well. Hope you are too. Maria told me you would be calling home this morning. So, I came over before going to see my first patient, and Eshwari asked me to pick up the phone."

She thought this was a regular phone call and he was just calling his family to say hello. Maria had not wanted to ruin the surprise. He asked her about her family and her work. She was more eager to know about his life and his work and did not want to waste time talking about her, but she realized how important it was for him and so she humored him. Eventually, she said, "Enough about me, dear. I want to hear about what's going on in your life."

That was when Senthil realized he had forgotten why he had called home after he heard her voice.

"I passed my boards and now have a permanent PT license," he blurted.

"Wow! Congratulations honey! I never had any doubt, but it sure is nice to hear it officially." Tears ran down her cheeks. She did not want to ruin the surprise for others. She placed the receiver down and ran to the kitchen to get Eshwari, who had left to give her some privacy. Eshwari had made a cup of coffee for Sumathi in the meantime.

Sumathi took it from her hand and told her to get the phone, and she would take care of the coffee for the rest of the family. Eshwari ran to the phone. Sumathi finished up in the kitchen with six cups of coffee and went to the kids' room to wake them up. She sat on the floor next to Rathi, gently shook her, and whispered, "Wake up sleepy head!" Rathi opened her eyes and was surprised to see Sumathi.

She said, "Hi *anni*, when did you come?"

"Your brother is on the phone. Wake the guys up, and please let your parents know."

Rathi was not as quiet or gentle as Sumathi. She kicked the two brothers lying on the other side of the room and yelled, "Wake up! *Anna* is on the phone." She then ran to her parents' room to wake them up. Just as she was about to knock, her *amma* opened the door. "*Anna* is on the phone," she announced and ran to the phone. She pestered Eshwari, who finally gave the phone to her. Nanda and Bala joined her, and it became raucous. Gentle rain gave way to a hurricane. They were all screaming over the phone, and the cacophony only simmered down when they heard their *appa* say, "One at a time. He won't be able to understand anything you say."

Senthil's parents patiently sat down for them to finish, and they all yelled at the same time: "*Anna* passed his board exam." They gave the phone to their *appa* then, and he congratulated Senthil, asked how he was doing, and handed the phone over to his *amma*. Even though she was pretending to be calm and patient, he knew how anxious she was.

Sumathi walked out with a cup of coffee and the morning paper and handed them to Senthil's *appa*. She then bent down to touch his feet for his blessings.

"Long live, my child. I am so glad you were able to come and share this good news with us. Please stay for breakfast."

Sumathi smiled and nodded, and then went back to the kitchen to join Eshwari. They quickly prepared some *idli,* coconut chutney, and *kesari*. They all sat down to eat an early breakfast, which was rather unusual for a Sunday morning. They knew Sumathi had to leave soon.

"I wish *anna* were here with us now," said Bala.

"Sumathi is here in his place. We should be happy about that," Rathi said.

"Well said," added their *amma*, and Sumathi blushed.

After breakfast, Sumathi helped Eshwari clean up. She then took leave, as she had to go to see her patients for the day. Senthil's parents asked her to convey their regards to her parents and siblings. Nanda came back hurriedly. He had run down to the corner store to get a small string of jasmine flowers for Sumathi. He gave it to his *amma*, who affectionately pinned it to Sumathi's wavy hair. She thanked them and took leave. She could not wait to be a part of this loving family. She felt lucky that his parents adored her.

Work in the Haven was busy as usual. Senthil had more free time on his hands during the weekends now that he did not have to spend the days and nights studying or worrying about his license. A few weeks later, on a Saturday morning, Senthil heard a knock on his door as he was getting out of the shower. He donned his clothes and rushed to the door. He was not expecting anyone and had no clue who could be knocking at his door at 7:00 in the morning.

He opened the door and was surprised to see Shiva. Before he could welcome Shiva into his house, the latter grabbed his hand and dragged him down the stairs. He pointed to a shiny new Toyota Camry and said, "1994 Toyota Camry V6 LE. What do you think?"

Senthil was impressed by the new car. Like a kid in a candy store, he opened the car door and began to fiddle with the features. The car had a sunroof, a cassette player, and automatic windows and locking system. It still smelled new.

Shiva asked Senthil to take a picture of him with the car. He wanted to send it to Maria. They enjoyed the weekend driving around Glasgow. They drove to Moberly and had a buffet at KFC for lunch. They spent the rest of the weekend playing cards, talking about home, and watching TV. Shiva left late at night on Sunday.

Senthil felt no need to buy a car anytime soon. He wanted to save as much money as he could. He continued to walk to the Haven and the grocery store and explore Glasgow on foot. He knew that every penny he saved was a step closer to Sumathi.

Senthil stayed busy the rest of the summer; he was getting used to life in America. He continued to impress the people at the Haven with his work ethic, bedside manners, and friendly nature. His only regret was that he was wasting his time on the weekends. He was used to working seven days a week in India. Until the boards, he was content with his work schedule. Now that he had passed the exam, he wished he could work during the weekends too. But there was no other facility around Glasgow that Hema had a contract with.

Everything was fine until the last week of October when Senthil received that fateful call from Hema. He felt the rug was pulled from underneath his feet when Hema told him that she had lost the Haven's contract to a bigger company that underbid her. She told him she had tried her best, but there was no choice other than finding another contract for him.

Senthil talked to Kathy to see if he could work directly for the Haven without a contract company. She promised to look into it. They decided not to tell anyone until they knew for sure. Kathy called her company and Hema to discuss the options and the possibility of hiring Senthil directly without a contract company. Senthil was working under an H1-B visa filed by Hema. Haven or the new company that had secured the contract would have to file a new H1-B visa and also reimburse Hema $10,000 for all the expenses incurred in bringing a foreign-trained therapist to the country, something which the Haven or the new contract company could not afford.

The Haven was sad to learn of Senthil's impending departure. Penny was devastated. She pleaded with Kathy to do something to keep Senthil back.

Senthil was the most heartbroken of all. Within a few months, Glasgow had become a home away from home for him; the thought of leaving Glasgow and the Haven made him sick to his stomach. He had come there on a contract for three months and had voluntarily extended his contract twice, which was unheard of in the Haven's recent history. He would have been happy to stay there for the rest of his time in America.

Amanda and Rachel were grief-stricken.

"Who is going to co-treat with me? It is all just business for them, and they care only about their bottom line. They don't care about the Haven or our patients." Amanda lashed out. Amanda and Rachel did their part and tried to talk to their respective companies to retain Senthil but to no avail.

The residents of the Haven were upset. Ms. Jones and Ms. Hillman were inconsolable.

Ms. Hillman who had been there the longest said, "I have seen many therapists come and go but none like Senthil."

Ms. Jones wondered if a bake sale would help to keep Senthil at the Haven. The staff and residents at the Haven understood that Senthil was not deserting them and felt helpless.

Friday, September 30, was his last day at the Haven and in Glasgow. Kathy, on behalf of the Haven, its residents, and employees hosted a big farewell party. The last few days had been bittersweet. Senthil thanked all the patients he had worked with in the Haven for giving him the opportunity to be their physical therapist. He thanked Penny for being a friend and his partner in crime, and for making the Haven such a fun place to work. He made a pot of chicken biryani for Pat to thank her for driving him to work in the winter. He thanked Kathy and all the staff members for being so supportive of him and Larry for furnishing his house. He left a note for his landlord, as he was out of town. Amanda and Rachel volunteered to take him to the airport.

Chapter 16 — Prince in Princeton

HEMA SECURED A JOB FOR SENTHIL IN PRINCETON, Indiana.

Princeton, with a population of 7,500 people, was a little bigger than Glasgow but still met his criterion. He was going to be working in a community hospital this time. The hospital did not have any therapist, and the administrator was desperate after firing his current physical therapist and occupational therapist for excessive tardiness and numerous complaints from patients.

Princeton Hospital was a small community hospital with a forty-bed inpatient medical and surgical unit. With a newly started seven-bed intensive care unit, the administrator was desperate to staff the Therapy Department with at least a physical therapist, to begin with, and then expand to include an occupational and a speech therapist. This was also a new contract for Hema.

The closest airport to Princeton was Evansville, Indiana, which was about forty miles south. Senthil flew to Evansville on Friday, September 30. He took a cab to a motel on Dixon Street and spent the weekend walking around Princeton. His first order of business was to check out the hospital. He asked the front desk for directions to the Princeton Hospital and was pleasantly surprised to learn that it was only a mile away. He walked to the hospital to acquaint himself with the route so he wouldn't get lost on Monday or be late.

Princeton was definitely larger than Glasgow, but he felt safe here. He hiked to Lafayette Park and walked around the large pond and the trails. On the way back to the motel, he stopped at McDonald's and got two Big Macs for $2. He could not believe the amount of food he got for $2. He was famished and ate both of them while watching the TV. In the evening, he walked to the nearest gas station to get the apartment guide. Unlike Glasgow, Princeton had a few apartments to offer, and he marked the two prospects that looked promising.

Monday, October 3, was Senthil's first day at Princeton Hospital. He woke up early, got ready, and walked to the hospital. He was supposed to meet the hospital administrator, Mr. Blazer, in the lobby at 7:00 AM. Senthil arrived in the lobby at 6:30 AM. He sat down and perused the newspaper and magazines. Mr. Blazer arrived on the dot.

"Hi, you must be Senthil!"

"Yes, Mr. Blazer. Good morning. How are you?"

"I am doing great, and please call me Mike."

Mike gave him a quick tour of the four-story hospital. The first floor housed all the administrative offices and the cafeteria. The second floor was occupied by the four operating rooms, the PACU, and surgical waiting rooms. The third floor had the ICU and the inpatient units, and finally, the fourth floor was home to the Rehab Department and a sixteen-bed skilled nursing facility. Even though the skilled nursing wing was a part of the hospital, the place was leased and run by a private group.

Mike walked him around the Rehab Department. It was nothing fancy, but it had all the basic amenities such as therapy mats, weights, TheraBand, wax therapy, ultrasound, TENS unit, infrared lamps, and interferential therapy units. He informed Senthil about the previous therapist from a different company whom he had to let go due to their tardiness, inconsiderate behavior, and inability and insensitiveness to meet the patients' needs.

Mike then introduced him to Connie Gibson, the marketing director. He asked both of them to work together to create a new identity for the Therapy Department and gain the trust of Princeton citizens. Connie took him back to the Therapy Department, where Jennifer, the rehab secretary, was waiting. Connie introduced him to Jennifer and told him that she would pick him up for lunch with the administrator, the chief of staff, and a few physicians.

After exchanging pleasantries, Jennifer told him that his first patient was to see him at 9:00 AM. Their chief complaint was back pain. Senthil did not have time; he wanted to be ready. He began to clean the therapy mat and the equipment. Jenny stopped him, asked him to look over the schedule, and took over dusting the mat and the equipment.

His first patient arrived on time. Joseph Martin was fifty-four years old, and at 6'2", he was a burlesque version of Sean Connery. Looking at his upper body, it was obvious that he used to work out in his younger days. His beer gut and chubby face, however, made it obvious that he had let himself go.

"Good morning, Mr. Martin! My name is Senthil. I am the new physical therapist."

"Call me Joe. What did you say your name was?"

"Ah, Senthil. It rhymes with lentil."

"Oh!"

"Please tell me about your back pain. When did it start and how long have you had it?"

Joe was a truck driver and had been cruising the highways for the past fourteen years. He reported developing a dull lower backache approximately two years ago while he was behind the wheels. His pain eased off when he was off the road and taking some ibuprofen. The pain gradually worsened and became present when he was off the road too. Over the past two months, it had been crippling, and he had to cancel his routes.

"Did the pain start after a particular incident?"

"No, I didn't have an accident if that's what you mean, and I watch my back when I lift anything."

"Is the pain present at all times or does it come and go?"

"It used to come and go, but for the past three months, it's constant."

"Does anything make it better or worse?"

"Any kind of activity, especially bending, even to put on my britches or tie my shoelaces, makes it worse, and rest and ibuprofen make it better."

"Does the pain radiate anywhere?"

"Yes, to my right cheek."

For a second, Senthil stood stunned like a cow on astroturf. "Right cheek?" he muttered to himself. He must have heard it wrong. "Where did you say it radiates again?"

"I said right cheek."

Senthil heard him but could not comprehend it. He could see Joe was getting frustrated with having to repeat himself. "I am sorry, could you please repeat that again?"

"RIGHT CHEEK!" yelled Joe.

As the last straw on the camel's back, Senthil asked, "Could you please spell that?"

"JESUS CHRIST! CAN I GET SOMEONE WHO SPEAKS ENGLISH? I am tired of these foreigners coming into my country without speaking A LICK OF ENGLISH! I need to speak to the administrator." Joe got up from his chair. He had had enough. Jenny rushed in, looking alarmed.

Like a frightened turtle, Senthil retracted. He became anxious and nervous. He thought he was going to get fired on his first day. He might not know English, but he knew his anatomy pretty well. Sumathi always failed to stump him while asking questions about the origin and insertion of muscles and its nerve supply. He knew for sure that there were no lumbar or sacral nerves that supplied the right cheek or any other part of the face for that matter.

As a last-ditch effort, he said, "I am really very sorry, Mr. Martin. Could you please point with one finger where the pain is radiating to?"

Somewhat enraged, Joe turned, and pointing to his right buttocks with his middle finger for emphasis, he said, "Right there! Is that enough or do you want me to draw a picture? Goddamit!"

Senthil let out a big sigh of relief, smiled, and raised his hand to stop Jenny who was trying to say something to calm Joe.

His smile only infuriated Joe, but before he could say anything, Senthil said, "Well Mr. Martin, that makes sense, and I can fix that. I was confused because there is no nerve from the lumbar or sacral spine that innervates the face."

Though they were speaking English, they realized they were indeed speaking two different languages. Senthil explained to Joe why he was confused: he had never known that the gluteus maximus was also referred to as the cheeks. Joe laughed out loud. His frustration quickly dissipated into amusement.

"Leave it to me, doc. I'll teach you American slang. By the time you are done with me, we'll replace your British English with American English."

Senthil tried to explain that he was a physical therapist and not a doctor, but his efforts were in vain. Senthil performed his physical examination on Joe. He documented all the pertinent positives and negatives. He discussed his findings with Joe and decided on a treatment plan. He taught him some back precautions and back stretching exercises. He also educated Joe on the importance of reducing his belly.

Joe was impressed. "That was the most thorough examination and explanation anyone has ever given me. I understand what's going on now, and that helps. Thanks, doc!" he said.

Senthil again told him he was not a doctor, and Joe replied, "Dammit, you are my doc! Besides, I don't want to butcher your name."

Senthil was relieved. He told Joe his fear of getting fired the way things had started, and Joe apologized for his rant. But Senthil said it was not necessary, as it was only miscommunication.

After Joe left, Jenny exclaimed, "I am impressed you turned an adversary into an admirer."

Senthil smiled. "Phew! That was a close call."

They looked at the appointment book. Jenny was very organized; she had filed all the inpatient PT orders and all the outpatient PT orders separately. The inpatient orders had the patient name, diagnosis, reason for the consultation, the room number, and the physician's name. The outpatient had similar information with the appointment time.

His outpatients for the day included a patient with periarthritis of the shoulder for mobilization and pain relief, a patient with plantar fasciitis, and a patient with ACL repair for mobilization and weight-bearing exercise. On the inpatient side, he had a stroke and a hip replacement patient. In between his outpatients, Jenny showed him the patients on the schedule.

Connie came back to take him for the lunch meeting. She took him down to the hospital cafeteria. Since she was the marketing director, she wanted to know his thoughts about expanding the market for the Therapy Department. He wanted her to notify all the hospital physicians and nearby clinics that Princeton Hospital now had a working PT Department. He emphasized the importance of hiring an occupational therapist and a speech therapist to increase clientele.

Connie asked him if he would like to be the one visiting the local clinics. Senthil told her that he did not have a car and his first order of business was to find an apartment close to the hospital so he could walk to the hospital. Connie informed him that the hospital guest house was available for rent. It was a fully furnished one-bedroom house, and she said that she would be happy to take him there after work if he was interested.

Senthil asked about the rent and was pleasantly surprised to learn it was $375 a month. He agreed to take it without seeing it. After all, the one-bedroom apartments he had seen in the apartment guide ranged from $350 to $450, and they were unfurnished.

Connie came back later in the day to give him the keys. She asked him if he needed any help moving into the house, and Senthil thanked her and said that he just had two suitcases and nothing much. That evening, after work, Senthil went back to the hotel and checked out. He called a cab and took a short ride to his new home.

The house was cozy; it was furnished with all the basic amenities, including a TV. He asked Connie to disconnect the cable, as he had no need for it. He was more than happy with the basic channels received with the rabbit antenna. The kitchen had dishes, including pots, pans, plates, and silverware.

Connie worked on a full-page ad on the *Princeton Daily* newspaper about the Therapy Department. Senthil screened all the inpatients in the skilled nursing facility and was able to identify the need for physical therapy in seven of them. He contacted their physicians for an order for evaluation and treatment. He met the surgeons in the hospital and talked to them about a postoperative physical therapy order for early mobilization of patients, especially elderly and patients with multiple comorbidities. He was able to convince them, and within a matter of a couple of weeks, all patients admitted overnight after surgery were ordered to be cleared by physical therapy before discharge.

Senthil became very busy very quickly. He prioritized the outpatients and remained flexible with the inpatients. Outpatients were able to come in as early as 6:00 AM and as late as 6:00 PM, so they did not have to miss work. He came in early or stayed back until late, depending on the patient schedule. Mike became aware of this when he came to the hospital at 6:00 AM one day for a board meeting and met Senthil in the elevator. He was surprised to see Senthil in so early. Senthil briefly told him the measures he had taken thus far to increase the caseload. Mike was impressed and gave him a pat on the shoulder.

Within a month, Jenny and Senthil could hardly keep up. They had built a sufficient caseload to convince the hospital to hire an occupational therapist and a speech pathologist. Senthil was instrumental in talking to Hema and securing her the contract for them too. Hema gave him a referral bonus of $250 for each contract, which was a surprise for Senthil. She thanked him for earning a good reputation for the company.

Mike also promoted Senthil as the interim director of the Rehab Department, which came with a raise of $500 a month. Senthil was very thankful, but both Hema and Mike assured him that he had earned it.

Senthil could not dismiss Jenny's help with the schedule and taking phone calls, so he gave her a $100 check for being his partner in the success. He was able to talk to Mike and convince him to give her a raise as well. This only motivated both of them to work harder. Hema sent Shelby Rogers, who was a native of Darien, Illinois, as the occupational therapist and her friend Heather Bramble as the speech pathologist. Heather was from Darien too. They rented a two-bedroom apartment in Evansville since the social life Princeton had to offer did not quite meet their expectation.

It was not a surprise that at the end of three months Senthil's contract got extended at Princeton Hospital.

Shelby, Heather, and Senthil worked well as a team to improve the quality of the therapy services provided at Princeton Hospital. Thanksgiving Day was approaching, and Mike invited Senthil to attend the Executive Officers' Thanksgiving dinner. This was his first Thanksgiving dinner in America. He learned more about the significance and the meaning of the day; it reminded him of Pongal, the Hindu harvest festival that was held to celebrate the first harvest of the year in January.

The hospital dinner was on Friday night the week before the actual Thanksgiving Day. Senthil declined Jenny's offer to ask her cousin to attend the dinner with him. He went stag instead. He got to meet most of the physicians, surgeons, and administrators working at the hospital. They had all come with their spouses, except for Connie's husband who was out of town.

There were two Indian physicians: Dr. Srinivasa Reddy, a cardiologist, and Dr. Girish Nair, an internist. Mike introduced them to Senthil. Everybody was surprised to learn that Dr. Reddy, Dr. Nair, and Senthil could not speak to each other in their native language. They spoke different languages. Senthil spoke Tamil, Dr. Nair spoke Malayalam, and Dr. Reddy spoke Telugu. After all, India had close to 1,500 spoken languages, 150 of which had a sizeable speaking population and 22 enjoyed official status.

Dr. Nair and Dr. Reddy's families were planning to get together on Thanksgiving Day and asked Senthil to join them for dinner. He accepted their invitation. Dr. Nair explained the directions to his house and asked him to be there by noon.

Jenny, Shelby, Heather, and Senthil worked that Sunday so that they could take Friday off and make it a long weekend. Heather and Shelby were driving home for Thanksgiving. Jenny and her husband were going to her parents' house to celebrate Thanksgiving. Senthil went to Dr. Nair's house. Dr. Reddy's family was already there. Dr. Nair welcomed him and introduced him to his wife Menaka and his children Ajith and Roshini. He also got to know Dr. Reddy's wife Mayuri and their children, Prakash and Banu Priya. All the kids were in middle school.

Dr. Nair had marinated a 12 lbs turkey in Indian spices. He removed it from the refrigerator and placed it in the oven. Menaka and Mayuri made all the fixings, including both the traditional stuffing and cranberry salad, along with vegetables cooked in Indian style, and rice. There was beans *porriyal*, potatoes, and peas masala, *bisibelabath*[43], and *avial*[44]. Accompanying the pumpkin and apple pies were Indian desserts: *rasamalai, basundhi,* and *laddu.*

The kids were getting restless. Senthil escorted them to the backyard to keep them entertained. He taught them some Indian games, and they were hooked. They played seven stones, cricket, and *kabaddi*. They lost track of time until Dr. Nair came out and said, "Come in guys, the table is set."

---

43 Spicy rice dish with lentils and boiled peanuts

44 plantains, carrots, snake gourd, pumpkin, yam, and brinjal in a coconut and curd curry

The kids wanted to continue playing seven stones, but Senthil promised them that he would stay back and play with them after dinner.

Everything was delicious. The parents were surprised to see how all the kids sat down and how well they ate everything. It was usually a struggle to get them to eat anything that was not pizza, chicken nugget, or pasta. It looked like they were all trying to get on the good side of Senthil so that he would teach them more Indian games.

Senthil became their official babysitter. He was called on whenever the parents had to go out, and he obliged. For the kids, it was a break from monotony. They enjoyed both the outdoor and the indoor games that Senthil introduced them to. Menaka and Mayuri tried to set Senthil up with every Indian girl they knew. Senthil told them about Sumathi and how much he was in love with her and how he was looking forward to going back to India once his financial goals were met.

The year went by fast. Senthil enjoyed a good reputation for his management of the Rehab Department. His skills as a physical therapist were recognized by the physicians and surgeons at the hospital and the patients and their families in the community.

He shared his success with his family and Sumathi through his letters. Even though it had been two years since he had left India, it had not become any easier to live away from Sumathi. His letters were more elaborate, and Sumathi enjoyed hearing about all his achievements and adventures. Sumathi had news to share too. She had climbed the ranks and was promoted to the position of a senior therapist, which came with some additional administrative duties and a raise. Senthil was immensely proud of her.

In early December, on a Friday, Dr. Nair stopped by the Rehab Department. He asked Senthil if he could come over to their house as they were going to a Christmas party that was going to last until late in the night. Senthil told him he would be glad to. Dr. Reddy and Mayuri came over to drop off Prakash and Banu Priya. They were going to the same party. Senthil played board games with Ajith, Roshini, Prakash, and Banu Priya. They reminded him of his two brothers and sisters back in India. He kept them occupied with stories about his siblings and about India.

Dr. Nair had ordered pizza for dinner, left a tip on the kitchen counter for the delivery man, and rented *Toy Story* from Blockbuster. The pizza arrived at 8:00 PM. There were three large pizzas—enough to feed four hungry kids, Senthil, and then some. As soon as Senthil got the pizza into the kitchen, the kids ran to grab plates and raided the fridge for more toppings and ranch dressing to dip the pizza.

After dinner, they settled in front of the TV to watch *Toy Story*. It was a feel-good movie. Senthil recognized the voice of Buzz Lightyear. It was Tim Allen from his favorite TV show *Home Improvement*. When the movie ended at about 10:30 PM, the kids were feeling sleepy and were slumped in the big, cozy sofas. Senthil stayed on the recliner, watching TV. He turned the lights off and decreased the volume, so he did not disturb the kids.

After a while, he got up to use the restroom. The TV was bright enough to subtly light the living room. He was able to find his way to the powder room and back without turning on the lights. On his way back, he saw all four kids lying on the sofas, peacefully asleep. He plopped down on to the recliner and fell asleep watching TV.

He woke up in cold sweat. He had not had that nightmare in a long time. Terrified, he looked at the kids and was relieved to see them asleep. He got up slowly to wash his face when he heard the front door open. It was 12:15 AM. Dr. Nair and Menaka walked in, Dr. Reddy and Mayuri following close behind. They thanked Senthil for staying and watching the kids. Mayuri unsuccessfully tried to wake up her kids. Menaka told her to let the kids sleep and pick them up in the morning. Dr. Reddy and Mayuri drove Senthil back to his house on their way home.

Princeton Hospital continued to grow, and with it, the Rehab Department expanded too. Both the inpatient and the outpatient caseload increased so much that Senthil had to frequently work a few hours during weekends to complete his evaluations. He wanted to keep up his principle of completing the evaluation within twenty-four hours of the order. Mike approved overtime for his commitment. Work and life in Princeton could not be better. Senthil only wished Sumathi was there to share all this with him.

Chapter 17 — Trouble in Paradise

IN THE FALL OF 1996, PRESIDENT CLINTON WAS CAMPAIGNing for reelection. Senthil remembered watching Clinton and the presidential debates with President Bush back home. Senthil thought Clinton was charismatic and hoped he would win. Now, he was able to follow the election more closely. He watched the Sunday news religiously, but to get more balanced news, he watched Fox, NBC, and ABC news specials. He was amazed at how the same piece of news was delivered by different networks with their own spin.

He was fascinated by the American two-party political system that was in stark contrast to India's multiple political parties, with an astonishing involvement of more than one thousand registered political parties. Also, the vast majority of American politicians were well-educated, primarily lawyers, compared to Indian politicians who rose to prominence either through the movie industry or by inheriting political clout through family members already in politics. Though there were tremendous differences, he was surprised by the similarities in the campaigning process, including smear campaigns, pandering, misrepresentations, and flat-out deceit and lies. The only difference was that things were a little more sophisticated in America.

Mike called for a meeting with the Rehab Department. He wanted to share the information he had learned from his meeting with Princeton

Hospital's board of directors and trustees. It was not good news, and Mike tried to be as politically correct as possible. The takeaway point was that the hospital, in an attempt to cut cost, was considering doing away with contract companies and would be hiring employees directly. This included the Rehab Department as well. Mike told Senthil, Shelby, and Heather that they had been the most successful group of therapists he had ever worked with and promised he would do everything in his power to keep them on board.

Senthil called Hema to update her regarding the situation. Hema assured him that she had been in communication with Mike and the Human Resources Department. She told him this situation was not unique to Princeton Hospital but was happening nationwide. It was a knee-jerk response to a legislation under consideration in the United States House and Senate. This piece of legislation, called "The Balanced Budget Act," aimed to cut health-care costs and reimbursement. She mentioned that the number of H1-B visas issued for health-care workers had decreased considerably compared to previous years. Hema sounded optimistic, though, and Senthil was reassured.

"I would encourage you to apply for your green card. My company can sponsor it," said Hema. Senthil reminded her of Sumathi and his family and his plans of returning to India as soon as he had enough money saved. Hema informed him that while a green card would guarantee him permanent residency in America, it did not require him to relinquish his Indian passport or citizenship. She told him that he could always go back to India, and a green card would give him the option of coming back if he chose to, without any requirement for a visa. Besides, the processing time of green card for health-care workers was only four to six months.

Hema filed the I-140 Immigrant Petition for alien workers for Senthil. Although there was some uneasiness in the Rehab Department, business went on as usual. Senthil did not let the uncertainty of the future interfere with his work and the present. He did not tell his parents or Sumathi about the political turmoil or about his need to apply for a green card. He did not want to worry them.

The board of directors and trustees held regular meetings with the hospital administration to discuss strategies for the future. Princeton Hospital had undergone a big expansion and met unprecedented economic success, and they were apprehensive of the impact the Balanced Budget Act would have on their ventures and financial success in the future.

Mike looked into the possibility of filing an H1-B visa for Senthil and learned that a moratorium had been placed on health-care worker visas for physical therapists, occupational therapists, speech pathologists, and nurses. This was indefinite and pending development of further guidelines for the issuance of health-care visas.

Incumbent President Clinton was reelected for a second term in November 1996 over former Senator Bob Dole. The winter of 1996 brought a blizzard, with the northeast wind blanketing the east coast with over four feet of snow. Princeton, Indiana, got its fair share of snow and freezing temperatures. Senthil hoped that 1997 would be his best year yet in America.

Thanks to his frugality, he was closer to his financial goal than the timetable anticipated. Another year and he could return home to his family and Sumathi. He even planned to return to India on the same day, and the same month he had left: December 8, 1997.

He dreamed of taking Sumathi to their favorite dessert shop on his motorbike and opening a physiotherapy clinic with her so they could have their own private practice after work instead of practicing home health. Until then, frequent long letters and periodic phone calls would console their longing hearts.

He called home the night of December 31, 1996. It was a Tuesday night—quite different from his usual schedule of calling home on Saturday night so that it would be Sunday morning in India. Even though it would be Wednesday morning there, New Year's Day was a holiday, and he had a hunch that Sumathi would come with a box of sweets early in the morning to wish him and his family a Happy New Year, as she had in the previous years.

He was right. Sumathi answered the phone. They were very happy to hear each other's voice. He also talked briefly to his family. He told neither her nor his family anything about the uncertainty brewing at his workplace. He wished them all a happy and prosperous new year and told them he was very optimistic for 1997.

The new year only brought more uncertainties with it. Senthil learned that his contract at Princeton had not been renewed; it was the same for Shelby and Heather. Mike assured Senthil that it was not a reflection of their work in the Rehab Department and told him he was doing everything he could to convince the board of directors to extend the contract. Senthil would have loved to stay in Princeton, as Hema did not have any new contracts owing to the possible legislative changes.

Heather and Shelby were not that worried. They could secure a license in any state, which increased their job market and Hema's flexibility to find them a job. Heather and Shelby held a current license in Texas, Michigan, Illinois, Indiana, Ohio, Missouri, and Florida. Even though Senthil had taken the national board exam, foreign-trained physical therapists were licensed and recognized only in a handful of states, which made his situation more precarious. He had a license in Missouri, Indiana, and Michigan.

Heather and Shelby decided to go on a road trip for a mini vacation if their contract did not get renewed, hoping that Hema would be able to secure them a contract somewhere soon. If Hema was unsuccessful, they were debating about either joining a national contract company that had more clients or heading back home and accepting a permanent position.

For Senthil, even though Hema would fly him back to the company's apartment in Texas, having no assignment even for a month meant a setback in his estimated timeline. It would not be a bad thing, but he wanted to go back with his mission accomplished and not with a shortcoming, small though it might be. To him, their sacrifice would hardly mean anything if he failed to reach his financial goal before returning.

On January 15, Mike and Connie stopped by the Rehab Department one afternoon.

"Senthil, I would like to introduce to you and your team to Samantha Crowley and Alexandra Bailey," said Mike.

Sam was a speech therapist, and Alexa was an occupational therapist. They were there to interview for a permanent position at Princeton Hospital. Mike and Connie wanted him to show them around the Rehab Department, the skilled nursing facility, and the surgical floors and answer any question they had about work in the hospital and life in Princeton in general.

After Senthil gave them a tour of the facility, Heather and Shelby talked to them about the type of patients they see, the average caseload for outpatients and inpatients, and their relationship with the staff members and the doctors. They were not merely painting a rosy picture; there was actually nothing negative to say, as they had created a positive work environment. Jenny maintained their schedule very well, and all their work was well received by the patients, nurses, and doctors.

It came as no surprise that Sam and Alexa accepted the position. While it was a testament to the work culture created by the current rehab team, it also meant that February 28, 1997, would be the last day at Princeton Hospital for Heather and Shelby. Senthil felt sad at the thought of leaving Princeton. Hema had told Heather and Shelby that she might have a contract for them in Florida. The girls were excited about the road trip to Florida; they eagerly sought an escape from the snow and the unrelenting cold weather. Senthil weathered the cold and the uncertainty.

A little hospital in the neighboring Oakland city was in talks with Princeton Hospital regarding sharing resources. Oakland city hospital was a 20-bed hospital with limited inpatient and outpatient services. With its population being only one-third of Princeton and the impending legislative changes in the Balanced Budget Act, Oakland City hospital was looking at options to stay viable. After all, the Balanced Budget Act aimed to decrease government spending by $160 billion, which included a $112 billion cut in Medicare and a $44 billion decrease in the reimbursement of hospital inpatient and outpatient services.

Heather and Shelby got word from Hema that their next assignment was in Gainesville, Florida. It was a three-month contract in a skilled nursing home with an option for renewal. It was a twelve-hour drive, and they had to start on March 1. They planned to finish work on Friday, February 27, and leave early Saturday morning so that they had time before they joined work.

Senthil was not so lucky. Mike came up to the Rehab Department and pulled Senthil aside. "I wanted you to hear it from me. I am aware of your contributions to the success of our Rehab Department. But this is beyond my control, and there is no easy way for me to say it."

"What is it, Mike? Whatever it is, you can tell me, Mike," Senthil added.

"Well, it looks like the physical therapist from Oakland City Hospital will come and work here. So, we will not be able to renew your contract. I am really sorry Senthil."

Even though he knew this was coming, to actually hear it with only a week more left was a little devastating. He thanked Mike for his support and the opportunity to work in Princeton. Mike told him he was going to call Hema to let her know. Jenny was the one who took it the hardest. She was in tears. Senthil calmed her down and went back to finish taking care of the patients for the day.

At the end of the day, Senthil called Hema. She told him Mike had called and she was working on securing an assignment for him. Senthil had only one week to finish up his work and vacate the house. He lived off two suitcases, so it would not be hard—but it was difficult emotionally.

Senthil had never used the dishwasher as he wanted to save electricity, but he made an exception this time. He loaded up the dishwasher with all the dishes in the cabinets, even the ones he had never used. He cleaned the nooks and crannies of the stove, microwave, and refrigerator. He dusted the TV and

VCR, washed the comforter, sheets, and the pillowcases, and vacuumed the carpet. Although Connie had told him not to worry about cleaning the house, as she was going to get it professionally cleaned, he wanted to leave the house like he had found it on the day he moved in.

Hema called Senthil on Wednesday. "I have good news and bad news," she said. She had found him an assignment in Evansville, which was only forty minutes down south. The catch, however, was that the contract was only for four weeks. An acute rehab facility was looking to continue coverage while one of their physical therapists had gone on maternity leave. Hema assured him that she would get him a long-term assignment by the end of this temporary assignment. Senthil was just glad to continue working without a break.

On their last day at Princeton Hospital, Senthil, Heather, and Shelby saw both inpatients and outpatients. They made sure all the progress notes were up to date and even wrote up a short summary so that the incoming therapists could familiarize themselves with the patients.

Dr. Nair, Dr. Reddy, and the many other physicians, along with Mike and Connie, stopped by the Rehab Department to bid goodbye to them. Jenny and some of the nurses had baked some goodies for a potluck, to send them off with sweet treats. It was a gloomy afternoon. Senthil thanked everybody who stopped by.

He was the last one to leave. As he walked out that evening, he stopped to take one last look at the hospital. With a heavy heart, he slowly walked back to the house. Since it was only for four weeks, he took Hema's option of finding him an apartment instead of the $1000 monthly allowance.

He slept on the sofa that night, as he did not want to mess up the bed. Connie had asked him to leave the keys in the mailbox. Heather and Shelby were going to drive right through Evansville, and they offered to drop Senthil off.

They came at 6:00 AM on Saturday morning. With his luggage ready, Senthil was waiting on the porch. He had to stuff his leftover spices, lentils, rice, and other groceries in a few plastic bags. Heather drove a Jeep Cherokee, and Shelby had a Honda Accord. When he saw them pull into the driveway, he locked the house and placed the keys in the mailbox. He walked down the porch and piled his stuff in Heather's jeep.

Before leaving town, they stopped at Dick Clark's restaurant on Prince Street for breakfast. Jenny and her husband joined them. After tearful good-byes and hugs, Heather, Shelby, and Senthil hit the road. The girls dropped him off in his apartment complex in Evansville.

His apartment was luckily on the ground floor, so he did not have to lug his suitcases up the stairs. He just lay down in the bed, emotionally drained and clueless about what awaited him on Monday. An acute rehab facility was somewhere between a hospital and a nursing home. Evansville was a much bigger city in comparison with Glasgow and Princeton, and so, he did not venture out too much.

Work at the rehab facility was all right. It was not the Haven or Princeton Hospital. He was not sure if it was big city mentality or the fact that he was only a temporary at work, but people seemed cold and distant. He tried his best to fit in, worked hard, and cared for his patients as he always did. He kept to himself and wondered what was going to happen at the end of the month. He did not establish a phone connection, ate at the cafeteria, walked to work, and tried to save money in every possible way.

Four weeks at the Evansville rehab facility seemed like an eternity, but time flew. It was the last week of March and Senthil was hoping to hear either from Hema about a new contract or from the rehab facility about an extension. He was hoping it would be the former. He did not want to call Hema and bother her. He knew she was doing her best in this post-Balanced Budget Act volatile market. The option to go back to Lewisville, Texas, was always open, in case Hema failed to secure an assignment.

Hema called him at work on Wednesday, March 26, two days before, to tell him that she was working on an assignment for him in Indiana, and if things are not confirmed before Friday, he might have to stay there in the apartment for another week. She reassured him that she would bring him back to Texas if the Indiana assignment did not pan out.

Hema caught him on Friday, just as he was leaving the rehab facility on his last day. Senthil could sense a reassuring elation in her voice. She said, "I am so glad I caught you before you left. Otherwise, I would have had to wait to hear from you since you don't have a home phone."

"What's going on, Hema? You sound very happy."

"Of course, I am happy. I have some great news," she replied. Before he could ask her, she said, "Your next assignment is confirmed! I have a job for you in a skilled nursing facility in Terre Haute, Indiana, for the next three months." Senthil was thrilled. Hema continued, "And the best part is, if they are impressed with your work, it could turn into a year-long contract."

He was so excited that all he could manage to do was thank Hema repeatedly. Not only would he get to work without a break, but he also did not have to worry about another assignment until it was time for him to head back to India.

He promised Hema that he would do his best and work very hard to impress them and get the contract extended. "I don't doubt that, Senthil. I am sure your work ethic is going to win them over."

She asked him if he wanted her to get an apartment for him or if he wanted the $1000 tax-free allowance instead. Senthil knew he could save more with the allowance and told her that he would find a place once he reached Terre Haute.

Hema told him that the only catch was the rehab director of Golden Manor was going on vacation the first week of April and would like to meet him Saturday by 12:00 PM before she left. He did not have a lot of time, as he would have to leave Evansville early the next morning.

He said goodbye to his coworkers and went to the administrator's office to thank her for giving him the opportunity to work at this facility, and then he hurried back to his apartment to pack. He took out his Rand McNally map; it would take him approximately two hours to get to Terre Haute.

He had a few leftovers. He had lived only on eggs, ramen noodles, and peanut butter and jelly sandwiches for the past four weeks. He was able to make six peanut butter jelly sandwiches and boiled the five leftover eggs. After packing and cleaning the apartment, he set the alarm for 7:00 AM and went to bed with a sense of peace that had eluded him the entire month.

On Saturday morning, he took a shower and got dressed. Two blocks from his apartment, there was a rental car company. He walked there and rented a car. It was a Toyota Corolla, which was just big enough to fit his two suitcases, carry-on, and a few plastic bags. He dropped the apartment key in the front office mailbox.

He had mapped out his route on his Rand McNally map. It was a pretty straight drive up US 41 North. The air was chilly, the skies were clear, and there was not much traffic on the road. Occasional mounds of dirty snow lined the way. He popped an audio cassette that played both his and Sumathi's favorite songs in the car. Kamal Hassan was his favorite movie star, but Sumathi liked Rajinikanth more. Both were the top two actors in South India. Warm and pleasant memories flooded his heart when he saw the exit to Princeton.

It was an easy drive. As Senthil took the exit to Terre Haute, he almost gagged at the sudden stench. First, he thought it was coming from the car and rolled down the window in a hurry to get some fresh air. But then it became clear that the stench was from outside and rolled the window back up.

He did not know where he was going to stay. As he took the exit for Terre Haute, he saw a sign for a Super 8 motel. He knew it was economical and followed the signs. The motel was on First Street. He checked in for a room and asked the clerk about the smell. The clerk laughed and said, "Ah! This must be your first visit to Terre Haute. It's our paper mill factory. You'll get accustomed to it in a few days if you are planning to stay longer."

Senthil told him he was moving to Terre Haute to work in the Golden Manor as a physical therapist. The clerk told him that the Golden Manor was only a mile away on Margaret Avenue.

He carried his suitcases to his room. He wanted to change into something professional to meet Lauren McNair, the rehab manager. He picked out a yellow shirt and a maroon tie with tiny yellow dots to wear with his black pants. It reminded him of Sumathi, as she had picked this out for him. He called the Golden Manor and asked to speak to Ms. McNair.

After a brief hold, he heard a "Hello" on the other end.

"Good morning! May I speak to Ms. McNair please?"

"This is she."

"Hi, my name is Senthil. I am—"

Before he could finish, Lauren said, "Oh yes! Hema told me about you. Are you in town?"

Senthil told her he could be at the Golden Manor in ten minutes. He hurried down to the check-in desk and asked for directions before hopping inside his rental car.

The Golden Manor was at least five times bigger than the Haven. As he entered the doors, he felt as though he was inside an upscale hotel. There was a big visiting area with many sofas, and chairs with tables and walls adorned with beautiful flowers and paintings. He walked past it to the main area where Lauren, who was standing by the nurses' station, greeted him with a handshake. She said, "Hi you must be . . ." She paused, afraid to butcher his name.

"Hi, it's Senthil. Like lentil with an S. And you must be Ms. McNair."

"Please call me Lauren. Let's go to my office. Thank you for coming in on a Saturday."

"My pleasure. Thank you for giving me the opportunity to work here," he replied.

She gave him an overview of the Rehab Department. When she learned that all his family was back in India, she said, "You are going to like working here. We have a dynamic and outgoing group of therapists. They are all young, single, and adventurous, and even though this is a skilled nursing facility, you get to see a wide range of patients."

Senthil was encouraged.

Lauren told him about Alina Pawlowski (Lina), a physical therapist from Poland, Mirasol Mercado (Mira), an occupational therapist from the Philippines, and Sofia Gonzalez (Sofi), another occupational therapist from Argentina. Emma Roberts and Monique Jackson were speech therapists who had been born and raised in America. Emma was from Kansas City and Monique was from Saint Louis. With Senthil in the mix, the Golden Manor's Rehab Department was a melting pot of cultures and languages. Lauren told him that she would be back in a week and had already appraised her therapists about his arrival.

Senthil stopped at the check-in counter at the Super 8 motel to inquire about apartments. The clerk told him about a new apartment complex on 25th Street, which was only a mile away from the Golden Manor. Senthil did not waste any time; he wanted to find an apartment while he could still drive around in his rental car. He looked up the apartment in yellow pages, so he could call and check if they were open. Lucky for him, they were open until 3:00 PM. He called a few more apartment complexes, but the one on 25th Street was the closest and the cheapest.

He got a one-bedroom apartment for $400. With another $200 spent for groceries and utilities, Senthil was confident he could easily save $400 from the $1000 tax-free allowance Hema gave him. With lady luck on his side, he could go home to Sumathi at the end of the year. It was an unfurnished apartment, but he signed the lease anyway. He hardly cared about furniture. His only goal was to save money.

The first week at the Golden Manor was a breeze, and if it was any indication of the time to come, Senthil felt happy. Lina gave him an orientation of the patients and the paperwork. The other therapists were very outgoing and easy to talk to and work with. They all worked well as a team. The physical therapists and the occupational therapists co-treated many patients—the former with regards to functional mobility and the latter with activities of daily living.

At the end of the week, the girls were planning a day in Indianapolis. They convinced Senthil to join them and told him of their ritual of hanging out together at least once a day during the weekend. They went out to eat, had potlucks, watched movies, played games, and took day trips to Chicago, Saint Louis, or Indianapolis. They were all single and had no family that lived close by. Above all, they celebrated their diversity and enjoyed each other's company. Even Lauren who was a tad older than them joined in on potlucks and local get-togethers.

Senthil had a great time in Indianapolis. The girls opted for Indian food for lunch. They felt adventurous because Senthil could explain the food to them and tell them what was good and what not. Senthil was more excited to see an Indian store next to the Indian restaurant. He asked to be excused, ran over to the store, and got a calling card to India. They all enjoyed the lunch buffet at the Indian restaurant. For $6.99, they got a culinary tour of India. The girls loved his explanation of the different dishes featured in the buffet.

After lunch, they went shopping and were surprised to see Senthil actually having a good time and not complaining as they went from one store to another in the mall. He was just taking mental notes on what would look good on Sumathi. Besides, he had grown up with two sisters, and Rathi frequently took him window shopping.

They came back late Saturday night, but it was not too late to call India. However, he was trying to save money, and he felt guilty about spending $6.99 for lunch. He would not have been able to talk to Sumathi anyway. The next day, he wrote long letters to his family and Sumathi. With all the tension and stress of the last three months, he had neither called nor written, as he neither wanted to lie and say everything was okay nor tell them how worried he was. They would only worry, and nothing good would come out of it.

Now, since things had calmed down and looked more promising, he wrote a long letter telling them about the last two months in Princeton, and the time in Evansville. He told them about Terre Haute and his colleagues.

He let Sumathi know that he had saved $75,000 and was hoping to make it to $100,000 by the end of the year.

Lauren came back from her vacation and was very impressed with how her new team member had assimilated. Their chemistry with each other reassured her that the patients of the Manor were in good hands. Senthil's sense of humor and work ethic fit in well with the rest of the gang. The caseload was diverse, including strokes, joint replacements, postsurgical patients, people coming to live, and people coming in as a transition from the hospital to their homes. The volume was enough to keep the two PTs, two OTs, and two SLPs busy.

Senthil and Lina often co-treated with the occupational therapists Mira and Sofi, especially the patients whose functional mobility and endurance were very limited to tolerate separate PT and OT sessions. The nurses were very understanding and maintained a good rapport with the therapists, thereby creating an ideal work environment. Given the diversity among the therapists, every other day was a potluck at the Rehab Department. Food was the best way to acquaint oneself with other cultures.

The night of April 19, Senthil sat down to call home. His heart jumped with anticipation as the phone rang. It was 8:00 AM on a Sunday morning in India, and he knew what they would be doing. Rathi answered the phone and screamed, "C'mon everybody! It's Senthil *anna*!" He talked to her, Eshwari, Bala, his *amma*, and finally his *appa*. They talked about his letter and told him how happy they were that everything was back to normal. Senthil was sad to learn that Sumathi was not there.

He understood. She probably had a patient she could not miss. After all, she would have gotten his letter only a couple of days ago. He asked Nanda to stop by her house and let her know that he would call again in a month. He said, "Tell her Sunday, May 18 at 8:00 AM." He did not want any ambiguity or guesswork; he already had to wait another four weeks to talk to the love of his life.

Coming to America, he had been aware of the perils of a long-distance relationship. However, he was confident their love would persevere despite the distance.

In the meantime, all he could do was focus on his work, and that was exactly what he did. He volunteered for all overtime opportunities during weekends. If a patient got admitted during the weekend, he was there to complete the physical therapy evaluation. All the other therapists worked for a large national company with which the Golden Manor had a longstanding contract. Senthil was the only therapist from Hema's company. However, Lauren was impressed with his dedication and teamwork, and to his relief, she reassured him that his contract would get extended.

He was thankful to have Lina as his partner at work. They complemented each other well as physical therapists. He liked treating patients with neurological disorders, while Lina liked treating orthopedic patients. She came from an affluent family in Poland and work was merely an adventure for her. She was not interested in overtime or money and loved to travel and enjoy life. She was blonde haired and blue eyed, with a petite frame, an infectious laugh, and a Polish accent. She knew about Sumathi, but then, so did everyone else as Senthil always talked about her. However, that did not stop her from playfully flirting with him just to see him squirm.

On April 29, Emma invited everybody to her apartment to watch a baseball game. Her hometown Kansas City Royals was playing the Toronto Blue Jays. Senthil had no idea about baseball. He was used to cricket and had a basic understanding of American football. Apart from their rehab gang, Emma had three friends visiting from Saint Louis: Katelyn, Madison, and her boyfriend, Scott. Madison was one of those girls you wished you had not started a conversation with at a party. She had a high-pitched nasal voice and was so self-centered that she could not talk about anything other than herself or her boyfriend Scott. She was extremely possessive and hung on to him like a poster on a wall most of the time.

The whole Rehab Department was going to be there. Senthil made some tandoori chicken drumsticks and took it to the game. They were all used to wings, and his chicken drumsticks, different and spicy of a different kind, were a big hit.

The game started, and he could not follow. It was unusually slow to be dubbed as America's favorite ball game. Cricket was much faster and contained a lot of action in comparison with baseball.

Emma said, "You are not able to enjoy it because you don't know the rules of the game."

She explained the rules to him, starting with how Major League Baseball was divided into American and National League. She decided not to overwhelm him and stuck to the basics. She told him about the pitcher, who was similar to the bowler in cricket, the catcher who was the counterpart to the wicket-keeper in cricket, and the mound, which was similar to the stumps. The bat was cylindrical, unlike the flat one in cricket. She explained to him the pitch, strike, safe, hit, run, and home runs. She told him about the first, second, third, and fourth bases and their significance when they were loaded.

Armed with the new knowledge, Senthil was able to tolerate the game but still not quite enjoy it. He had more fun socializing and sampling the different food items people had brought.

As usual, Lina was busting Senthil's chops. She was teasing him and making fun of him and his proper English. Senthil tried to defend himself by saying that he too could speak slang but just chose not to.

Just then, Madison walked in and asked in her shrieking voice, "Has anyone seen my boyfriend Scott? Where is my boyfriend Scott?" She asked the questions at least four times before anyone could answer her.

Senthil thought this was his perfect opportunity to show off his repertoire of slangs. "He is down with a fag!" exclaimed Senthil.

The entire room gasped and grew silent. "What? What did you say?" asked Madison.

"He is down with a fag," replied Senthil, a little louder than before. He did not realize that people asked him to repeat things not because they did not hear him, but because they did not understand him.

"My boyfriend, Scott? I don't think so!" scoffed Madison.

Parting the curtains and looking down the window, Senthil claimed, "Of course he is. He has one in his mouth right now."

Madison pushed him aside and rushed to the window. She saw Scott smoking a cigarette. She turned around, scowled at Senthil, muttered "Idiot," and walked downstairs to talk to her boyfriend.

Confused, Senthil asked, "What's wrong with her?"

Everybody started laughing. Emma asked, "Why did you say what you said?"

Senthil said, "I was just trying to prove to Lina that I too can use slang in conversations." He looked around and asked, "Where is she?" Lina was rolling on the floor laughing.

"Do explain, English professor," she mocked.

"Now you know how I feel! Fag is slang for a cigarette. None of you knew that, and for once, I can teach you some slang." He retaliated, feeling vindicated.

Emma laughed and said, "It may mean that in India, but here, fag is a derogatory term for a homosexual man."

Senthil's jaw dropped. "I am so sorry. I had no idea. I'd better stick to my proper English."

Katelyn came to his rescue. "Don't be so hard on yourself. You did well, and you speak good English. I am sure we sound foreign to you. Don't worry."

"Thank you, Katelyn. I am glad somebody understands," said Senthil.

Emma and Monique explained that each state in America had its own unique slang and sayings and that even though they were born and raised in America, they did not understand all the sayings. They thanked him for a good laugh, though.

They all went back to watching the game. It was tied at 5–5 and was dragging on until the tenth inning when Chilli Davis hit a home run, giving Kansas City Royals a 6–5 win and scoring his 300th career home run. Emma was ecstatic, and she ran to the phone to call her family and friends back home to share the win with them.

Since the next day was a working day, everybody left on time. Senthil told Scott and Madison he was sorry for the fag remark, but they laughed and asked him not to worry about it. To his relief, they said it was more funny than offensive.

The following week, Emma told Senthil, "Hey, remember my friend Katelyn from the baseball party? She asked me for your phone number, and I gave it to her. Hope you don't mind."

"Oh really? Did she say why she wanted my number?" asked Senthil.

"Something about a recipe for an Indian dish she wants to make."

"Oh, that's okay," he responded.

Hearing this, Lina came to Senthil and said, "Be careful. I hear Katelyn is a wild one." She was confident that between her Polish accent and him taking everything in the literal sense, he was not going to notice the hint of jealousy in her voice.

Katelyn called him on Saturday morning.

"Hey, Senthil like Lentil! Remember me? This is Katelyn from the baseball party."

"Oh yeah, Emma's friend from Saint Louis!"

"Hope you don't mind me getting your number from Emma and calling you out of the blue."

"No, it's quite all right."

"I am coming into town this evening, and Emma is going to be busy. I thought we could hang out, play some games, and have some fun. You could tell me all about cricket, Indian slangs, and teach me the Indian ways."

She talked for half an hour. Senthil had no clue she was coming on to him. He was completely oblivious of her advances. He told her he did not have any plan and would be happy to talk to her about any recipe she wanted. "We can even play baseball if you want," he said.

"Hmm, that sounds so good," she said. "Well, if you play it right, you could easily get to first base. Who knows? Maybe even to second base!" she added, laughing. She told him she would see him at 6:00 in the evening, got his address, and hung up.

Senthil heard a knock on his door and looked at his watch. She was right on time. He opened the door, and she looked puzzled. Senthil was wearing a T-shirt and a pair of track pants tucked into his crew length socks. He wore sneakers and a baseball cap. They did not match, but that was the best he could do to mimic baseball uniform. He had borrowed a baseball bat and a ball from his neighbor.

Senthil had the same puzzled look when he saw Katelyn. She was wearing a short black dress with red high heels. "You are going to play in that? Forget first and second base, I am going for a sixer. Sorry, that's cricket. I am going for a home run!"

"What did you think we were going to do this evening, Senthil?" Katelyn asked.

"Well, weren't we going to play baseball and talk about Indian food and recipes until Emma got back? I thought we could play while there was still light outside," he replied.

She could not help but laugh at his naiveté. She slipped into a pair of jeans and sneakers that she had in her car. She then drove him to Deming Park. They took turns pitching and hitting. When they had had their fill, she drove him back home and told him she was going to check on Emma. Before leaving, she asked him to write down the recipe for the chicken drumsticks he had made for the baseball party and give it to Emma.

The following Monday, Emma came straight to Senthil, gave him a hug, and kissed him on his forehead. "You are such a nice guy. Your girlfriend is so lucky to have you." He looked at her in confusion.

"I am the lucky one, Emma. She is all I could ever ask for." He did not understand why she said that, but then again, he needed no rhyme or reason to talk about Sumathi. He could barely wait for May 18 to call home and talk to her. This was the longest he had ever gone without talking to her. Even though he kept busy with work and his friends, he had an emptiness and a sick feeling in his stomach that only Sumathi could cure.

On May 17, Senthil could not wait for the clock to strike 9:30 at night so he could call home. It would be 8:00 AM on Sunday in India. He pictured his siblings waking up to TV, Eshwari making coffee, his *appa* reading the newspaper, and Sumathi and his *amma* preparing breakfast. When the phone rang, Rathi would be the one to fight to answer it first.

The phone rang a few times. Eshwari answered, and right off the bat, he could sense that something was wrong. She tried to be cheerful in her greeting, but the tremble in her voice screamed that the situation was dire. He asked her if everything was okay, and she began to cry. He did not know what could be wrong; a million things crossed his mind, but the first thing he muttered out was: "Is *appa* okay?"

Between bouts of crying, Eshwari finally spoke the dreadful words that she knew would be a dagger to his heart: "I am so sorry, but Sumathi got married to someone."

She wanted to make sure she said it clearly, and Senthil heard it clear as a bell. He could not comprehend it, however. He did not believe his ears. His heart sunk to the pit of his stomach, and like a skier taken down by an avalanche, he collapsed to the ground.

While he was going through a period of uncertainty, insecurity, and a volatile health-care market, he had no idea Sumathi herself was going through hell, surrounded by opportunists and no one to help. How could he have known? In his haste to leave Princeton for a very brief stint in Evansville, he forgot to let the post office know his forwarding address.

Sumathi had penned a desperate letter to the Princeton address, the last address she knew, only to have it returned to her twenty-seven days later. This was enough for her vulnerable status to succumb and make the ultimate sacrifice for her family.

Chapter 18 — Mayhem in Madras

WITH SENTHIL GONE TO AMERICA, LIFE WENT ON AS USUAL for Sumathi. She went to work in the morning, took care of a couple of private patients before coming home, hung out with Gauthami, read Senthil's letters for the hundredth time, and looked at some of their old photos just before falling asleep, only to repeat the same cycle all over again the next day. Her favorite pick-me-up that always brightened her day was Senthil's attempt at poetry. He claimed it was corny but to her it was Shakespeare.

When I look into your deep, dark and dreamy eyes
I find them brimming with love that never dies
The hours without you are long and dreary
And our time together seems far and bleary
I look behind me and your shadow fades away
Like a crippling house made foolishly out of clay
I chase your footsteps that vanish in thin air
All the while thinking, 'If only you were here!'
But you are oceans away, and I live only with hope
Holding on to it tight like a strong, heavy rope
In times like these, to your memory I cling
Knowing in my heart that there will come our Spring!

On weekends, she visited the temple with her *amma* and sister, helped in the kitchen, caught an occasional movie with Gauthami, and sometimes went window-shopping with her. Once every two weeks, she went out with her friends from work. Her memories of Senthil and dreams of a future with him helped her persevere through a mundane schedule. After all, there was a bright, warm light at the end of the cold tunnel.

Little did she know that she, her love, and her family would be dealt an unexpected deadly blow. On Monday, February 10, 1997, the week began as usual, with nothing out of the ordinary. Sumathi finished sessions with her two private patients and returned home at around 9:00 PM. She was greeted by her *periyamma* and *periyappa* who had dropped in, as they happened to be in the neighborhood. She was not too thrilled to see them and was too tired to socialize. However, being her polite self, she greeted them with a smile and answered their barrage of questions about where she had been and why she had come home so late. She answered patiently and told them about the two home-health-care patients she took care of. She looked at her *amma* to bail her out.

Her *amma* understood her plight and came to her rescue: "Go freshen up, Sumathi, and help your sister set up the dinner table. It's time to eat."

She looked at her *amma* thankfully and replied, "In a minute." She walked to the bedroom as fast as she could.

Gauthami was studying inside. She whispered, "Did you see the witch and the sorcerer outside?" Sumathi rolled her eyes and went into the bathroom.

When she came out, she and Gauthami could hear their *periyamma* and *periyappa* harassing their *amma*.

"It's not good for Sumathi to come home so late. It's time for her marriage. What are you all waiting for?" asked *periyamma*.

Then *periyappa* added, "One of our friends' family is very interested in Sumathi. They are Brahmins and even belong to our subsect. Their oldest son is an engineer; he is a strict vegetarian and a teetotaler. They are well connected, and Subbu would be able to get a job in his firm. Best of all, their second son is only a couple of years older than Gauthami, and when the time comes, I am sure they will ask for her hand too."

Her *amma* was trying to be polite. She replied, "Sumathi wants to work for some time before thinking about marriage, and Gauthami wants to pursue a graduate degree. They are in no rush to get married." She was caught alone with them. Sumathi and Gauthami walked out of the bedroom, and their *amma* said, "It's getting late. Let's sit down for dinner."

"Where is *appa*?" Sumathi asked her *amma*.

"He complained of a headache. So I gave him some Aspirin, and he is lying down now. You girls set the table, and I'll go get him."

Periyamma and *periyappa* sat down as Sumathi and Gauthami set the table. Their *appa* came out reluctantly, only to be polite to the guests who would take offense if he did not join them at the table. Sumathi and Gauthami served the food before joining them at the table.

When they began to eat, *periyamma* again said, "You should seriously consider the grooms we are talking about for Sumathi and Gauthami. There are a lot of benefits in the sisters getting married into the same family. You know what will happen if Sumathi continues her friendship with that boy. Not only is he a non-Brahmin, but he is also from a lower caste. You all would be ostracized by the rest of the family."

Just as her *amma* was about to say something in response, Sumathi interrupted in horror, "Are you alright *appa*?"

She rushed towards her *appa* who was drooling from the right side of his mouth. Just as Sumathi approached his side, he slumped down his chair and became unresponsive.

There was panic in the house. Sumathi knew exactly what was happening: *appa* was having a stroke. She tried to remain calm and think about what to do next, which hospital to take him to. Her *amma* was in a shock, and *periyamma* was hysterical. *Periyappa* helped Sumathi lift her *appa* from the chair, carry him to the living room, and lay him on the sofa. She asked Gauthami to get a taxi. Gauthami was crying, but she listened to her sister and ran out of the house.

She returned within a couple of minutes. She ran into Subbu who was coming home and told him what had happened, so he went to hail a cab. Sumathi tried to prop up her *appa's* head and keep it turned to one side so that he would not aspirate. When Subbu got back with the taxi, he and *periyappa* carried *appa* to the car. *Periyamma* stayed home with Gauthami, while the rest of them huddled into the taxi and rushed to Vijaya Hospital. It was a private hospital that was going to cost a lot of money, but it was closer than the government general hospital. Sumathi knew that every minute counted when dealing with a stroke.

He was admitted to the ICU. CT scan of the brain revealed a large ischemic stroke in the left cerebral cortex, the dominant hemisphere. He was intubated. The doctors administered *Heparin*[45] to see if they could help reestablish circulation in the damaged part of the brain.

For the next five days, Sumathi and her *amma* did not leave her *appa's* bedside. Sumathi wished Senthil was here to support her. Cases of strokes were his specialty. Sumathi was aware that once her *appa* pulled through this acute phase, he had a long road to recovery, which would require intense physical, occupational, and speech therapy.

Gauthami cooked at home, and Subbu delivered the meals to them in the hospital. They all tried to be there for each other. All their relatives took turns visiting them in the hospital and at home. The private hospital was expensive, and Sumathi handed checks signed by her *amma* to her *periyamma* and *periyappa* who managed the finances at the hospital.

Sumathi felt helpless. Even though she was not a doctor, she was accustomed to taking care of patients with similar conditions and helping stroke victims on their road to rehabilitation. Her *amma* and her siblings looked up to her to make sense of everything that was happening. The doctors told her that following the administration of *Heparin* to restore circulation in the

45 Blood Thinner

left side of the brain, the CT scan showed a hemorrhagic conversion of the stroke, worsening his condition. The doctors told them the supportive care they were providing was futile and keeping him intubated was only prolonging the inevitable.

Sumathi had to convince her *amma* to agree to one-way extubation. Before making the decision, she took her *amma* and her siblings to the temple. They prayed that their *appa* should survive the extubation and continue to breathe on his own and slowly recover. With the entire family surrounding him, Sumathi's *appa* was extubated. He never regained consciousness and died shortly afterward.

It was a devastating blow—something Sumathi's family was entirely unprepared for. All of their relatives descended upon their house. Sumathi's *amma* could neither handle the grief nor the stress. She was emotionally crippled, and it took a toll on her health. She was confined to the bed, and Sumathi's *periyamma* and *periyappa* took charge of the final ceremonies. Sumathi had to get in touch with Senthil and his parents to let them know what had happened. She had to put up a brave front and hold her head up high for her *amma* and her siblings.

However, she felt she could let her hair and guard down and grieve in front of Eshwari and Senthil's *amma*, and Senthil's *appa* would help console her. With all the relatives at home and her *periyamma* closely watching her every move, Sumathi could not find a reason to leave the house. Subbu was busy with his *periyappa*, as he was the only son and had to perform all the last rites for his *appa*'s cremation and funeral ceremony.

The house was crowded. The men slept in the living room and on the terrace. Many of the women slept in Sumathi's *amma's* room. Their *periyamma* shared Sumathi and Gauthami's room. As a domineering matriarch, their *periyamma* ran the household and kept a fervent watch over the girls. Sumathi had to stay up late at night and hide in the bathroom to pen a letter to Senthil. She sat on an overturned bucket and sobbed as she poured her heart out in the letter. She managed to give the letter to Subbu as he was going to the post office to mail the notification of their *appa*'s death to relatives who lived in different parts of the country.

A few days after the cremation, many of the relatives left. Sumathi went to check on her *amma* in the bedroom and told her that she was going to make a phone call to Senthil's house to let his parents know. Hearing her speak, her *periyamma* came rushing inside and yelled that Sumathi would do no such thing. She and her *periyappa* would never allow her to drag their family name down in the mud by mingling with a boy from a lower caste.

Sumathi was upset and furious. She tried to explain that while she and her family were grateful for all the help from them, this was her life and she intended to marry Senthil when he got back from America. Gauthami came to her rescue, but their *periyamma* would hear none of it. She turned around and screamed at their *amma* who was in no position to respond and simply started crying.

Their *periyamma* threatened how they would become outcasts in their community. She warned that they would never be able to find a suitable groom for Gauthami and would also have a tough time surviving without the relatives' help. Gauthami refused to let herself be used as a pawn to blackmail her family. She told her *periyamma* she did not care and that she was confident her family would be in good hands with Senthil. Her *periyamma* shot back saying that once Sumathi became the daughter-in-law of that lower-caste house, she was going to be engulfed by them and all her earnings would go to that house. Senthil had four siblings of his own to worry about, and he would not care about Gauthami or Subbu. Sumathi could see their *amma* was suffering and was rendered helpless with grief at this moment. She let her *periyamma* have the last word and walked out with Gauthami.

She hurried to the phone booth down the street to call Senthil's parents. Eshwari answered, and Sumathi began to cry as soon as she heard her voice. She barely managed to tell her what had happened. Eshwari tried to console her and reassured her that as soon as her parents returned, they would visit Sumathi. After hanging up, Sumathi hesitated to turn back. She did not care about the gawking of the man managing the phone booth. She knew it was going to be an expensive international phone call. But nevertheless, she called Senthil, hoping to hear his voice—the voice she knew would vanish all her pain, melt the burden, and instill hope in her.

Instead, she got a message: "This phone number is no longer in service." It was Senthil's Princeton phone number. She thought the stress and grief had somehow failed her memory, and dejected, she returned home.

All the conservative and traditional relatives admonished Sumathi and Gauthami into the kitchen while they managed all the post-cremation ceremonies and traditions. Subbu wanted to be home with his sisters and *amma* and alleviate some of the harshnesses meted out by their *periyamma*, but their *periyappa* made sure to take him everywhere he went, to show him what the real world was going to look like without his *appa* to support and protect them. He was intimidated, blackmailed, and brainwashed. In reality, the poor kid, even though he was not the eldest child, was scared about the future, as he was the only son. His *periyappa* made sure of that.

That evening, Eshwari told her family the devastating news. They were all upset for Sumathi and her family. Rathi pestered her parents to visit Sumathi's house to offer emotional comfort. Her *amma* told her that while she understood her concern, it was better for the elders to first go visit before the entire family went there.

The next day, Senthil's parents bought some fresh fruits and went to Sumathi's house. As they opened the gate downstairs, Gauthami saw them first from the balcony. She screamed, "Sumathi, *athimber's* parents are here." As soon as Sumathi heard that, she ran to the door, only to be stopped by her *periyamma*. Her *periyappa* hurried down and stopped them midway up the stairs. He told them while he appreciated the thought behind visiting the mourning family, he hoped they would understand that their lower-caste presence was not appropriate when they were performing rituals. He told Senthil's parents that they would not understand their upper-caste customs and that it would be better if they left now so that the rest of the relatives did not create a scene.

While Senthil's parents had not expected a warm welcome, they were quite taken aback by this insult. They stood stunned on the stairs. They did not dare go upstairs but stood there, peering up to see if they could catch a glimpse of Sumathi or her *amma*. Eventually, they turned back, and as they reached the gate, they saw Sumathi run down the stairs. She was sobbing and reached down to touch their feet. Senthil's *amma* hugged her, while his *appa* patted her shoulder tenderly.

"I am so sorry for what happened. Please forgive me for what *periyappa* said."

"Don't worry about it, Sumathi. It's not your fault. Here, please take these fruits and tell your *amma* that we came."

"I'll go get my *amma*," said Sumathi, but Senthil's *amma* stopped her and told her it would not bode well in this situation and assured her that they were only a phone call away whenever she needed them. They would do anything to help.

Sumathi and Gauthami felt extremely ashamed of their relatives and were sad for Senthil's parents, but they felt helpless. The following couple of weeks were like hell for Sumathi and her family. *Periyappa* and *periyamma* fed Sumathi and her family with guilt, shame, the fear of being chastised, and the uncertainty of the future. Some relatives even threatened harm to Senthil and his family if they ever set foot in Sumathi's house.

Sumathi's *amma* was crumbling to pieces. She was left alone with three children. She was more worried about the girls. With their *appa* gone so unexpectedly, it was her responsibility to make sure they were all settled well in life. She was aware of the uphill battle against her relatives when it came to Senthil, but both she and Sumathi's *appa* had been impressed with Senthil and his family and were happy for Sumathi. They did not care about the difference in caste. That resolve and strength started to waver with the untimely passing away of her husband; she needed her relatives now.

Sumathi could not stand seeing her *amma* have a nervous breakdown. That was more torturous than the guilt and shame her relatives were putting her through. Sumathi and Gauthami felt like they were on house arrest. Their *periyappa* and *periyamma* arranged for a meeting with the family that had the two sons who were interested in Sumathi and Gauthami. They made the girls dress up in their best saris and adorned them with their best jewelry. The girls reluctantly complied, just so that their *periyappa* and *periyamma* did not harass their *amma* for their defiance.

Sumathi thought about running away and seeking sanctuary in Senthil's house. She trusted them to act for her and her family's best interest more than her own relatives. But she knew what her relatives would do to her *appa's* reputation and her family, and she could not be that selfish. Within weeks, the relatives changed the house of mourning to a house of festivity. They wanted to impress the family that was visiting to see Sumathi and Gauthami. The onlookers were having more fun than the participants.

Sumathi and Gauthami went numb. They did what they were told mechanically. They served the family and the two sons with coffee, savories, and sweets. Unsurprisingly, the boys and the family liked both Sumathi and Gauthami. Their *periyappa* and *periyamma* did all the talking. Sumathi's *amma* was reduced to a puppet. The visiting family left with a favorable impression of the girls. The *periyappa* and *periyamma* gathered all the troops and spent days convincing Sumathi's *amma* that this was the right thing for Sumathi and Gauthami and their family's future, to preserve their position in the Brahmin community. They saw as their duty to prevent one of their own from getting mixed up with a lower caste-family and having their reputation dragged down.

Sumathi's letter to Senthil returned to her with the stamp "Unable to find recipient." It was the last straw that broke the camel's back. She succumbed to her relatives' pressure and to her *amma's* incapacity and made the ultimate sacrifice for her family by agreeing to marry the groom her *periyappa* and *periyamma* had selected. Her *periyappa* and *periyamma* had struck while the iron was still hot and did not waste any time in setting up the marriage.

Her last note to Senthil, which she managed to get through to his parents in a sealed envelope, read, "I am sorry for not being stronger. I am sorry for shattering our dreams. I am not asking for forgiveness but only for your understanding of my failure. I wish you and your family nothing but the very best. There is a girl out there who is luckier than me. Please do not come to see me until you are married too."

Chapter 19 — Hermit in Terre Haute

DISTRAUGHT AND DISHEARTENED, SENTHIL SPENT THE weekend in his apartment. He was numb with pain. He barely got off the bed sheets he had spread out on the floor, even though he had not slept at all. He realized the future he had been working for was only a mirage. He was freefalling without a parachute. Amidst the barrage of emotions and uncertainties, all he could do was feel sorry for Sumathi. He was not sure what had happened, but he was absolutely certain that she had not betrayed their love. Dire conditions must have compelled her decision. The more he thought about it, the angrier he got at himself. He felt he had let her down somehow and could not forgive himself.

Tears soaked his pillow as he cried over the future he would never have. He was ready to sell his soul to the devil just to see Sumathi one last time and ask her what had happened. However, she was a married woman now, and he knew he would only be a tornado in her life.

The weekend seemed to last forever. Monday finally arrived. He did not feel like going to work at all. He did not want others to see him this way. But he thought work would be a good cure for his grief, and so he mustered up enough courage and strength to get up.

Lina was the first one to notice something was wrong. Senthil was polite to the patients and courteous to the staff as usual, but he seemed mechanical.

Lina did not ask questions and thought he probably had a bad weekend. It was a busy day. There were quite a few admissions over the weekend, and there were new patient evaluations. Senthil masked his feelings. Interaction with his patients helped him focus his troubled mind elsewhere. He worked through lunch. At the end of the day, all the therapists sat down in their respective corners to complete their evaluations, progress notes, and billing. This was the time the Rehab Department was at its loudest. Everybody would be busy chatting.

Senthil did not want to draw attention to himself. He tried to make as much small talk as he could. The rest of the week progressed similarly. It was finally Friday evening. Glad that the busy week was over, they were all making plans for the weekend: dinner and then a movie at the $1 Indiana Theater. As Senthil tried to talk himself out of joining them, Lauren walked in with a big cake. "Hey, guys! Mrs. Piper is going home today, and her family wanted me to give this to you guys."

"Caaake!" the gang shouted and ran to attack it. Nothing could beat a sugar rush after a long day.

Senthil who usually led the charge did not move a muscle. Lina turned around and was surprised to see Senthil buried in a chart, writing a progress note. She knew then something was definitely wrong. The dessert connoisseur had not even bothered to find out what kind of cake it was. The rest of the gang was too busy cutting into the white chocolate raspberry cake. Lina brought over a piece for Senthil.

"Hey, this is scrumptious. Let me know what you think of it."

Senthil said, "Thank you, Lina," and absentmindedly placed the small plate next to him.

The gang was disappointed that Senthil was not joining them. Lina asked them to get a table at the restaurant and said she would bring Senthil. Everybody left; Lina stayed back with him to finish her notes. She realized he was not going to start a conversation, so she said, "Is everything okay?"

Senthil looked up and replied, "Yes Lina. Everything is okay."

"Bullshit. You can fool others, but not me, Senthil. I know something is bothering you. You haven't been yourself this whole week. Is your family okay back home?"

Senthil did not look up to see her sitting in front of him. Without taking his eyes off the chart, he just blurted out, "I just learned that she got married."

"Who got married?"

"My girlfriend Sumathi got married to someone. I don't know who."

"Did you guys break up?"

"No, we didn't. Something bad must have happened, and her relatives must have forced her into an arranged marriage."

"I am so sorry, Senthil. I had no idea it was this serious." She gave him a hug and asked, "When did you find out?"

"Last Saturday."

"Oh, you poor thing. You have been dealing with this all by yourself? You know you have friends who care about you."

"Thank you, Lina. I just need some time alone to think and sort some things out in my head."

Lina asked, "Is it okay to tell the gang? They all are wondering why you are so aloof." Senthil nodded, and on her way out, Lina said, "If there is anything I can do, please let me know."

Reality sunk in as he said the words out loud. Senthil came home and called Hema. He told her what happened and asked what he had to do if he wanted to go home. Hema was shocked and sorry to hear it. She told him she would help him in any way she could and asked him to do what he thought was best. She told him she could send someone to cover his assignment. Senthil said he would talk to his family and let her know soon.

He called home and talked to his family, especially Eshwari. She was the closest to him in age and the one who knew Sumathi the best. She told him everything that had happened to Sumathi's *appa*, their parents' visit, Sumathi's predicament and her inability to reach him, with her letter being returned to her, and Sumathi's last note. She told him that as much as everybody was eager to see him, he was better off in America for now, as there was nothing he could do if he came home. She told him it would not be a good idea to go see Sumathi, that her guilt would only torture her even more if she saw him. Visiting India and not being able to see her would be torturous for him too.

Eshwari was right. Eloping with him or getting a divorce was not even an option. Neither he nor she had been raised that way. Senthil might be a little forward in his thinking, but he respected the traditions and the sanctity of marriage. Arranged marriages were still the norm in India. While their love was true, he knew Sumathi would eventually learn to love her husband; while she might be miserable now, Senthil would eventually become a ghost of her past. This was his longest phone call to India. He was on the phone for nearly an hour and a half. It was going to cost him, but it felt worth every penny.

After hanging up, he called Shiva. He was talking to him after a long time. Shiva was working in a nursing home in Bay City, Michigan. He asked him about his work, his car, and life in Bay City. He then asked him about Maria. Shiva told him that she was not in Madras anymore and had moved back home to Kerala. He added that she was doing fine and that her parents had agreed to their wedding on one condition: they wanted him to get baptized and convert to Christianity. Shiva was not giving up Hinduism. He was only going to convert to appease Maria's family, have a Christian wedding, and bring Maria to America. They were going to celebrate Diwali and Christmas and go to the temple and church on Sundays. He told him he was going home in November and would return only after marrying Maria. Senthil was very happy for Shiva.

"Wait. Enough about me. Tell me what's new with you. How is Sumathi? How are your parents and siblings?"

Senthil told him that his family was doing well. Then in a cracking voice, he told Shiva what had happened to Sumathi. Shiva was shocked and saddened. Shiva told him he would come to visit him soon.

Senthil was emotionally drained when he went to sleep. It was a strange feeling. After talking to Hema, to his family, and finally to Shiva, he felt sad and a little light all at the same time. He felt light talking about Sumathi, but it had also made him sad as reality finally kicked in. It was around midnight when his phone rang. He wondered who would call him at this hour.

It was Lina. She said, "There is something at the door for you," and quickly hung up.

Puzzled, Senthil opened his apartment front door and saw a take-out bag. She had left him dinner with a card that read, "Dear Senthil, I care about you. You still have your whole life ahead of you. If you need a friend to talk to, I'll always be there for you." He called her back and thanked her.

She said, "I don't want to bother you, but I want you to know that I am here if you need a friend to talk to." Senthil thanked her for being so caring and understanding.

After much deliberation, he decided to stay in America. He decided to continue his pursuit of securing a bright future for his siblings and a comfortable and worry-free life for his parents. He immersed himself in work. He worked all the unclaimed overtime at the Golden Manor. While he was not his jolly old self, his work did not suffer. He forced himself to be as social as he could be.

His patients enjoyed his banter and the sense of humor that naturally came to him, but with his friends and colleagues, he had to try to be social. Often, they found him not eating properly, not mingling during downtime, not joining in their silliness at day's end and not participating in their weekend escapades. They gave him space and understood he was heartbroken. They wished he would get over his funk soon and join them.

Nine months of Senthil being a hermit passed. Summer ended, and autumn revived people from the heat. People began to prepare for Christmas. Work at the Golden Manor was going well. The community preferred the Golden Manor for their needs partly because of the success the Rehab Department had with their patients. Case managers at the local hospitals had the Golden Manor on their speed dial for patients who were getting discharged but were not quite yet ready to go home and could use more therapy. Lauren was happy with her team's results and productivity and the reputation they had earned for the Golden Manor.

On Friday, December 19, 1997, Lauren returned from her company's annual regional rehab managers' summit held at Indianapolis. The corporate headquarters had honored her as the "Rehab Manager of the Year" for her results in the Golden Manor and awarded her a bonus and a pay raise. She entered the department with a cake in her hand only to see all the therapists frantically catching up with their notes, productivity reports, and billing. They were gearing up for their weekend.

Lauren walked into the middle of the room with the cake held up high.

"Caaake," the gang shouted as they scrambled to gather plates and procure forks and a knife.

"I have some really good news for everybody," said Lauren.

"What can be better than cake?" asked Lina.

Lauren asked everybody to gather around. She saw Senthil slowly folding his charts. "Hurry up Senthil; this is going to impact you the most." Lina turned around and motioned for him to hurry up. When Senthil joined the circle of the therapists around Lauren, she said, "I am so proud of you all. With your hard work and dedication, you have made the Golden Manor the best-skilled nursing facility in south-west Indiana, and the headquarters has extended all your contracts for two more years. No more worrying every three months."

The room broke into cheers, laughter, high-fives, and hugs. In the current state of uncertainty in the therapy market, a long-term contract was unheard of. Even Senthil was swayed by the infectious mood and spirit. He high-fived back and tried to get to Lauren so he could thank her.

Lina ran to him and gave him a bear hug. "This is absolutely great. Don't you think? I am so excited!" Senthil agreed.

"Let's celebrate this with a night on the town. My treat. Irish pub at 7:00 PM. Be there or be square!" said Lauren.

Senthil hurried to meet her at the door and said, "Thank you very much, Lauren."

"No, thank you! See you at 7:00," she replied.

"You are going to come out tonight, right?" Lina asked.

"I'll try Lina," he replied.

Lina became angry. She told him it had been nine months since he had become a recluse, and it was not healthy to be a lone wolf. She reminded him that this great accomplishment was only because of teamwork and he was a part of the team. His absence would only put a damper on the celebration. While she understood the pain he was going through, she made it clear that he had mourned enough, and it was unhealthy for him to continue to wallow in self-pity.

"I am not wallowing in self-pity," Senthil said defensively.

"I know I sound harsh, but it's time somebody said something before you wither away from loneliness," Lina fired back. "You spent Thanksgiving alone in your apartment when we invited you to join us. I know you loved her, and I am sorry it ended the way it did, but it's time for you to move on."

Senthil kept quiet and hung his head low. Deep down he knew she was right. Lina told him she was going home to freshen up and then would come to pick him up at 7:30 PM; if he was not ready then, she was not going to go either.

As promised, Lina knocked on his door at 7:30 PM but got no response. She knocked again and waited. She thought he was being rude and began to walk away angrily when she heard the door open. She stopped but did not turn around.

"Lina?" he called. She turned around and saw him tucking his shirt and fixing his belt. "I am sorry I was getting dressed in the bathroom."

She smiled and said, "I was going to curse you. I'll wait in the car."

Everyone was excited to see him. This was the first time in nine months he had joined them. They gave him a hug and told him how happy they were to see him come out. Lauren had made reservations for them, and they settled down at the table. As they looked at the menu, Lauren walked in, and the whole table went wild. They had a great time.

Lauren ordered some pretzels and beer cheese dip, Irish nachos, beef, and Guinness hand pies and Rueben fritters as appetizers for the table. She reminded the gang that it was her treat and they could order whatever they wanted. Monique suggested a family style dinner, and everybody agreed. They ordered Shepherd's pie, Boxty, unstuffed cabbage, bangers and colcannon with Guinness onion gravy, and corned beef. They unanimously elected Senthil to order four desserts for everybody to share. He was happy to oblige, and ordered the Irish apple cake with custard sauce, soda bread pudding, chocolate biscuit cake, and orange-scented soufflé pie.

While Senthil sipped on lemonade, the rest of them got hammered. They partied late into the night. They realized it was late only when the bartender yelled "Last call." They decided to head home. They were in no position to drive. Lauren called her husband to come and pick her up. Since Mira and Sofi lived close by, they hitched a ride with them. Senthil drove Lina, Emma, and Monique in Lina's car. He dropped off Emma and Monique on the way. He was going to drop off Lina and her car and walk back to his apartment that was less than a mile away. He parked the car and handed her the keys.

"Are you going to let me walk up by myself?" she asked coyly.

Senthil helped Lina out of the car. She leaned on to him as they walked up the stairs. She did not want him to walk home alone at this hour; it was cold outside. He told her his leather jacket was good, and if he walked briskly, he would not feel the cold and be home in about thirty minutes. He said that he could drive her car and bring it back in the morning, but she insisted that he stay over. She would not take no for an answer, and Senthil finally agreed.

Senthil sat down on the couch as Lina went inside.

"You can turn on the TV if you want," she yelled. Lina had cable TV.

As Senthil was flipping through the channels, Lina walked out in her red floral silk pajamas. The first two buttons on the top had come undone, revealing the middle of her black brassiere against her milky white skin.

Senthil did not want to embarrass her by telling her to button up. So, he continued to look at the TV and surf the channels. He moved to one side of the couch, but Lina came and plopped herself right next to him with her head bent between her hands and her fingers interlocked in her thick wavy blonde hair.

She tilted her head and looked at him with her dreamy eyes. In a sultry voice, she asked, "What are we watching?"

"You are about to fall asleep. You should go to bed," he replied.

She grabbed the remote from his hands as though to tell him that he was not going to get rid of her that easily; she was not drunk, just a little tipsy. She came across the movie *Good Will Hunting*. The movie had just started, and Matt Damon was sitting in a chair, reading a book.

"I love Matt Damon!" Lina screamed and cuddled next to Senthil.

It was an interesting movie. Just when Will met Skylar in the bar and took down the snobbish guy for embarrassing his friend Chuckie, Senthil noticed Lina was asleep on his shoulder. He muted the TV. Without waking her up, he tried to gently get up and lay her down on the couch, but he ended up waking her.

"Did I miss the movie?" she asked sheepishly. He told her that they were only twenty minutes into the movie.

"Can we watch it together later? I don't think I can stay awake any longer." Senthil agreed and turned off the TV.

Lina held on to his hand and walked towards the bedroom. Senthil told her he would sleep on the couch.

"You don't trust me or don't trust yourself? It's a queen size bed, and there is enough room for both of us."

Senthil tried to reason with her, but it was just a moot point. He lay on his side on one end of the bed. Lina lay down and cuddled up to him. Just before falling asleep, she said, "Don't leave in the morning as soon as you get up. We can have breakfast and finish watching the movie. I'll drive you to your apartment later."

Lina woke up to the smell of bacon. Senthil had taken the liberty of making breakfast. With the things he could find in her kitchen, he made home-style potatoes, eggs, and bacon.

"I could get used to this," she said as she poured out two glasses of orange juice and set the table. "I know you are too much of a gentleman and would never take advantage of a girl who is tipsy but did the thought of kissing me ever cross your mind last night?"

Senthil almost choked on the potatoes. Clearing his throat, he replied, "No Lina, I am sorry."

"Am I not pretty?" There was some disappointment in her voice.

He said, "Lina, you are gorgeous! I am still not over Sumathi, and she is still on my mind and in my heart." He explained to her that it would be unfair to her if he kissed her while he was still thinking about Sumathi. Lina told him that she really liked him and would like him to take her out on a date. She told him it was time he moved on, but she understood if he was not ready and would be patient in hopes that he would come around.

"You are not going to act weird around me now since you know how I feel about you, right?" she asked.

Senthil smiled and said, "Of course not, Lina. I am flattered and really appreciate your candor."

They finished watching *Good Will Hunting*, and Lina dropped him home.

Even though he was not over Sumathi and missed her terribly, Senthil had come out of his shell, thanks to Lina. He began to hang out with his colleagues again and live his life. It was a big relief to not have to worry about the next assignment for the next two years.

The Golden Manor and his fellow therapists, especially Lina, turned out to be the best remedy for Senthil's broken heart. The gang did something or other every weekend. Lina found ways to hang out with Senthil alone. It was usually at her apartment, either playing cards or watching movies. She taught him how to cook Polish food, and he taught her a few Indian dishes.

They became very close friends, albeit platonic. Senthil was enamored by her Polish accent, her blonde hair, and her charming personality. Then there was her affection for him. However, he just could not make the transition from being a friend to a boyfriend. He felt he was betraying his love even though she was married and had perhaps moved on with her life by now. He also felt he would be cheating Lina if he went out with her while he still had strong feelings for Sumathi. He simply could not bring himself to do that.

Life could not be any easier. Senthil had great job satisfaction, an appreciative manager, caring friends, and a steady paycheck. However, he was not truly happy—content but not happy. Lina was the beacon of hope in his life. She motivated him without smothering him. His gang and Lina kept him from spiraling down into an ascetic life of labor. However, with Sumathi gone from his life, he could not help but become a self-abnegating brother and son.

Chapter 20 — Culture Shock

SENTHIL WORKED HARD AND DID NOT TURN DOWN ANY opportunity for overtime. The next year and a half sailed by smoothly. He sent money home every month so that his *appa* did not have to work overtime. His parents thought it was time to get Eshwari married. She had graduated from college and begun working as a teacher in a school. They asked Senthil when it would be convenient for him to come home so that they could schedule the wedding accordingly.

It was not an arranged marriage. Karthik's parents were family friends whom they had known since childhood. They had moved away to Pondicherry after Karthik graduated from high school. Karthik had stayed in touch with Eshwari through letters and visited them whenever their family came to Madras to see their relatives. Karthik was working as a medical technologist at JIPMER hospital in Pondicherry.

When Karthik and his parents asked for Eshwari's hand in marriage, the answer was a no-brainer. Senthil would not miss his sister's wedding, but he did not see a future for himself in India, so he did not want to jeopardize his job or the green card process. He called Hema to check with her. She explained that his I-40, the immigration petition, had been approved and since his priority date was current, she was able to file for an I-485 for the adjustment of status and apply for employment authorization card; his six-year limit on the H1-B visa was to end this year. However, since the Balanced Budget Act, green card processing for health-care workers was being held in abeyance until further regulations were clarified. She told him she would file for advanced parole for international travel and asked him to check with Lauren regarding his time off from the Golden Manor.

Lina stepped up and said that she would work as many hours as needed if it helped Senthil take three weeks to attend his sister's wedding. Lauren promised to not cancel his contract and that if they needed help for Lina, she could ask their sister facility Meadow Oaks to send a physical therapist on a PRN basis. Grateful, Senthil prepared to go home.

Hema helped him book his tickets through Lufthansa Airways and got him her corporate discount. He would be flying out of Indianapolis. The wedding was set to be on September 17, 1999. Senthil was flying out on Friday, September 3, and returning on Saturday, September 25. He started shopping. Lauren loaned her Sam's Club card, and Lina drove him there. He bought a lot of candies, chocolates, cookie tins, and chewing gum. They went to Walmart, and Senthil got his *appa* and *amma* watches, and a couple of jeans and body sprays for his brothers. Lina helped him pick out perfume and nail polish for his sisters. Other than a few change of clothes and underwear, he did not pack much of his stuff. He had to make sure his suitcases were within the weight limits.

On the day of his flight, both Lina and Senthil went to work at 6:00 AM so that they could finish their work and leave early. Lina drove him to Indianapolis, dropped him off on time, and reminded him that she would be back to pick him up. He hugged her and thanked her for her help with shopping and the ride to the airport. Lina kissed him on his cheek and said, "I'll miss you. Have a safe trip and a great visit with your family."

He had a three-hour layover in Frankfurt, Germany. Unlike his first time, he just sat down by the gate and did not venture into the stores. He was returning home almost six years later, under circumstances he had not imagined. Although he was looking forward to seeing his family, he was anxious.

He did not know if he could restrain himself from going to meet Sumathi. He sought closure, but at what expense? What good was going to come of it? How was it going to affect Sumathi, and what would she have to face after he left? The thoughts overwhelmed him.

He landed in Madras and exited the plane. He was immediately hit by the heat and the smell that his skin and his nose had forgotten. It took him a few minutes to get used to it. After collecting his suitcases, he headed towards immigration. People returning from Malaysia, Singapore, Dubai, and Saudi Arabia had a much more difficult time with the Indian customs than the people coming from America.

Gold and electronics, including TVs and VCRs, video cameras, and cassette players, garnered the most custom taxes and duties. Unlike India, America had 110-volt appliances and the most popular jewelry was made of 14-carat gold. Other countries such as India had 22-carat gold jewelry and 220-volt appliances. So, the customs officers did not target people coming from America. They concentrated on passengers who were most likely to return home with 22- or 24-carat gold jewelry and electronics so they could demand bribes to let them through without hassle. People obliged because they did not want to unpack and pack again.

When a customs officer approached Senthil, he said to him in Tamil, "I don't have anything to declare. I am coming from America and didn't bring any gold or electronics."

The officer just waved to gesture him to keep moving, as if to say, "You are wasting my time."

After getting his passport stamped, Senthil stepped out of the double glass doors, pushing his suitcases in a cart.

There was a sea of people outside, all trying to get a glimpse of their loved ones. Senthil scanned the crowd. Bala was the first to spot him and jumped up, waving his hand. Grinning, Senthil hurried in his direction. He waved him to keep moving forward to the walkway and then, in a split second, jumped over the ropes, paying the guard no heed, and ran towards him. He hugged him and said, "Everybody is here. They are on the other side. I'll get the luggage. You go ahead."

"Oh, my goodness, you are almost taller than me and even have a mustache now!" Senthil exclaimed.

Senthil ran towards his family. Rathi was waiting with a rose in her hand. He hugged his *appa* and *amma* and touched their feet to pay his respects. He then hugged his sisters. His parents looked older than when he had left. The past six years, he had remembered them the way they had looked when he left India. His siblings were all grown up too. Tears welled up in his eyes; he was not prepared.

"Where's Nanda?"

Nanda had to go to their grandparents' village to secure the marriage hall and pay an advance deposit to the cook and the priests. "He'll be back tomorrow morning. He didn't want to go but had to," his *appa* said.

They had hired a taxi. Bala came on the motorbike—Senthil's motorbike. When they got to the parking lot, Senthil saw his bike and was flooded with memories of Sumathi. He stroked the bike, reminiscing. Everybody was quiet; nobody wanted to address the elephant in the room.

His *appa* broke the silence, "Let's go home. He must be starving."

The taxi was an Ambassador and had bench seats. Senthil sat in the front with his *appa*. His *amma* and Rathi sat in the back. Eshwari went on the motorbike with Bala. She wanted to get home ahead of them to start preparing breakfast.

As the taxi exited the airport and entered the main road, Senthil clenched his fingers on his *appa*'s thigh and screamed, "Oh my goodness!"

Everybody in the car got alarmed, including the driver. He braked the car and pulled over to the side of the road, but Senthil realized what had happened. Everybody in the car was relieved when he said, "It's okay, keep going. I just forgot that we drive on the left side of the road here."

Eshwari had made *idli, dosa, pongal*, and *vada* with coconut *chutney*, *sambar*, and tomato *chutney*. His *amma* had made *kesari* for dessert. The aroma made Senthil salivate. He took a quick shower, and everybody sat down at the table to eat. His *amma* was the last to join the group and sat down as she set a big 2-liter Coca-Cola bottle in the middle of the table.

Senthil was surprised and asked, "Why did you get a Coke?"

Bala replied, "Do you prefer Sprite? We have that too."

He thought they had got it since he was returning from America but was shocked to learn that drinking soft drinks with meals was the norm in most households in India now. He reminded them of the time when sharing a bottle of soda on a hot summer day was a luxurious treat. Rathi said that things had changed in India slowly over time since he left and they had not really noticed the change. She asked, "What do you drink in America when you eat?"

Much to their dismay, Senthil replied, "Water."

They sat around and talked about life in America. They wanted him to narrate everything that had happened. They were all very careful to avoid talking about anything that would even remotely remind him of Sumathi. He gave them a glimpse of his life in America. He gave them a synopsis of his time in Dallas and took them on a journey to Missouri and Indiana. He told them about all the people who had helped him.

Rathi asked, "Did you go to Disneyland? How about New York or Hollywood?"

Senthil told them that he had been busy working and saving and never had the time or the desire to be a tourist.

Eshwari said, "I know you went to make money for all of us, but I wish and hope you take some to time to smell the roses and enjoy yourself too."

Senthil's eyes were glazed from the jet lag; it was past midnight in America. His *appa* asked him to take a nap.

Even the smell of his *amma* and Eshwari cooking lunch did not wake him up. It was quiet, and the sun had set when he woke up. He freshened up, and when he came out of the bedroom, he found Eshwari in the kitchen and his parents sitting on the porch. Eshwari was making tea for her parents.

"What time is it?" he asked, walking into the kitchen.

"It's 6:30. I can't believe you still haven't taken up drinking tea or coffee. I am sure America has many different types to offer."

He just smiled and walked out to the porch. He sat on the floor next to his *appa*. He told his parents that he had brought his checkbook and asked them how much the wedding was going to cost.

"You just came. We don't have to talk about money today. We are just glad you are here."

Senthil was surprised to hear that his other siblings had gone out with their friends. As they were discussing wedding plans, Senthil saw a motorbike come to a screeching halt in front of the gate. Rathi had her arms around the guy riding the bike. As they came to a stop, she hopped off the bike and high-fived the guy who waved at the porch, turned around, and took off. Senthil was speechless. He looked at his parents and was even more shocked when they asked her, "Did you have fun?"

"When did you wake up, sleepy head?" Rathi patted Senthil on his head as she ran inside to change.

"Who is that guy?" Senthil asked.

"Oh, it's her friend," his *amma* replied.

Senthil reminded them that he used to drop Sumathi three streets away from her house and stop by the main road and walk the bike with her when they came home. He was surprised to see how things had changed since he had left India. This was the first time Senthil had brought up Sumathi's name, and there was an awkward silence.

His *appa* said, "Things have changed, so slowly that we hardly noticed it. Not all of it is good."

Everybody went to bed after dinner. Senthil tried to sleep but could not. He stayed up watching TV, and around midnight, he heard the gate open. It was Nanda. He had worked fast and managed to catch the evening bus. He had not wanted to wait until the next day to return. They chatted for a long time. Senthil was glad that Nanda had stepped up and was helping with the wedding duties.

The wedding was approaching fast. Senthil deposited $25,000 in his *appa's* bank account. Eshwari, Rathi, and their *amma* were busy shopping for sarees and jewelry. The boys and their *appa* were busy shopping for everything else. With the computer and Internet boom and call centers in every corner, Madras had become the Silicon Valley of India. People who had bicycles had upgraded to motorbikes, and the ones who had motorbikes had upgraded to cars. There were malls and high-rise shopping centers everywhere. However, the roads and space had not changed, resulting in pollution, congestion, and traffic jams. Senthil had coughing and sneezing fits and burning eyes whenever he went out during the day.

His parents did not want him to fall sick before the wedding, but he could not just sit at home. Besides, keeping busy took his mind off Sumathi. He longed to see her, but he could not imagine what good their interaction would bring. He was torn by the hope of running into her when he was out and about, but at the same time, he prayed for it to never happen. After all, she was not *his* Sumathi anymore. He could not bear to see her with another man.

They went out in the evening to eat. All his favorite little restaurants and snack spots had been replaced by McDonald's, Pizza Hut, KFC, Subway, Taco Bell, and Burger King. The youth of India not only flocked to these joints but also dressed like their western counterparts. Indian girls had traded modest, traditional clothes for western wear. He saw kids, both boys and girls, smoking and drinking in public. He had never seen an Indian girl smoke or drink before. Boys and girls sported hair with blonde and brown highlights. He looked at his conservative *amma*, and she did not seem to be bothered by any of it. He realized how much the culture had changed in Madras.

The days when debt was dreaded had given way to an age of reveling in credit. Gone were the days where one had to save enough to buy what one wanted. People had become accustomed to just charging their credit card whenever they needed something. Going out on the weekend had been a once-in-a-while affair and a treat, but now it was expected. Senthil was shocked to hear Bala pestering his parents to go out to eat just because it was a Saturday. Even TV in Madras had changed. It was inundated with western soap operas and TV shows. People of Madras had become like the cat that saw the tiger and branded itself to be striped like a tiger. They were emulating westerners and going way overboard.

The wedding went well without a hitch. Senthil was very happy to get acquainted with Karthik who he realized was the best suitor for his sister. Eshwari had not been swept away by the wave of westernization. She remained grounded and was the only stable thing that Senthil found solace in his return from America.

His siblings had taken time off from school for the two weeks Senthil was there. Rathi spent most of her time at home on the computer, chatting with her friends online. Bala was more interested in going out than staying home, and Nanda was just busy helping with all the errands. Once the hustle and bustle of the wedding days were over, Senthil had a few days to relax before heading back to America. He came to realize two things: Madras was not his home anymore, and he did not see a future for himself in India.

Eshwari and Karthik wanted to become stable, and therefore, they had postponed their honeymoon. Eshwari told her new husband that she wanted to stay back until Senthil left for America. Karthik understood and told her he would be back to see Senthil off to the airport. She was the most responsible one of his siblings. Now, with her newly embraced maturity as a wife and daughter-in-law, she found a quiet moment and advised Senthil to think about his future. She asked him to slowly forget about Sumathi and assured him that there was a lucky girl somewhere waiting for him. Senthil just listened and nodded.

A few days before his return, Senthil wanted to go shopping to buy some souvenirs for his friends in America. They all decided to make it a family day out. They went to Poompuhar, the Tamil Nadu handicrafts development store to buy some traditional crafts that were unique to India. He got several figurines, letter openers, and objects made of sandalwood. He bought several Thanjavur art plates—handicraft plates made with a combination of silver, copper, and bronze, embossed with figures of elephants and peacocks. He wanted to buy enough for his friends in Glasgow, Princeton, Terre Haute, and his company.

Eshwari helped him pick a *Kancheepuram Pattu* sari for Hema, while Rathi helped him pick a beautiful *Banarasi* silk *churidar* with handmade embroidery for Lina. The *churidar* was a rich two-toned peacock blue color, which he thought would complement Lina's blonde hair and blue eyes. He was still living with the same clothes he had bought the first time he had left India. It was time to revamp his wardrobe. He bought fabric for shirts and pants. He stuck to the basics: dark pants and matching pastel shirts. As he was sifting through pant materials, he was inundated with memories of shopping with Sumathi before he had first left the country. Tears trickled down his cheeks; he was careful to hide them, though.

The next morning, he took some chocolates and candy bars he had brought from America and the pant and shirt fabrics and headed to see his friend Venkat at Masculine Tailors. He could not recognize the store when he reached there. It was very upscale and had sprawled to include the two neighboring stores. It looked more like a showroom and less like the tailor shop he had last seen.

He stepped inside and was greeted by a young man. "Welcome, sir. How can I help you?"

Senthil told him he was there to have seven pants and seven shirts stitched for him. The young man replied, "Sure sir, we can have it done in five days."

Senthil told him he would need it in two days since he was leaving. The young man scratched his head and said, "It's wedding season, sir, and it is very hectic."

"Is Venkat here?" asked Senthil.

"Boss is upstairs, but I'll call him for you."

Venkat came down, and his face lit up like a 1000-watt bulb. He shook Senthil's hand vigorously and was glad to see him. He told him he had expanded his business and now lived upstairs with his wife and one-year-old son. He asked one of his boys to get a Coke for his favorite customer. Senthil gave him the bag with chocolates and candy bars. Venkat said he would share the sweets with his wife later. He brimmed with happiness as he talked about his wife and how lucky he was. He inquired about Sumathi, and Senthil just told him she was doing fine before changing the subject. He did not want to repeat his sob story. Senthil said that he would need his pants and shirts in a couple of days but would understand if he could not manage to deliver it due to the wedding season rush.

"Don't worry about it. One of my boys will deliver them to your house tomorrow evening. You don't even have to come back to the store." Senthil thanked him profusely. After Venkat took his measurements, Senthil paid him and took leave.

The night before his departure, Senthil stayed up late. He could not believe he had experienced a culture shock coming back to his homeland. His biggest regret was that he was leaving without seeing Sumathi. He could not forget her, and knowing she was only a few kilometers away made it all the more difficult to bear.

It was a wholly different affair leaving India this time around. The first time, he had left with a heart full of promise, a bright outlook for the future, and a warm embrace from Sumathi that had quelled his fears. This time, he left with a void in his heart, an unsure future ahead of him, and an unexplained fear. The only thing he was confident of was his ability to take care of his parents and make his siblings' dreams come true.

When he reached America, Lina was at the airport to receive him. She ran towards him excitedly and hugged him. On the way home, she enquired about his family and Eshwari's wedding. Senthil gave her a detailed account of everything. As she took the exit 7 for US-41/U/150 toward Evansville/Terre Haute, Senthil exclaimed, "Ahh! There is the smell of Terre Haute."

Lina laughed. "Looks like you missed it more than you missed me."

She took him to her apartment and asked him to freshen up while she made him breakfast. She made a typical Polish breakfast with sausage, potato pancakes, and scrambled eggs. As they ate, Senthil thanked her for covering for him. She replied that all was well at work and everybody was awaiting his return. Senthil opened his suitcase and gave a box to Lina. She looked at him in confusion. Senthil asked her to open it and told her that he had especially got it tailored for her.

"Wow! It's gorgeous! I love the unique colors."

"I am glad you like it. I picked the colors because they complement your blonde hair and blue eyes."

Lina was thrilled and suggested that they should soon take a picture dressed up in Indian outfits. Senthil agreed.

"I hope you took a lot of pictures in India."

Senthil pulled out the albums of pictures he had taken at home and at the wedding. He showed her the pictures and explained to her all the rituals surrounding a South Indian wedding ceremony.

"You have a lovely family. I can see why you love and care for them so much." Without looking up and in a monotone, she asked, "Did you see Sumathi?"

Senthil didn't answer. After a brief silence, Lina looked up and saw Senthil staring into the corner. "Are you okay? I am sorry if I asked something I shouldn't have."

"It's all right Lina. I am okay. I didn't see Sumathi. I really wanted to, but I realized nothing good would come from it."

He told her about Eshwari's advice of refraining from going to see Sumathi and avoid creating a cyclone in a heart that was beginning to feel solace with time. Eshwari was close to Sumathi's age and was as steeped in traditional values as Sumathi. She knew best, and Senthil did not think twice to abide by her counsel. His love for Sumathi and his desire for her to be happy and peaceful quelled his desire for closure.

His brief absence had made Lina more enamored of him. However, Lina kept quiet. She told herself there would be a better opportunity when Senthil would be more receptive to her love and reciprocate her feelings.

Chapter 21 — Ultimatum of the Millennium

AS THE YEAR 2000 APPROACHED, Y2K BUG FEAR REACHED its peak. From the sudden influx of Indian and Chinese computer programmers overwhelming the national visa system and causing lopsided annual visa quotas, to people buying guns and ammunition and bunkers to protect themselves from the end of the world, Y2K fear had far-reaching effects. People were turning off their VCRs to prevent the internal clock from turning to "00" after "99." Many were panicking that their cars were going to die when the clock struck 12:01. Computers were going to crash, and planes were going to fall from the skies.

Amidst this uncertainty, daily life went on as usual. The therapists at the Golden Manor continued to enjoy a good volume of caseload and a wide variety of patients. They worked well together and hung out on most weekends. Whether the entire gang got together or not, Lina made every effort to spend as much time with Senthil as possible. They ran together, went to the local YMCA gym, went grocery shopping, visited the $1 Indiana Movie Theater, and hung out at home watching TV.

Senthil was immensely grateful for Lina's friendship. He did not realize Lina had feelings for him. He still had Sumathi on his mind and could not even dream of anyone else taking her place. Even a goddess like Lina, with her kind heart, head over heels for him, could not remold his broken heart.

Lina would hold his arm during long walks or while watching TV. She had changed her life in the hopes of winning his heart one day. She ignored her friends and spent all her time with Senthil. Thanksgiving Day and Christmas rolled by. December 31, 1999 was a Friday, and everybody made plans to ring in the new millennium with their family or loved ones. Senthil had no plans; he was not worried about the Y2K bug. He had no TV or VCR, and he intended to unplug his Sony cordless phone before midnight, just in case. Hema invited all her therapists for a party in Dallas, but Senthil did not want to attend.

A couple of Lina's PT friends from Poland, who were working in Chicago, planned to go to Times Square in New York to watch the ball drop; they were pestering her to join them. Lina wanted to spend the night with Senthil and knew he would not be willing to go to New York. All the other therapists were skipping town early Friday. Lauren told them they could all leave as soon as they had seen all their patients for the day.

Every TV in the nursing home was tuned to play the celebrations across the world. This New Year celebration was a global event. After all, it only happened once in a thousand years. Besides, this was probably the first time the new year was also speculated to be a doomsday. People were curious. There were thirty-nine time zones in the world to welcome the millennium at thirty-nine different times. New Zealand and Australia had already celebrated the birth of the millennium before breakfast was served at the Golden Manor. People breathed a big sigh of relief to see no devastation unleashed when the clock struck midnight. The lights were on and partying continued without a hitch. Australia was followed by Japan, South Korea, North Korea, China, Philippines, and Singapore.

Lauren had a TV set up in the therapy gym so that the patients interested in watching live broadcast celebrations did not miss it. They showed every country ringing in the new millennium with their traditional music, dance, and festivities. China had a dazzling display of people dressed in traditional dress cheering to their music and dragons. Senthil was hoping to catch a glimpse of the Indian celebration, with people in traditional clothes, classical Indian music, and all forms of Indian traditional dance styles: *Bharatanatyam, Kathak, Kathakali, Kuchipudi, Odissi, Manipuri, Mohiniyattam*, and *Sattriya*.

Lauren came by with a big cake to wish everyone in the Rehab Department a happy new year. She was going to Indianapolis with her husband for New Year's Eve. She asked everybody their plans and told them to be safe.

Lina said, "Looks like everybody is leaving town except for Senthil and me. Maybe we'll hang out if he doesn't have any plans."

She looked up to see his reaction and was pleased to hear, "Of course! I cannot think of a better way to spend New Year's Eve."

They decided to cook at Lina's apartment. She picked him up, along with his spice box and a bag of basmati rice. They went grocery shopping. Senthil wanted to make something special for Lina. He bought frozen meatballs, garlic, ginger, tomato, onions, peas, and coconut, while Lina got a bottle of champagne; since Senthil did not drink, she got a bottle of sparkling apple cider for him.

They hurried home so that Senthil could call his family. Senthil called exactly at 1:30 PM, which was midnight in India. Only his parents were there; Nanda, Rathi, and Bala were out with their friends. He wished them a happy and prosperous new year. He then called Eshwari and Karthik to wish them. Eshwari told him she prayed the new millennium would bring a special girl into his life. He knew she was sincere, but he did not say anything.

Senthil was chopping some onions when Lina screamed, "Senthil! Come! Hurry up!" He went to wash his hands when Lina came running to the kitchen, dragged him into the living room, and pushed him on to the couch. She landed on his lap as he plopped down on the couch. She was in no hurry to move. She had her arms around his neck and pointed to the TV. "Look they are featuring Indian celebrations!" she exclaimed.

To his dismay, they featured Indians dressed in suits and dresses, dancing to Mambo #5 with streamers in their hands. "This is not fair. I am sure the rest of India is celebrating with traditional dances, classical songs, and temple visits."

Lina laughed and said, "It's hilarious, but I am not going to judge India based on this."

Disappointed, Senthil went back to finish cooking the curried meatballs and biryani with vegetables. At 6:00 PM Lina called her family in Poland, as it was midnight there. Senthil set the table. Lina poured herself a glass of wine and joined him.

They played Scrabble, chess, and cards until 11:45 PM. After that, they settled on the couch to watch Dick Clark's countdown of the crystal ball. Lina brought the chilled champagne bottle and the sparkling apple cider. As the countdown began, they popped open the bottle. When the clock struck 12:00, they raised their glasses and wished each other a happy new year. Lina kissed Senthil on his lips.

"Aren't you going to kiss me in return? It's a new millennium," she said.

Senthil kissed her on her forehead.

They stayed up late talking about what the new millennium was going to bring—their hopes and fears and professional goals.

Lina said, "I am going to ask you something, and I want you to be totally honest with yourself and with me."

"Of course, Lina. What's it?"

"What do you think of me?"

"I think you are very smart, kind, intelligent, beautiful, and an exceptional PT. You're also a great friend."

"You are very kind, but do you like me?"

"Who wouldn't like you, Lina?"

"Senthil, you can't answer a question with a question. I am not sure if I am going to regret saying this, but I just want to be honest with you and with myself. I have fallen in love with you."

Senthil remained silent. He dared not look at her.

"Please say something, Senthil."

"I don't know what to say, Sumathi. I mean Lina. I am sorry."

"Don't you find me attractive? Is it a cultural thing?"

"Lina, you are every Indian guy's dream. You know what happened with Sumathi. I just can't get over her. Even now I accidentally called you Sumathi. That's the only name that comes out whenever those feelings are evoked."

"She's married. She has moved on."

"I know Lina, but I can't help it."

"You have to take a chance."

"If I go out with you, it'll be only physical, and I can't do that to you. Maybe time will change me. I hope it does, at least."

"I am not looking for a physical relationship, Senthil. I want to be with someone who loves me. I have been hopeful, thinking that time will change you. I don't want to use the cliché that my biological clock is ticking, but I can't live like you do. I don't want to have regrets when it's too late. I opened my heart to you, but now I realize that you don't have any room for me in yours. I don't want to compete with your memory of Sumathi."

"I am sorry Lina but—"

Lina interrupted him, "Don't apologize, Senthil. It is what it is. If there is no place for me in your life, I don't want to be here in Terre Haute anymore."

"Lina, please don't make it harder than it already is."

"It's easy for you to say. I made myself vulnerable to you. I don't regret it. Waiting was worse than knowing. I need to move on, and I hope you do too."

"You don't have to leave because of that, Lina."

"I have no choice. I have to, Senthil. It's going to be hard if I keep seeing you every day. I don't want to live in the past, thinking of 'if only' or 'what if' like you. I am not that stupid."

Senthil just hung his head and said, "Hmmm."

"I am so sorry, Senthil. I did not mean to insult you or your memory of Sumathi. It's just—"

Senthil interrupted her, "It's okay, Lina. Don't worry about it. I need to hear more of that."

Lina gave him a hug and went to bed saying, "I may sleep in tomorrow. Please don't leave without saying bye."

Senthil settled down on the couch. He felt horrible to have caused Lina pain. He was not sure when he drifted off to sleep, but he woke up to the sound of sniffles. Lina must have been crying. Her bedroom door was partially open, but he hesitated. He hoped she would stop, but when she did not, he felt compelled to comfort her. He was the reason why she was crying.

He walked towards her room and stood by the door. The faint night light cast a soft glow on her body. She was lying on her stomach, with her head turned to the other side. Her golden hair was sprawled over the pillow. Senthil went in. He gently stroked her head and said, "I am really sorry, Lina. I did not mean to hurt your feelings."

"I don't blame you for anything, Senthil." She rolled over to the other side of the bed to make room for him.

Senthil lay down, and Lina turned towards him. She placed her head on his chest while he gently patted her head. They did not speak. The silence was comforting to both.

Lina was not bluffing. She had talked to Lauren about leaving but had asked her not to tell anyone until her company found another assignment for her. She wanted to go to Chicago for its large Polish population, to feel close to home. Lauren was disappointed, but she understood.

And just like that, Lina was gone. She did not tell anyone, not even Senthil, until Friday, January 28, 2000. A new job waited for her in Chicago the following Monday. She wanted to just fade away rather than have a big farewell party. She did not want any drama and anyone blaming Senthil for her departure.

The Golden Manor was not the same for Senthil without Lina. He felt lonely at times. As much as she was the life of the party, she was tamer than all the other therapists; with her, Senthil did not feel out of place when they went drinking or dancing. He wondered if he had made a mistake. But then, he felt bad as his guilty conscience rebuked him for betraying Sumathi's memory. He consoled himself with the thought that Lina deserved someone better than him—someone who came without any emotional baggage and would be true to her and only her.

Lauren called a rehab meeting to tell all the therapists about the corporate decision to hire therapists permanently and directly rather than through contract companies. Given the uncertainties that surrounded the reimbursement for therapy by Medicare which, through the Balanced Budget Act of Clinton, aimed at reducing cost, health-care institutions were taking a second look at how they staffed their rehab departments. To add to that, freezing the processing of new H1-B visas and green cards for therapists until new standards were established was wreaking havoc on the therapy market that had once thrived, bringing in a lot of foreign-trained therapists. With baby boomers aging, the market was expected to see an increased need for therapists taking care of the elderly.

Thanks to the impetuous greed of many rehab companies and home health agencies that fraudulently billed Medicare and Medicaid for services, the government decided to implement some corrective measures. The victims of this were honest and hardworking foreign-trained therapists who had left their country and desired to call America their home through hard work and loyalty. Just like Senthil, many of them had filed for their green cards, but their processing had been frozen until new standards for regulating the influx of foreign-trained therapists and credentialing them were put into place.

Contract companies were finding it difficult to place their therapists, and many were taking permanent jobs for stability. Hema's workforce had also dwindled down to only five therapists, with Senthil being the only one who was foreign-trained and under a visa, pending green card. Even Shiva got a permanent job a while back in 1998 after he got married and brought Maria to America. Both of them worked for the same nursing home in Bay City, Michigan. The nursing home had filed the green card for both of them.

Hema was considering the idea of settling down in India. The only reason she struggled to stay afloat in this market turmoil was to not jeopardize Senthil's green card process. He was very thankful for her kindness and support. If Hema called it quits, Senthil would have to find another company to sponsor his green card, which would be a setback; with all the uncertainties involved, it seemed too risky.

Hema had to find another assignment for him starting in May. Meanwhile, the Golden Manor was in mourning. All the patients and staff members were upset that the entire rehab team was going to be replaced by new therapists. They held several potlucks and farewell parties. It was painful to say goodbye, and Senthil understood why Lina had left quietly the way she did.

Emma and Monique negotiated with their company and were able to accept a permanent position with the Golden Manor, which had to pay $5,000 each to their company to buy them out. Lauren convinced the corporate office that it was worth having some stability and therapists familiar to the Golden Manor to orient the new crew. The big national company of Mira and Sofi was able to find them an assignment in Arizona. Senthil's license limited him to Indiana, Michigan, and Missouri, which made it more challenging for Hema.

April 28, 2000 was his last day at the Golden Manor. Senthil still did not have an assignment. Hema said that he could come to Texas and stay in the company's apartment until his next assignment, but he would have to pay his way there. His apartment rent and the price of the flight were almost identical. Senthil decided to stay in Terre Haute for the time being. Besides, he did not have a license to practice in Texas and just wanted to be near a place where he could get a job.

He joined the YMCA and the public library to maintain his sanity. When he called home, he did not tell them that he had no job. There was no point in alarming them. He kept himself busy. He would pack himself a peanut butter and jelly sandwich and a bottle of water, walk to the YMCA, and work out there until noon. Then, he would walk to the Terre Haute public library.

It had a few computers, and he spent hours scouring the Internet for therapy jobs. He created a yahoo email account and emailed Hema regarding leads of job openings.

Hema was not sitting still. It was just her, as she had down-scaled her company in a difficult market. She was on the phone all day, calling different companies and facilities. The entire month of May passed, and there was still no job in sight for Senthil.

Senthil was already frugal, and since he no longer had a job, he took his frugality to new heights. He only purchased the bare essentials when he went grocery shopping and bought only things that were on sale. He clipped coupons, skipped meals, and lived off cereal, eggs, and ramen noodles. He made himself a strict budget and tried to live within it.

June 23, 2000 was his fifty-sixth day without a job when Hema called. She told him she had some good news and some bad news. The good news was that she had found him a job, and it was a long-term contract for two years. The bad news was that the job was in Detroit and he would have to take a significant pay cut.

Hema was doing all the talking. Senthil stayed quiet on the other side of the phone. The word Detroit triggered a PTSD-like reaction in him. How could he forget being mugged by a fake pregnant woman?

"Hello! Senthil, are you there?"

"Yes, Hema! I am sorry. I don't mean to look a gift horse in the mouth, but is Detroit the only place that has an available assignment?"

Hema explained how hard it was to get an assignment. While she understood the agony of taking a pay cut, she assured him that two years without a break would make up for the difference. Besides, the other four therapists were looking for permanent jobs, and very soon, he would be the only client. She consoled him by saying he would have his green card before the end of this assignment and would then be able to find a better job and settle down.

Senthil reassured her that he did not question the placement because of the pay cut, but because of the mugging. He told her that he was more street-savvy now and did not want to hold accountable an entire city because of one person and one incident. He told her he would make the best of it and promised to work hard and represent her company well. Hema told him he had ten days to get to Detroit, Michigan, as the assignment was set to start on Wednesday, the day after the Fourth of July. She recommended he buy a car, as he would have to go to two schools.

Senthil thought about it. Sure, he wanted to save money so that he could help his siblings and parents. But the future he had planned out with Sumathi would now remain a pipe dream. He did not want to depend on others. One must spend money to make money. All these rationalizations went through his head, but the only one that made sense to him was that we could no longer deny himself the basic necessities of the present for a future without Sumathi.

The next morning, he walked to the Toyota used-car dealer in Terre Haute and drove back in a 1996 V6 XLE Camry in silver leaf metallic color, with gray leather seats. It had a cassette player and power windows. He could have bought a new car, but this one came loaded and was a lot cheaper. The best part was that it had only 41,300 miles and was without even a scratch. Even though he did not know much about cars, coming from India, haggling came naturally to him, and he was able to wear down the salesman. That evening, he drove the car to the park and took some pictures of it to send home.

He called Hema and told her that he had bought a car. After hearing the details, she told him he had got a very good deal. She told him to check the odometer when driving to Detroit and report the mileage as she offered to reimburse 0.30 cents/mile.

Chapter 22 — Destined in Detroit

AFTER TWO DAYS IN MOTEL 6, SENTHIL FOUND AN APARTment in Warren, Michigan. It was a twenty-five-minute drive to the special education school in Detroit. This assignment was different from his previous work. The issues faced by the special education children ranged from developmental delay to congenital deformity and physical handicap. They required various degrees of assistance. Some were mobile with altered gaits, some required assistive devices, and some used wheelchairs. There were classrooms designed to teach the usual subjects, vocational classrooms to teach different trades, and some classrooms dedicated to greater custodial care for children with minimal to insignificant function.

It broke Senthil's heart to learn that some children had been severely affected physically and mentally because of parental drug and alcohol abuse. He could not fathom how a mother could be that irresponsible and selfish. In his mind, he favored abortion over a lifetime of such torture. He kept his opinion to himself, however, and just focused on helping those unfortunate children the best he could.

Although it was emotionally taxing, being a therapist at a school was a lot easier than at a hospital, rehab center, or nursing home. Only, he could not deal with the pessimism of the people caring for these children. He spent hours stretching their contracted extremities, making splints with the limited resources available, and educating the teachers and teacher assistants regarding proper positioning of affected joints.

His actions were met with skepticism and comments such as: "We have tried something like this in the past," "What's the point? The parents are not going to follow this at home," "You are wasting your time," "The joints are going to be back where you started when the kids come back after a break," and so on. None of this negativity affected Senthil and the other dedicated therapists who continued to do their best.

School started at 8:00 AM and ended at 3:30 PM. He always went to work early to help kids get off the school bus and wheel them to their classroom and stayed back to assist the teachers and teaching assistants to buckle the children in the wheelchairs and strap them down in the bus. Even after that, the work hours in the school were less than those of his previous contracts. Additionally, he had days off on weekends and holidays as well.

Hema called Senthil to update him on the process of acquiring a green card. She informed him of a new agency called the Foreign Credentialing Commission on Physical Therapy (FCCPT) that was being formed to regulate the green card process for international physical therapists. She told him that he would need to get an approval certificate from them for the INS to approve his green card. The FCCPT would require credential evaluation, original transcripts from his college in India, and clearance of the Test of English as a Foreign Language (TOEFL).

There were growing concerns that the FCCPT might not recognize the bachelor's degree from India. Hema informed him that his Bachelor of Physiotherapy had thirty credit hours more than the American counterpart with regards to physical therapy subjects but fell short in terms of general subjects such as language, arts, and humanities. That was a drawback of getting into professional degree programs straight out of high school. Since his working hours were not taxing, Senthil began to take some classes in the local community college. He signed up for classes in the evening and during the weekend. He just wanted to be prepared if the FCCPT did not approve his green card application because of the credential evaluation. He called Nanda and asked him to get three original transcripts from his college in Madras. As soon as he received the transcripts, he sent his application to the FCCPT for clearance.

Senthil enjoyed being back in school. The special education schools were closed for two weeks for Christmas. When he resumed work in January 2001, Senthil realized why some of his colleagues were so pessimistic and why they had said he was wasting his time. Many of the children he worked on, especially the two with fetal alcohol syndrome, were back to square one. Their contractures had worsened, the splints he had made for them were in shambles, and his six months' worth of work had gone down the drain.

This was the first time Senthil felt tired of being a physical therapist; his outlook towards his career became gloomy. He did not know where he would end up after this assignment or if this was the only option left for him.

From his kindergarten days, Senthil had wanted to be a doctor. Even his favorite subject in school had been biology. As soon as he finished high school, he had every intention of applying to a medical college. He knew he wanted to become a surgeon eventually but had not decided on a specialty. At that time, he was unaware that a few simple words from a stranger would abruptly and unexpectedly catapult him to a different path.

At his high school graduation party, Deepak, one of his *appa's* friends, asked Senthil about his plans. Senthil replied that he had been accepted into a medical college and was going to become a doctor. When Deepak asked what kind of a doctor, Senthil quickly said that his ultimate goal was to become a surgeon. Deepak pressed on and asked him what specialty he had in mind. He had stated, "Maybe orthopedics." Senthil was an avid sports fan and enjoyed playing cricket, tennis, and soccer. He had often seen his friends break bones that needed to be fixed surgically, and this seemed to be his natural choice.

"But why? Why do you want to become a doctor or a surgeon?" Deepak asked.

"Science and the human body fascinate me. It's a noble profession, and most of all, I want to help people." His tone turned a bit defensive. However, he was not prepared for what he was about to hear.

Deepak said, "If you really want to help people, you should become a physiotherapist. Doctors and surgeons provide patients with anatomical continuity. Physiotherapists endow them with physiological function. Anatomical continuity is irrelevant if there is no physiological function."

He didn't quite understand the significance those words would have on the rest of his life, but he knew they carried a profound meaning that he wanted to explore fast. He had never seen or even heard of a physiotherapist until then and had no idea what this profession was. He shared his thoughts with his *appa*, who helped him shadow a friend of a friend, an orthopedic surgeon at Madras Medical College.

Senthil spent the next three weeks observing the surgeon while he examined patients, perused X-rays, and worked in the operating rooms. He was enamored by the skill and the precision of the surgeon in fixing and mending broken bones. He also witnessed a total hip replacement. Senthil was in awe, but what happened next inspired him even more. On the post-operative days, Senthil noticed the surgeon writing orders for physiotherapy.

He requested the surgeon to let him follow the patient to the Physiotherapy Department. A whole new world and discipline of medicine opened up to him that day. Senthil met a few physiotherapists and saw them helping patients regain range of motion, muscle strength, and functional mobility. He also noticed the bond the patients formed with their physiotherapists—an emotional connection that he had not seen them share with the surgeon.

The surgeon spent very little time with his patients, and most of his amazing work was done when the patient was under anesthesia. The physiotherapist, on the other hand, helped them through their recovery process. The patients were still helpless after the surgeon fixed a fracture or gave them a new hip. Without the help of physiotherapists, patients would not be able to enjoy their new lease of life. Senthil now realized the difference between anatomical continuity and physiological function. His mind was now clear regarding the profession he wanted to pursue.

His *appa* not only wanted him to be an example for his siblings but also wanted him to pursue a career he was passionate about. It was much harder to convince his *amma*, who was disappointed that her son was not going to become a doctor. But he was eventually able to wear her down.

It was physiotherapy that had brought Sumathi into his life, and he could not have imagined a better future for himself. It was her love that had helped a frightened, insecure introvert in becoming more outgoing. Since then, he had never looked back—until now. With the recent market trend, the questionable future in his line of work, and above all, with Sumathi's departure from his life, he was ready to take on a new challenge and keep his dreary mind occupied.

Senthil no longer wanted to be a physical therapist, so he went to Wayne State University to inquire about his first passion: surgery. Senthil sought the advice of a student counselor at the university. She analyzed his transcripts and advised him regarding all the prerequisite courses he had to take to be eligible for medical school.

Senthil busied himself taking courses at the Macomb Community College, thanks to the shortened workdays and free time during weekends and holidays. The classes would help him meet the requirements for applying to medical school and also satisfy the FCCPT requirements by making his Bachelor's degree from India comparable to an American degree. He was aware that he would not be able to apply to medical school unless he got his green card.

In April 2001, the FCCPT declared the final uniform standards to evaluate the credentials for foreign-trained physical therapists. Senthil had to send in his application along with original transcripts from India and forward his test scores from the National Physical Therapy Exam, PT license verification, and credential evaluation from the agency approved by the FCCPT. The only new requirement Senthil was yet to meet was take the TOEFL. He managed to study for it while keeping up with his obligations at work. TOEFL was not hard, but it provoked some anxiety.

He was thrilled when Hema called to tell him that the FCCPT had cleared him and sent the approval to the INS. It was the fall of 2001, and all the requirements for his green card were met. It was only a matter of time before he got the card. However, his student counselor at Wayne State University noticed his enthusiasm dwindle every time he saw her.

"You keep taking courses to meet the prerequisites, and yet you seem less sure each time you come to see me. What's the matter?" she asked. She was right; Senthil was worried about the time frame.

He was pushing thirty-one years, and even if he got his green card by the end of the year and finished his prerequisite courses by the following year, he would be thirty-two years old when he entered medical school. His *appa* was nearing retirement, and he had to consider being there for him if there was any financial emergency. Four years in medical school and then another five to six years in a surgical residency program—he would be forty-one or forty-two by the time he finished, and that was a conservative estimation. At that age, with the massive college debt, he was afraid he would lose his passion for helping people and focus only on paying off his debt. That possibility bothered him. He was concerned about upholding the nobility of the profession.

The counselor patiently replied, "Well, you should think about becoming a physician assistant instead."

Senthil was confused and taken aback. "I am trying to move up in my profession, not down." He had never heard of the profession of a physician assistant before. There are no PAs in India, and he thought she was referring to the medical assistant he had seen in physicians' clinics.

She explained to him what a PA was. It required a two-year master's degree, and he could work in any specialty. He thought she was only teasing him. When she offered him the opportunity to shadow a PA, he readily accepted.

Grace Hospital in Detroit was a busy place even at 6:00 AM on a Saturday. Senthil found his way to the Internal Medicine ward on the second floor. He was dressed in a shirt and a tie, his black shoes were freshly polished, and he wore a big smile on his face as he stood in a corner. He was both nervous and excited.

"Are you San-teel?" he heard a soft, friendly voice from behind him.

Senthil turned around and saw a tall, slender young Filipino lady in a pink floral dress and a long white coat. She was wearing glasses, and her hair was pulled back in a sleek bun. "Yes, I am."

"Hi! I am Anne Baker. The Wayne State University student counselor told me you are coming in today to shadow me. I am a PA in internal medicine. I am sorry if I butchered your name."

"That's quite all right. I am Senthil. It rhymes with lentil. Thank you so much for letting me shadow you."

"Let's go to the staff lounge to chat for a bit and then you can follow me on my morning rounds. Do you want some coffee?" she asked, pointing Senthil to a chair as she poured herself a cup.

"No, thank you. I don't drink coffee or tea."

"Really? I am surprised. Anyway, what do you do now?"

"I am a physical therapist, and I currently work as a consultant for Detroit Public School."

"Oh! That's fascinating. I was an athletic trainer for three years before I joined PA school. In fact, PA is the second career for many."

"There are no PAs in India. I don't know what PAs are or what they do. The student counselor seems to think it would be a good fit for me. Any help you can provide is much appreciated."

Anne wanted to spend an hour explaining who PAs were and what they did but decided it would make sense for him to tag along for her morning rounds. Senthil followed her like an eager puppy. He did not want to intrude or disrupt Anne's work, so he maintained a healthy distance, and spoke only when spoken to.

Anne had her rounding list in her hand. She went to the nurses' station and sat down in front of her computer, gesturing Senthil to grab a chair. She checked the labs and wrote them down across each patient. She examined the X-rays and the CT scans and pointed out some abnormalities and interesting findings to Senthil. She proceeded to check on each patient, update them on the results, and examine them. She reviewed the vitals documented by the nurse, listened to the patients' hearts and lungs, and updated the nurses of new orders for the patients. She used her ophthalmoscope and her otoscope to check some patients' eyes and ears.

Senthil was awed. She did everything a doctor would do. Her skill, her bedside manners, and how grateful the patients were to see her impressed him. He even saw her discharge a patient, write a prescription for medications, and call the case manager to give her a prescription for setting up home health physical and occupational therapy.

This was too good to be true. Senthil did not know if Anne was putting on a show for him or if this was what she actually did. When taking leave for the day, Senthil hesitantly asked, "Anne, if you are working the next weekend, would it be okay if I come to shadow you?"

"Of course," she replied.

Senthil returned the following Saturday. Anne was impressed to see he had researched all the diagnoses he had come across the previous week and had neatly written down in a notebook the definition, incidence, pathophysiology, signs and symptoms, and treatment for each diagnosis. She realized that he was committed towards his aim. He spent the entire fall and winter shadowing Anne every weekend she worked. He was convinced that physician assistant was the right profession for him. This resolution was only strengthened when Anne told him about her friends who were surgical PAs in different specialties.

The only thing that stood between him and the application to the PA program was his green card. Senthil was hopeful and continued to work hard towards completing the prerequisites for application and studying for the

GRE. By early spring of 2002, he had completed his prerequisites and begun his application process. He was thrilled when Anne offered to write a letter of recommendation for him. He needed two more letters of recommendation to attest to his discipline and work ethic and contacted Lauren McNair from the Golden Manor and Mike Blazer from Princeton Hospital.

Senthil woke up to his phone ringing one early Saturday morning in April 2002. It was 5:00 AM, and he wondered who could be calling him this early. It was Hema. Senthil sat up on the floor and leaned against the wall.

"I am sorry to call you so early, but I couldn't wait!" She sounded ecstatic. "Your green card has been approved!"

Senthil was speechless—happy beyond words. Hema could not see him grinning from to ear to ear.

"Senthil? Did you just hear what I said?" she screamed.

"Oh yes, Hema! I did! I don't know what to say. Thank you for all your help and for seeing me through this."

She told him she was going to mail the I-485 approval to him and that he had to take that and his passport to the INS office to get the I-551 stamped in his passport. This would be the temporary proof of his permanent residency status. The actual green card would be mailed to him later.

A couple of weeks later, this happiness was topped by the letter he received from the Wayne State University's PA program inviting him for an interview. He wanted to be prepared, and so, he went to the Henry Ford Centennial Library to learn more about the profession.

The PA profession had been born out of necessity. Due to a national shortage of physicians and a population boom after World War I, America was hard-pressed to meet the medical needs of those in need. Dr. Eugene Stead Jr., the chairman of the Department of Medicine at Duke University, noticed that highly trained navy hospital corpsmen, who provided invaluable medical care during the war, returned home and had no place to utilize the skill and experience they had gained. Dr. Stead created a curriculum to augment the clinical knowledge these corpsmen had gained and established the first physician assistant program in October 1965 at the Department of Medicine at Duke University.

During this time, Duke University established the new Department of Community Health Sciences and appointed Dr. Harvey Estes Jr. as the chairman. Dr. Estes assumed the reins of the PA program as the first three PAs Kenneth F. Ferrell, Victor H. Germino, and Richard J. Scheele graduated from the program on October 6, 1967. In 1970, the Duke PA program accepted the first female student, Joyce Nichols who was a nurse at Duke Hospital. She created history for not only being the first female PA but also the first African–American to do so.

Following the addition of postgraduate residency in family medicine in the 1970s, the clinics of Duke Hospital were transformed into centers of excellence in training MD/PA health-care teams. Dr. Estes's tireless efforts with extensive writing and traveling across the country for promoting the new philosophy to deliver health care paid off: the medical community eventually embraced this new profession and set accreditation standards and established national certification standards.

Since then, PAs nationwide have provided care to medically underserved communities and have helped elderly patients maintain and improve their health and dignity. With the growing number of aging baby boomers and the ever-increasing cost of delivering health care, the PA profession was bound to grow immensely and become a cornerstone and a game changer in the health-care sector.

After taking notes on its history, Senthil left the library with a new respect for the PA profession as well as an unbridled ambition to become a PA.

On the day of the interview, he got up early in the morning, brushed up on the notes he had taken, and memorized some of the dates. He got dressed in his favorite outfit: black pants, light blue shirt, and a tie—Sumathi's favorite. Even after five years, he still missed her. Her beautiful face and eyes, her smile and her fragrance were still fresh in his mind. He realized physical therapy was the only thing left in common between them now, and if he managed to get into the PA program and embark on a new career, he would, at least symbolically, put his past behind him. The thought sent shivers down his spine. He shrugged and told himself not to think about it.

He arrived fifteen minutes early. There were about one hundred applicants for the forty-five spots available. It was a very diverse group of people. Some of the applicants were very young, right out of undergrad, without a previous career, and had solely gained the thousand hours of health-care work experience—a prerequisite—through some part-time work as a nurse's aide or a medical assistant. Some were a little older, with careers unrelated to the health-care field, but had completed all the prerequisites. There were even a couple of applicants who were physicians from different countries. One was from China, and one was from Lithuania. He spoke to a few applicants who were nurses, athletic trainers, and respiratory therapists. It was a very competitive field, and anyone could be a potential candidate.

They were seated alphabetically in the hall and called into a boardroom for the interview by the admission committee comprising the program director and four faculty PAs. Each applicant was interviewed for ten minutes. Senthil knew he was going to be interviewed towards the end of the day. He was worried that the committee could potentially find their forty-five students even before it was his turn. He tried to remain calm, pacing down the halls and trying to engage in small talk when fellow applicants asked him a question. He spoke to the applicants who came out of the interview. The questions ranged from addressing ethical concerns of health care, motivation to apply to PA school, prior health-care experiences, difficult patients they had dealt with in the past, their undergrad experiences, and where they saw themselves five years from now.

Eventually, it was his turn. He took a deep breath as he entered the room to try and calm his nerves. He ran his mind through the history of the profession and the dates of the historical milestones of the PA profession. He shook hands with the panel and took the designated seat.

The program director spoke, "I don't want to butcher your name. How do you say it?"

"Senthilvelan Rajashekaran," he replied slowly, emphasizing the syllables. "But please call me Senthil, like lentil with an S," he added.

"Great. Thank you, Senthil, for making that easy. You have a very strong application with good experience in health care, a well-written essay, and good recommendation letters, one of which is from an alumnus of our program. But there are many applicants like you. So, tell us why we should select you out of the hundred applicants?"

Senthil was caught off guard. He was not expecting this. He told them what came to his mind first: "I learned to spell my name in kindergarten."

As soon as he said it, he was shocked that he would joke at the biggest interview of his life. He thought he had ruined his chances and was bracing himself for the response from the committee. They all laughed out loud and the program director, unable to control his laughter, said, "Get out of here; we are done." He did not sound angry or disappointed. In fact, all the members of the committee seemed genuinely amused. Senthil sat there in disbelief, but when he was told again that the interview was over, he thanked them for the opportunity and left with his head hanging low.

He was in the room for only a few minutes while others were in for at least ten minutes. As he exited the room, he could see the concern etched on the face of the applicant who was going in next.

"What happened?" she muttered, but Senthil was in no mood to speak.

He just shook his head and said, "All the best," as he walked away.

The next few days, he contemplated his next move. With the green card being approved and Hema finally closing her company for good, he was free to look for a permanent job and finally settle down in a place he could call home. Until now, he had been busy taking classes and studying. He had never thought of a plan B in case he did not get into the PA program. He blamed himself for not applying to the other PA programs in Michigan.

His grief over his performance in the interview lasted only about two weeks, until the time he received a letter from the PA program. He was afraid to open it and stood to stare at it for a while. Finally, exhaling, he opened it.

"Dear Senthil,
We are pleased to inform you that . . ."

Senthil stopped reading. He was trembling. The first few words, "pleased to inform," sent him on an emotional roller coaster. Through a few deep breaths, he learned that he had been accepted into the program. As soon as it sunk in, he called Hema to share the news. She was thrilled for him, and he thanked her again for keeping her company open for him until he got his green card. That night, he called home to let his family know about his new career path. He had to do a lot of explaining as the PA profession did not exist in India. It was not the same as a medical assistant, and he was not going to be a secretary for a physician. He had to convince his family that he was moving up in his profession.

The faculty of the Wayne State University PA program had put together a well-balanced class, and Senthil reveled in its well-planned diversity. The students became a very tight-knit group very quickly, and their diverse backgrounds played to their strengths in helping each other out. The program was well supported by visiting lectures from leaders in their respective disciplines from various hospitals associated with the Detroit Medical Center.

After a year of endless tests, practical exams, simulated case scenarios, handwriting hundreds of history and physical exams, they were finally ready to begin their clinical year.

As the clinical year neared its end, everyone was not only looking for jobs but also preparing for their Physician Assistant National Certifying Examination (PANCE). The faculty reassured them that they were more than adequately prepared and should not have any trouble passing the PANCE. They were expecting a 100 percent pass rate as usual.

Senthil could not make up his mind. He was not looking for a job; he wanted a career. He had decided to pursue a career as a surgical PA but did not know what specialty to choose. His surgical rotation at Henry Ford Hospital had been in general surgery, but there were so many surgical specialties and subspecialties that he could not figure out which one he was the most passionate about or the one he would excel in and be the best PA he could be.

He had no special ties to Michigan and was free to go and settle down anywhere in America. He had fond memories of Terre Haute, and one day while looking at job opportunities in a Journal of the American Academy of PAs (JAAPA), he came across an ad that read, "Postgraduate Surgical Residency for PAs."

Intrigued, he started to research more regarding postgraduate surgical residencies and found that they were a year-long course and there were residencies in general surgery, emergency medicine, obstetrics and gynecology, orthopedic surgery, and cardiothoracic surgery. The general surgery residency interested him the most, as it offered a wide range of possibilities and rotations through various subspecialties. He figured that it would be best to be cross-trained in different specialties to keep his options open.

He researched the top surgical residency programs and narrowed down his choices. His goal was not to become a technician but a skilled clinician who would not only be able to assist in the OR but also, most importantly, take care of complex surgical patients during the preoperative and the postoperative periods. The Durham Memorial Hospital's PA surgical residency program was 13 months long. A didactic month preceded twelve months of surgical rotations, which involved general surgery, trauma, neurosurgery, cardiothoracic surgery, urologic surgery, vascular surgery, a month in SICU, two months of dedicated OR time as well as an elective month.

Senthil figured each rotation was a month-long interview in that specialty, so he could learn and see if the particular specialty could be a career choice. It was going to be an intense year, and if PA school was like putting a fire hose in one's mouth and turning it on at full blast, the surgical residency was going to be like two fire hoses in one's mouth. He concluded that he would be better trained and prepared to take care of complex surgical patients at the end of the residency. Most importantly, he hoped to decide on a specialty he would see himself practicing for the rest of his career.

He received mixed responses when he told the faculty members and his friends about his decision to pursue a postgraduate residency. "You don't need to do one since you can get a job in any specialty you want," "It's cheap labor since you get paid only around $50,000 but work eighty hours a week," "It's about time you get a life and settle down" were just a few, but he had made up his mind.

He left Detroit on a Thursday morning and drove to Durham for the interview. Around thirty applicants were vying for the thirteen available spots.

His interview went well, and the panel was impressed with his desire to build a career path for himself and his goal to become a clinician over a technician. At dinner following the day-long interview and the tour of Durham Memorial Hospital, the program director and the medical director told Senthil unofficially that he had a spot in the residency if he chose to attend their program. He was ecstatic and also felt relieved when they said he had a week to think about it.

He returned to his hotel, feeling he was on cloud nine. Senthil was impressed by the southern hospitality of Durham and the down-to-earth surgeons and physicians. Durham had all the charm of a small town, with the amenities of a big city. He felt at home.

He called the medical director to let her know he was accepting the offer and it would be a privilege for him to attend their surgical residency.

After graduation, like the majority of his class, Senthil took the PANCE on the very first day it was made available. Just as the faculty of the Wayne State University PA program had hoped, the Class of 2004 had a 100 percent pass rate.

The PA surgical residency at Durham Memorial Hospital was set to start on September 1. Senthil found an opportunity to cover for a PA who was on maternity leave at Henry Ford Hospital ER, where he completed his last two months of preceptorship. It worked out perfectly. He was able to work for three months, save some money, and head to Durham.

Chapter 23 — Determined in Durham

WITH GREAT ENTHUSIASM, SENTHIL ARRIVED IN DURHAM a week early. As a physical therapist, he had worked long hours and even on weekends, but he had never been on call for twenty-four hours or worked the nights. The PA surgical resident class of 2005 were a cohesive group from different universities from across the country and had come to Durham with a common goal: to train with the best to be the best they could be.

Senthil's first rotation was in the Neurosurgery Department. The surgical interns were foot soldiers, the junior residents, lieutenants, the chief-residents, generals, and the attending surgeons were presidents. This was the golden chain of command and a system that was essential for taking care of complex surgical patients. The foot soldiers supervised autonomy and addressed the day-to-day care of surgical patients under their care. It was like throwing someone into the deep end of the pool to teach them swimming. While a life preserver and a lifeguard were always available, it forced one to learn swimming faster and better than others who took swimming lessons. That was the analogy Senthil used to compare surgical residency to learning on the job with the comfort of three to six months of protected orientation, with a gradual increase in responsibilities.

Just when he was getting a little comfortable with taking care of complex neurosurgical patients, his one month of rotation in neurosurgery came to an end. The neurosurgery residents and the attending surgeons were impressed with his work ethic and potential.

He was better prepared for his second rotation: general surgery. By the end of three months, he and his fellow PA surgical residents had traded angst for anticipation as their insecurity gave way to confidence. Senthil was surprised at how much he had learned in such a short time in three different specialties in comparison with the friends he had graduated with from Wayne State University, who were just finishing their orientation in their own jobs.

The year was flying by, with each rotation essentially serving as a thirty-day job interview. Senthil bonded with several residents and chief residents. There was no shortage of job opportunities, with each chief resident asking him if he wanted to join his or her new practice. Senthil had completed rotations in neurosurgery, general surgery, cardiothoracic surgery, trauma, vascular surgery, transplant surgery, plastic surgery, SICU, and a month of night shifts cross-covering multiple services. As fate would have it, for his tenth rotation, he was scheduled to neurosurgery again.

What a contrast it was between his first month and now! The nurses and the residents were amazed at the progress Senthil had made. It was not his dedicated OR month, but since he was able to accomplish his daily tasks more efficiently, the residents encouraged him to visit the OR and scrub in with them. They developed good chemistry. They were impressed by Senthil's reliability and knowledge base. All the residents urged Dr. Papavero, Chairman of the Department of Neurosurgery, to hire him since there were no PAs in their department.

Dr. Asaph Papavero was a brilliant neurosurgeon. He towered over Senthil even after years of operating under the microscope—specializing in gross total resection of malignant brain tumors—had resulted in poor posture and a slightly hunched back, decreasing his vertical stature. A full head of salt-and-pepper hair, a thick mustache, and a deep husky voice added depth to his unique personality. The residents and nurses affectionately referred to him as "Papa." He had a straightforward manner and never sugarcoated anything while dealing with his patients. Though he was a man of few words, no one cared about patients' health and a good surgical outcome more than him. The man practically lived in the hospital and would operate 7 days a week, 365 days a year if the hospital allowed him to. Even after earning the reputation of being one of the best neurosurgeons in the country, he remained involved in all aspects of patient care. He rounded on his patients twice a day, even if it was just to stop by to say his catchphrase: "Hello! Why aren't you out of bed?"

Though he could be intimidating, everyone admired his commitment. He was a stickler for efficiency and commanded his operating room with surgical precision. No task was too small for him if it helped the surgeries to be performed in time. Many times he would be found inserting a Foley catheter or an arterial line to get the process going. He demanded as well as inspired excellence.

One afternoon, Senthil found himself scrubbed in a craniotomy for resection of a glioblastoma. He leaned in with the bipolar to cauterize a small bleeding vessel when the footstool he was standing on slipped. He dropped the bipolar to balance himself as he held on to the operating table.

"Are you a klutz?" sneered Papa.

Embarrassed, Senthil replied, "No Sir. I am Indian like from the country India."

The entire OR burst out laughing, albeit only for a brief moment as an irked Papa asked: "What's funny?"

One of the older scrub nurses said, "Looks like Senthil doesn't know what klutz means. He thinks it's a nationality."

Papa couldn't contain his amusement and just said "Hmm."

Senthil's lack of familiarity with American lingo did not overshadow his technical skills in the OR. Papa was impressed.

At the end of their evening rounds, Senthil asked Papa if he could name him as a reference. Papa said, "Sure, but my residents tell me that I would be an idiot to not hire you. Would you be interested in working for us after you finish your residency?"

"Of course, Dr. Papavero. I graduate from the residency on September 30 and will be ready to start on October 1," Senthil enthusiastically replied.

"Terrific!" Papa exclaimed.

Senthil wanted to hear more about the offer. Since the Neurosurgery Department did not have any PAs, he was curious about the position and the job description. Having spent two months as an intern in the service, he had an idea regarding where he could make the most impact and become a valuable team player.

His last two months constituted his dedicated OR period. Whenever the General Surgery administrative chief resident did not have a case for Senthil to scrub in, he scrubbed in with the neurosurgery residents. Three weeks away from graduating from an arduous but immensely educational experience, Senthil was getting anxious that he had not heard more about the offer from Papa.

He talked to his trusted neurosurgery residents who warned him to be careful while negotiating a salary and his responsibilities. Their exact words were, "Papa is shrewd with money; so, make sure you get a good deal." If Senthil had been a fresh graduate right out of PA school, this proposition would have been a bit daunting—intimidating even. The postgraduate residency had given him a great amount of confidence and the time to reflect on his strengths and weaknesses and had transformed him from a naïve to an astute PA with a stellar job description and remuneration to go with it. The question was, could he successfully convince Papa, the savvy and brilliant neurosurgeon?

Senthil did not know if Papa was serious when he asked him to work in neurosurgery. He did not want to lose an upper hand, if he had one at all, by asking Papa about the job offer before he brought it up first. Besides, he did not want to put all his eggs in one basket. Some of his classmates from Wayne State University who had got a job right out of PA school were already looking for another job. Either they did not like their job or realized they had a passion for a different specialty. Unlike them, the postgraduate residency had helped Senthil decide on a career—a specialty he could focus on for the rest of his life. In the alumni newsletter from Wayne State University, he noticed an ad for a job opportunity in neurosurgery in Detroit. Senthil applied for that position and named Papa as his reference.

Two more weeks were left for the residency to end. Senthil was scrubbed in a pancreaticoduodenectomy, a long surgery for pancreatic cancer. He was assisting with the procedure, and towards the end of the case, his pager went off. One of the OR nurses, who was the circulator, was holding his pager.

She called back the number and said, "Senthil is finishing up in OR 22 with Dr. Watson. Can I take a message for him?" After hanging up, she said "Senthil! That was Dr. Papavero. He asked you to go to his office as soon as you are done."

"You must be in some kind of trouble for Papa to be paging you," quipped Dr. Watson.

"I hope not, sir," Senthil replied as he closed his end of the abdominal fascia.

When Senthil was finally closing the skin, Dr. Watson asked the circulator to get the patient's family to the surgical consultation room so he could update them about the surgery. Senthil escorted the patient with anesthesia to the surgical ICU and gave the receiving resident and the nurse a sign-out.

Then he walked up to Papa's office, wondering if it was about his offer or if someone from Detroit had contacted him for reference. He knocked on the door. Papa always cut to the chase, so as he opened the door turned to walk towards his chair, he said, "I thought we had an agreement. What's this call I get about a reference for you from a hospital in Detroit?"

"Yes sir, but I didn't hear anything more from you after that and didn't know if you were serious."

Papa motioned for him to sit down and picked up the phone. He called the HR Department and said, "I want to hire this PA." He reached forward, pointed the phone's mouthpiece to him, and said, "Tell them who you are. I don't want to butcher your name."

"This is Senthilvelan Rajashekaran. I am one of the PA surgical residents."

Papa hung up the phone and said, "They'll get in touch with you."

'Thank you Dr. Papavero, I would like to sit down and talk about my role, expectations, and responsibilities."

"How about this Saturday after my morning rounds?"

"That would be great. I'll come to your office at 11:00 AM. Thank you again, sir."

The next day, he got a call from the HR about the job offer. He was disappointed when he heard their salary offer. While the offer took into consideration his one-year experience at the hospital, he believed it did not consider the extensive training of the residency and the eighty-hour week, which essentially was comparable to two years' on-the-job training.

Over the next few days, he researched national PA salary survey based on location and specialty and visited the American Association of PA's website to check out their salary survey based on specialty and other private sites, which boasted of carrying the current up-to-date data about PA salaries across the nation.

Armed with all the information he needed and the practical knowledge he had gained firsthand from his rotations in neurosurgery twice, Senthil knocked on Papa's door with optimism and confidence, which he credited to the residency program. When Papa came to the door and saw Senthil dressed up in a suit, he exclaimed, "You look dapper! I didn't realize I had to dress up on a Saturday."

Senthil replied, "Thank you, sir. This is a very important meeting for me." He told Papa that the HR had sent him a job offer and he was disappointed with the salary they had quoted.

"I think they quoted the current standard and fair market rate," replied Papa. Senthil replied that the offer fell way too short of his expectation and he couldn't even consider it. When he shared the figure he had in his mind, Papavero replied, "I am not sure what PAs make, but that sounds more like private practice. This is an academic institution, and I don't think they would go for that. Besides, I am not even sure what your role is going to be to justify that pay."

Senthil was prepared to make his pitch. He explained to Papa that the department would save three months of orientation since he had been trained here. He not only knew the system but also the two months in neurosurgery and the time spent in scrubbing in neurosurgical cases had made him familiar with the attending surgeon's preferences, not to mention the rapport he had built with the neurosurgery residents and nurses. With the current model, he explained, with an intern from different departments rotating each month, there were too many moving pieces. His presence would ensure continuity of care and a familiar go-to face for patients and attending surgeons. He elaborated that he would come early in the morning to round with the residents, assist the interns, and then cover add-on or scheduled cases to ensure a timely start of the OR so the residents were not spread thin.

He explained that his twelve months of taking care of complex surgical patients in all specialties had put him in a unique position to manage all sorts of preoperative issues and postoperative complications. He assured Papa that he could assist the inexperienced interns in the management of myocardial infarction, cardiac arrhythmias, diabetes, shock, postoperative hemorrhage, pulmonary embolism and prevent the residents from having to scrub out of cases when there was an emergency or a new consult in the ER. He concluded, "In short, Dr. Papavero, I can enable both the senior residents and the attending surgeons to be in two places at the same time, and I would be nothing short of an extension of your will."

Papa had heard enough. "Okay! I thought you would come in at 8:00 AM and do a couple of discharges, and by 11:00 AM, you would put your feet up, drink coffee, and eat bonbons until the preops start coming in around 3:00 PM. But now I get the idea of what a PA can do for me. You win. I understand why my chief resident said that it would be a mistake to not hire you.

However, I cannot convince the hospital to pay you more. Do you care if you get two paychecks instead? I'll pay you the difference."

Senthil was ecstatic. He credited the surgical residency and the experience and confidence it provided for negotiating this deal with Papa. While Sumathi's love had helped him with his fear and insecurities, the surgical residency had helped him masquerade as an extrovert, albeit in the hospital setting.

Chapter 24 — Neurosurgery: A New Beginning

IT WAS MONDAY, OCTOBER 3, 2005. THE FIRST DIFFERENCE Senthil noticed in the neurosurgical service was that the nurses were relieved to have a go-to person for the little fires they had to put out all day. Through his hard work and dedication, Senthil quickly became an integral part of the Neurosurgery Department.

Senthil made it a priority to learn each and every attending neurosurgeon's preference in different matters that impacted the care of complex neurosurgical patients—the simplest of wound care choices, steroid taper, the timing of anticoagulation, removal of surgical drains, preoperative needs, and postoperative complications.

The OR staff welcomed his addition, as they were able to start add-on cases and emergency cases that came through the ER or as a hospital-to-hospital transfer. He assured Papa that he was able to handle all the in-patient needs, the demands from the ER, and the challenges of the OR. The surgeons were not only impressed with what he did but also how he did it. Even though he had been hired for a forty-hour work week, he came in early and stayed back late until the time he was needed, which the residents on call appreciated.

He had special skills to manage pediatric neurosurgical patients and was very good with children. He realized early on that for every pediatric patient he had, there were an additional two and sometimes three more patients: the nervous parents, the concerned grandparents, and if the parents were divorced, the biological parents and the stepparents. His little patients appreciated his sense of humor. Even while performing invasive procedures, he was able to not only put the parents at ease but managed to placate their little ones too.

One such day, he was holding a consultation with the parents for a lumbar puncture on eight-year-old Abigail; she was readmitted with high fever ten days after a craniotomy for the resection of a cerebellar medullo-blastoma. The fever workup included chest X-ray, blood cultures, and urine culture, which were all negative. While the incision appeared well healed, it was imperative to rule out meningitis.

"Hi, Abigail! My name is Senthil. It rhymes with lentil. Some people call me Mr. Bean." Little Abigail laughed uncontrollably. She loved that Senthil treated her like an adult and explained to her, instead of just talking to her parents, why it was important to check the CSF (cerebrospinal fluid).

While the prospect of sticking a long needle in the back of her spine was terrifying, Abigail felt sure that Senthil would not hurt her. She wanted to lie on her right side so that she could face the TV and watch *Finding Nemo* during the procedure. Abigail chose her mom to help with the procedure. Abigail rolled over to her right, and Senthil helped her curl up like a ball, with her hips and knees bent and her chin tucked. Her mother held her hands. Senthil marked a spot in the midline between the third and the fourth lumbar vertebra.

He scrubbed and put on the mask, hat, sterile gown, and gloves, telling Abigail what was happening the whole time. Before prepping the site, he told her that the betadine was going to feel very cold. As the prep was drying, he drew up some lidocaine with an insulin syringe, as it had the smallest needle. He told her that she was going to feel a tiny ant bite, followed by a burning sensation that would last a few seconds. Abigail squeezed her mother's hand, shut her eyes tight, and braced herself for the sting.

He asked Abigail about her school, her friends, her favorite cartoon, and Disney princesses as he performed the lumbar puncture, checked the opening pressure, and drained a total of 5 ml of CSF in two sterile tubes. It was a single pass, and it was all over in a few minutes. Senthil was applying a band-aid when Abigail said, "Let me know when you are going to use the big needle."

"I am done, Abigail. You can roll on your back if you want to. In fact, you can lay any way you want to as long as you remain flat and don't lift your head for the next hour."

Abigail rolled on her back and said, "What? You are done? I didn't feel a thing!" Her eyes grew wide, and she forgot his advice and jubilantly tried to sit up to say something. Senthil put his hand on her forehead in time to prevent her from sitting up. "But I discovered something new," Abigail said as he applied the labels on the CSF tubes.

"What is it Abigail?" he asked.

"Well, your name rhymes with gentle more than with lentil. Your new name is 'Gentle Senthil,' not Senthil like lentil." His new moniker spread in the hospital like wildfire.

Having been a physical therapist himself, Senthil forged a special bond with the physical therapists, occupational therapists, and speech pathologists who took care of his patients.

He worked well with all the charge nurses who were responsible for the bed flow and running the busy neurosurgical ward to accommodate new admits, transfers from ICU, and postoperative patients. He identified potential discharges the night before and let them know so they could plan the next day accordingly. Nurse Sherilynn took on the role of his elder sister. Though she pulled pranks on him, she also looked out for him at all times. She was a widow in her early 50s, with wavy hair, glasses that sat low on the bridge of her nose and were attached to a necklace, and a Bostonian accent that had successfully thwarted off the southern drawl for thirty years. Senthil affectionately called her "Pepto," as she always wore pink-colored scrubs.

Pepto constantly busted him for being single. She often said, "You should be dating. If you are not going to plow the field and sow wild oats, you might as well marry me and be a father to my grownup children."

Senthil would laugh and be amused by her constant efforts to play matchmaker with the nurses or residents in the unit. Senthil was content being single. The thought of displacing Sumathi from his heart was unfathomable.

However, he did not sulk or isolate himself. Senthil enjoyed being in the hospital. He arrived early and did not leave until all the patients were tucked in. The residents appreciated his constant presence in helping them and guiding the interns. Even though he worked long hours and averaged around seventy hours a week, he went out with the residents, nurses, and therapists when invited. He was the designated driver when they went to the bars. He loved to eat out with them and frequently hosted potluck dinners in his new house.

Senthil considered it a privilege to be able to take care of patients with brain tumors. In the brief time he spent with them, he did everything he could to give them hope. His sense of humor was infectious, and his patients and their families appreciated his efforts to lighten up their spirits. Now, his encounter with his patients started with him introducing himself as "Senthil, like gentle with an S." He shared with them his embarrassing stories, and his self-deprecating humor was well received in their times of need. Patients and their families routinely stopped by long after they were discharged to meet "Gentle Senthil" when they came back for a follow-up appointment with their neuro-oncologist or radiation oncologist.

Once, Senthil had to place a stereotactic frame on a young patient with a tumor in the left frontal lobe, very close to the motor cortex that controlled the movement of the right side of her body. Diana was a twenty-six-year-old anthropology student and was nervous about the prospect of having a cage screwed on to her head before the MRI for preoperative localization. Papa explained to her and her terrified parents and husband that the frame was necessary to be as accurate as possible since the tumor was near the motor cortex. As he was walking out, he said, "Don't worry, my PA will take good care of you."

Pepto offered to help, as she was the charge nurse and did not have patients of her own. Senthil asked her to get 2 mg of Morphine and 1 mg of Ativan to premedicate Diana. From the time he had walked in, he could tell that the patient was anxious and afraid.

He used his usual spiel. "Hi, my name is Senthil, like gentle with an S. I am Dr. Papavero's physician assistant." Diana smiled nervously. "Have you had this done to you before?" he asked.

"No, I have not. This is the first and hopefully the last time."

"Oh, we have something in common. This is my first time too, but don't worry, I stayed in Holiday Inn Express last night." The initial shock gave way to a laugh.

"Don't listen to him. He is an expert and just like his name, he'll be gentle. Don't you worry," said Pepto as she walked in with the drugs.

Senthil instructed her worried husband to sit by the bedside and hold her hands. He gently placed the frame over her head to mark the spots for the screws: two on the forehead, well above the eyebrows, to avoid the supra-orbital nerves, and two on the back of her head. The frame looked like a square helmet.

Diana noticed his badge and asked, "What does that 'C' next to PA mean?"

"Oh, that C stands for charming," he quipped.

Diana laughed. Pepto administered the Morphine and Ativan as Senthil drew up Lidocaine and assembled the stereotactic frame. As he came closer, Diana's husband and her parents chorused, "But she is still awake."

Senthil explained that the medications were just to take the edge off and help her relax and that they were not meant to sedate her. He came close with the syringe and said, "You are going to feel a prick," adding, "I meant the needle, not me." Diana laughed again as he injected Lidocaine in each of the four spots he had marked earlier. Pepto held the frame in place over her head as he placed the screws to secure it in place. He tightened the screws all the way to perch on the skull so that they would not move. And just like that, it was over.

"It's all done. This is the worst part of the day. I have the hard job, and Papa has it easy. But he gets paid more than I do. Go figure," Senthil said.

Diana's husband and her parents were worried about the frame and how she was going to tolerate the procedure, but they were impressed with Senthil's calm demeanor and bedside manners as he kept her laughing through the entire process.

After assisting Papa with the biopsy, Senthil and the CRNA (certified registered nurse anesthetist) brought Diana back to the room to sign-out to the nurse taking care of her.

Pepto interrupted Senthil to say, "Please see me before you head back to the OR." When he stopped by the nurse's station, Pepto said, "Transfer center called. We are getting a new patient with a brain tumor for Papa. The patient is coming from Charlotte and should be here within the hour." The remaining ORs were staffed with residents. He asked Pepto to page him when the new admit came in and went to dictate some discharge summaries.

It was around 3:00 PM when his pager went off: "The new patient is here in room 4130."

Charles McCormick was twenty-three years old. He had presented to his physician with progressively worsening headaches and vomiting, which prompted a CT scan of the brain revealing a brain tumor. Senthil popped the CD into the player and loaded the CT scan that came from the outside hospital. His heart sank to see a big tumor involving the right frontal and temporal lobes and surrounded by cerebral edema.

His gut feeling said it was a primary brain tumor, and he was afraid it was glioblastoma multiforme (GBM), an aggressive high-grade brain tumor. He felt bad that Charlie had a devastating tumor at such a young age. He did not want to share his concerns while Charlie was alone and wanted to wait until his family arrived. He made small talk as he noted the patient's history and conducted the physical exam. Charlie said that he and his family had left at the same time, but the ambulance brought him to the hospital faster.

Charlie was lying in bed. He was slim and had the face of a baby. It looked like he was trying to grow a mustache, as he constantly kept stroking his peach fuzz of a mustache with his thumb and his index fingers. He was tanned and had thick dark brown curly hair that had some sun-bleached blonde streaks in it.

"Looks like you got some sun," Senthil commented.

"Oh yeah! I should get some more so I can look like you."

"Really? This is hard work, my friend. It takes twenty-two minutes of tanning every day to get my color," Senthil shot back.

"Well, can we do this up on the rooftop of the hospital so that we can knock two birds with one stone?" said Charlie, keeping up with him.

"So, how much do you drink in a day?" Senthil redirected him to his history.

"I am a pastor. I don't drink alcohol," Charlie replied.

"Hmm. Interesting! What are you going to do with that six-pack?" Senthil asked, pointing to Charlie's abs.

"Hahaha, good one," replied Charlie.

He told Charlie that his first order of business was to get an MRI of the brain and then complete a tumor workup with a CT of the chest, abdomen, and pelvis to rule out any sign of malignancy.

"In the meantime, I am going to order some IV steroids."

"Steroids? I'll just drop down and do a couple of pushups if I want some muscles. I don't need steroids," replied Charlie.

Laughing out loud, Senthil said, "No Charlie, the steroids are for the brain swelling around the tumor, and they'll help with nausea and headaches too." He reassured Charlie that he would come back to update him as soon as the MRI and the CT scans were done.

"Are you claustrophobic? The MRI of the brain will be forty to forty-five minutes long. I don't want to sedate you for the MRI but wouldn't mind giving you something small to take the edge off."

"I'll just close my eyes. I think I'd be okay but thank you."

Senthil knew that waiting was worse than knowing. He was reluctant to leave Charlie alone with so many uncertainties. "Are you okay being alone in the room? I can ask a nurse to keep you company. Or you are welcome to sit by the nurses' station."

With a smile, Charlie replied, "'So do not fear, for I am with you; do not be dismayed, for I am your God. I will strengthen you and help you; I will uphold you with my righteous right hand.' Isaiah 41:10. I am never alone. Please go tend to whatever needs tending."

He did not seem to be in denial but rather someone who was sure of his faith and beliefs. Senthil was amazed at Charlie's emotional maturity and conviction.

Senthil was saddened as he reviewed the MRI of the brain. Radiographically, the tumor screamed GBM. As expected, the CT of the chest, abdomen, and pelvis was negative. Papa was still in the OR. He was aware that Charlie and his family were waiting.

Pepto paged Senthil to let him know that Charlie's family had arrived. Charlie's wife, Mary, their six-month-old daughter, and Charlie's parents were in the room. Even though they were obviously concerned about Charlie, they appeared calm. Senthil pulled up the scan and showed them the large contrast, enhancing tumor occupying the right frontal and temporal lobes. He told them the significance of the findings and shared his concern. He reassured them that Dr. Papavero was aware and would be visiting as soon as he was out of the OR.

"Do you have any questions I can answer in the meantime?" he asked.

"Is this operable? What are our options?" Charlie's father asked.

Senthil informed them that there were three options. The first was a minimally invasive stereotactic brain biopsy, where a three-sixteenth-inch hole would be drilled into his skull to retrieve a small sample, smaller than a grain of rice. The second way involved waiting and following with surveillance MRI brain. The third entailed surgical resection.

"Dr. Papavero is an aggressive surgeon. He'll definitely put surgery on the table, and I am confident that he'll be able to get a gross total resection, but . . ." Senthil paused. He certainly did not want to overwhelm them with information and had to make sure they were able to follow.

"But what?" asked Mr. McCormick, Charlie's father.

Senthil said that he wanted to make sure they had enough time to process the information he had provided so far. He thought they perhaps wanted to hear further details from Dr. Papavero.

"It's not rocket science . . ." started Mr. McCormick.

"It's only brain surgery," Charlie chimed in. Proud of their tag team, Charlie and Mr. McCormick high-fived each other.

"Kids!" Mrs. McCormick admonished them, and then turning to Senthil, said, "Please proceed. We would like to know as much as we can from you so that we can ask the right questions when Dr. Papavero is here."

Senthil looked at Mary, who was holding her daughter and intently listening. "Well, like I mentioned, Dr. Papavero is an excellent surgeon and is the best in removing brain tumors. But even if he manages to remove the entire tumor you see on the scan, it is not a cure."

Seeing their puzzled faces, Senthil continued, "This tumor is not like a cherry in a bowl of Jell-O. It's more like a handful of sand being dropped on the table. You see a mound of sand in the middle, but there are scattered grains of sands around. We would be able to take out the mound but will not be able to go after the individual grains that are not visible even under a microscope."

Senthil could see the tears welling up in Mary's eyes as she rocked her daughter on her lap. He looked directly at her and continued, "This means that even after a total resection, we need to zap the rest of the remaining cells with radiation and chemotherapy." He wanted to be very careful and chose his words carefully to make sure he was not giving them false hope while giving them hope at the same time.

"So, when can we cut out Lucifer?" asked Charlie, sitting up in bed.

Senthil looked puzzled. Mary got up from the chair with her daughter, walked over, and sat on the bed beside Charlie. She tousled his hair and said, "My dear husband has named his tumor 'Lucifer.'"

Senthil smiled and nodded. He told them he would be back with Papa once he was out of the OR. If any questions came up in the meantime, he instructed them to ask their nurse to page him. As he was leaving the room, he turned around and pointing to their daughter, asked, "What's the little girl's name?"

They answered, "Hope."

Senthil felt chills run down his spine and rubbed the goosebumps on his arms.

He tended to a few more patients and looked over the labs and notes from consult services in preparation for his evening rounds with Papa. He was on the other end of the unit when his pager went off.

"Papa is on the floor. Nurses' station A. Hurry." It was from Pepto.

Senthil rushed off to meet him. Papa was sitting in the middle of the nurses' station. He had changed out of his scrubs and was dressed in a shirt and tie. In his deep husky voice, he said, "What you got? Let's round."

Senthil pulled up the MRI on the computer and briefed Papa about Charlie and his family. After scrolling over the MRI, Papa turned to Senthil and muttered, "It has to come out, but it is going to be tricky."

Senthil led the way to Charlie's room. Papa pulled a chair on one side of the bed and sat down next to Charlie, as his family huddled around the other side of the bed. He looked at Charlie and said, "I am sorry to meet you under these circumstances. My PA has updated me about you. Where do you want me to start and what questions do you have for me?"

Charlie looked up at his father, and Mr. McCormick started the conversation. He told Papa that Senthil had explained to them about the tumor, the location, and treatment options, and after discussing as a family and praying, they had decided on surgical resection. "What does the surgery entail and what are your biggest concerns?" he asked.

Senthil had pulled up the MRI on the computer screen in the room. Papa pointed to the scan and explained in detail the location of the tumor, the significance of the insula, and the middle cerebral artery. He also briefed them regarding the challenges of the surgery. He told them about the risk of paralysis on the left side of the body, chances of failing to get all the tumor out, and potential personality changes. He told them about the three options, and since Charlie was young, he recommended an aggressive surgical resection. He told them that he would do this surgery with an asleep motor mapping, which would help him preserve function while trying to obtain gross total resection. Papa added, "I can do the surgery tomorrow."

Mr. McCormick asked Papa, "When will they start radiation and chemotherapy?"

"I can tell you with 85 percent accuracy what type of tumor this is tomorrow. Final pathology takes about five to seven days. If it is indeed what I think it is, we will get the ball rolling by consulting neuro-oncology and radiation oncology. However, the treatment would start only after two to three weeks." Before Mary could ask about the delay, Papa said, "We got to wait for the final pathology and give time for the incision to heal."

After answering all the questions to the family's satisfaction, Papa got up, and like he always did with each patient, he stuck his hand out to Charlie and said, "You and me. Tomorrow." He then shook his parents' and Mary's hand as well before leaving the room.

The next day, Papa and Senthil met Charlie and his family in the preoperative area.

"Any last minute questions?" asked Papa.

"No, sir. We are all set. Let's get rid of Lucifer."

Mrs. McCormick said, "We hope everything goes well. There are a lot of people praying for Charlie, including us."

"We'll take all the help we can get," replied Papa.

When Mr. McCormick asked if they would join his family for prayer, Papa and Senthil readily agreed. They all held hands as Mr. McCormick said a prayer. After the "Amen," Senthil and the anesthesiology resident rolled Charlie into the OR.

"Please take good care of him," Mary pleaded.

Senthil said, "I promise. He is in good hands. Papa is the best. Please don't worry."

Papa was like a maestro in the OR. Under the microscope, he skillfully removed the tumor piecemeal with motor mapping. When Papa was convinced he had a gross total resection, he asked the OR nurse, "Please bring the family into the conference room so I can update them." As he was headed out of the OR, he told Senthil, "Keep him on high dose steroids and get a postop MRI tonight."

"Yes, sir!" Senthil replied as he proceeded to sew the dura (paper thin membrane covering the brain).

Papa met the anxious family in the waiting room and told them that the surgery had been successful and exceeded the objective. He told them that the preliminary frozen pathology confirmed the initial diagnosis GBM.

"Did you get it all?" Mary asked.

"Everything I could see. We'll get an MRI tonight to prove it. Senthil is closing him up and will bring him up to the ICU."

Senthil and the anesthesiology resident rushed the patient into the ICU and gave a report to the receiving nurse and the intensivist. Senthil then went to the lobby to find Charlie's family. They were as elated to see him as marooned islanders would be to spot a ship. He brought them into the ICU. Charlie was sitting up in the bed; he was a little groggy but was awake and conversant.

Chapter 25 — Vivacious Red Encounters

WITH THE ARRIVAL OF JULY 1, 2006, THE HOSPITAL BRIMMED with fresh interns. Aspiring surgeons enthusiastically embarked on their respective surgical services. Even though it was a Saturday, Senthil came to work to help the interns who were not only new to the hospital but also new to neurosurgical service. To the relief of the nurses, he stayed until 10:00 PM to make sure all the patients were tucked in and even gave a little orientation to the night intern.

Over time, a symbiotic physician–physician-assistant partnership was born. Through hard work and dedication, Senthil earned the trust of his surgeons. From then onwards, he gained the liberty to manage patients without having to check with the surgeon for everything. All the residents, the nurses, and the ancillary staff members consulted him regarding the care of neurosurgical patients. It was a responsibility he took very seriously and a right he never abused.

Senthil was walking down the hall one day when he heard a lady's voice behind him ask, "Are you Senthil?"

He turned around and said, "Yes. How can I help?"

"Hi! My name is Annabelle Kingston. I am a new speech therapist. Mr. Dickerson in room 4123 failed the TBI[46] screening. Could I please get an order for cognitive and communication evaluation and treatment?"

"Oh hi!" Senthil smiled. "Welcome aboard! I'll enter the order as soon as I get to a computer."

Annabelle Kingston was assigned as the dedicated speech pathologist to Neurosurgery. She was a vivacious twenty-six-year-old with wavy cinnamon hair always rebelling to break free from her up-do. She had an infectious laugh, and a vibrant face, peppered with faint ginger freckles, and a petite frame. A pair of slightly oversized glasses, along with her white coat, negated her Southern drawl. The surgical residents always found an excuse to talk to her, and the bold ones flirted with her unabashedly. While she welcomed the attention, she did not encourage it since she had a boyfriend.

Annabelle was born and raised in Benson, a small town in North Carolina. The place had a population of approximately three thousand people. Brian, her high school sweetheart, was an assistant county ranger in Harnett County. She was the first one to venture out of Benson to go to school in Chapel Hill and now work in Durham. While Brian offered her everything familiar and the stability of a small town, part of her always wondered about life outside Benson. She had been content with living with her parents and driving an hour to Chapel Hill for school and now to Durham for work.

With her outgoing nature, she quickly became friends with all the nurses. Her striking persona was complemented by her overt animation when she talked and laughed. Besides Senthil, she quickly became Pepto's favorite, who practically adopted her. Annabelle's interaction with Senthil was strictly business-related. He called upon her when consulting speech therapy for swallow studies and cognitive evaluations. Annabelle was impressed with his knowledge about the role of speech therapists, realistic expectations for his patients, and his respect for physical, occupational, and speech therapists.

46 Traumatic Brain Injury

The nurses and the residents invited Annabelle to join them in their regular outings to Raleigh or Chapel Hill. As usual, Senthil was the designated driver. Annabelle always teased him for not being able to relax and have a drink or two. She always tried to get him a fruity drink to mask the taste of alcohol. He would oblige and take a sip or two, but he never could get past the taste of alcohol. His taste buds were too sensitive. Besides, he always believed that one hardly had to drink to relax or have fun. His choice of poison was desserts.

Annabelle usually crashed in one of the nurse's places when she went out instead of driving to Benson on a buzz. She invited Brian all the time and encouraged him to go out of Benson occasionally to experience life outside the small town, but he was content. This was a constant source of strife between the two. She loved Brian but did not want to settle in Benson. Brian, however, had no intention to leave. Her parents favored Brian and admired his patience with their daughter. She had had a rough childhood, and they wanted her to be happy, so they did not interfere in her life.

Jenna was one of the nurses working in the Neurosurgery Department. She had married her high school sweetheart and was a mother to two children. Raised with puritanical standards and married into a similar household, she always longed for excitement and constantly complained that she had missed having fun in her younger age. She befriended Annabelle and constantly reminded her that she lived vicariously through her. Annabelle did not want to have regrets or live an unsatisfied life like Jenna who was not happy even with her nice house with a white picket fence, good husband, and two beautiful children.

"Will you marry me?" Brian proposed one evening, going down on his knee with a ring. Annabelle had no spontaneous answer. The proposal came on the heels of one of their spats about living in Benson and moving to Raleigh or Durham. She was not plagued by the hour-long drive to and from work in Durham, but the thought of settling down in Benson did not sit well with her.

Instead of giving him an answer, she asked him a question. "Will you move out of Benson and come to Durham or Raleigh?"

Brian was not surprised by the lack of emotion, but he was taken aback by her ultimatum. She was not ready to break up with him but could not settle down in Benson either. She was happy with the status quo and felt angry at him for proposing and forcing her to choose. She was hoping that the excitement of the night-outs in the city would eventually wear out and she would be ready to settle down.

There were a lot of "country girls" (as Annabelle put it) who were interested in Brian—girls who had no desire to venture out of Benson, girls who were perfectly content with being a homemaker, dote over their able-bodied provider, and make babies. She did not want to hold him back and told him he would be better off with one of those girls. She was twenty-seven years old, and when she told her parents she was moving into an apartment in Raleigh, they were concerned but held back their reservations.

Unlike their other daughter Virginia, Annabelle was not domesticated. Virginia was married and settled with two boys in Dunn, North Carolina. Virginia was married to Dan, a simple man who worked as an independent contractor fixing houses. Buddy was in eleventh grade and Landon in eighth. Virginia owned her own beauty salon that had a loyal following.

While Annabelle took care of her laundry and shopping, she did not know how to cook or clean. Her only responsibility had been taking care of her red Yorkie Poo Cinnamon whom she had had for thirteen years. Since Annabelle lived only an hour away, her parents comforted themselves with the thought that she would come home whenever she got tired of frozen and canned foods. They came down with her to Raleigh to make sure her apartment was in a safe neighborhood. Annabelle's parents, Lydia and Ben, were retired. They consoled themselves with the thought that they would visit Annabelle between his fishing and hunting and her quilting and bridge club.

Pepto wasted no time after she learned about Annabelle's breakup. "Hey Senthil, you should ask Annabelle out now that she is single," she told him.

By this time, Senthil had grown used to Pepto's antics. "Annabelle who?" he asked.

"You know, Annabelle, the pretty red-headed speech therapist."

He merely shook his head and walked away to check on a patient.

It was a well-known fact that just like slangs, Senthil did not have any idea about double entendres or sexual innuendos. He took everything literally and often ended up being teased. However, he took it in stride. Pepto and Annabelle led the charge and often ganged up on him since he was such a good sport.

Pepto's kids were attending school at Appalachian State University. She lived alone at home and often entertained. She had a pool in her backyard and a hot tub in her sunroom. Pepto and Annabelle had a strong penchant for lying out in the sun and drinking all day. She cooked a mean prime rib and delicious apple pie and walnut brownies. She invited Annabelle and Senthil at least twice a month to come and hang out with her by the pool on hot days and in the hot tub on cool nights.

Senthil had never had the opportunity to learn to swim, and at the age of thirty-seven, it was only getting harder. He loved the water though, and stayed in the pool, learning to doggy paddle, while Pepto and Annabelle watched as they sipped on mai tai and an Aunt Roberta cocktail respectively. Senthil was content with lemonade, brownies, and ice cream. Pepto and Annabelle also made fun of him for being too modest and wearing a swim shirt with his swim trunk. The longer they sipped on the drinks, the more handsy Annabelle got with Senthil. Pepto egged her on; watching him squirm amused her. Annabelle was always too tipsy to drive back and crashed at Pepto's place.

Annabelle was entrusted with the charge of organizing the weekend shenanigans. There was a core group of single nurses and therapists who regularly went to out to bars in Chapel Hill and Raleigh. Her signature event was "Thursday's Girls' Night Out." The nurses and therapists who frequented this weekly bar-hopping event with Annabelle always called it an "epic night."

On Friday night, Annabelle called Senthil, "Hey, do you want to go to the library in Chapel Hill?"

Senthil was still in the hospital. Looking at his watch, he was surprised to see it was 7:30 PM. He replied, "It's open this late?"

Annabelle laughed and said, "Of course. It's open until 2:00 in the morning."

When he asked her where it was, she said, "Nancy just handed over her charge to the night nurse and wants to come. I'll tell her you'll pick her up. She knows how to get here."

Nancy was the navigator. It was not easy to find a parking spot on Franklin Street on a Friday evening. Senthil and Nancy walked the sidewalk, and she came to a stop in front of a building with a white façade. "The Library" read the black letters that adorned the top of the building.

"Here we are!" said Nancy as she opened the door and walked in. Senthil followed. As soon as he entered, two things caught his attention. It was loud, and there were no books. It was a nightclub.

Annabelle had reserved a table for them. She waved and motioned for them to come over.

Senthil said, "When you said the library, this is not what I thought."

With her signature boisterous laughter, Annabelle said, "Gosh! You are always so uptight."

She loosened his tie and unbuttoned his collar. Annabelle and the others had already had a couple of drinks. Nancy ordered two shots to catch up.

"I'll take some ice water with lemon please," said Senthil, and Annabelle rolled her eyes. She grabbed his hands and dragged him to the dance floor. He was like a fish out of water with his two left feet, but she was too tipsy to care. He humored her for a couple of minutes by moving side to side but eventually came back to the table.

Even though bars were not his cup of tea and he could not dance to save his life, he did join them occasionally, mostly because of Annabelle's constant barrage. Even though they all went to the bars as a group, as the evening progressed, after everyone had downed a few drinks, the girls and the guys began flirting with other patrons in the bar and hit the dance floor with them, leaving Senthil alone, sipping on water. On days he was not the designated driver, Senthil usually slipped out without saying bye, went home, and settled in front of the TV. He preferred that over watching his friends make out with acquaintances.

He had never understood the need to go to a bar to have fun. Nothing about the bar scene was appealing for him. Loud music, the need to yell just to have a conversation with someone standing right next to you, and the ridiculous price of the drinks hardly made sense. Eventually, he began to join them when they went out to a restaurant and bailed after dinner as the rest of them hit the bars.

The days Annabelle did not see Senthil because both of them were too busy, she called him at night to talk about their day. What started off as a quick hello and a chat gradually transformed into long phone calls that went on until late in the night and sometimes even early dawn. The subject matter ranged from gossip at work, to patients, politics, family, religion, and movies. No matter what they talked about, the conversation always ended up with Annabelle teasing him about being a virgin at thirty-seven. She told him that she and Brian had a healthy sex life and could not believe someone would choose not to partake in something so pleasurable.

He told her about Sumathi, and she could not believe that they had had a four-year relationship without even kissing. She was shocked he had not been on a single date since she had gotten married in 1997. He told her about his responsibilities and how he was focused on saving for his family's future. She could not relate to that either.

"So, in the past nine years, you haven't gone out with anyone?"

"No, I haven't. It won't be right to marry someone while I still think about Sumathi."

"Who is talking about getting married, dude? You don't have to get married to everyone you date."

"Well, I can't go out with someone with whom I don't see a future."

"So, there was no one special, no one you connected with since the girl from India?"

He told her of his time in Terre Haute and his friendship with Lina.

"Wait! A beautiful girl is not only interested in you but is in bed with you and you didn't do anything? Are you gay?" she asked.

"No, I am not," he replied.

"Life is too short. You, my dear, need to get laid."

Chapter 26 — Unfamiliar Territories

MONDAY, SEPTEMBER 3, 2007, WAS LABOR DAY. PEPTO arranged for a potluck barbecue and invited some nurses and the therapists. She threw some hamburgers, hot dogs, and bratwursts on the grill. The rest of them brought in all the fixings that go with barbeque. Senthil made a new dish, his own creation, with meatballs and called it "curried meatballs"—meatballs in a spicy and creamy sauce, full of Indian spices and flavor. Annabelle walked in with all the ingredients to make her favorite and signature drink: Aunt Roberta cocktail.

The best ingredient for the party was the weather. The temperature was just right to enjoy the pool under clear blue skies. It was picture perfect, and everyone was taking pictures and uploading them to Facebook. Pepto made a punch with frozen lemonade, Sprite, and some generous slices of oranges, lemons, and limes for Senthil. She was a good host from behind the grill, making sure everybody had their fill. Senthil played cornhole by the pool with others while Annabelle played beer pong.

By 7:00 in the evening, the last few stragglers bid farewell. Pepto finally sat down and said, "Now I am ready for my drink." She was so busy entertaining that she had not had the time to eat.

Senthil jumped up. "You poor thing. Let me fix you a plate."

"I know exactly what you need," said Annabelle as she sprinted to fix a mai tai for Pepto.

Flanked on either side by Annabelle and Senthil, Pepto enjoyed a plate of food while sipping on the mai tai. "I can see why people were raving about these. Your meatballs are delicious. They pack some heat. I like it."

"What about my mai tai?" asked Annabelle.

"It's delectable, sweetie," Pepto laughed.

"Where is my camera? We should take a picture." Annabelle remembered leaving it on the lounge chair by the pool. She hopped up and ran to the side of the pool, tripped on her sarong, and fell in. Senthil laughed but hurried to help her.

"I am glad you didn't fall with the camera," he jested.

"You are very funny," she replied.

"What happened?"

"I have no earthly idea," she said. She reached out her hand, and when Senthil tried to pull her up, Annabelle pulled him into the pool instead.

"What did you do that for?" he screamed.

"Who is laughing now?" Annabelle shot back.

Realizing she was at the six-foot end of the pool and the reason he was vigorously splashing water was that his feet were not touching the bottom of the pool, she went behind him, pulled him on to her, and swam to the shallow end of the pool on her back.

"I would have managed to reach the wall, you know," he said, standing at the four-foot side of the pool."

"You are so cute," she said, placing her hand on his head as though she was trying to push him under. She gazed into his eyes, lifted his chin with her other hand, and as Pepto turned around to see what the hoopla was all about, Annabelle quickly planted a kiss on his lips. It was brief, but it was the first kiss ever on Senthil's lips. As she got out of the pool and walked towards Pepto, she turned around, looked at a stunned Senthil, and coyly asked, "Aren't you going to come out of the pool?"

Senthil grabbed her sarong that was floating nearby and got out of the pool.

"I am going to take a quick shower. I'll be right back," Annabelle said.

"Okay honey. There are fresh towels in the linen closet next to the bathroom," Pepto yelled.

Senthil sat gazing at the pool quietly.

"She likes you," Pepto broke the silence.

"She's tipsy," Senthil replied.

"Maybe. But that doesn't change the fact that the two of you are made for each other."

Annabelle remembered the kiss the next day. She had kissed other guys in bars after a few drinks and had given neither the kiss nor the guys a second thought. Last night was different, and she was mad at herself for feeling emotional about it. She was concerned he was going to be all weird at work even after Pepto said to her, "Don't worry. He is more mature than your average Joe."

She continued to call him every night though she could not explain to herself why she felt the urge to, even the nights she stayed out late, even after having kissed a random guy in the bar. Their conversation always ended with her teasing him about how he "needs to get laid."

Laughing, she told him, "This may sound weird, but I wish I could be a fly on the wall when you do it for the first time. I bet with all your bottled-up sexual tension, you are going to explode within a few seconds."

One night she asked him, "How come I am the one who always calls? Why don't you call me?"

"I don't like to bother people. I am very predictable, and you know my schedule. I am either at work or at home."

They had nothing in common and held completely opposite views on almost all matters. Still, they got along very well.

After working as a PA for two years, Senthil had saved enough for a down payment on a house. He bought a small three-bedroom single family home with a small backyard in Durham. It was his first investment, and he was very proud. He would not have to sleep on the floor anymore. Every evening, he scoured the furniture stores lining Glenwood Avenue. With High Point, the home furnishings capital of the world, only an hour away from Durham, he hoped to find some quality and affordable furniture.

He did not have any trouble deciding on his living room and dining room furniture. This would be the first time he was lying in his "own bed," so he wanted it to be perfect. He haggled successfully at one of the stores for a discount for furnishing the entire house.

It was a Saturday delivery. Senthil had agreed to work that day as there were some sick patients on the service. He was relieved when Annabelle volunteered to go to his place and receive the furniture. He drew up a floor plan so she could instruct the delivery crew regarding the placement of each piece of furniture. She felt like royalty and, much to the amusement of the delivery men, spoke in a fake English accent.

The master bedroom was the last one to be fitted in with furniture. It had a king-size bed and two end tables. One of the delivery men exclaimed, "Wow! This is a Louis Phillipe sleigh bed." It had a leather embossed headboard and footboard and looked very regal. Annabelle looked at the receipt to check the price. It was $900. He continued, "Your boyfriend has good taste."

She chuckled and was about to say that he was not her boyfriend, but she stopped herself and instead said, "He got himself a great bargain."

"Yes, ma'am. The manager gave him a good deal since he furnished the whole house," the delivery guy acknowledged. She lay on the pillow top mattress. It was very comfortable.

On the occasion of Halloween, Annabelle and her posse were planning to attend the big party at Franklin Street. Annabelle got herself a nurse costume, and she wanted Senthil to dress up like a doctor and come with her. Senthil did not see the amusement in adults dressing up. He thought that Halloween costumes had morphed over the years from being cute or scary to blatantly sexy. He told her that a nurse would never wear an outfit like that. He thought Halloween was just an excuse for good girls to dress slutty—another view of his that diametrically opposed hers.

She knew he was not a prude, but he took life too seriously. She pitied him for not being able to cut loose and relax. He did not drink because he hated the taste of alcohol. He did not think it wrong to have a few drinks but just did not see the point in getting drunk in the name of fun, doing things under the influence of liquid courage and not remembering what happened the morning after. Sorrow was no reason to drink, and normal emotions should be experienced rather than being drowned temporarily in alcohol. He did not dress up and joined a much tamer party thrown by one of the neurosurgery residents.

Annabelle and Senthil always exchanged their different beliefs and opinions only as friendly banter and never argued or tried to impose their views on each other.

He was not surprised when his phone rang at 1:00 in the morning. It was Annabelle. She had gotten separated from the gang and Nancy had her purse and could not be reached on the phone. She had tried calling a cab a few times but had not heard back. She sounded inebriated, and he did not think it was safe to leave her there alone. Luckily, he was still at the party, and the resident's house was only a few miles away from Franklin Street. Senthil told her he would be there in ten minutes and hopped into his car.

She was sitting on the curb and was relieved to see him. She did not have her purse or her car keys and would not be able to get into her apartment. He offered to take her to Pepto's house, but she did not want to wake her up this hour. That left them with only one option. "Let's go to your house," she muttered as she got into the car.

Senthil buckled her seat belt and drove her to his house. He gave her his bathrobe, placed a glass of water by the night table, grabbed his pajamas, and closed the door. He gave her his room as the master bedroom had an attached bathroom and retired into the guest room.

Sometime during the night, he woke up startled as he realized that Annabelle was lying next to him. It was dark. She had her arms around him, and she was not wearing any clothes. She caressed his head and pressed it against her bare bosom. He did not know what to do and just kept still. From lying on his side, she slowly moved to lie on top of him. He had to summon all his self-control and will to not act upon his body's physiological response to her overtures. She fell asleep on top of him, and he gently slid her to the side.

Early the next morning, Annabelle woke up before him in a panic—ten minutes before his 4:30 AM alarm went off.

"Oh shit! Oh God!" she muttered as she sat up, clutching the bedsheet to her chest. Everything about last night was a blur. She remembered waddling into his room and lying next to him. She gingerly lifted the sheet covering him and breathed a sigh of relief to see he still had his pajamas on. She slid out of bed, wrapped herself in the sheet, and began tiptoeing to the door.

"Good morning!" Senthil said.

She froze. "Oh shit!"

He did not want her to go through the dreaded walk of shame and said in a soft but clear voice, "Nothing happened last night."

She grabbed her head with one hand and groggily said, "Don't say a word." She hurried out of the room and shut the door.

He waited for a few minutes until he heard her downstairs. Then he went to his room, took a shower, and got ready for work. As he was fixing his tie and climbing down the stairs, he found her sitting on the couch, her head buried in a pillow. He handed her some Motrin and a glass of water.

Without looking, she held her hand up. "Do you have the time to take me to my car?"

He looked at his watch. It was 5:10 AM. "Let's go," he said.

After work, Annabelle called him at night as usual. "I am so glad you didn't act all weird at work today." She told him he was more mature than the guys she knew. They were glad that they could laugh about the incident and be comfortable with each other. "Hey, what did I really do last night?" she then asked. Senthil briefly told her what she had done. Annabelle laughed and said, "I don't know if I should be happy or sad." She added, "I am not sure if you have great self-control or if you don't find me attractive."

"Oh, Annabelle! Please don't say that. You are very pretty. You were inebriated, and what kind of a man would I be if I took advantage of you? You wouldn't have done it if you weren't drunk."

She said, "I'll let you in on a little secret. Alcohol only reduces your inhibition to do something that is deep down in your heart. It does not make you do something you have never thought about doing," and laughed. When she stopped laughing, she said, "Oh my goodness, you wouldn't know what to do anyway."

Senthil just laughed and replied, "Just so you know, I got an 'A' in anatomy."

Annabelle told him that theory is different from practical and asked, "Promise me you will tell me everything and not spare any details when it happens."

"I can't talk about stuff like that. A gentleman doesn't kiss and tell."

Annabelle was surprised to learn that he did not share their night with any of his friends. Anyone else in his shoes would have bragged about it.

When she pestered him to promise to tell her everything after his first tryst, Senthil said, "The only way you are going to know such personal details is if it happens with you."

After a brief, awkward moment of silence, she abruptly said, "Oh, it's getting late. You got to get up early. See you tomorrow. Good night."

This time, there was no usual teasing about him needing to get laid.

Chapter 27 — Change of Heart

THE MCCORMIKS HAD FINISHED THEIR APPOINTMENT with the neuro-oncologist and were stopping by to see Senthil as usual. Since discharge, the McCormiks had come every month to see Senthil. They must have thought of it as a social visit, but they did not know Senthil was thankful to them for refueling his spiritual quest.

Annabelle was impressed by Senthil's constantly growing fan base and admired his commitment to go the extra mile for his patients. Senthil realized that even though they had different outlooks in life, different moral standards, and a decade between them in years, he was falling in love with Annabelle. With her, he intuitively knew that there was more than met the eye. He did not care if Annabelle felt the same way. He was just happy there was love in his heart again. With all his siblings married and settled, he could finally think about himself. Annabelle's little tugs had rocked the pedestal on which Sumathi had reigned supreme in his heart. She flirted with him but had not opened her heart to him.

In November 2007, Pepto asked Annabelle if she was taking Senthil home for Thanksgiving.

"Take him home? Where is this coming from?"

Pepto replied, "I know you are falling for him."

"I am falling for him? What makes you say that?"

"For starters, you are repeating everything I say, and that high-pitched voice gives it away. You just keep denying to yourself what you know deep down inside."

"You know me. I don't know what I want. I am here today, and I can easily up and leave tomorrow."

"What are you afraid of, Annabelle?"

"I have no earthly idea. I just don't want to hurt that poor boy."

Pepto asked her if her parents knew about Senthil.

Annabelle said, "Of course they do. I have told them so much about him—how funny and caring he is and what a great PA he is."

"Hmm . . ."

"What? I tell my parents about all my friends. I have told them about you too. Besides, I go out a lot and make out with random guys."

"Yes, but have you gone home with them or brought them back to your apartment?"

Annabelle remained quiet.

"Cat got your tongue? Answer me," Pepto persisted.

"No."

"Why not?"

"I have no earthly idea."

Not wanting to push her, Pepto just told Annabelle there was more between her and Senthil than she acknowledged and that she hoped Annabelle realized it before it was too late.

Even though the OR was closed and there were no elective cases on Thanksgiving Day, the service was busy. Senthil and the on-call resident took turns going to Papa's house for dinner.

The following day, Annabelle brought to work two Tupperware containers with turkey and all the fixings in one and apple pie and blueberry pie in another for Senthil. He was in the OR with Papa. Annabelle was doing a fiberoptic endoscopic swallow study (FEES) on a patient in the ICU, who had undergone an acoustic neuroma tumor resection, when Senthil passed her room with his postoperative. She was in the middle of the study and could not leave to tell him about the food she had brought for him. They kept missing each other throughout the day.

Annabelle gave the containers to Pepto and asked her to make sure he got it. "There are so many people here, and you are friends with a lot of them. But you brought back food only for him. What's up with that, Annabelle?" asked Pepto.

"Well, he doesn't have family here, and I just wanted him to have some homecooked food," Annabelle replied, but she could not hide her smile. Pepto noticed but did not say a word.

Annabelle called him late that night. "Did you like the food?"

"I just ate that for dinner. It was amazing. Thank you so much. Did you cook it?"

Annabelle laughed heartily and asked, "Me? Cook? I can't even boil water! No, my mom did all the cooking. I just did all the chopping and cutting and cleaning afterward."

Senthil shared with her what Papa had told him about him being a part of the family.

"You are in love with the man and married to your job," she joked. She always teased him about his bromance with Papa, which Senthil never denied.

He replied, "After my father and grandfather, Papa is the most influential man in my life."

He admired Papa because he was a gifted surgeon and a caring physician. Papa realized the importance of Senthil's role in the care of his patients and acknowledged him as his eyes and ears outside the OR. Through his hard work, he had gained Papa's trust, and Papa, in return, rewarded him with the reigns to navigate preoperative and postoperative care. It was a beautiful symbiotic relationship, and they served as a model for a physician–physician-assistant relationship for the rest of the hospital.

Chapter 28 — Happy New Year

ANNABELLE WAS A COMPLEX INDIVIDUAL. SHE CALLED Senthil every night without fail, and they would talk for hours. He had developed strong feelings for her and made no secret of it. He knew she did not reciprocate, and he did not want to scare her. She was very friendly, but there was a slight difference in her behavior in person and when she was on the phone.

Initially, he was uncomfortable whenever she bantered about his virginity. But like waves gradually erode the seashore, Annabelle gradually eroded the foundation of the throne Sumathi had occupied for long.

During one such late-night phone call and teasing session about his need to get laid, Senthil interrupted her, "Would you like to come to the Neurosurgery Christmas party? As my guest?" He had phrased it carefully; instead of "my date," he said, "my guest."

Annabelle was still caught off guard. She stuttered. "People talk about us already. What do you think they'll say if you bring me to the party?"

"I don't know. Does it matter?"

"It's different for you."

"It is not complicated. It is a yes or no question."

"It's not that simple. Are any therapists or nurses invited?"

"No, not for this one."

"Can I think about it and get back to you later?"

They both agreed to leave it there.

Annabelle recounted their conversation to Pepto, and she asked: "What are you going to do?"

"I have no earthly idea," Annabelle replied.

"But you have to give him an answer."

"I know. You know how Senthil feels about me. I am not like him. Everybody revers him; they'll kill me if I hurt him."

"Don't worry about them. He is not delusional, and this is no puppy love. As much as you don't want to hurt him, you should also be true to yourself."

"All the surgeons are going to be there. Papa is going to be there. What if I end up embarrassing poor Senthil?"

"Exit stage left, Annabelle. Exit stage left," Pepto said.

Annabelle went shopping. While her short cocktail dresses were fine for a night out on the town, she wanted something more elegant for this party. She went to Black House White Market at the Southpoint Mall, and after deliberating over the choice of several dresses, she walked out with a black knee-length asymmetric pleat-front A-line dress—it was conservative yet sexy.

"I am on my way to pick you," Senthil texted her. Annabelle played with the double shot of vodka in her hand. She felt nervous and needed some liquid courage. She had tamed her burnished copper tresses and pulled them back into a sleek bun. A tendril of hair adorned the left side of her face. A simple pair of pearl earrings and a pearl necklace completed her ensemble. He pulled up in front of her apartment.

Annabelle took one final look at herself in the mirror, and raising her glass, she said, "Here's to whatever." She downed the vodka in one big gulp. She did not want him to see her messy apartment, and so, she grabbed her clutch, jumped into her high heels, and walked out of the apartment as Senthil was getting out of the car.

She took his breath away. He walked towards her as she smiled coyly and twisted the loose tendril of hair. She felt shy—a feeling that was completely new for her. As she hugged Senthil, a hint of Japanese honeysuckle lingered.

"You are gorgeous, and you smell great!" he exclaimed. He opened the car door for her.

The Christmas party was at the posh Umstead Hotel in Cary. Annabelle was unusually quiet. She turned the radio on. After a couple of commercials, Bonnie Raitt's song came on.

"People are talkin', talkin' 'bout people
I hear them whisper, you won't believe it
They think we're lovers kept under covers
I just ignore it, but they keep saying
We laugh just a little too loud
We stand just a little too close
We stare just a little too long
Maybe they're seeing something we don't, darlin'
Let's give them something to talk about . . ."

She noticed a smile on his face and turned the radio off. He started laughing. "Somebody is having a lot of fun," she said.

The department had arranged for complimentary parking, so he pulled up at the entrance.

After they got out of the car, she grabbed his arm and said, "Let's do this."

Everybody was used to Senthil attending social gatherings without a date and began to whisper, "Who is Senthil's date?" as soon as they saw her. They were the talk of the evening; people assumed she was his girlfriend.

Senthil introduced her to Papa. "Sir, this is my friend Annabelle Kingston. She is a speech pathologist and takes excellent care of our patients."

Papa shook her hand and said, "Oh yes. I have seen the two of you together in the wards. I don't know who hit the jackpot here between the two of you. Merry Christmas. You two have a good time."

Annabelle blushed and smiled at Senthil. She was a social butterfly, and Senthil was happy to see her at ease with the best of the party's attendees. She sipped on a glass of wine and chatted up all the curious surgeons, residents, anesthesiologists, CRNAs, and OR nurses.

That evening after Senthil dropped her off, she immediately reached for the phone to call Pepto.

"I had a great time," she said.

"Do tell," Pepto replied.

Annabelle told her about the party, what Papa had said, and how different it was from the parties she was used to. It was mature: there were no drinking games or mindless banter, only thought-provoking conversations. Gourmet food supplanted pizza and wings. Most of all, she saw firsthand how much Senthil's peers loved and respected him. She always teased him for his long hours in the hospital, for being a slave to Papa, and for getting paid for only forty hours a week when he worked close to twice as many hours. She understood that evening that Senthil had earned something far more precious than money: the admiration and respect of everybody in the hospital. She did not tire of hearing everybody tell her their favorite story or encounter involving Senthil.

Senthil knew well that Annabelle coming to the party with him had changed nothing between the two of them. He downplayed the story to surgeons and his friends whenever they asked him about Annabelle. "She is just my friend," he would say.

"Leave him alone. I am sure they'll get married soon. Senthil doesn't do anything halfway," Papa interjected.

Christmas 2007 fell on a Tuesday. Annabelle took the preceding Friday and Monday off and went home. Senthil worked so that the residents with families, kids, or significant others could enjoy Christmas Eve and Christmas Day.

Annabelle called him on Saturday night. She told him she was busy helping her parents with shopping and wrapping gifts. She was also baking cookies with her sister Virginia and promised to bring him some. Her brother-in-law and nephews had brought a big beautiful Christmas tree to the house. As she was calling from her parents' house, she refrained from her usual antics. "Good night Senthil. I hope you have a Merry Christmas."

"Same to you. I love you, Annabelle."

There was a pause, and then she said, "Please don't say that. Those words scare me. I cannot say it back."

"Annabelle, you don't have to. I just wanted you to know how I feel. I don't expect anything in return."

"Honey! Can you come down and give me a hand?" Lydia yelled from the kitchen.

"I am sorry, I gotta go Senthil. My mom needs me. I'll talk to you later."

Senthil called Shiva and Maria on Christmas Eve to wish them Happy Christmas. They were both jubilant to catch up with him and happy for his success in his new career.

Even though he worked the next day, he went to a local church for the Midnight Mass.

Annabelle returned to work the day after Christmas. She was relieved to find that Senthil did not act awkward. She told him she could up and leave anytime and had a huge fear of commitment. Senthil reassured her that he would not bother her.

"I feel bad, Senthil."

"Annabelle, I can't blame you for not feeling the way I do as much as I can't blame myself for feeling the way I do."

2008 was days away. The service was not busy at all. The OR was closed for New Year's Day, and there were no elective cases posted for New Year's Eve on Monday. Since he had worked Thanksgiving Day and Christmas, the

Neurosurgery residents told him to not work New Year's Eve or New Year's Day. They requested him, instead, to host a New Year's Eve party with Indian food. Senthil agreed and invited all of them. Annabelle told him that she had a previous commitment and was going to a New Year's Eve party in a club at Raleigh. While he was disappointed, Senthil did not show it and replied, "Oh okay. I hope you have fun. If there are any leftovers, I'll bring them on Wednesday." Annabelle too did not show her disappointment over his lack of insistence that she come to the party.

He spent that weekend cleaning and sprucing up his house. On New Year's Eve, he cooked a delicious Indian spread. The guests brought drinks. To make the evening a true Indian experience, Senthil played songs from Bollywood. It was around 11:30 PM when Annabelle walked in.

"Hey, I thought you were at a bar in Raleigh!" exclaimed one of the therapists.

"Well, I was. But not anymore."

Senthil fixed her a plate of food while she poured herself a glass of red wine. They all gathered around the TV to watch Dick Clark's *New Year's Rockin' Eve '08*, featuring Carrie Underwood, Miley Cyrus, and the Jonas Brothers. John Lennon's "Imagine" played as they waited for the ball to drop.

Senthil and the gang joined in on the countdown, and just as the clock struck 12:00, streamers and confetti exploded all over his living room. One of the guests popped a champagne bottle. There was no time to waste on the bubbly by looking for cups, and so, the bottle was passed around for everybody to take a sip directly from it.

Everybody thought it was a great party and helped themselves to second helpings of whatever food was left. Senthil was relieved. After playing the busy host for the whole night, he sat down with a slice of peanut butter pie. He declined offers of help in cleaning up. "Don't worry guys. I got this. Please help me by taking home any food you want, as there is no room in the refrigerator. Just leave the desserts alone."

He laid out some Tupperware containers and ziplock bags for people to help themselves. Gradually, people thanked him for the delicious food and bid farewell.

Anabelle said, “I can stay and help clean up.”

“Oh, don’t worry about it, Annabelle. There is little leftover to pack. I’ll just clean up in the morning.”

She was the last one to leave. “Are you sure you don’t want me to stay and help clean up?”

“I am sure, Annabelle. I have my method. It’ll just take me a few hours in the morning, so I’ll be fine.”

He walked her to the door. She gave him a hug and wished him a Happy New Year.

“Happy new year to you too. Drive safe.” He locked the door, and started heading back to the kitchen when there was a knock on the door.

Puzzled, he opened the door. It was Annabelle. “Hey, did you forget something?” he asked.

Annabelle stepped in, held his face with her hands, and kissed him on the lips. She caught him off guard.

“Let’s go upstairs,” she whispered, grabbing his hand and leading him to his bedroom.

When she entered the bedroom, he turned the lights on. She turned them off and said, “No.” She walked towards the bed and lay on it. Even though the lights were off, moonlight filtered through the blinds to cast a faint glow over the bed.

He paused at the bedside and asked, “Are you drunk?”

“I am tipsy but not drunk. I am aware of what I am doing,” Annabelle replied.

“I don’t have any—”

She interrupted him and said, “I am on the pill.”

“Are you sure about this?”

Annabelle sat up, put her finger on his lips, and said, “Shh . . .”

He hesitated but did not resist. For the next hour, he just followed her lead. She led him into a blissful night, and he followed her every step with rapturous delight.

Like the calm after a storm, they quietly lay next to each other, staring at the ceiling. She broke the silence first. "Are you okay?" she asked.

He cleared his throat and said, "Yes, I am." After a brief pause, he turned towards her and asked, "You?"

Without taking her eyes off the ceiling, she said, "You and Papa were right."

"How so?"

"You were right when you said you know your anatomy, and Papa when he said you don't leave anything halfway." She started getting dressed in the dark.

"What are you doing?" he whispered.

"Going home," she answered.

"It's middle of the night!"

"I need to let Cinnamon out before she makes a mess inside. Thank you for a great night." She leaned down to kiss him on the forehead as he sat up on the bed, and said, "Just stay. You don't have to walk me down."

Annabelle was apprehensive of how things were going to be at work. She expected to be greeted by sly grins from Senthil's friends and the male Neurosurgery residents he worked with, but to her surprise, he went on about his work, as usual, not drawing any attention to himself or her. Any other person would have bragged. It made him more desirable in her eyes.

Annabelle was out with her friends for the usual Thursday girls' night out the next day. It was around 10:30 PM when Senthil's phone chirped with a text message from her. "Can I come over?"

He was working on a research paper he was writing in collaboration with a Neurosurgery resident. He smiled and replied, "Sure." He was at the dining table with textbooks and articles sprawled all over. As he tried to finish up, there was a knock at the door. He looked at his watch. It had only been five minutes since Annabelle's text. *Sure, it can't be her. But who could be at the door this hour?* he thought.

He opened the door. It was Annabelle; she must have texted him from the corner of his house. She stepped in wordlessly and kissed him before leading him up the stairs. It was 2:00 AM when he was woken up by the ruffling of sheets. Annabelle was getting out of bed.

"Shh. Go back to bed. I'll see you at work later today," she whispered.

Her trysts with him became frequent. Weekdays or weekends—it did not matter. She came over, and he welcomed it. He loved her and was happy to be with her every chance he got. The only thing that bothered him was that she left in the middle of the night. When he asked her to stay and not leave at odd hours, she said, "I am not your girlfriend. We are just friends with benefits."

When he told her he loved her, she would say, "Please don't say that. I don't like to feel smothered."

Senthil remained patient. He never once called her on his own. He thought his love was enough for both for them.

Their strange relationship worked, because they were both honest with each other. Valentine's Day came on a Thursday, and Senthil left work on time. He stopped by the grocery store on his way back home and cooked up a romantic dinner complete with heirloom tomato salad with balsamic vinaigrette, medium-rare garlic butter steak, roasted fingerling potatoes with herbs and garlic, sautéed broccolini, strawberries, and chocolates. He chilled a bottle of sparkling apple cider and set the table with a white tableclot, and a single long-stemmed red rose in a slender vase as the centerpiece. He showered and dressed up with hopes that Annabelle would come over on this special day.

He waited until 10:00 PM before he proceeded to eat dinner by himself. He was not terribly disappointed. He knew how she felt. He packed and put the food in the refrigerator. Annabelle had gone out with her single girlfriends to a bar in Raleigh that hosted a "Single ladies' night" on Valentine's Day.

The next day, as he was getting ready for work early in the morning, he noticed a text on his phone. "Hey, I was out late with the girls and just got home. Have a good night." It was sent at 1:30 AM.

Friday was busy with a couple of emergency surgeries that were added on from the ER, and he had to hop from one OR to the other. He did not even have a chance to grab lunch or come up to the ward.

That night, he received the familiar text earlier than usual: "Can I come over?"

"I am starving," she said as she walked in. He warmed up her share of Valentine's Day dinner.

"Oh, steak? I thought you would eat Indian food at home. This plate is so American."

He told her he had made it the previous night as a special dinner for Valentine's Day in case she came over. She paused momentarily and then started laughing. He felt annoyed and said, "That's not funny."

"I am sorry. I just realized something and couldn't help laughing." He was curious to know what it was all about. Still laughing uncontrollably, she said, "You are the girl in this relationship!"

He did not find it funny, but he did not argue and just shook his head.

"Don't get mad. I am just teasing you," she said.

Pepto had them over for dinner the following weekend. Annabelle set the table while Senthil helped in the kitchen. Pepto whispered, "I hear you are quite the stud in the sack."

Even his brown skin could not hide the blush. He was mortified and did not know what to say.

Senthil was quiet during dinner.

"Cat got your tongue, honey?" Annabelle asked.

Pepto interrupted and said, "He is upset that you told me about his prowess."

She asked him why she could not tell their mutual friend about them if he could tell his friends about the affair. He told her he had not told anyone and that it was too personal a subject to discuss with others. Annabelle was surprised. She had never thought that a guy would get upset if his girl talked about how good he was. What was sacred for him was simply a fun affair to remember for her. They were cut from a different cloth. She said that he just proved her point that he was the girl in the relationship.

She continued to come over and appreciated the space he gave her. She was thankful that he did not stifle her with his love. They were still discreet when they went out with friends. Gradually, she began to change. Instead of leaving after what she had come for, she started spending the night. She brought Cinnamon with her so that she did not have to leave to let her out. When she spent the night on weekends, she slept in, and Senthil got the time to treat her to homemade breakfasts. She loved his cooking. Impressed by his presentation, she would snap pictures of her breakfast.

They both came from humble beginnings but had different outlooks. He had not grown up eating gourmet foods and had never been to any fancy restaurant. Through his hard work, he had made a life for himself. After helping his siblings settle down and achieving his self-dictated goals for his family, he finally found someone he loved, even though she did not share the same sentiment. Now, he wished to enjoy the little niceties life had to offer.

While she enjoyed the elaborate breakfasts and dinners, she longed for just donuts, bacon and eggs, spaghetti and meatballs, canned Chef Boyardee products, and canned tuna. He liked for them to dress up and treat her to dinners in nice restaurants, while she wanted to just go to a bar or order pizza and settle down in her pajamas in front of the TV.

"You just want to be seen with me all dressed up," she often joked. While it hurt him when she said that, he did not argue.

When they went out with friends, the evening would usually start well—until they ended up in a bar. She and their friends would drink while he sipped on lime water. After a couple of Aunt Robertas, she would usually get a little loud and overtly friendly with the other patrons at the bar. Their friends did the same, and very soon, Senthil would be left feeling alone. He found it difficult to watch other guys flirting or getting too close to her on the dance floor. When she caught a glimpse of him sulking in his chair, she always said, "Lighten up. This is nothing. I am just having fun. At the end of the night, I am going home with you. So, you shouldn't worry about it."

Yes. That was the difference. Annabelle only thought of their relationship as "going home with Senthil for the night," which implied merely a physical relationship, while Senthil longed for more. He was in love with her, but she was not. She reminded him at every instance that she would leave any time, and that she was not his girlfriend and just wanted to keep things simple.

The nights she did not go out, she came over to his place with a bottle of wine.

"I wish you would have a glass of wine with me. It would make the evening so much better. It's no fun drinking by myself," she complained.

"Honey, I don't like the taste of alcohol."

Chapter 29 — Ebbs and Flows

ANNABELLE WAS FULL OF SURPRISES, AND THERE WAS NOT a dull moment in their relationship. The first six months were a little strange: he wanted an emotional connection while she was just happy with their physical compatibility. However, it gave both something they were missing in their lives.

Annabelle and Senthil appreciated that there was no hidden agenda; they were open in their demands from each other, without any pressures or deadlines. They did not dwell on their disappointments or shortcomings and appreciated the ups and downs of their strange but real relationship. He got used to being the "girl in the relationship," and she respected him for keeping his word of not interfering in her life.

"Honey, you know there are a couple of nurses who have huge crushes on you," Annabelle said one day. Senthil just nodded. He was taken aback when she said that he should go out with them.

"Are you intoxicated?" he asked.

"No honey! You are so skillful. I feel bad for keeping you all to myself."

He was appalled by her suggestion. He said he was not in love with them and the only reason he went to bed with her was that he was madly in love with her. "Why did you?" he asked.

"Honestly, it was because I knew I was in control and more importantly because you were safe," she said.

"What does that even mean?" he shot back.

She did not hide from him the fact that she had made out with random guys in bars. Some he had even witnessed firsthand before they had embarked on their relationship. Right after she broke up with her boyfriend Brian, she used to party hard and drank more than she did now. During one such outing, she had gotten too drunk and separated from her friends. She woke up the following day next to a random guy she had met at the bar. She did not even know his name. It was a one-night stand, and she had to visit the Planned Parenthood in Raleigh to get tested for STDs.

"With you being a virgin, I didn't have to worry about anything," she said.

"Let me get this straight. You started this whole thing because I was clean and safe?"

She said, "Come on, it's not just that. Don't make it a big deal."

Even though he had always known Annabelle was not in love with him, this admission was hard for him to digest. What could he do? He had no grounds to fight or argue. So, he just kept quiet. Silence did not bother him, but she could not stand it.

"I told you this wouldn't work. I told you I am not cut out for love and relationships. I don't need this kind of emotional blackmail. It's over. We better part ways now before we end up hurting each other."

"I am not fighting with you. I know where I stand; you have made your intentions very clear from the beginning. I know if it weren't for alcohol we wouldn't be here today. I am not delusional, but that doesn't mean I can't have hope. I am only human, and when you say something that bothers me, I just need the time to process it."

She had no answer. This was their first fight. She left with Cinnamon. It was a restless night. After a fitful sleep, Senthil woke up early the next morning. It was a Saturday. He started cleaning his house that needed no cleaning;

it was therapeutic for his weary heart. He was halfway through when there was a knock on the door. It was Annabelle. She led him upstairs. In the end, she said, "The best way to make up after a fight is in bed."

He wanted to tell her that her past did not matter to him. He too had been in love with another girl in the past but had put everything behind him. He wanted to clear the air, but she was not interested in talking.

Things went back to usual. Their fight was nothing more than a lovers' spat and did not have any lasting ramifications. However, this would not be the last of it. His biggest gripe was her affinity for alcohol, and hers was his nature to clam up when she would rather have him engage when they fought. She did not care that their squabbles always progressed with her saying it was over and that they should part ways only for her to come back and make up in bed.

He understood that every relationship had its ebbs and flows. They had their occasional quarrels, but what bothered him more was Annabelle's reaction. He questioned why it must end with her saying that it was over.

"Honey, we still make up, don't we? I wouldn't worry about it," she downplayed the seriousness of her behavior.

On Halloween of 2008, Senthil was pleasantly surprised when Annabelle said she would rather go to the Halloween party hosted by one of her fellow speech pathologists than her usual Halloween bar-hopping in Raleigh. She also chose a more conservative outfit: Dark Phoenix instead of the usual provocative outfits. He was invited to the party as well and accepted since costumes were optional.

There was no shortage of ghoulish creative foods to fit the Halloween theme along with a different variation of Jell-0-shots with alcohol, spiked punch bowl that mimicked a witch's brew, and mixed drinks with fake eyeballs floating on them. Spider webs and little ghosts adorned the walls. Senthil was happy with the Devil's food chocolate cake with ghostly Rice Krispies and marshmallows that made it look like a cemetery with tombstones. Annabelle chose to drink her calories.

At the end of the party, Senthil literally had to carry her back home. Even though this was a common occurrence, it was something he could not get used to. He assisted her up the stairs. She managed to get out of her costume when a wave of reflux hit her, and she ran to the bathroom to vomit. She missed the commode, however. Concerned, he followed her and held her hair. He cleaned her up and helped her to bed. He then mopped up the bathroom and went to bed himself.

Annabelle slept in while Senthil got up early as usual. He searched online for breakfast ideas to cure a hangover. He let Cinnamon out in the backyard and cooked a rice bowl with fried eggs, avocado, sriracha, scallions, and vinegar. Even though it was Saturday, he wanted to go to the hospital to check on a couple of his sick patients. He placed the food on the kitchen table with a note that read, "Good morning. Warm this in the microwave for forty-five seconds. Going to the hospital to check on a couple of patients. Will be back by noon."

Annabelle was sitting at the kitchen table with his computer and Cinnamon on her lap when he returned.

"How are your patients, honey?"

"They are okay."

"Thank you for breakfast."

"You are welcome."

"Are you okay?"

"Hmm."

He started to wash the dishes. Annabelle asked Senthil to come sit with her. She had seen his search history on the computer about foods for curing a hangover and could vaguely recall throwing up last night. He finished the dishes and sat down next to her. She turned the laptop towards him, showed him a YouTube video, and said, "Hit play, honey."

It was a clip of comedian Jim Breuer's take on alcohol. It was pure comic genius, with Jim explaining a party in the stomach where different types of alcohol came in as guests. Even though it was hardly funny in real life, Jim's caricature of alcohol and throwing up was undeniably hilarious. As he laughed, she placed Cinnamon on his lap and said, "Cinnamon, please tell your daddy that we are sorry for last night." He sat quietly cosseting Cinnamon. "Don't be mad. I'll try to be mindful of how much I drink."

His first instinct was to quote an adage in Tamil, his native tongue, "*Kudikaran pechu vidinja pochu,*" which translated to "A drunkard's words are gone when the next day dawns." But this was the first time she was not defensive about her drinking and had expressed a desire to change. So, he held his tongue and replied, "I sure hope so."

A weekend before Thanksgiving, Annabelle asked, "Would you like to join me for dinner with my sister and her husband?" This was the first time he was going to meet someone from her family. Virginia liked Italian food, and so they met at Maggiano's at Southpoint Mall. He was a little nervous about meeting her family, but Virginia and Dan made him feel right at home as soon as they met him.

"Thanks to you, Dan learned to pamper me on the weekends," Virginia said. Senthil looked puzzled. She explained that Annabelle texted her pictures of all the fabulous breakfasts he fixed, which had inspired Dan.

Senthil was surprised. He did not know Annabelle spoke about him to her family. Virginia said that every time Annabelle went home, he was the topic of conversation at the dinner table.

Their kids were staying with her parents, and Virginia and Dan planned on spending the night in a motel and driving back the next day. It was their getaway, as they were celebrating Dan's birthday. They had plans to watch the new James Bond movie: *Quantum of Solace.*

After a leisurely dinner, they strolled through the mall. "We don't want to be late to the movie," Dan said.

"Yes dear! Let me powder my nose before we head to the theater," said Virginia.

"I'll join you, sissy," Annabelle said.

"They are not going to powder their noses. They are going to gossip," quipped Dan and Senthil agreed.

On their drive back home, Annabelle said, "You are invited to come home with me for Thanksgiving dinner. My parents want to have you over."

"Really?" he asked.

"Would you be able to forsake Papa's Thanksgiving dinner to join the Kingstons?" Annabelle asked.

"Of course. Papa will understand," he said.

Senthil made some *samosas*[47] to take to the Thanksgiving dinner. He was anxious and wanted the Kingstons to like him. He laid out his dress shirt, pants, and a sports jacket. "Honey, my folks are very simple. You don't have to wear a coat," Annabelle said.

"It isn't for vanity; it is for respect," he replied.

She reassured him that they already knew about him and he could relax. She left very early in the morning to help with the dinner and asked him to reach around 2:00 PM. She warned him not to comment on politics or guns even if it came up in the course of the conversation. She also told him that her folks did not know that she spent the nights at his house.

Even though Annabelle suggested that he address them by their names, he stuck with the Indian tradition and called them Aunt Lydia and Uncle Ben, which they found adorable. They made him feel like he was a part of the family; they were also impressed with the eloquence with which he described life in India.

"I feel like I have been to India and back!" exclaimed Lydia.

Buddy and Landon were more interested in the gory details of brain injuries and brain surgery and asked him to tell them details about his patients with gunshot wounds and trauma to the head.

Since Annabelle had told them about his sweet tooth, there was peanut butter pie and chocolate pecan pie along with the traditional pumpkin pie. It was a great dinner with scrumptious food and great conversation. The *samosas*

---

47 Fried pastry with a spiced filling made of onions, potatoes, and peas

were a big hit. The kids called it Indian totinos. Senthil got along well with the adults and connected with the kids by horsing around in the backyard with football and baseball.

"I am so glad she found you," Lydia said. She told him that Annabelle always spoke about him and had told them a lot of stories about his patients and the respect he had earned in the hospital. She requested him to be patient with Annabelle.

Annabelle gave him a quick tour of the house before he left and showed him her room, which had been left untouched since the day she moved out. Lydia gave him a box with a slice of the pies and some cookies for him to take home.

Annabelle came over on Monday night with some leftovers from home. As they were eating, she said, "I am screwed."

When he asked her the reason, she said, "Everybody in my family is in love with you." She told him that they had talked about him the entire weekend and could not wait to have him over for Christmas.

"If I up and leave now, they are going to be upset. I am afraid I am going to let everyone down."

"I am sorry. Should I have been a jerk to them?" he asked.

"Of course not. Thank you for being so kind and loving. I am thankful my family got to see what a wonderful man you are." She tried to tell that she felt added pressure now but could not articulate her fears in words.

It would have been easy for her if he had been a jerk. He satisfied both her emotional and physical needs. She had strong feelings for him, but unlike him, she was unsure about the future. It was like she was constantly in struggle with herself. Sometimes, she felt like she had hit the jackpot with him, and at other times, she felt he was just a safe and good lay who was just a fleeting moment in her whirlwind of a life. Part of her wanted to settle down, get married, live in a house with a white picket fence, and have children. The other part wanted to live a carefree life without any responsibilities and without any emotional tie-downs. Both parts were trying to suppress the other. And now with her family in love with him, she felt like she was losing control.

As much as she was outgoing and free-spirited, Senthil could sense that there was someone frightened and lost underneath that façade. When it came to her, he always sensed that there was something more than met the eye. Even though he masqueraded as an extrovert in the hospital, it was a façade and an illusion he had created with self-deprecating humor. Deep down he was a frightened, insecure introvert plagued by his childhood nightmares. He would have been lost without Sumathi's love, and he dared not imagine where he would have been without her impact on his life.

Senthil did not believe in Christmas gifts. He believed Christmas was about faith, Jesus, family, and communal spirit. He always showered Annabelle with attention and constantly invented reasons to spend on her. He struggled to find appropriate Christmas gifts for the Kingstons. Annabelle squashed his struggle and told him he need not get them anything.

"I can't come empty-handed when you are coming with a car full of gift boxes for your family," he protested.

"Well then, why don't you make some of the famous Indian food that you make for your parties?" she replied.

The Kingstons relished the *samosas* he had made for Thanksgiving; it was not a bad idea. He made chicken biryani and mutton curry and invented a new dessert. He made the classic South Indian dessert *kesari*, filled it in a pie shell, and created fresh whipped cream flavored with cardamom and saffron. Annabelle left with the gifts on Christmas Eve. Senthil drove down on Christmas day with the delicacies he had prepared. He arrived just as they were setting the dining table.

When they all sat down for dinner, the chicken biryani and curry lasted only a hot minute. He had made it with just the right amount of spices and exactly enough for everyone to have second helpings. Even Buddy and Landon, who were picky eaters, licked their plates clean. The *kesari* in the form of a pie was a big hit too, and they could not get enough of the cardamom-and-saffron whipped cream. The Kingstons thanked him for bringing some culture into their lives and thought it was the perfect Christmas gift.

Senthil returned home early with the neckties that Lydia and Ben had got him as a Christmas present. He had to work the next day. Annabelle came back straight to his house that weekend. Senthil was looking up Biltmore House, the largest home in America and the most famous tourist attraction in Asheville, North Carolina. Biltmore House was a Châteauesque mansion built by George Washington Vanderbilt in 1895.

"New Year's Eve is coming up, and I think this would be the perfect place to celebrate our first anniversary," he said. "Of course, it's on a Wednesday, and we must wait till Saturday," he added.

"What anniversary? The night we had sex?" With that callous remark, Annabelle brought him crashing down to reality.

He did not know what to say. "I can't believe you said that," he responded in a timid voice.

"Say what, the truth?" She added insult to injury.

She always gave him a reality check whenever he got carried away with their relationship. She said it was immature of him to assume that their relationship had changed in any way with her introducing him to her family. "Why can't people be happy with things as they are? Why do they have to push it?" she questioned.

"Some see things as they are and ask why. Others dream of things that never were and ask why not," he replied.

"Quoting Bernard Shaw? Two can play that game. We must always think about things as they are, not as they are said to be," she fired back. "I really can't do this anymore. This is over," Annabelle added.

She reached for the cabinet to get her bottle of wine, and after finding out that there was barely a glass left, she said, "I need a drink." She grabbed her keys and headed for the door.

"It's illegal to have an open alcohol container in the car," he yelled. She stopped in her tracks, gave him a death stare, and slammed the bottle on the end table before storming out.

Work was busy, and Senthil was in the OR for the most part of the day. They did not have any common patients, and so they did not need to speak to each other at work. They spent New Year's Eve apart and did not even talk to each other. After a week of silence, Annabelle called him to say that she was going to drive in a U-Haul with a friend who was moving to Austin. She was going to be away for a week, and after helping her friend settle down in Austin, she would be flying back the following weekend. She did not want to go away without telling him.

"This time away from each other will be good for us, honey. It will help us put things in perspective," she said. She was thinking about boarding Cinnamon for the week but was discouraged by the $250 bill.

"I can watch her. Why don't you leave Cinnamon with me?" he asked. She hesitated but then agreed.

She came very early Saturday morning. She was in a hurry and did not want to come in. She apologized for waking him up on his day off. She dropped off Cinnamon and a bag of dog food with instructions.

2009 started off much differently compared to 2008—at least for the two of them.

He kept himself busy at work as usual and barely had time to think about her. He missed her late-night phone calls and talking to her before going to bed. He responded to Pepto's questions about Annabelle with "I don't know."

Annabelle broke her silence with random texts: "Hope Cinnamon is not causing too much trouble," to which he just responded with a picture of Cinnamon curled up with a little pet pillow he had gotten for her.

She came back on the evening of the following Saturday. As soon as she entered the house, she wordlessly led him upstairs. After they were done, she rolled over and said, "I am sorry, but I panicked."

She was overwhelmed by her family constantly talking about him after the Christmas dinner. They told her he was a good catch and that it was time for her to settle down as her biological clock was ticking. Annabelle felt pressured; the last straw on the camel's back was him wanting to celebrate their anniversary. This week apart, while it was fun hanging out with her friend and partying in Austin, made her realize that she missed him. While she was not ready to settle down, she did not want to throw away something that had so much potential and promise. She needed more time and wanted to make sure she was not making a mistake. She did not want to become another Jenna.

He told her he was not in a hurry and that he had not waited this long to get married and then be miserable.

"I'd rather be single than be a divorcee," he said. "I am sure this is not going to be the last of our fights. But next time, let's talk before we head upstairs. Everything would be better that way," he said.

"The only thing better than make-up sex is drunken sex," she joked.

"Yes, it's called make-up because you make up before you hop into bed," he said. She just rolled her eyes.

"I saw that," he said.

She laughed and exclaimed, "You are the girl in this relationship!"

She was an enigma. He could not understand why she based her self-worth solely on her physical characteristics and sought to resolve disputes in the bedroom instead of the living room.

Chapter 30 — Pipe Dream

ONE DAY IN THE SUMMER OF 2009, ANNABELLE TOLD HIM, "Honey, pack your bags for a weekend trip."

"Where are we going?" he asked.

Annabelle had planned a surprise getaway; she refused to tell him where. She left Cinnamon at her friend's place and came over Saturday morning to pick him up. He offered to drive, but she would not have any of it. She knew it would give away the destination.

"Nice try. I am going to drive, and you don't ask any questions. You'll know when we get there."

She hopped on I-40 and headed west. "Can you give me a clue?" he asked.

She just smiled and asked him to be patient and just sit back and relax. She drove for more than three hours. "We are almost there, but for the last ten minutes, I want you to close your eyes. Do not open them until I tell you to."

He reluctantly obliged.

Eventually, she parked the car and said, "No peeking."

She held his hand and led the way. From the noise, he could sense that there were a lot of people around him. She finally stopped and said, "Okay honey, you can open your eyes now." They were standing at the far end of the lawn as he opened his eyes to the panoramic view of the majestic Biltmore House in Asheville.

He was elated; this was the place he had wanted to bring her for their so-called anniversary. They embarked on a two-hour-long self-guided tour of the Biltmore and were in awe of its sheer scale and magnitude. They walked the entire 175,000 square feet together. There were three floors and a basement, which included thirty-five bedrooms, sixty-five fireplaces, and forty-three bathrooms. His favorite room was the two-story library with the eighteenth-century ceiling painting by Pellegrini titled "The Chariot of Aurora." Her favorite was the 70-foot-high banquet hall with three majestic fireplaces and a 1916 Skinner pipe organ.

Annabelle had made a reservation in the inn on Biltmore Estate. On Sunday morning, they toured the Biltmore Winery and savored the complimentary wine tastings. They came back home exhausted late Sunday night. Senthil thanked her for a great weekend. She could have chosen any other place, but he thought it was symbolic that after mocking him when he had wanted to commemorate their one-year anniversary, she chose to go there. He was hopeful about their future, but he refrained from telling her that, as he did not want to rock the boat.

A few weeks later, he took her to Wilmington beach for a weekend getaway. Neither of them advertised these escapades, as she still was not ready to make their relationship public. They were spending more time together and were getting closer, albeit too fast on her account and not fast enough on his. They still had their walls up to protect themselves from getting hurt.

It was a smooth sail for their relationship. When her family happened to call Annabelle while she was with Senthil, she pretended to be in her apartment. For his part, he did not tell his family in India because he did not want to get their hopes up.

His *amma*, after Sumathi's departure from his life, pleaded with him to agree to an arranged marriage, but he had declined. She hoped he would find a good Tamil girl and settle down. Then as he fulfilled his family responsibilities and helped his siblings settle down, she agreed to accept a daughter-in-law from anywhere in South India, even if she did not speak Tamil. A few years later, she was willing to accept any Indian girl—north, south, east, or west did not matter. He was turning forty the next year, and she just wanted him to get married to any girl "even if it's a foreigner." That sentiment was shared by everyone in his family.

Even though Annabelle and Senthil did not announce their relationship, their colleagues and friends knew something was going on between them. They neither denied nor confirmed it and just let everyone assume whatever they wanted to. They maintained a healthy working environment and disproved the adage "Don't get your meat where you get your bread."

Annabelle continued to fight with herself. She hesitated to make herself vulnerable and feared what might happen. "What if I can't live up to his standards?", "What if I let him down?", "What if he gets bored with me and leaves?", "What if I am not marriage material and I am better off being single doing what I want and when I want?" For one reason or another, his patience and understanding were not enough to assuage her fears.

"I fight with you a lot and have broken up with you many times. How do you put up with me?" she asked him the weekend before Thanksgiving Day as he prepared some food in advance to take to the Kingstons' family dinner. He decided to explain it with a practical experiment.

He took out a sewing thread from the drawer and cut a long segment of it. He asked her to hold one end while he held the other. "Go ahead, try and break this thread," he told her.

"That's easy," she said, and as she yanked on the thread, he gave some slack to the thread by taking a step towards her. She tried again, and he did the same. "How can I break it if you keep taking a step towards me and cause a slack?" As soon as she finished her question, she realized the answer. "But why?" she asked.

"Why? I love you Annabelle, and I can't think of a future without you," he replied.

She was not as eloquent and found it hard to put all her fears into words.

The second Thanksgiving dinner at the Kingstons eclipsed the first. Annabelle did not reveal much to them, but they embraced him as part of their family since her actions spoke louder than her words.

Christmas was fast approaching. Annabelle wanted to get a real Christmas tree, and since her apartment would not allow it, she asked Senthil if he would keep the tree in his house. He did not believe in Santa Claus or Christmas trees, but he saw no harm in it if it made her happy. So, they went to a farm in Raleigh, and Annabelle was like a kid in a candy store. Senthil did not know what made a good tree and so he just followed her as she studiously examined each tree. She gently grabbed the inside of a branch and pulled her hand towards her to check the freshness of the needles. She tapped the branches to see if the needles fell. She bent the needles between her two hands. She commented on how one tree was not fresh, or another was too tall or too short, how one was a spruce tree and had sharp needles and she was looking for pine or fir with softer needles.

"Honey, this tree looks good, but maybe there is a better one at the back," she said a couple of times and asked him to mark the snow on the ground by the tree. She had walked to the end of the farm but did not have a tree in her hand.

"Honey, I think the one you marked with a smiley face is the best one so far."

They hurried back to the front of the farm. "Dammit, someone bought it already!" she cried. "Oh, there was the one in the middle that you marked with an 'X,'" she said as she hurried to the middle of the farm. "I don't believe it. That's gone too." She then half-heartedly settled on one and said, "I am tired. Let's just get this one."

They stopped by her apartment, and she got the box of ornaments she had collected and saved over the years. They carried the tree in together and placed it in the living room. Senthil went out to get the box of her ornaments, while she went to the mailbox to get his mail. "Look, honey, my parents have sent you a Christmas card."

He was filling water in the tree stand. She opened the card after he said it was okay. There were two cards. One was signed by Virginia, Dan, Buddy, and Landon. The other was from Aunt Lydia and Uncle Ben. Annabelle was surprised to see a separate note tucked inside the card. She read the card aloud but paused on the note. She read it to herself first:

Dear Senthil,

We are so glad that you and Annabelle found each other. She speaks very highly of you, and after meeting you, it is clear why. Please continue to be patient with her. We welcome you into our family with open hearts. Uncle *Ben and I wish you a Merry Christmas and a Happy New Year.*

With lots of love.
Aunt *Lydia and* Uncle *Ben*

PS: Thank you for asking Uncle *Ben for his approval, and we are glad to hear that you are willing to be patient until our little girl comes around.*

She told him she was leaving the card on the coffee table and then looked through the rest of his mail and said, "You have another Christmas card. This one is from Lina."

"Oh really! Open it, honey," he said.

"Isn't Lina the girl from Terre Haute who was interested in you?"

He replied that it was a long time ago and she had moved on.

Annabelle opened the envelope. It was a family picture card with her and her husband standing in front of a Christmas tree with their daughter in her arms. The caption on the card read,

Merry Christmas and a Happy and Prosperous New Year to your family from ours. Lina, Jeff, and Elzbieta.

He was crouched on all fours, securing the bolt on the tree stand. He extended one hand and said, "She's got a child? Let me see." She handed him the card. "Her daughter looks just like her," he said as he got up and put the card on the coffee table. He then picked up the card from the Kingstons.

Much to his surprise, she said, "I am tired. I am going to take a shower and go to bed. We can trim the tree tomorrow."

He swept the floor and put the needles and debris from the tree in the trash can. He logged into his computer to check labs and consult notes on his patients and make sure they were okay. When he went upstairs, Annabelle was already in bed with the lights turned off.

It was Sunday, and Senthil woke up early. He was brushing his teeth when Annabelle walked in with her eyes half shut. She sat on the commode to tinkle.

"I am sorry if I woke you up, honey," he said. She was sitting with her head down, and her sunset-red locks hung over her face like a rusty waterfall. She shook her head no.

"You are up early. You must be excited about trimming the tree," he said.

She furtively glanced through her locks and asked, "Do you miss her?"

"Miss whom?" he asked.

"Lina, your PT friend from Terre Haute."

"Sometimes. Lina was my best friend from that phase of my life. She helped me through the toughest time in my life, but I haven't thought about her for a long time. Why do you ask?"

"Do you think you met her at the wrong place at the wrong time and should have met her in Durham instead of me when you were over Sumathi?"

"What are you talking about?"

"I have no earthly idea. Just answer me."

He did not know whether there was jealousy or self-deprecation in her tone as she posed the question, but he quoted Shashi Tharoor, the acclaimed Indian writer: "There is not a thing as the wrong place or the wrong time. We are where we are at the only time we have. Perhaps it's where we're meant to be." He added that he had not fallen for her after getting over Sumathi, but it was she who had helped him get over his past.

She said that he would be better off with someone more wholesome and without vices, like Lina, instead of her who came with some baggage. Senthil tried to clarify that even though his love for Annabelle was unrequited, he had no regrets. She stared at the ceiling, and asked: "What if I up and leave tomorrow?"

"I hope you don't, and if you do, I'll be sad. But I also know that life goes on."

"How long would it take for you to get over me?"

He was not a serial monogamist. It had taken him almost a decade after Sumathi to develop feelings for another woman. "I don't know. I don't plan these things," he replied indignantly.

"You, my friend, jumped off a burning train on to a sinking ship," she said.

He replied that everything happened for a reason.

They went downstairs. Senthil fixed her a cup of coffee. Sipping on the coffee with her legs crouched up on the couch, she told him that she had read her mom's note in the Christmas card. Senthil sat down next to her with a bowl of cereal and said that it was very magnanimous of Aunt Lydia and that he was very appreciative. She told him that he and her family were colluding against her and she was mad at him for going behind her back and asking her dad. He told her that it was out of respect for her and her parents that he had asked Uncle Ben if he had his blessings to ask for her hand when the time was right.

His attempts to mollify her only fueled her rage. "Damn you! I thought this was going to be a one-night stand, but you had to be good at everything you do." She had embarked on this relationship with the thought that they were merely going to be friends with benefits. Senthil, on the contrary, had hoped that she would eventually feel the same way he did. The only reason they had managed to survive was that they were honest with each other and did not try to convince the other that they were right.

"I don't want to make you mad, but I am thinking of becoming a traveling speech therapist," she sheepishly said. "I don't want to settle down and regret I missed something or get rejected," she added. There were so many places she wanted to see.

He told her he loved to travel and see new places too and told her he would take her anywhere she wanted to go. "You are married to Papa and your job, and you have never taken a day off or called in sick all these years. You would only hate me for taking you away from what you love doing."

He explained that he had four weeks of paid vacation each year and that he could take a week off every three months and whisk her away for a vacation. He never took a vacation simply because he did not want to travel alone. She was not convinced. "How do you know I am the one for you? What if there is someone better out there? You have never been with any other woman for god's sake!"

"You didn't learn anything from what happened at the Christmas tree farm yesterday?" he asked. She looked at him in confusion. He told her that she kept passing on good trees that she liked thinking she would find something better in the back and when she did not find a tree that was better, she came back to find that someone else had already bought the good ones that she had initially liked.

"Are you telling me that you won't wait for me?" she asked.

"You are missing the point," he said.

"I have to go. I need some space to think." She abruptly left.

He could not understand why a couple of Christmas cards had spooked her so much, but there was nothing he could do.

Chapter 31 — Reality Check

ANNABELLE WAS NOT CRYING WOLF THIS TIME. WITHIN A few days, she found a traveling company and signed a contract. Her first assignment was in sunny California. She could not get any further away from the east coast. She applied for her California license and was all set to leave in two weeks. Like yin and yang, guilt and liberation wreaked havoc inside her. She felt guilty for leaving behind what could be the love of her life and her aging parents, but she felt liberated from the ball and chain of her relationship and the fear of failure.

Annabelle's three-month assignment was to start on Tuesday, January 19, 2010, in a hospital in San Francisco, California. Finally, her dreams of living in a big city were coming true. It was either 2,817 miles and a 42-hour drive via I-40 West, or 2,849 miles and a 43-hour drive via I-80 West.

Since Christmas 2009 fell on a Friday, Senthil volunteered to work the day and the weekend. Besides, he did not want to face the Kingstons when Annabelle told them her decision.

"Are you sure you know what you are doing?" Lydia was visibly upset when Annabelle told her. "You are thirty. Aren't you worried about your biological clock ticking?"

Annabelle downplayed the significance of her decision by saying that it was only temporary and that it would give her a chance to see the places she had always wanted to see. Lydia cautioned her about the perils of long-distance relationships but knew not to push her. Seeing her family upset that Senthil could not join them for Christmas weirdly validated her decision. She was only sparing them from more heartache and disappointment down the road.

She left Cinnamon in her apartment since she had plans of returning after the Christmas dinner. But she could not just leave after telling them about her decision. She texted Senthil at night to ask him if he could let Cinnamon out. She had spare keys to her car and her apartment at his place. Senthil went to her apartment and was shocked by what he saw inside. It was like a tornado had ransacked the place. There were clothes on the floor, couch, and bed. The sink was littered with dishes and plastic glasses with red wine stains. Half-eaten canned soups and pizza boxes lay on the counter, and several empty wine bottles and bottles of vodka were strewn across the floor of the living room and the bedroom.

He could not understand how someone could live in such filthy conditions. Cinnamon was curled up in a ball on a pile of her clothes. She ran up to him, wagging her tail as soon as he walked in. He walked her around the complex, and after she finished her business, he brought her back to his house.

Annabelle came back to Senthil's house on Saturday night with tons of food and desserts that Lydia and Virginia had packed for him. "What are you going to do when I am gone?" Annabelle asked.

Senthil told her that he was probably going to work more and keep himself busy with work and studying for his PANRE (Physician Assistant National Recertification Exam), which he needed to take every six years.

"You didn't try to stop me from going. Is this what you wanted too?"

The question upset him. He told her it was her decision—he was ready to spend the rest of his life with her—and she had not asked him about taking up the traveling job but told him.

"I love you. But I can't be in it for the both of us. I want to be with someone who wants to be with me. There is no point in me begging you to stay. You should want it too," he said.

He was okay with her scratching her itch and was confident that when she came back to him, it would be forever, and if she did not, he reassured her that he would have no regrets. He told her that she had no reason to feel guilty, as she had warned him about this day for the past two years.

Pepto took it the hardest. Annabelle promised to stay in touch and asked her to take care of Senthil.

He offered to help her pack and clean her apartment. He told her that she could leave her boxes in his garage instead of renting a storage unit. "You are just making sure I come back to you," she joked.

He did not find it amusing and simply said, "Three months' rent for a storage unit is a flight ticket home."

He asked her how she could have kept her apartment in such a mess. She dismissed him, saying, "Honey, I lived in much worse conditions when I was growing up, and I don't want you judging me."

Other than her essentials that fit in her car, they packed everything else in boxes and put them in his garage. She moved in with him for the last ten days of her stay in town to avoid paying apartment rent for January. She came from work one day to find a gift box on the dining table. It had her name on it. She looked at him with curiosity. "Go ahead. Open it. It's a going-away gift," Senthil said.

She sat down and slowly opened the gift box. "Garmin GPS unit!" she exclaimed. "Honey, you shouldn't have."

"I got the GPS to not only help you know where you are going without getting lost but also to help you find the shortest and fastest way back to me if and when you decide to come back."

She just nodded, and with tears in her eyes, she asked, "What are you afraid of the most with me traveling?"

"Your drinking," he unhesitatingly answered. He had not realized the extent of her drinking until he helped clean her apartment. He was afraid that with no loved one around, in a big new city where no one truly cared, she might get too drunk and jeopardize her safety.

"Don't worry. I always wear dirty granny panties and don't shave above my knees when I go out drinking. I have no intentions of going home with any guy," she said, laughing. Again, he did not find it amusing. He had come across the horror stories in the news involving abduction and killing.

With Monday, January 18, being Martin Luther King Jr. Day, which was an OR holiday, no elective surgeries were posted. He offered to leave with her on Friday to keep her company during the long drive to San Francisco and fly back in time to get back to work on Tuesday. She told him that one of her friends had offered to go with her. Senthil kept quiet.

"Are you sure?" Annabelle asked.

When he nodded, she said, "You can't protect me all the time."

"I know. I just wanted to travel with you as far as I could. Besides, driving coast to coast was always a dream of mine," Senthil responded.

"Honey, if it means so much to you and you are okay with it, sure," she said.

Cinnamon hopped on to the back seat and snuggled over the comforter Annabelle had used to cover the suitcases. Annabelle insisted on driving. Senthil suggested the scenic I-80, but she preferred I-40, as it was an hour shorter. They left very early on Saturday morning. He set up the GPS on her dashboard. She hardly spoke once they hit the road. They only had pit stops for gas, restroom breaks, and food tops at fast-food joints.

He tried to read her face as she sped down the highway. Was she just anxious about reaching there on time? Or was she in a hurry to get as far away as possible from North Carolina? After twenty hours of pretending to enjoy the radio or be immersed in the sceneries and having loud conversations inside their heads that made up for the silence between them, they stopped at midnight at a motel to get some rest.

They hit the road again at 4:00 in the morning on Sunday and drove for another twenty hours. Senthil was amazed at the vast, varied landscape of the country. He realized that he and his problems were minuscule to the cosmos. They rolled into San Francisco Monday morning, and reached the high-rise apartment her contract company had secured for her. It was a tiny 600-square-foot studio on the seventeenth floor. They had only enough time to freshen up and grab a bite to eat before he had to reach the airport at 1:00 PM.

He wanted to take a cab to the airport. "Don't be silly. I'll drive you there."

Unlike the cozy Raleigh-Durham International Airport, San Francisco International Airport was busy. She dropped him off at the curb and was immediately ushered out by the security. Senthil got out of the car, waved her goodbye, and asked her not to get out of the car. She ignored both him and the security guard and got out of the car and yelled back, "Tow it if you want to." She ran around the car to give Senthil a hug. "Let me know you reached home safely."

Senthil reached home at 11:30 PM and texted Annabelle, "I'm home. Good luck with your new job tomorrow."

"I know it's late there, but it's only 9:30 PM here. Please get some sleep and thank you very much for riding with me," she replied.

Annabelle made friends with two other single traveling therapists from her company. Casey Miller was an occupational therapist from Wisconsin, and Miranda Schuster, a physical therapist from Nebraska. At last, she felt liberated. She explored the city of San Francisco with them. They engaged in people watching and frequented the bars. She enjoyed the carefree city life. Having an apartment downtown meant there was no need for them to drive, and they could easily stagger back home after a night on the town.

Life went on as usual for Senthil. With Durham being three hours ahead of San Francisco, Annabelle called him after work during the weekends and on her way out for nights on the town. She told him about the magic of the city, and about Casey and Miranda who had quickly become her partners in crime. She talked about the unique bars that were open twenty-four hours a day and how men in California were better dancers than the men in Raleigh. The distance did not seem to bother them, and they comfortably settled on this rhythm.

It was 11:30 on a Saturday night in February and Senthil was fast asleep when he received a text. Before he could reach for the phone, his phone lit up again with another text. He sat up on the bed and grabbed the phone before it went off ten more times. His first thought was Annabelle's safety. He turned the phone on to find Neurosurgery residents, the nurses, and the therapists texting him with, "Congratulations, Happy Valentine's Day!" He was confused.

As he was texting one of them to ask what it meant, Annabelle called him. "Honey is your phone blowing up?" she asked, laughing.

He told her it was, and he had no idea what it was that people were congratulating him about. She said, "I have been getting the same texts too from our friends, but I know why." She then hurriedly said, "I am out with Casey and Miranda. I'll call you tomorrow. Check Facebook, and you'll know. Happy Valentine's Day, honey!" She hung up.

Curious, he logged into Facebook to find "Annabelle updated her status from single to being in a relationship with Senthil."

It was the first time he felt his love validated; he was on cloud nine. He responded by changing his status too. It was official now. He no longer had to tiptoe around with his friends at work whenever Annabelle's name came up.

He was a little disappointed when she extended her contract in San Francisco for another three months but was glad that she would be coming home before starting on the new contract.

"Honey, do you mind if my parents pick me up from the airport and I go home first?"

Senthil told her he understood family came first. She arrived and went home with her parents. They had a little family get-together and sat around her and listened to her stories about the big city in awe.

Senthil had made a breakfast spread early Saturday morning. He set the table and waited anxiously. Dan dropped Annabelle off at Senthil's house on his way to Raleigh. As soon as she entered the house, she grabbed him and led him upstairs. They came back downstairs for breakfast. She did not tire of talking about the exciting city life. He was a little disappointed when she said that she did not miss Durham or home.

He had planned a quiet day, cooking some of her favorite foods for her and hanging out with her at home to talk and catch up. He did not show his disappointment when she told him that she had texted some of their friends to meet up at a bar in Raleigh. He offered to have them over so that they could all be at home. Her flight back was at 7:20 PM on Sunday night, and he wanted to spend as much time with her as possible.

"I used to go out every night in San Francisco. I haven't been out the last two days that I was stuck in my parents' house. I have to get out," she insisted. He did not argue.

Pepto had them over for breakfast on Sunday morning. "Please tell me he doesn't mope around the hospital," Annabelle asked.

Pepto laughed and said, "Oh no honey! When it comes to work and his patients, he is all focused. If I didn't know any better, I would think that he doesn't miss you at all."

On the way back to the airport, she invited him to California before the end of her assignment. "I want you to experience the city. I want to take you to all the places I have been to. It'll be a lot of fun. That is if you could part with Papa." Senthil was excited and told her that he could take a week off and come to visit her.

Senthil planned his week off during the time that Papa would be gone for the 78th American Association of Neurological Surgeons (AANS) Conference in Philadelphia—from May 1 through May 5. Annabelle worked a couple of weekends so that she could take the week off while he was there.

During the day, they walked around downtown, rode on the cable cars, biked across the Golden Gate Bridge, and went to China Town. He took his camcorder everywhere they went and captured her and the city on video. He wanted to go to the California Academy of Sciences, San Francisco Museum of Modern Art, Asian Art Museum, and the Alcatraz. She indulged him during the day, and he returned the favor at night by accompanying her to the bars she frequented. She introduced him to Casey and Miranda. It was a whirlwind of a vacation.

"I can never get bored of this. There is so much you can do in a big city. Don't you get bored in little Durham, honey?"

Senthil told her that while San Francisco was great, it could get old very quickly. It was a great vacation, but nothing could beat the charm of the little city and the laid-back, stress-free life and the cost of living that came with it.

"What if I want to settle down here? Would you move for me?"

He paused for a second and said, "Sure honey. If that's the way we can be together, of course, I will. I am sure I can find a job here."

"Papa and everybody in Durham will kill me if I steal you away. You have built a reputation there, and I would never do that to you. But I am glad to hear that you would do that for me."

She told him that she was just kidding and when she indeed decided to settle down, it would be back home. She just wanted to travel and see the world on her own and get the wildness out of her.

The day before he left, she made dinner reservations at the romantic Forbes Island restaurant between Pier 39 and Pier 41 in Fisherman's Wharf. They dressed up and rode a little ferry to the floating island. She insisted that she pay, as it was her treat. She knew how much he liked dressing up and having dinner at fancy restaurants.

It was time for him to fly back. They continued to have a hot-and-cold relationship. The second half of her contract did not go as well as the first. More than the distance, the time difference began to take a toll on them. When Annabelle called, she was always on the go and in a hurry to catch up with her friends. They always had to cut their conversations short. On weekends, he would be up late waiting; she would call him from bars which were loud, and he could barely hear her. He thought she did not care to take the time to call and talk to him, and she thought she never got enough credit for calling despite being busy.

It bothered him when she called after a night on the town, drinking—not because it was late but because she barely remembered the conversation the next day. She argued that he was being paranoid and asked him to lay off her drinking. She was not an alcoholic, and she really did not need him to constantly remind her about the harmful effects of alcohol. She could quit at any time.

She was young and was having fun, and since he was ten years older, he could not understand. She told him that several guys hit on her when she went out and yet she remained true to him. He interpreted it as her doing him a favor. He never argued with her, but he never had to. She accused him of always having a tone of disapproval with her or sensed sadness in his voice whenever she told him she was out or was going out. She interpreted his patience as being passive-aggressive.

There was a trend. Senthil was dating three different personalities, and they came in a predictable sequence:

There was the "indignant Annabelle" who was angry and annoyed and perceived judgment or ridicule from him for her drinking and partying or for having a free spirit. She was childish and defensive, and no reasoning could get through to her.

She was followed by the "desolate Annabelle" who was mature, pensive, and lonely. She would feel remorse and longed to have a purpose in life.

Finally, there was the "happy Annabelle" who was born out of self-reflection. She was cheerful and optimistic and wanted to live life to the fullest while she still could before courting the perils of married life. "Happy Annabelle" always went overboard and perfectly segued to "indignant Annabelle," and the cycle continued.

Senthil was a hapless romantic. The only reason they were still together was that he took all three of them in stride. He understood that one did not come without the other two. He hoped his patience would exorcize the "indignant Annabelle." He knew alcoholism was a disease of denial. He did not want to be an enabler or an accuser; he trod a fine line, albeit unsuccessfully at times.

One of the low points of his love life was when he learned that she sat with a bottle of wine when she had called him late at night years ago. Those long late-night conversations during the initial stage of their friendship were what had made him love her. She would finish the bottle by the end of the conversation. Had she been friendly because she was inebriated? Was his love predicated on a false impression?

Chapter 32 — Collision Course

ANNABELLE HAD HAD ENOUGH OF SAN FRANCISCO. AFTER the second stint, she did not extend her contract. June 25 was her last day on the job. She was going to have one last hurrah with her friends in Napa Valley that weekend before driving back home. She wanted to spend the summer at the beach and was elated to learn that her company had a contract with hospitals in the US Virgin Islands. They told her that the earliest a contract would be open was in August. She told Senthil and her family that she was coming back home and that Miranda was hitching a ride with her to her next assignment in Charlotte. She refrained from telling them her plans for her next assignment, as she did not want to ruin their excitement.

Pepto's kids had come home for a week to be with their mother for their father's death anniversary. They had always spent the week together to commemorate the last week he had returned from the hospital with home hospice. Senthil learned that Pepto's son's car had died on the way and had to be towed. Luckily, it happened close to Durham. Senthil's 1994 Toyota Camry had served him faithfully. Even though it had 180,000 miles, he had taken good care of it with regular maintenance, and it was still in good condition. He decided to give the car to her son and buy himself a new car. He wanted to help a kid in school, and besides, he did not have the heart to sell his first car to some stranger or a car dealer. Pepto had always been there for him, after all.

When Annabelle called, he told her he was thinking about buying a new car.

"It's about time you upgraded your ride, honey," she said. She wanted him to get a luxury car to reflect his status. "How about a Mercedes or BMW?"

Senthil was thinking about another Camry since it had served him well and he could not really bring himself to spending close to $50,000 on a car. "You live only once and should enjoy it," she said. She was thrilled when he told her he was going to give away his Toyota to Pepto's son.

"That is very generous of you, honey. I am so proud of you, and I bet you made Pepto's day."

After a night of research on the computer, he settled on an Acura TL. It was marketed as a luxury car, and a price tag of $33,000 to $35,000 did not give him a sticker shock even though the difference of the monthly installment between a Camry and an Acura TL was $150. He wanted Annabelle to be a part of the new car buying process, so he suggested that she just stop at a local Acura dealer in San Francisco and pick out a color for him. He wanted to get the car before the end of the week so that Pepto's son could drive his Toyota back to school.

He was a little disappointed when Annabelle said that she did not have time to stop by an Acura dealer. He was upset that she had time to go to bars every day and hang out with her friends but could not spare a few minutes for him. She got angry when he said, "our car." She emphasized, "It's YOUR car, not ours. I can't deal with this with all the stuff that's already going on. We'll talk when I come back in a few weeks."

Annabelle texted Senthil a few times while she was on the road with Miranda to update him on her location. She reached home in the afternoon of Thursday, July 1. She called Senthil that night and told him that her parents had rented a property on Cabin Lake for the Fourth of July weekend and had invited him to join them. Her entire family left very early Saturday morning, but Annabelle stayed back and asked Senthil to pick her up first so they could drive to the lake together.

He was very excited to see her after three months and was looking forward to having a great time with the Kingstons. He reached her parents' house at 9:00 in the morning. Annabelle welcomed him at the door with a warm embrace and a long passionate kiss. He asked her about the drive back, where they had stopped, and if she had had enough rest. Annabelle was fooling around the whole time that he was trying to talk to her.

"Let's go up to my room," she said.

"Don't we have to go to the lake, honey? We shouldn't keep your family waiting," he replied.

Annabelle was disappointed. She had stayed back so she could be alone with Senthil before they went to the lake. "You didn't miss me? Aren't you excited to see me?"

"Of course, I am honey, but this is your parents' house. It would be disrespectful."

Annabelle sighed and said, "Fine. You are so uptight. Let's go then."

When Annabelle stepped out of the house, she exclaimed, "Wow! That's your new ride? It looks great." She was even more impressed with the interior. "I love the new car smell!" she exclaimed.

They had a great time at the lake house. Lydia and Virginia cooked an excellent spread of food, while Ben and Dan organized backyard games that the family could play together. They put up some fireworks over the lake.

Everyone congregated around the fire pit for s'mores and stories. To Senthil's delight, along with the traditional s'mores with Hershey bars, they made s'mores with Reese's peanut butter cups. As a contribution, he created a new version using Oreo cookies and Nila wafers. It was a bit nippy, and Annabelle snuggled next to Senthil who wrapped his arms around her. Lydia was happy to see them together. She grabbed her camera and said, "Now that's a picture worth framing."

"When are you two getting hitched?" Landon blurted out.

Annabelle broke the awkward silence that ensued by saying, "Hey look, your marshmallow is getting burnt."

Senthil changed the subject by telling them about Diwali, the Indian festival of lights, which also had fireworks as part of the celebration. He reminisced about his childhood days in his grandparents' village. Annabelle shared her adventure in San Francisco and the cross-country drive.

As the sky became shades deeper and stars came out, Lydia and Ben retired to the house. Annabelle and Virginia were waiting for this. As soon as their parents disappeared into the house, they grabbed the hidden bottle of wine and went on a stroll along the moonlit lakeshore. Dan and the boys asked Senthil about his work, especially trauma, and were enthralled with the details about gunshot injury to the head, car accidents, and traumatic brain injuries.

When Annabelle and Virginia returned from their stroll, Virginia whispered into Senthil's ear, "Mom and Dad are in the master suite downstairs. There are three bedrooms upstairs. You and Annabelle can have one, and the boys can share one. Just keep it quiet." She then hurried back in with Dan. Senthil just laughed and shook his head. Annabelle nestled next to Senthil with a throw around her. Dan had put out the fire, but the pit was still warm.

"You guys should hit the sack. It's getting late," Annabelle urged Buddy and Landon, and then whispered to Senthil, "Let's go in honey."

In a low voice, he told Annabelle that as much as he wanted to, it would be best if they did not sleep in the same room.

"Honey, my parents, now know that we have been sleeping together," she said.

He said that he did not want to set a bad example for the boys of such an impressionable age. She understood it but was obviously upset. "You should really get off your high horse, honey," she said as she walked into the house.

The boys were excited when Senthil said, "Hey guys, I saw some sleeping bags in the garage. Who wants to sleep under the stars?"

Annabelle wanted to spend the week with her parents to catch up and make them happy, especially her dad. Within four days, she was struck with cabin fever. She enjoyed spending the day with her parents, but in the evening, she was restless. She wanted to go out, but Benson did not have much to offer. She felt bad leaving them and driving to Raleigh just for the evening.

On Friday evening, Senthil came back from work and sat down with his PANRE prep books in front of the TV for some white noise. Working in neurosurgery, he had been associated with a subspecialty for the past six years. The national recertifying exam was designed to test the general medical knowledge of PAs and included questions from all aspects of medicine.

It was around 9:00 PM when a knock sounded on the door. "Surprise!" Annabelle squealed. He was extremely excited to see her. Dropping a Tupperware container in his hands, she said, "Here you go. Your Aunt Lydia especially made this for you. Now let's hurry upstairs."

"Let me put this in the refrigerator," he said hurrying to the kitchen while she waited impatiently at the stairs.

As he walked towards her, she said, "What are you watching?" She saw herself on TV.

"Oh, those are the videos I shot when I came to San Francisco. I just put that on when I study for my exam."

"That is so sweet." She turned off the TV. "You need to get a life, honey. Now let's go upstairs." Senthil gave her a piggyback ride upstairs.

They lounged in bed the whole weekend. On Sunday night, Annabelle asked, "Do you have to go to work tomorrow? Can't you just tell Papa that your woman is in town?"

Senthil promised her that he would hightail out of the hospital as soon as his work was done.

Annabelle caught up with sleep and TV shows when he went to work. She dressed up and waited for him in the evening. They went upstairs as soon as he came and then she sat him down in the kitchen and tried her hand at cooking. She made spaghetti, grilled cheese, and tuna salad. He ate everything she made and complimented her on how delicious it was. She knew he was lying, since she ate the same thing. He took a break from his preparation for the board exam to enjoy her company.

After a week, she said, "I don't know how you put up with my food. I called friends and have arranged a get-together on Friday night." They went to a pizza place in Raleigh. After dinner, they wanted to go to a bar; Annabelle wanted to go since it had been a long time.

"Let's go with them for a couple of drinks, honey. Then we can then go home and watch a movie."

There was a pool table at the bar, and Senthil played pool with one of their friends while Annabelle and the rest of them hit the dance floor. A couple of Aunt Roberta cocktails led to a couple of shots. One of their friends came and told him, "Hey, it's time you take her home. She is getting out of control." Senthil turned around to see her dancing sandwiched between some guys who had their hands all over her. Her eyes were glazed over, her limbs were jerking to the music, and she was very tipsy. One of her friends escorted her from the dance floor and handed her over to him.

"I just had some fun, honey. Do we really have to go?" she whined. He told her it was getting late and helped her to the car. Annabelle talked the whole way but did not make much sense.

He understood when she said, "Honey, pull over!" But he was in the middle of Glenwood Avenue, and there was no shoulder. Suddenly, she threw up in the car. "I am sorry. I threw up in your new car," she kept mumbling until they reached home.

He brought her some ice-cold water to drink. She took a sip and then plopped on the bed. Senthil did not want the putrid smell of vomit to ruin his car, so he tucked her in bed and went to the garage to clean up.

Saturday morning, she walked downstairs, groggy and hungover, and sat down at the dining table where he was studying. He was only able to give her one-word answers as she tried to make conversation. He made pancakes for breakfast alongside bacon and scrambled eggs.

After they had breakfast, she said, "I don't want to bother your studying. I am going back to bed." She did not remember what had happened the previous night and wondered why he was quiet. He was hurt but did not want to bring up the previous night's events. She spent the rest of the weekend in bed, and he spent it with his books.

The more he avoided a fight by being quiet, the more her rage was fueled. At times, she wished he could call it off and break up with her. She thought he deserved someone better.

"Why do you put up with my nonsense?" she asked.

He told her it was because he loved her, but that did not satisfy her.

Chapter 33 — Childhood Nightmares

AFTER ANOTHER WEEK OF WALKING ON EGGSHELLS, Annabelle was the first to drop her shields. The following Saturday morning, she woke up before he did for a change. She made toasts with butter and jelly, poured out a glass of orange juice, and then came back to the bedroom.

She stopped him from jumping off the bed to brush his teeth. "You could for once eat breakfast in bed the way it is meant to be." When he finished, she said, "My company called. I have accepted another assignment, and this time it's in Saint Thomas, US Virgin Islands." There was silence as they lay next to each other, staring at thc ceiling.

She had to leave in a week. Getting an assignment on the island was very difficult; there was a lot of competition as it was a favorite destination for traveling therapists. The contract was for three months with no extension. It was only for three more months, and she had to know if he was the one. She had to know if she was meant to settle down or if marriage would elude her for the rest of her life. The past few weeks had scared her. She missed her life in San Francisco—the freedom to do whatever she wanted, whenever she wanted, without being held back by anything.

She realized it was easier to change her status on Facebook than in real life. He had put up with her faults, but she wanted a clean slate and wanted him to know everything about her if they were serious about taking the plunge. So, she let her guard down and opened up to him.

Lydia and Ben were not her biological parents. She was adopted. She was born to a couple who were not ready to be parents. Teenagers themselves, they were addicted to alcohol and drugs, and she was neglected and starved. Being raised around drug addicts and abandoned for days when her parents would go off on a binge, Annabelle had developed the proclivity to fend for herself.

When she was seven, Annabelle came from school one day to find her mother lifeless after a heroin overdose. Little Annabelle blamed her father for her death and grew to hate him. She called him by his first name instead of calling him Dad. He could not handle the stress of being a single parent and did not know how to cope or care for precocious Annabelle. Short tempered and high on one drug or the other, he held a gun to her head one too many times. "Pull the trigger mother fucker!" would be her response.

She reached puberty early and became an expert in fending off perverts. She realized quickly that guys were nice to her only because they had ulterior motives. She also learned that by wrapping these guys around her finger, she could get what she wanted. She was skillful in creating an illusion that made them think the odds were in their favor and was thus successful in maintaining her innocence in a manner that was not completely innocent. Being unkempt and having a potty mouth was her defense mechanism.

She lived in filth and ate canned food. She learned not to trust anyone. Eventually, the state took custody of little Annabelle when she was ten. The school nurse had complained to the authorities regarding her hygiene, and the social worker found her living alone in a ranch house. Her wild survival instincts, coupled with little understanding of her temper and language from others, meant she scurried from one foster home to another.

Grace came in the form of Lydia and Ben who learned about Annabelle's plight and adopted her at age twelve. They tolerated her outbursts with patience. She was initially a recluse in their home and never came out of her room. The turning point came when they rescued a puppy, a little red-haired Yorkie Poo, from the pound. The two vagabonds immediately gravitated towards each other. Lydia and Ben asked Annabelle to name her. Cinnamon, as she called her, brought Annabelle out of her shell.

Lydia, Ben, and Virginia welcomed her into their home and their hearts. Although their unconditional love and generosity helped Annabelle grow up in a stable home and go to college, there was always a storm brewing inside of her. She feared rejection, feared she was going to let her loved ones down, and also feared abandonment.

Even after unloading her heart to him and telling him things no one other than her family knew, she felt heavy. Tears rolled down her cheeks. She stared at the ceiling, afraid she might see disgust in his eyes. Having grown up privileged and in a loving home, how could he understand?

Then, to her utter surprise, he said, "I love you now more than I ever did."

He wanted to be the rock in her life. He was willing to give her space and the time she needed to fight her demons.

Little did she know he too had a past he was living with as well. It was time for him to drop his shields too and open up to Annabelle.

Despite their modest means, Senthil's parents always had philanthropic hearts. Teenage girls in villages were looked at as a financial burden for a family. They were subjected to manual labor; and to circumvent dowry, desperate poor parents gave them up in arranged marriages to older men. Boys were made to work in paddy fields and rice mills to add to the family's income. They remained illiterate.

Senthil's parents temporarily adopted these teenagers and young adults down on their luck, one at a time. They provided food, clothing, and shelter. His mother taught them to read and write, and they put away some money each month in a bank account under their name. When they were of marriageable age, they sent them home with enough money to help their families with the wedding. The young adults came to learn a new trade so they could return to their village with a new skill to earn a living.

Senthil was nine years old when his parents welcomed into their house Ambika, a twenty-three-year-old girl from the village. She was saved from being married to a forty-five-year-old widower with two kids. Eshwari was seven, Nanda was four, and Rathi was two, and Bala was not born at that time. Senthil and his siblings slept on the floor in one bedroom, while Ambika slept in the spare room. One night, he woke up with a start to find Ambika fondling him. He was not old enough to even have a physiological reaction to her touch, but that did not stop her. Her suction was uneasy and painful. He was scared that he was going to get dismembered.

He was too afraid to tell his parents. He did not know what or how to tell them. His silence only emboldened Ambika and encouraged more nightly visits. He did not want his brother and sisters to be subjected to the hellish experience that he was going through. He could not sleep at night. He always made sure to sleep close to the door and push his siblings closer to the wall on the farther side. Whenever Ambika seemed to move towards his siblings, he coughed or made some noise that would halt her. This torture went on for a year.

He was immensely relieved when it was time for Ambika to leave. However, the relief was only temporary, as Raju came to live with them shortly afterward. Raju was twenty-one years old and had been laid off from a rice mill that had burned down. He was the sole breadwinner for his family and got in trouble for harassing the village chief's daughter. Senthil's father got Raju an apprenticeship at a mechanic and welding shop nearby so that he could go back to the village with a new trade.

Everything was fine for the first month. Even though Ambika had left, his nightmares continued. He had grown accustomed to waking up in the middle of the night in cold sweat. After a month, Senthil's nightmares took a new turn. Raju did more damage than Ambika and caused him greater pain. Senthil was scared to see blood in the toilet. He was afraid he was going to die. Fear took over him every night, as he kept vigil in the bedroom to protect his siblings from the predator. He felt ashamed and did not know how to confide in his parents. He contemplated suicide at that young age but convinced himself to be resilient for the sake of his siblings, especially Rathi who was only a toddler.

Although it felt like an eternity, this nightmare was shorter. Raju left after eight months when he got word of his father's death. With the birth of Bala the following year, his parents did not have the time or the means to accommodate anyone from the village. With five kids, they had to save for the future. Putting five kids through a good school was no small feat, and they began to practice the idea that charity began at home.

During that troublesome phase if his life, Senthil fervently prayed not just to the Hindu gods but also to Jesus and Allah, but to no avail. He felt forsaken by the gods who he felt were punishing him. He felt betrayed and stopped believing in them. He became withdrawn and silent and grew up to be a scared introvert. He could not trust anyone and was afraid of making new friends. Sumathi's love was the first to break a window on the wall he had erected around himself.

He had never shared this with anyone—not even Sumathi. Annabelle hugged him as he sobbed like a child. He felt lighter, as though a mountain had been lifted off his back. They felt closer in their pain.

While Annabelle wondered if two wrongs can make a right, Senthil believed they were meant for each other: two souls plagued by childhood nightmares seeking solace in each other. Perhaps the power of love would erase the nightmares, and they could dream of a new future.

"I can understand your pain and why you are afraid. While I cannot fathom what it must have been like growing up until Aunt Lydia and Uncle Ben took you in, I can certainly see why you are on the run all the time. You would rather leave than be left behind," Senthil said.

Annabelle was quiet for a few minutes as she rested her head on his chest. She could hear his racing heart gradually slow down. She eventually broke her silence. "I am a lost cause, Senthil. I am constantly afraid that I am going to let down the people who love me."

"That's not true Annabelle. Look at you. You have made something of yourself. You have put yourself through graduate school. As a speech pathologist, you help so many people and make a difference."

"Well, that's all your Aunt Lydia and Uncle Ben. If it was not for them, Virginia, and Cinnamon, who knows which crack house I would be in now. I studied for them as I didn't want all their love to become meaningless. I live in constant fear that my past is going to catch up with me and I am going to disappoint everyone dear to me. It's in my blood, in my genes."

"Oh, Annabelle. Please don't let your past define your future. We have to learn from our past and move on."

"Easy for you to say Senthil. I don't know how you do it. After all you have been through, how did you become so normal? You are so confident. I am afraid I don't have your resilience."

"Normal? Hmm . . ." Senthil let out a big sigh as he stroked her wavy lava locks.

"What does that mean? I am still trying to figure out all your hmms and ahhs," Annabelle said as she lifted her head to look at him.

"Normal and confident? Those words are not even in my vocabulary. You strip away my white coat, my title, you take me out of the hospital, and all you have left is a frightened nine-year-old boy. I am like a log drifting on water. I have only learned to stay afloat. I don't change course; I don't affect any change. I just let life come at me at the pace it chooses: a gentle stream or a raging sea, I remain the same. I have lived my life just like how I laid still and lifeless during those horrific nights. That is not normal, Annabelle." Overwhelmed with emotions, he paused. Annabelle gently stroked his chest. It was like a lullaby to a crying child. Sighing, Senthil continued, "I don't even know if I am a good brother full of love for my siblings and a good son for my parents or just a protector whose purpose in life is to have responsibilities and care for the well-being of them. I am afraid I am just a programmed robot."

"That is not true. Please do not be so hard on yourself Senthil. You are a kind man who wishes only the best for everyone. I don't know your parents or your siblings, but I am sure they know you love them very much. You are a dedicated PA, and you make a big difference in all your patients' lives."

"I cannot take credit for all that, Annabelle. Sumathi was the first person in my life to give me hope. She stopped the downward spiral, and to this day it is her gift of love, albeit, for a short time, that gave me some buoyancy to stay afloat. Papa's support and trust in me and the valuable assistance from the residents, therapists, nurses, and case managers make the workplace a haven for me. And the truth is, patients like Charlie and his family touch my life far more than I do theirs."

"You deserve someone better than me Senthil, someone more stable. I am only going to become a disappointment and cause you heartache," Annabelle sobbed. "Your protective instincts and desire to help someone in trouble is clouding your judgment."

"No, Annabelle. I have lived my life without taking charge and let time and chance dictate terms. I have lived in the past worrying about the future and forgot to live in the present. You have lived in the present not worrying about the future and forgot your life in the past. Together we can change that."

Annabelle's eyes opened wide. She raised her head and kissed him. "I do feel safe when I am in your arms. I trust your love, but I just can't trust the devil in me. You always know what to say to make me feel better. I am just worried you are going to get lost trying to rescue me. I believe it's worth taking the chance."

They found solace in each other's embrace and in the newfound lease of their love. Annabelle pleaded with her company to delay her assignment in the Virgin Islands for a couple of weeks, and her company was able to convince the speech pathologist she was going replace to stay another two weeks. Annabelle did not go out or touch a drink for the next two weeks. She kept herself busy watching TV and cleaning the house when he went to work.

Senthil took a hiatus from his studying to spend time with her after work. They explored Durham, a city known for its eclectic restaurants, took some cooking classes, and enjoyed each other's company. Order was restored in their life.

Chapter 34 — The Last Straw on the Camel's Back

ANNABELLE PROMISED HERSELF THAT THIS WAS HER LAST assignment. As it was not possible to drive to the island, they placed in her car her stuff that had been stored in his garage and parked her car inside. From the fall weather of Durham, she moved to the year-round summer of Saint Thomas Island.

On her first day off, she put on her swimsuit, a big hat, and sunglasses. She grabbed a towel and headed to the beach. The people on the island were very friendly. There was a constant flux of new people from cruise ships. She made friends with people from the hospital she worked in. Some were traveling like her, and some were permanent residents.

There were so many beaches that they never got tired. The days they were not working, they lived in bathing suits and drank alcohol all day at the beach. Annabelle's resolve to limit her alcohol intake did not last very long. She posted a ton of pictures of the beautiful island on Facebook and tagged Senthil with the line, "Wish you were here with me." Senthil was busy studying for his PANRE. He wanted to finish his exam before she returned.

Like bar-hopping in Raleigh, she and her friends hopped from one beach to the other. Most of the games they played included alcohol. A month flew by. It was carefree and filled with nothing but sunshine and alcohol. She felt liberated again and did not feel the pressure she felt when she stayed with her family and Senthil. Her strong feelings for Senthil conflicted with her desire to be a free spirit. *What if he gets tired of me? What if I have the tendencies of my drug-addicted parents? Maybe he deserves someone better than me.* All these thoughts only made her drink more. She thought she was doing the right thing by staying away from home. Her fear of abandonment always pressured her to leave rather than be left behind.

One weekend, she and a few of her friends chartered a boat to the nearby Saint John Island. The boat was captained by Jimmy. He was a local who had lived in Saint Thomas all his life. It was a party boat, and Jimmy flirted unabashedly. Single and successful, he attracted a lot of girls on the island. Annabelle was mesmerized by the blue waters. They had a blast, and when they returned, they were all too tired to walk back.

Jimmy told them they could sleep on the boat before he went home. The tide rocked them to sleep. The next morning, Jimmy came to the boat to find Annabelle still fast asleep. All her friends had left. He had to go on a run for some whelk, conch, and langoustes for a local restaurant, so he woke her up. Annabelle apologized and got up to leave. "Hey, you want to tag along? I know a great snorkeling spot." Annabelle did not have to work that day and decided to join him.

Coki Beach was amazing with abundant coral reefs. He told her that she had an open invitation to come aboard Jimmy's Paradise. She thanked him for a great time. He was going to Brewer's Bay next week and invited her. He gave her his card to call him if she was interested.

Unlike her time in San Francisco, she was on the same time zone this time. She called Senthil that night and told him about the snorkeling. He was glad for her and wished she had an underwater camera to take pictures. He agreed to take a week off to visit her as soon as he was done with his recertification exam. She felt a little guilty for not telling him about Jimmy. She then called Pepto to tell her about life on the island. When she told her about

Jimmy, Pepto warned her that he was nothing but trouble. She told him that they were just friends and he was like a tour guide.

Brewer's Bay was even more fabulous. She could get used to traveling on the boat and would hardly regret it if she did not have to set foot on land again. Jimmy fixed her an Aunt Roberta. She was flattered that he had paid attention to what her favorite drink was. She did not reject his advances but did not reciprocate either. She did not object when he kissed her on the cheek. He was different from Senthil in so many ways. He was a road scholar with extensive travel and practical experiences. He did not live by a schedule and was spontaneous. He could fly by the seat of his pants and be perfectly happy to live in his swim trunks. He was a kindred spirit.

"Honey, what would you do if I don't come back?" she asked Senthil during one of her phone calls.

He was getting tired of this line of questions. "I can only hope you do."

"That is not an answer to my question," she insisted.

He said that he had had a life before her and that his life would go on if she did not come back. It seemed to him that she was looking for a fight.

Out of the blue, she said, "Christina told me what happened when we went to the Raleigh bar the last time I was there." She was only having fun; some drunks had misbehaved, and it was not her fault. She accused him of being uptight and said that he would never understand. She blamed it on their cultural differences and their age gap. He told her that he was not mad but upset. Yes, he was upset that strangers had their hands all over her, but he was more upset that she could drink so much that someone had to tell her what had happened. She was thirty years old and not a teenager. He contended that in any culture, at any age, and in any relationship, it would hurt anyone to see their loved one in the state she was in. Love and relationship were universal, whether it was between a man and a woman or between two women or between two men.

"You never told me I threw up in your new car?" she asked him.

"I didn't want you to feel bad," he said.

She would rather have him fight with her than be nonchalant. He saw no point in fighting and just needed some space and time to get over things. He understood that she would not behave the way she did if she were not under the influence of alcohol. She was upset that she was stuck alone at home and that he did not like going out to have fun. She was not ready for a monotonous life with work and predictable weekends that included a trip to Sam's Club, the grocery store, and cooking for the week.

Annabelle contended that his behavior for the few weeks she had stayed with him made it difficult for her to choose that life, as she feared monotony. She tried being what he wanted her to be. She stayed home, cooked, and did not drink, but she felt miserable when he was away at work. She accused him of not asking her to stay when she told him she had an assignment. He said that she had never asked his opinion and had merely informed him of her decision.

He tried to explain that some of their misunderstandings had emerged because they were living parallel lives. Annabelle was on vacation mode. He, on the other hand, was juggling work and studies for an exam. Some of these clarifications temporarily made sense to her, but she was still in denial about alcohol being a problem. She felt something was wrong with her, and her childhood experiences had something to do with it.

Phone calls like these continued. Annabelle rehashed old events. "I am only trying to understand, and your unwillingness to talk about it is not helping," she lashed out. She told Senthil that he had never once asked her to come over, never called her once, and never made the first move. She had to ask him if she could come over, she had to call, and she had to initiate sex. He politely reminded her that those were her demands when the affair started, and he never wanted to lose her by making her feel smothered.

He was yet to hear her say that she loved him. She told him that she tried showing it to him during the weeks she had stayed with him. He told her that he had fallen in love with her a long time ago and was miles ahead in their relationship and just a couple of weeks were not going to help her catch up. She hated it whenever he made sense. She hated that deep down in her heart there was a string that he could tug, and no matter how far she strayed, she recoiled, albeit temporarily.

After taking his recertification exam, he told her that he was ready to visit. He just asked her to give him two weeks' notice so that he could plan his trip. Annabelle stalled; she did not think this was a good time for him to visit her.

Annabelle could not resist hanging out with Jimmy. It was weird, but she thought he was the perfect test for her. If she could resist his advances, then she could be 100 percent sure about her decision to settle down with Senthil. Pepto warned her not to go to Jimmy's house party. She told her she was not going to be alone and her friends were going to be there. And they were, but she was the last one to leave. She stayed back to help him clean up. One thing led to another, and she woke up the next morning next to him in his bed.

Was it a mistake? Was it deliberate? Jimmy's carefree attitude triumphed over Senthil's thoughtfulness. Did she just use Jimmy as an excuse to set Senthil free? Anyway, a decision had been made. It was finally over. She knew Jimmy was not the future, but she realized that Senthil was the past now. She was not going to be a disappointment to anyone. She was not going to give them the opportunity to find out. It was better for her to leave than being the one left behind. Besides, after hearing Senthil's revelations, she believed he deserved someone more stable. She felt empty, but a strange feeling of calm inundated her.

Pepto was devastated when Annabelle told her what had happened. She worried it was going to break Senthil's heart. Annabelle confessed to her that she did not know how to tell him. She needed some liquid courage.

She wrote him an email first. She was sorry to hurt him. It was probably for the best, and now he could move on with his life instead of waiting for someone crazy who was too scared to come to her senses. He deserved better, and she ended it by saying that she would always be there for him if he ever needed her. Even in her drunken state, she could not bring herself to tell him that it was over or that she had slept with someone. The last line she wrote was, "Honey, what you always feared has come true."

Senthil sat stunned, staring at her email. He could not sleep. It had not happened because she was drunk; she had wanted it to happen. She had always warned him that she would leave one day. She had never lied to him, and so he could not be mad at her—he was never mad at her. He was hurt that she had tried to blame him for her decision. He was sad for her that she had not learned anything from her parents' mistakes.

He finally realized that it was over. After a long deliberation throughout the night, he decided to rewrite history, more specifically, *his story*. He booked a flight to Saint Thomas and a return flight for the same day. If this was over, it must happen face to face and not over a drunken phone call or an email. Unlike with Sumathi, he wanted closure this time. That morning, he caught Papa in his office before he went into the OR. He told him that he and Annabelle were through and that he would not be at work that day since he was going to Saint Thomas to break up in person. Papa was sorry for him. He gave him a hug and said, "Don't let a girl ruin you. You'll be fine. Take as many days off as you need."

Pepto, on the other hand, told him that this was a bad idea and pleaded with him to not go. He said, "Even if God grants your wish, the priest doesn't."

She looked at him puzzled. He told her that Papa was okay with him going, but she was trying to stop him. Even though he presented a calm façade, she knew he was an emotional wreck inside. Pepto knew he was very sentimental and feared what might happen to his fragile heart. After all, he was the girl in that relationship. Pepto said, "I am worried. If you go there, I am afraid you are going to get hurt more than you are now."

"That's not possible," he said, and added, "Once you drown, another ten feet of water does not make a damn difference."

Pepto was stunned. She had never heard him use a curse word in all the time she had known him. *Is this a new Senthil? What else is going to be new?*

she wondered. As he walked away, she yelled, “What are you going to tell her in person that you can’t tell her over the phone or email?” His reply was stoic. “I have no earthly idea.”

A Note About the Author

S.K. Radhakrishnan trained and practiced as a physical therapist in India before coming to the United States. After thirteen years of practice as a contract physical therapist, he attained physician assistant training at Wayne State University. The Wayne State University PA Program Faculty selected him as one "who is most likely to achieve clinical excellence while advancing the ethics & standards of the profession" and presented him with the "Professionalism Award" for the Class of 2004.

He came to Duke University Hospital after being accepted into the Duke Postgraduate PA Surgical Residency Program. After successful completion of the residency program, he began his career as a neurosurgical PA for Dr. Allan Friedman in the Department of Neurosurgery. Shortly thereafter, S.K. Radhakrishnan was invited to be a guest lecturer for the Duke PA students.

In 2006, he was a recipient of the Duke Strength, Hope and Caring Award for the extraordinary provision of compassionate care for patients. In April 2018 he received the Meritorious Service Award for distinguished service to Duke. Currently, he is the administrative chief and clinical neurosurgical PA in the Department of Neurosurgery.

His volunteered contributions include work with Special Olympics and Duke Global Health's neurosurgery mission to Uganda.

Readers can interact with the author on the following social media.

skradhakrishnan.com
facebook.com/IHaveNoEarthlyIdea
twitter.com/SKRad007
instagram.com/skrad007